TICKING

A TALE OF TWO TIME TRAVELLERS

CRAIG VANN

 FriesenPress

Suite 300 - 990 Fort St
Victoria, BC, V8V 3K2
Canada

www.friesenpress.com

Author drawing by the author's son, Clark G. Van Alstyne
Editing by Kate Juniper and Erin Carpenter

ISBN
978-1-5255-2350-2 (Hardcover)
978-1-5255-2351-9 (Paperback)
978-1-5255-2352-6 (eBook)

1. FICTION, ACTION & ADVENTURE

Distributed to the trade by The Ingram Book Company

For my dad, Clifford, who gently touched a lot of lives while he was here with us. I used to scold myself when I found myself doing things the way he did them. Now, I find myself hoping that I'm doing things as well.

And for my beautiful wife Audrey, as we travel through time together, forever.

To Shannon,
Merry Christmas and
happy reading.

Craig Vann

∞

"It was the best of times, it was the worst of times."
—Charles Dickens, *A Tale of Two Cities*

PROLOGUE

HE AWOKE TO A blood-curdling scream. The acrid smell of smoke hung in the humid air. The night had been moonless and dark, but was now lit by the golden light of fires dancing on the wall. He sat up quickly: more screaming now and angry voices. He swung his bare feet to the dirt floor.

Quietly, he shook his wife until she woke, wondering how she could have slept through that. He kept her from speaking, with a firm hand over her mouth and a finger to his lips. Satisfied that she understood, he released his hand and led her into their son's room.

The 12-year-old boy had not slept through the noises. He sat in his pajamas, curled up in a ball in the corner of the small room, shaking and sobbing. They rushed to comfort him, and the three of them crouched together: a sobbing, frightened circle. Outside, the screaming had almost stopped, replaced by the sound of angry male voices.

The father peered cautiously out the window. He saw a group of men in the common, armed with machetes and swords. Some of the intruders carried torches that they had used to ignite the houses, now fully engulfed. They were talking loudly over the chant of others in the group;

"Kuua wachawi! Kuua wachawi!"

Even with his limited knowledge of Swahili, the father knew that the vigilantes were chanting, "Kill the witches!"

Sweat now glistening on his face, he turned and said, "We don't have much time. We have to leave... NOW!"

With no time to dress or to take their few valuables, the missionaries cautiously opened the only door in the small hovel just a crack. The father held his breath as he looked out. Trying to fathom what was happening, he gasped in horror. People ran here and there, some being chased by men with weapons. Many had already been caught and cut down, lying in black puddles that turned gold in the flickering firelight.

A large figure, an old woman, appeared on his left, running and puffing violently; her breath almost gone. And then it was, as her pursuer caught her and sliced her down with a red-stained machete. He then slowly walked away—away from the group huddled at the door, looking for more victims.

With a grimace, the father turned and whispered, "Okay, we run together into the forest. We'll be safe there." He looked deep into his wife's eyes, stroked her hair and kissed her. He wiped her tears from her cheeks and hugged his young son, saying, "Joni... and dear Sky, I love you both."

He opened the door wide, taking the hands of his wife and son, and began to run toward the trees; away from the blazing village, away from the chanting, angry voices. As they ran from the firelight, the darkness began to engulf them. A few more barefooted strides and they would be in the safety of the dark forest.

Suddenly, directly in front of them, a torch was lit. They had to stop quickly so as to not crash into the three men now looming menacingly within arm's reach. The father, in the lead, skidded to a stop; losing the grip of his wife's slippery hand. He found himself lying in the dusty soil at the foot of a leering black man. The man made a sound that combined the gasp of being startled with a guttural laugh. Two machetes flashed in the firelight.

The wife and son turned and ran, hand in hand, for the shadowy safety of the nearby trees, pursued by one of the men. She ran like she had never run before, but could not see her footing in the dark. She tripped over a tree root, losing grip of her son's hand. She fell to her knees and felt a sharp pain in her ankle.

"Run, Sky, run!" she screamed.

The torches approached – quickly at first, then more slowly as the pursuers realized that their quarry was caught.

Sky ran, leaving his mother. Through his sweat and tears, he ran through the darkness; through the invisible foliage with its cutting barbs. He ran until he too, fell. He fell, he guessed, into a deep ravine – down its bank and through the stunted scrub and thorny acacia bushes. Breathless, he rolled to a stop at the bottom; cut and bruised, his pajamas torn. He groaned until he passed out.

Of that night, that was all he remembered.

∞

1

Fraserdale, Canada
Summer 2018

IT WAS THE BEST at telling time, it was the worst at telling time.

Sky's antique Mickey Mouse pocket watch was a beaut. He turned it slowly in his hand under his desk, gazing at it furtively, admiring its silver patina – as his professor, Mr. Gauthier, rambled on about Canadian history. The watch had been his 13th birthday present from his grandparents. It featured a "Hippy Mickey" wearing bell-bottoms, a Nehru jacket and a flowery T-shirt, and carrying a bouquet of flowers in his famous white-gloved hands. *Carrying them to Minnie*, Sky had thought many times in the years since he received it – even now, eight years later. It had become a habit. Mickey stood proudly atop the date "1970" in small print. The watch hung on a large-link silver chain that Sky secured to his jeans belt loop.

But the watch was less than reliable, even though Sky wound it diligently every morning. Hence the problem with the actual telling of time. As Professor Gauthier turned once again, Sky held it to his ear to hear the metallic *tick, tick, tick*. He set the time, pushed down the winding stem and nuzzled the watch back into his pocket, face in.

The professor walked slowly from side to side at the front of the lecture hall, gesticulating with his omnipresent laser pen for emphasis as he described the Métis leader Louis Riel and the Red River Rebellion.

"The central element of the Métis flag is the infinity symbol. You've all seen the symbol before – it looks like a sideways figure 8 – but you may not have known that it is otherwise called a 'lemniscate'. The lemniscate on the flag represents the mixing of European and First Nations blood into a distinct Canadian culture."

The professor seemed oblivious to the entire class. *Content as "the sage on the stage,"* thought Sky as he stifled a yawn. He felt safe in tuning him out for awhile; while the lemniscate was new, Sky knew most of this already. He was taking the course for credits – easy credits, for him.

Sky enjoyed Canadian history, but enough was enough already! How many times did he have to study the same periods of history? First high school, now university… where was the history of the rest of the world? An epic novel is always better than a short story.

Sky fantasized about actually living in the past – long before the Trudeaus, Riel or even Canadian Confederation. As he loved to tell anyone who'd listen, one of his favourite historical eras was 18th century Britain ("The 1700s that is," he often would add). On the one hand, he'd explain, rarely noticing the eye roll of the person to whom he was speaking, there was the aristocracy – a small minority of the population – that owned most of the wealth. On the other hand were the poor. Most people were poor, living in squalor and often dying young. At no other time in Western history was the contrast between rich and poor so vast.

There was also so much happening at that tumultuous time in history – especially in and around London; the greatest city in the world! He'd give anything to be there, to see with his own eyes what it was like to live during that time.

He imagined himself as a member of the aristocracy, living in comfort amongst acres of land on a country estate, with servants and gardens and dogs for fox hunting. He would own at least three grand carriages, with footmen and prancing white horses. His mansion would feature a grand ballroom to host large parties, where guests wearing big wigs danced to a live orchestra.

His grades were a testament to his passion. At times he amused himself by posing probing and complicated questions that made his professor nervous. But he didn't push it; Mr. Gauthier had recently come to recognize when he was being played.

As he often did, Sky thought of that horrific night eight years ago when his parents were murdered. The couple had been Christian missionaries on a two-year service in southeast Kenya. They lived in a simple mud hut constructed of wood and coated with mud and straw. Most mornings, they would wake to find bits of mud ceiling in their hair and on their bed sheets.

One of his parents' more challenging duties was to visit the "Witch Camps," like the one in which they had perished. Anyone accused of witchcraft could find refuge in a camp. Many were accused. The outcasts were typically women, and most were elderly. They were mentally and physically abused in their former lives, so coming to the camp was, in some cases, a matter of life or death. The Church believed that part of its mission was to directly confront the concept of witchcraft by providing a benevolent alternative belief through the missionaries and the Word.

Thankfully, Sky could remember little of that night, but he knew that he had been found in the morning by the Kenya Police Service, then turned over to Canadian Embassy staff in Nairobi. An overnight stay at the hospital in nearby Mombasa revealed that he had suffered only minor cuts and bruises. The witch-hunting mob had killed

18 people that night. Some 90 had escaped into the night, including a bruised and cut and orphaned Skypilot.

The embassy had sent Sam Richter, a young diplomatic agent with full privileges and immunities, to see young Skypilot safely home to Canada. Sam was to return home soon, and so his plans were changed to accommodate taking Sky. Sam stayed with Sky until the boy ran into the arms of his sobbing grandparents at the Fraserdale Airport arrivals lounge. They were now his closest family.

While Gramma and Gramps were glad to take Sky into their care, they understood that it would dramatically change their lives. An orphaned child is, at any age, a challenge for the new caregivers. The elderly couple realized that that challenge might be greatest for caregivers of a budding teenager.

Sam kept in touch with Sky and his grandparents, and called in whenever he was passing through Fraserdale. Sky fell into the gentle rhythm of life provided by his maternal grandparents in their comfortable suburban home.

His hippy grandparents, to be exact. They had lived for years in a commune during the heyday of the Love Generation. In fact, they had been leaders there, although they'd never admit to being anything more than "part of a far-out committee." The commune had been turned into condos, though by now many of their friends had died or moved away; so they had sold up. Gramps had wisely invested his share of the proceeds from the sale, and so the two were comfortable – more than comfortable – in their golden years.

Gramma and Gramps still enjoyed facets of the hippy lifestyle. Just a few years earlier, Gramps had finally shaved his beard, although his grey hair remained tied in a neat ponytail. A huge peace sign (handcrafted from scrap metal salvaged from a munitions shop, his Gramps would proudly state) hung over the mantel in the living room. Daily conversations typically included old communal life and favourite tunes, peppered with the slang of the 1960s and 1970s. Impressionable young Sky had picked up aspects of his grandparents' speech over the years, and now, at 21, he considered his choice of language a way to honour them.

In fact, even his appearance harkened back to the Love Generation. His hair, a halo of tangled and unstyled brown curls, framed an intelligent and sensitive face reminiscent of his father. His frame was gangly – all arms and legs, as Gramma would say – and his clothes, while modern, hung loose. He still considered his Mickey watch to be the epitome of flashback coolness.

Sky was very much a geek for the things he loved – computers, video games, history, and music (especially classic rock). His grandpa had belted out late '60s and early '70s rock tunes from an old stereo with huge speakers. Sky had found himself loving the music by osmosis as his grandparents grooved away. One day, his grandpa brought him an old acoustic guitar. Sky quickly became proficient. As Bob Dylan might attest, the natural progression was to an electric guitar and amplifier, which his grandparents gave to Sky on his 16th birthday.

Both of the grandparents' daughters had been born in the commune. Their eldest, Joni (named after Joni Mitchell), became a nurturer at an early age, taking care of her little sister, Beatrice, and often some of the other children in the commune, too. They formed a tie-dyed, fast-moving clump of giggling merriment.

The sisters were, at first, inseparable. But as they developed into young women, their lives took separate paths. Joni found comfort and solace in the church, where she continued to nurture those in need. Beatrice eschewed most high school highlights, like dating and graduation ceremonies; immersing herself in her studies instead.

Beatrice became something of a recluse, which alienated her from her parents. Despite this, they continued to financially support their hard-working, genius daughter. This support, combined with the proceeds from scholarships and bursaries, allowed Beatrice to complete her education, which culminated in the graduate program at Cornell University and ultimately, her PhD.

Beatrice had even turned down an offer to join the Canadian astronaut program, saying that she was too busy.

In reality, she *was* busy, obsessing over a new project that many would consider even more exciting than blasting off into space: a project that she believed would one day propel her not only through space, but through time.

Aunt Beatrice had always been something of an enigma to Sky, and in his mind, that made her unmistakably cool. He had been all the more impressed when she returned from New York with a story about having met actor Christopher Reeve – or Superman, to Sky. He loved the Canadian-made superhero. Sky had seen all the movies and read all the books. He considered his own name, Skypilot, to be Superman-esque.

His bedroom was still scattered with some of his favourite Superman memorabilia. He still dreamed of flying – red cape flapping in the wind behind him – doing good deeds and defeating criminals.

In every man, young and old, there lives a boy.

At that moment Professor Gauthier uncharacteristically stopped pontificating and asked a question. Not of the entire class, but specifically of Sky! The collective attention of the lecture hall was tuned in on one tuned-out student.

"Skypilot! Again, why was Riel hanged?"

Sky was momentarily dumbfounded; lost somewhere between Africa, the 18th century, early Canadian history, and Metropolis. His teacher had obviously seized an opportunity to catch him off guard, perhaps as retribution for Sky's cheeky questions earlier.

Sky looked down toward his teacher and could only offer a weakly comedic answer: "Ummm, they thought he was a witch?"

As the class snickered, the teacher smiled wryly, and slowly walked up the stairs to Sky's desk, tapping it with his pen. "No, they didn't think he was a witch. Besides, being a male, he'd have been a warlock, no? Try again…"

A familiar voice rang out from beside him, strong and true. "He was convicted of high treason."

Sky tried to suppress a smile – Zac! Momentarily defeated, Professor Gauthier suggested that Sky should buy Zac lunch, and walked back down to his stage. With his back turned, he did not see Sky wink at his buddy, or the wide smile on Zac's face.

Skypilot Sewell, named after the song of the same name by Eric Burdon and the Animals, had grown to appreciate his unique name. His parents had named their only son after the song's military chaplain who blessed the troops prior to battle. The name reflected their Christian background, their love of peace, and the hippy attitude that even then, was so prevalent in the family.

In high school, his classmates – some of whom also had non-conformist names – got used to his name after some initial (and reciprocated) teasing. "High-in-the-sky-pilot" was a favorite taunt, especially when classmates thought that Sky was zoning out, as he admittedly often did. Typical schoolwork, with its rote learning and memorization, just didn't capture Sky's vivid imagination. He preferred experiential, hands-on learning. In either case, his marks were typically at or near the top of his class.

Thankfully, this class came to an end; the final page for the sage on the stage. It was only noon, but both Sky and Zac had the afternoon off. No more classes until Monday!

For second-year university students Sky and his buddy, Zachary Burling, weekends meant studying, reading, and when possible, some play time. And in just a month, they were due to leave for two weeks of summer camp on one of the Gulf Islands, a short ferry ride from Fraserdale, to be volunteer leaders for a third consecutive year. They always had a blast there and the kids were usually pretty well-behaved.

As Sky and Zac walked down the hill from campus, an idea occurred to Sky. "C'mon. I'll do as Professor Gauthier suggested and take you for lunch – at my aunt's house. She texted me, asking if I'd drop by to see something she's been working on. And besides, she makes a mean omelet, and the price is right."

∞

2

TWENTY MINUTES LATER, THE two arrived at Sky's aunt's home; a modest, unkempt split-level. The squeaky gate that they opened gingerly was in dire need of repair, and the front lawn resembled a hay field. Beatrice had lived alone in this house for years; a stranger to her neighbours.

Sky looked around at the overgrown bushes. "I'll ask Aunt Bea if I can cut the lawn and trim the bushes for her soon," he said.

He knocked on the door. Then again; louder this time. It was awhile until they could hear footsteps approaching from inside. The door creaked open, and Beatrice Westover smiled.

Like her sister, Beatrice was a tall, attractive woman. But few would see her as such, as she did not place much emphasis on her appearance. Obscured behind her ever-present, black-rimmed eyeglasses were sapphire-blue eyes. Her long auburn hair was typically pulled back into a practical bun. Fashion, under her white, stained lab coat, was not a concern.

She had never married. As she put it, "My work never leaves me any time to land a man." When pressed as to why she never married, the 40-something professional usually quoted Albert Einstein: "Men marry women with the hope they will never change. Women marry men with the hope they will change. Invariably, they are both disappointed."

In any case, Beatrice had little free time to pursue romantic possibilities. She spent most of her time working in her basement. When she did relax, she liked to curl up to read in her big chair with her silver British Shorthair cat, Hawking, on her lap. She loved romance novels, of all things. Not just any of the genre, however. She felt that she had graduated from the bodice-ripper type. Under that stained lab coat lived a die-hard romantic.

"Sky, you got my text! Great!" she exclaimed. Sky was pleased to see his aunt so animated. "Hi Zac," she called back, as she led them into the house and toward the basement door. "I was downstairs, but I heard you knock and saw you on the cam, " She motioned upward at the non-blinking eye of a small camera in the corner. The camera had been a gift from parents after one too many long waits at the door whenever they came to visit. Beatrice had quickly discovered that the camera was a godsend for a hermit/scientist like herself. It meant improved security and the ability to make an informed decision as to whether to interrupt work to answer the door; a decision that she usually made easily. Her work, however, was reaching the point where more draconian security measures would be required.

"I have something incredible to show both of you," she said.

Her cat, with its distinctively chunky body, dense coat and broad face, meowed his approval and purred loudly as he wrapped himself around Zac's leg.

"Hawk, scoot!" Beatrice clapped her hands and the cat ran just a few steps away, tail twitching in protest.

Beatrice walked to the door that led to the basement – which was, in fact, her lab. "Hawking is a wonderful pet, although he can be annoying at times. He has only two bad habits: wrapping himself around people's legs – sorry Zac – and hunting butterflies. He doesn't catch insects or even birds, just butterflies. He'll catch one live and proudly bring it home to me, before letting it go in the house. I then have to catch and release the butterfly. My own personal Butterfly Effect, but that's another story." Beatrice opened the door, sighed and said, with some authority or trepidation or both, "Come downstairs."

Trying to forget about the omelet for now, the guys and their stomachs rumbled down the narrow stairway behind Beatrice. Sky had only been in the basement a couple of times before, when he was much younger. His recollection was that it was almost too cluttered to have fun in. He hadn't stayed long.

But the space had changed. The basement was still windowless and large, but it was now crammed with a plethora of new technology – from computers and hard drives, to piles of scientific journals, to cages housing laboratory rats. This was where Beatrice spent much of her time, reading scientific journals, conferring with colleagues via Skype and conducting experiments. And, judging by the discarded pizza and Chinese food boxes, it was also where she ate many of her meals.

As a theoretical physicist, Beatrice had gained prominence amongst her peers for her cutting-edge work in the areas of space-time, relativity and quantum physics. She considered time travel by human beings to truly be the "last AND first frontier."

But, her colleagues did not know the full extent of her work to date. Nor did they know of the recent success she had had. Her family, including Sky, only knew that she was a hard-working research scientist who had met and worked – in some unknown way – with the likes of Stephen Hawking.

They also knew that she did not have a lot of time for family, working as she did all hours of the day. Sky knew that she missed his mom, too, and that part of the reason for her immersing herself in her work was an attempt to forget the pain of losing her sister.

Beatrice led the youths through a maze of boxes and piled books toward the far wall of the basement, where a large blue tarpaulin covered what they guessed to be her latest work. She stood with one hand on the tarp, facing the young men, almost giddy with excitement.

With a single motion, she pulled down the tarp, revealing what looked like an old English phone booth – bright red, with partitioned glass on all four sides. The word telephone was displayed prominently in black on white at the top of each side, topped by a regal gold crown.

"This K2 phone booth is…" she sighed. Beaming with pride, she motioned with her arm, "… a time machine."

Sky gulped and looked at Zac, not knowing what to say. Zac just stood there, dumbfounded.

Sky's aunt had obviously lost her mind. "Aunt Bea, I think you're spending too much time down here in the basement." He hugged her sympathetically. "Maybe you need some fresh air. Maybe a major shopping trip to the mall, or a vacation?"

Zac, still in a trance, tried a question. "Is there a phone in there? What's a K2? It kinda looks like the machine in Dr. Who."

"That would be the TARDIS, Zac." Beatrice removed her nephew's arm from around her shoulders and laughed. "That machine is dimensionally transcendental; that is, it's bigger on the inside than it is on the outside. No such magic here. The K2 – 'K' stands for 'kiosk' – you see before you is just a modified public phone booth, the type that was a common sight on the streets of the United Kingdom for decades. It is a British cultural icon. I got this one on eBay. With some modifications, like a rubber seal around the door, a phone booth is the perfect size and configuration for my purposes." She turned and smiled at Sky, "I guess that's why Superman and others have used them too."

Sky smiled back at the mention of his favourite superhero.

Beatrice continued, "I've been referring to it in my lab journal as 'K2' and I think I'll just keep calling it K2. I mean, Rocky, Bullwinkle and the Internet Archive have already claimed the name 'Wayback Machine'.

"And I don't need fresh air, Skypilot," she said to her nephew with mild disdain. "Not when I am so close to ultimate success. As I said, this is a time machine – a PROVEN time machine. It has the ability to transport an object or an occupant through time and space, but only when that occupant is wearing the catalytic device."

"The catalytic device?" asked Sky.

Beatrice propped her glasses further up her slim nose and held up a "wait just one sec" finger to his question.

"About 100 years ago, Albert Einstein – I'm sure you've heard of him – predicted the existence of something called 'gravitational waves' as a product of his ground-breaking general theory of relativity. Like light, gravity travels in waves, but instead of radiation rippling because of light, it is space itself that is rippling. Einstein thought that humankind, with its limited technology, would never be able to find the waves because you need a huge wave to be able to detect it. And huge waves are rare. The strongest grav waves – the only ones we have a hope of detecting – are formed when objects with enormous gravity undergo dramatic acceleration. Like when two black holes merge to form another!

"Our technology has advanced exponentially since then. So, we can now detect these large gravitational waves, made more visible through technological advancement. It is a monumental achievement. We're only going to learn even faster in the future."

Beatrice held up her left arm at an odd angle, pointing to the ceiling. "If technology during Einstein's time was here (she used her right hand to point to her shoulder) and we are here today (she pointed to her elbow) then future scientists will be learning at this accelerated rate." She pointed to her upstretched hand, a handy way to show exponential growth.

"But how do these gravitational waves work with... time travel?" asked Sky, looking over at the phone booth in a new way.

"Einstein's theory of relativity tells us that gravity is the curvature of space and time. These waves are ripples in the space-time continuum." As she spoke, Beatrice grew more animated. She seemed to forget that the guys were there. "My fellow scientists have been concentrating on how gravitational waves will usher in a new way to observe the universe and gain knowledge about enigmatic objects... like the nature of the very early universe, black holes, neutron stars and ancient stuff like that. I have simply used this new knowledge to look ahead, not back in time. And, to look here, within the confines of our little blue planet, rather than into the heavens."

Beatrice leaned forward on the desk. "I have found that it's possible to basically ride one of these waves through space-time. Like a surfer riding a wave. So..." She paused dramatically, "Do you guys want to ride a wave? It might be interesting," she winked roguishly.

Sky reminded her, "And the... ummm... catalytic device?"

"Oh!" Beatrice clapped her hands once, reminding Sky of his mom. She used to do that often, when she was happy, and her eyes would glitter and dance. His eyes welled up. Oh, he missed her and Dad.

"Yes, here, let me show you." Beatrice moved to a nearby desk, where an old-fashioned sterling silver food cover occupied almost half of the desktop. She motioned for them to approach. The young men slowly made their way to the desk, wary of even more surprises. She waited until they were beside her and then said excitedly, "You're gonna love what's under here. This food cover, called a 'cloche' by the way, is 18th century. Get used to it."

As Sky and Zac wondered about her reference to the 18th century, Beatrice grabbed the handle on the top of the cloche and, pausing dramatically, cried, "One, two, three, for chrononauts only. Behold!" She lifted the *cloche*; underneath was a small platform with a round silver plate in the middle. Just above the plate hovered – yes, hovered – a smartwatch mounted on a wrist-shaped support. As it hovered, it slowly rotated.

"This… is an anti-gravity smartwatch charger," Beatrice said. "The base creates an electromagnetic field that wirelessly transfers power to the smartwatch. I show you the charger only because it is so cool. A glimpse into the future before you venture into the past! And, a great way to present the catalytic device to you – and when the time is right, to others."

Zac and Sky exchanged glances. They had never seen a rotating antigravity charger. And, who says "Behold" anymore? Then, as if on cue, they looked back at Beatrice. She was assuming that they would agree to some trip through time and space.

"As cool as it looks," said Beatrice, "It's not the watch that is important, it's the app that a friend and I have developed that makes the watch so special."

She removed the smartwatch from the levitating charger. "Here, check out the "Ticking" icon. It still needs some work. My associate and friend, Alim, is a gifted senior researcher in app development at Apple. He's the only other one who knows about the depth of my research. He knows his stuff, but look at this: he should have been a graphic artist."

She handed the watch to Sky, who held it so that both he and Zac could see the watch face. Amongst the other recognizable app icons, the Ticking icon seemed to stand out. The bright yellow and black icon was a stylized, standard round clock face with the Roman numerals III, VI and IX displayed where they should be. The number eight – in its familiar Arabic form – sat awkwardly on its side where the number three is typically displayed.

"Why is the number eight where the number three should be on the clock?" Zac was leaning in to see the small number.

"That's not an eight," Beatrice replied, "It's the infinity symbol, which is also called a…" She paused, reaching for the correct word.

"Lemniscate!" Sky interjected, recalling Professor Gauthier's reference to the Métis flag.

"Wow! Impressive, Mr. Sewell. Yes, the symbol represents the infinite ticking of the clock and the infinite possibilities of time travel. Once activated by simply pressing the icon, the app works in conjunction with the time machine to propel the occupant through time and space. One does not – *cannot* – operate in the absence of the other.

"But together…" she lowered her voice to a whisper and looked at Zac and Sky mischievously, "… magic. I think it is time for a little demonstration."

∞

3

BEATRICE COULD NOT HELP herself. She was so excited to show the results of her long, laborious work. Work that she had not shared with anyone other than Alim. She walked to the area under the stairs and opened a kennel. Inside the kennel was a dog; a young beagle.

The dog strutted out, wagging his tail tentatively. Beatrice stooped, picked up the dog and kissed him on his snout, saying, "His name is Legal. I want him on my side if this whole time travel thing becomes a lawsuit. Also, beagles are smart and easily trained."

From the top of the kennel, Beatrice grabbed a sturdy harness. "This is what he'll be wearing for his visit into the past." She passed the harness to Sky, who noticed that she had modified it to include a large leather pouch on the side and a smaller one at the chest. Both pouches featured strings woven like shoelaces to secure their contents. *Aunt BEA-utiful handiwork*, thought Sky. Hand-made pouches like these, *sans* plastic and modern affectations, would present nothing too bizarre for a person living in the past.

With Zac looking on, Beatrice had Sky hold Legal while she attached the harness. The way she cinched up the belt, with one end of it firmly secured in her teeth, made Sky believe that she had done this a few times before. As he held onto the dog, Sky's hands got close to the small pouch on Legal's chest. The dog growled menacingly at Sky, who quickly pulled his hands away.

"Oh, keep your hands away from that pouch! It will be holding this." Beatrice held up the watch.

The harness now secured, Beatrice slid a piece of plain paper and what looked like coins into the large pouch. She then directed her attention to the smartwatch, touching the watch face repeatedly before placing it in the small pouch, without so much as a whimper from Legal. Beatrice tied both sets of strings, securing the pouches.

She picked up the dog and kissed him once again, looking into his canine eyes. "Legal is the world's first 'chrononaut'; the first living thing to travel through time. At least, I think that he is the first – unless of course, he is not. Farewell, my furry friend. I'll see you soon. Remember, time flies!"

With that, Beatrice placed the dog on the floor of the so-called time machine.

Talking louder from inside the phone booth, Beatrice spoke haltingly as she worked. "Now, I simply program the watch for a pre-determined time and space, and send the occupant there. My computer is linked to the... watch, so the specifications I submit to the... watch are automatically transferred to my computer. The K2 machine stays here, but constant contact is maintained with the occupant or occupants – it can hold up to three – through the computer via the watch."

She patted Legal one last time and stepped out of the machine, leaving the dog inside. She closed the rubber-sealed door with a deft twist of the lever handle. She ran her hands over the doorframe, checking for faults in the rubber seal. Satisfied, she walked to her computer desk, saying, "My computer acts as Mission Control. Once I've vacated the machine and ensured the integrity of its seal, I can begin the transference process."

Biting her lip while adjusting her glasses again, Beatrice began typing on the keyboard. "Upon completion of the mission, I can recall the occupant to this time and space from my computer," she said.

"If you are thinking that THAT is interesting, here is the really interesting bit: the occupant could be gone for a few weeks or even months, in terms of his time in the past or future, but could return here to whatever time I establish. What I mean is, you could go for a prolonged trip and be back for supper! But, in the meantime, you would experience an extended period in another time and space. I can set that all up in advance, but I do not yet know how to change the predetermined coordinates."

She sighed. "Okay, you ready? Here we go."

In the dim light of the basement, the bright red phone booth – lit by a ring of spotlights in the ceiling – had seemed like a beacon even before the time travel process began. Now, it began to glow from within with a bright, pulsating light. Sky and Zac stood watching, but each took a step back as the intensity of the glow increased. The only sound was low and undulating, like the sound of a distant emergency vehicle. The pulsating light corresponded to the sound. The pulsations quickened and the sound grew louder – until with just a small *pop*, it was over.

Beatrice rushed to the time machine and opened the door. With a sweep of her outstretched arm, she smiled and cried, "Ta Da!"

∞

4

THE DOG WAS GONE!

The suction created by Beatrice opening the sealed door drew steam out from the booth. The guys were incredulous. Had she trained Legal to walk out a false doggie door in the back?

Closing and inspecting the door again, Beatrice explained, "The dog has travelled through time, into the past. It has also travelled through space, to approximate assigned coordinates. I have programmed the watch to remain in that time and space for three hours."

Beatrice sat again at the desk, behind the computer, initiating the sequencing protocol. "But, for us here, the dog will return in… oh, lets see… 45 seconds. The sequencing is designed to run repeatedly until it detects the activated app in the smartwatch. Unlike a human user, who would activate the app himself, the dog's app is set to activate at a specific time."

Again, the time machine began to glow from within. Gradually, the intensity increased, as did the sound – and then, *POP*!

Beatrice ran to the machine and flung open the door. Heat and steam wafted out, and then out wandered Legal, hot and wobbly but still wagging his tail. He walked like a drunkard, seemingly getting his bearings.

"Good boy, Legal! Good boy!" Beatrice knelt down to pat the dog. "Gravitational waves are not like light waves travelling through space; they are actual waves. They stretch and squeeze space. Any objects in the path of grav waves rhythmically move further apart and closer together as the space they are in is manipulated, so, I suspect that Legal has been stretched and squeezed a bit too. Some ancillary heat and stream is generated in the process. He is dazed, but he seems okay. I had a local veterinarian conduct some blood work and other tests on him after an earlier mission. They confirmed that he had not undergone any trauma."

Beatrice kissed the dog's head before placing him on a table. Then, she removed his harness. The dog allowed his master to open the small pouch, without growling. She smiled; the watch was still inside! She extracted the watch and handed it to Sky, then reached into the bigger pouch and pulled out a newspaper and several coins, along with the original piece of paper.

"I needed to confirm that time travel for a passive occupant had taken place. The best way that I could think of was to simply include a handwritten note, with instructions."

She handed the paper to Zac. He scanned it, then cleared his throat and read it aloud: "Hello! My Master is conducting an experiment in social behaviour. He wants to see if people will obey a simple request for compensation. His request is that you place today's newspaper in my large pouch. Your compensation for doing so is found in the pouch. Please do not attempt to remove the collar as I have been trained to bite, as required. Thank you for participating."

Beatrice went on, "This only works, of course, at certain historical times and in English-speaking places. Yes, I could have translated into any number of languages, but that would just add suspicion to an already tenuous procedure. There is also a huge risk in exposing the watch, but I think I've dealt with that by training the dog to defend the pouch.

"You'll notice too, that the dog's 'Master' has to be a male, to correspond to gender roles in most societies throughout history." Beatrice slowly shook her head and sighed. "We've come a long way, baby!"

Beatrice emptied the old coins onto the desk and explained that she had visited a local shop to purchase coins from different eras in time and bought more online. "I just drop the date-specific coins into the pouch prior to a mission. Did you know that you could buy coins from ancient Rome? I didn't, until I recently went looking for them. And, you can get coins from any era since, more or less. Hmmm, maybe next time I'll translate my note into Latin or Aramaic," she chuckled.

"So, where and… ummm… to when did the dog go?" asked Zac, scratching the underside of Legal's soft muzzle.

"Aha! Well, according to the date on the front page of this newspaper," Beatrice proudly held the paper up high, "He went to the target date – January 8, 1942, which is, of course, Stephen Hawking's birthday. And, he went to the target space, I mean PLACE – and that is Oxford, England; the place of Hawking's birth."

She pulled the note out of the pouch and scanned it.

"I didn't know they had smiley faces in 1942!" Beatrice giggled to herself and then sighed. She handed the note to Sky, then walked to where Zac held the dog. She carefully lifted the dog's rear leg and inspected him for damage.

Someone had scrawled their own note below Beatrice's careful handwriting: "I'VE NOOTERD YOUR MUTT. HE TRYD TO BITE ME! ☺"

"Apparently, not everyone in Oxford is a brainiac! Some are just the class clowns. No harm to Legal. And, the joker even left my original coins. Commendable for war-torn England, I must say."

Sky quietly asked, "So, a beagle is one thing, but can this watch take a human back in time?"

"Uh huh, working with the time machine it can take one back in time or forward into the future. Going into the future, via time dilation, is actually easier. I've never tested it with a human, though. You know by now that that's why I want to talk to you both. Come here." She motioned for Zac and Sky to join her on a dusty old couch, which she first had to clear of boxes and piles of files. Beatrice then explained at some length her reasons for choosing them.

"I want you both to think about this tonight and come back here tomorrow morning, ready to go. This will be the biggest adventure of your lives. And, you'll be contributing significantly to the knowledge of humankind. The goal of the mission is simply to confirm that time travel for an extended period is possible. I do not want you to affect history in any way while you're there; that may be for a future mission."

Beatrice then lowered her voice for no particular reason.

"Don't tell *anyone*! This has to remain a secret, even after you return. While you will be gone for a scheduled 39 days in your 'real time', I'll be able to have you back here for dinner tomorrow night."

"Why 39 days?" Zac asked.

Beatrice rose from her seat. "That is the next time when a suitable geometry of space-time is available, based on recent patterns of geometric waves." The two young men obviously did not understand. "What I mean is that a predetermined sector of space-time must be warped in the correct way."

Sky looked more confused, "Okay, so when you really think about it, if you are 'inventing' time travel now for possible mass future distribution, why don't we have people from the future coming back to our time, showing us their way-cool 23rd century smartwatches? I mean, what if I went back in time to kill an ancestor of mine. He wouldn't be there at the top of my family tree anymore and I wouldn't be at the bottom because I had killed him, preventing my birth. So, I couldn't go back in time to kill him."

"A HA!", exclaimed Beatrice. "And there's the rub. Thank you for asking the billion-dollar question. You've nicely summarized the famous grandfather paradox. It basically says that time travel is impossible. How could it be possible if you're not there to murder him? Stephen Hawking has explained that time travel might only be possible when the conditions – the geometry – of space-time are perfect. Given perfect conditions, which I can assure you I have found, and a viable time machine, which you are looking at, time travel *is* possible. However, from this date, we may indeed have visitors from the future visiting us. We are, essentially, providing the springboard."

Beatrice continued her line of thought, now pacing back and forth. "Physics in or near time machines can only be consistent with the universal laws of physics, and thus only self-consistent events can occur. In other words, anything a time traveller does in the past must have been part of history all along, and the time traveller cannot do anything to prevent the trip back in time from happening, since this would represent an inconsistency. The point, however, is moot: our current mission is to just confirm that time travel is possible. Nothing more."

Numb from the sheer volume of information, Zac and Sky just sat and listened.

Beatrice continued, "Carl Sagan is a well known theorist who I met when I was a student and he was a professor of astronomy at Cornell University. I love his research," she said with an odd nasal twang. "I've read his stuff 'billions and billions of times'!" By the look on her face it appeared Beatrice had made a joke. She loved to laugh at her own jokes. *Perhaps a result of so many hours alone in her basement*, her nephew surmised.

Undaunted by the boys' blank faces, Beatrice continued; "Anyway, Carl Sagan suggested that time travellers could already be here amongst us. They disguise themselves though, because bringing unintentional changes to the space-time continuum might bring about harm to themselves. Or, if past events were changed, we might not notice because following events and our memories would have been instantly altered to remain congruent with the newly-established timeline."

All of this was not helping the two buddies understand the complexities of time travel. They began to think that perhaps they were better off without the details.

Sensing this, Beatrice brought them back to earth. "You've told us about how you fantasize about life in 18th century Britain, Skypilot. I assume that, given a choice, you'd like to travel to that time and place, if you were to go on this little adventure. Am I correct?"

Sky nodded, and still taking it all in, mumbled something about that time and place being a favourite of his. He couldn't face the prospect of somehow returning to the time in Kenya when his mother and father were killed, although the idea ran quickly through his mind.

Zac just sat with his mouth open, staring at the telephone booth.

"I have selected an 18th century target date at random," Beatrice continued, "using a random number generator. Randomness must be maintained for now. You'll be able to ascertain the date when you arrive. Maybe in a future mission you can meet Jesus, or watch the Allies land on D-Day, or witness the signing of the Magna Carta. The target space today is Middlesex, England, which is close to London, but far enough away to ensure your anonymity – at least initially."

Beatrice walked to an open wardrobe in a dark corner of the room. "I have taken the liberty of sewing some time-specific clothes for each of you." She grabbed two loaded clothes hangers from the wardrobe. "I've sewn two outfits that suit a middle-class Englishman of the 18th century:

a knee-length coat, breeches, a waistcoat (that's a vest, of course), a linen shirt with frills, and linen underwear. You won't stand out under any circumstances. No colourful 'Joe Boxers' there!" Beatrice giggled again. Except for the white linen shirt, the clothes were light brown. "They should fit well enough, although I just approximated your sizes."

She proudly held out a full hanger for each of the guys to take. Both took the hangers, but did not try on the clothes.

"And, I got these on eBay too," Beatrice picked up two pairs of odd-looking buckled shoes; one pair brown, and the other black. "These are hobnail shoes. Check out the soles."

She handed Zac the brown pair, and Sky the black. Turning the heavy shoe over revealed rows of "hobnails," the nail heads protruding to provide traction.

Putting the shoes on the floor and holding the clothes at his side with a touch of disdain, Sky growled, "Aunt Bea, I'm not gonna wear this stuff."

"Neither am I!" said Zac. "I'll take my chances with my regular clothes." He threw his hanger of clothes and the shoes onto the sofa.

Beatrice was taken aback, but carried on. She was so close to her dream. She sighed deeply. "Okay, no period clothes. But wear comfortable clothes. You'll have to get other clothes soon after you arrive there. Your appearance may create some questions, but I'm sure that you both will be able to deal with them. You'll have to. I won't be able to talk to you. You'll be on your own, with just each other for support."

She looked them each in the eye to drive home her point.

"I have some period coins for both of you. I'll give them to you tomorrow. The last thing involves recharging your watches. You'll be gone for an extended period, in your time that is, so you'll need to periodically recharge." Beatrice held up two small white units, just a bit bigger than a cell phone. "I have these handy portable chargers that will rapidly charge your smartwatch. The cable provided with the smartwatch plugs into the standard USB port on the mini-charging unit. You'll need to charge the units daily." Beatrice showed Zac and Sky how to re-charge by using the magnetic clasp on the back of the watch. "See? Simple! And the charger uses a lithium cobalt battery that holds a single charge for over a year, so that won't be a concern. It even has a flashlight! All the more reason to keep it hidden whenever you charge your watches."

Beatrice pressed on, "Oh and by the way, don't cut your fingernails while you're away. At least, not the nail on the middle digit of your dominant hand, as that is the one that grows fastest. I'll measure nail length before you go, and when you return. In this way, we can see if you have aged 39 days or just a single day. I'm 99 per cent sure that your fingernails will be longer – 39 days longer. "

"Won't our beards be a better way to gauge aging?" Zac suggested.

"They would, for sure. But you'll both want to shave, and perhaps cut your hair while you're gone. You'll need to abide by the fashion… I would love to give you both smartphones to take pictures with. In fact, you could take pictures with your smartwatches; they are now capable. And, you'd only have to speak to it to activate the photography mode. But again, I have to resist the urge to allow you to take pictures. The mission, as I've said, is simply to confirm that time travel for humans is possible. It's not to provide a greedy scientist with touristy snapshots of the original London Bridge. That, unfortunately, will have to wait."

Beatrice sighed. "Maybe I'll equip you each with a smart-phone next time. Now, you've taken in a lot of information. Go home, digest it. Have dinner with your families and I'll see you back here at 8 a.m. Don't be late!"

Zac looked at his buddy. Sky's facial expression could not hide his excitement.

Zac glanced at Beatrice, then stared at Sky, "Dude, no way! I'm not doing it!" he protested.

"Zac, we have to do this!" Sky was adamant., "I've got to see the past with my own eyes. It'll be far out, man! The biggest adventure of our lives, bud, better than summer camp! And we'll still get to go to summer camp, for probably the last time. Besides, I'll need you to save me from harm somewhere along the way. And, there's that little thing about 'contributing to the knowledge of mankind', too."

"Well, have fun then. And try to stay outta trouble." Zac pointed to the watch in Beatrice's hand. "Looks like there's only one watch."

Beatrice cleared her throat and pushed the persistent glasses back up her nose. Slowly opening the desk drawer, she pulled out a second watch and said, "Actually, there are two. These watches – well, the onboard apps – are prototypes. They are the only two of their kind, to date. We are refining the app now, but I'm happy with the results so far. Here, my chrononauts," she paused to let the word resonate. "Try these on." She handed each of them a smartwatch.

"A watch to slip us back through time. How apropos is that?" As he fastened the watch to his wrist, Sky whistled and playfully punched Zac's shoulder.

Zac knew that, despite his reservations, this was the opportunity of a lifetime. Holding up his watch to inspect it, he mumbled, "Okay, okay… 39 days. I guess this smartwatch will be ticking."

Sky thought, *These two smartwatches won't be the only ones ticking. I'm gonna bring Mickey too, for good luck.*

With his hand in his pocket, he ran his fingers over the ridges on the familiar silver casing. That always comforted him.

∞

5

London, England
Spring 1766

THE EVENING RAIN POURED down relentlessly as the trio emerged from London's Royal Theatre with the rest of the vacating audience. Only the woman held an umbrella, made of oiled black silk, over her head while the two men hurried ahead to their private carriage, which was waiting on Bridge Street.

A waiting coachman and two footmen sat soaked and sullen in the front of the carriage. Having just completed his walk-around inspection, the coachman turned to watch his masters and mistress hurry into the elaborately decorated coach. Purple with gold trim, it seemed to mimic the opulent fashions of its occupants with its phallic embellishments on each of the four corners and floral patterns ornamenting each side. Even the wheels were richly appointed, with the wooden spokes hand-carved and each hub lathe-turned into a cone.

The older of the well-dressed men turned to assist the woman into the carriage, the interior of which was upholstered in purple brocaded silk. She needed a hand. Her hooped dress, complete with layers of petticoats, was wet from the rain and had to be carefully gathered as she stepped up into the coach through its narrow doorway.

By royal decree, the Royal was one of only two theatres in London where people could attend a play where actors spoke their lines. No other premises were allowed to present plays with speaking roles. So, rival theatre owners got around the rules by presenting pantomimes, or "plays" that were primarily song and dance, with the spoken word taking a minor role.

Having attended a production of *The Beggar's Opera*, the group wore their most stylish evening wear. Both of the men wore wigs, while the young woman wore a luxurious patterned silk dress. The low-cut dress (her mother was not available to censor her daughter's fashion choices) had revealed her ample bosom.

Now, she was protected from the cool summer air by a gold-coloured shawl. The ruby-red dress was adorned with gold trim and woven with velvet ribbon, although most of those who beheld her at the theatre may have been too distracted by the aforementioned bosom to notice the intricacy of the dress's pattern. She required no corset; her naturally thin waistline was kept toned by frequent horse rides. Her richly embroidered tricorne hat featured pearl accents and white ostrich plumes that contrasted smartly with her shining auburn hair. Panting after her efforts to enter the carriage, she pushed aside a curly lock of hair, revealing deep brown eyes.

Although make-up was considered aristocratic, this particular young woman wore relatively little: only red lips, and rouge on the apples of her high cheeks. Pearl earrings, a pearl necklace and a gold pendant watch – signed and numbered by the watchmaker – completed her look. She was so proud of her watch. It was a birthday gift from her father, and she found a pendant watch useful on her frequent rides. The 22-carat cover depicted a woman in dressage, over whose shoulder stood a horse. Other animals, including a stag, a boar, a wolf, a lamb and a lion, comprised the background, and a pristine landscape completed the scene. She wore the watch everywhere and sometimes, like tonight, had to carry it hidden in a pouch sewn into her petticoats. In quiet moments, she was comforted by the sound of it ticking.

The older man, her father, muttered sentiments of gratitude under his breath: his daughter's hoop dress, though ungainly, had worked tonight to keep men at a chaste distance.

Like most aristocratic men, he wore a white wig, which he proceeded to remove once inside the carriage, complaining of the sweaty combination of rain and having to hurry through it. He sat down beside his daughter on the forward-facing bench seat and rapped hard on the roof of the cabin; the signal for the coachman to go.

The coach lurched forward, and the sounds of hooves on cobblestone replaced the gentle patter of rain on the roof.

The father's well-manicured beard, in the Van Dyke style, brushed against his frilly, white linen shirt as he looked down to sweep the rain from of his knee-length coat, under which he wore a long matching waistcoat. French silk stockings and leather shoes completed his outfit.

Their companion surpassed both of them in gaudy resplendence. Like his father sitting across from him, the young man was bedecked in a wig. His, however, was much higher than his father's, and pink. His face, powdered white, bore several pockmarks – though they had been decorated for the evening with boldly colored silk patches cut in star shapes.

He, with the assistance of his valet, had taken much time earlier that day to prepare. After he was finished dressing, his valet had helped him pull on a temporary silk coverlet designed to protect his clothing from the powder to be applied to both his wig and face. His man then scribed fine light-blue lines on his white cheeks, emulating veins and indicating a certain healthy clarity of skin. His lips had been reddened beneath a fine thin moustache.

From the theatre he had strutted in his high-heeled leather shoes, each fastened with a detachable buckle and embellished by a red ruby. The high heels made the wearer taller and provided a more pleasing physical proportion, as a semblance of balance was achieved when a high wig was worn. The heels also defined his social status; that is, wearing heels made it impossible for him to do physical labour.

For his theatre visit, he had, days ago, chosen a pale yellow coat with broad silver stripes. His vest of silver with broad stripes of the same yellow complemented the over-coat, which was shorter than most and cut in a curve at the front. He believed he had good legs. *Be damned if I am going to cover them up!* he thought.

His silver, knitted silk breeches fit close, and for him, served as a constant reminder of his innate elegance and other fine qualifications too numerous to mention here.

He had turned many a head in the Royal tonight, all with complimentary intentions, he thought, but most of which were not. One well-heeled man, sitting just two rows back from the young man, had whispered derisively to his female companion, "It appears that the young Lord has a chartered membership in the Macaroni Club."

There was no formal "club"; members were simply young men who dressed higher than high fashion and spoke in an outlandishly affected and effeminate manner. The "maca-roni" reference was to the fact that many of these men had travelled, or were planning to travel to, Italy. Our young lord, William Mansfield III, fit the mold perfectly.

The observer's female companion had raised a penciled eyebrow. "Wee Willy is a pompous ass. His mother would turn in her grave." She leaned closer to her friend and asked rhetorically, "What, pray tell, does his father think of him, parading around like that?" A droll thought came to mind and her eyebrow reached higher. "And if he and his prancing Macaronis were in parade, wouldn't they bring up the *rear* of the cavalcade?"

Despite himself, the gentleman had snorted, eliciting glances from near-by theatre-goers.

Now, Willy's walk/run from the theatre meant he resembled a wet peacock. His make-up had started to run about the same time that he had. Dripping, Willy stared at his father and sister sitting across from him. As his father knocked on the roof, the well-sprung and richly upholstered carriage lurched forward, rumbling along the cobbled street muffled with straw that had been strewn as a courtesy to theatre-goers and neighbours.

But as the carriage gained speed on the bare outlying streets, the clatter all but prevented conversation. Soon enough, the cobblestones disappeared along with the city and its dim light, as the carriage rumbled into the western countryside. The deafening noise was replaced by the muffled sounds of hooves on a sodden mud road, and the snorts of labouring horses. Conversation was easier here.

It had been a long day; the group had arrived early at the theatre, despite being subscribers.

"Can't we sit on the stage tonight, father?" the flamboyant son had asked on their earlier journey into London. To Willy's chagrin, the family had rented box seats for the season, just back from "the pit," the cheap seats closest to the stage. William loved sitting on the stage under the lights, where everyone could see him. All the best families did it.

"Not tonight, William. I've found that to be most uncomfortable," the father replied, rubbing his lower back. Attending the theatre was a way to reaffirm the Mansfield family's social standing. It had served to keep the family together since his wife's untimely death, but he was damned if he was going to suffer for it.

Willy's need to be seen was, however, easily accomplished without actually sitting on the stage, as candles and oil lamps brightly illuminated the auditorium throughout the performance. Although this created a certain intimacy between actor and audience, it also encouraged audience members to look around and chat instead of watching the play. The son and daughter had taken full advantage, with discrete waves and the occasional funny face directed at friends, despite their father's annoyed looks.

The young man, who spoke with a pronounced and unfortunate lisp, was discussing the play. "They say that John Gay wrote the play to satirize Italian opera. I just adore how it lampoons the classic Italian style. Father, we should have the theatre company stage a show at the estate!" He looked inquiringly at his dad and crossed his legs, which was not easy to do in the gyrating carriage.

"Absolutely not, William! While it may be humorous when it pokes fun at the Italians, it seemed to speak more to the lower classes than to you and me. I mean, that one character – what was his name? Peachy?"

"PeaCHUM, father," corrected Willy. "Think 'impeach him'; the one who manages a company of highwaymen."

"Impeach him, indeed! He is immoral, as were almost all of the characters. We are, I suppose, meant to revel in their depravities. Well, I cannot. I will not promote that type of thinking in my own ballroom. Besides, your birthday celebration is coming soon; you shall have a ball then." Sir William Mansfield II, the Duke of Chestney, stared into the distance and sighed deeply. "I just wish that your mother could be there with us."

Returning to reality, Sir William glared at his son, William III, then looked sullenly out the window at the growing shadows. Annoyed, he banged on the roof and yelled to the carriage man, "Faster, Daltrey, let's get through Hounslow quickly!"

Hounslow Heath was part of the wild forest of Middlesex and, quite possibly, home to the most dangerous roadways in Britain. Infested by highwaymen, the Heath provided attackers with many hiding places and many more potential victims.

"Yes, M'Lord!"

With a crack of the whip, the carriage picked up speed.

Staring out the window, Lady Rachel Mansfield was aware of her father's nervous agitation. Trying to calm him, she said, "Well, I have mixed feelings about the play. I loved the music. I knew every tune, I think. But, their characterization of women as scheming, utterly self-interested harlots left me cold."

"I'm cold too. Can't wait to get home," said Willy, rubbing his shoulders.

∞

6

Middlesex, England
Spring 1766

"WHAT O'CLOCK D'YA MAKE it? We've bin out in this pissin' rain since half past 8 o' the clock. Not much on the road tonight, mates. The only other thing we seen was that footpad awhile back. And he told us he'd had no luck either."

With a grunt, Harry Moody finished relieving himself against the huge oak tree under which they had hidden. He re-mounted his horse. "At least the rain's lettin' up."

The torrential rain had subsided to just a few drops of clinging haze. The waning light was barely enough to reveal the three dark figures on horseback waiting under the tree. Their overnight camp was just a stone's throw further into the bush. A passing traveller would need the light of the waxing moon to see them hunched over their saddles, although receding clouds still filled most of the tree-lined sky.

Waiting – highwaymen had to be good at it. They waited beside roadways, sometimes for hours, until a suitable victim came by. Suitability was based on the level of protection, the number of potential victims in a party and the caravan's appearance.

This successful trio had been together for some time, and their infamous leader had gained notoriety not only for getting what he wanted, but for doing so by using his charm.

French-born, he remained bilingual and spoke English with an accent. Rakishly handsome, mustachioed and elegantly dressed under his dripping raincoat and black tricorne hat, Jacques DuTemps had come to be adored by the ladies he robbed, and despised by the men.

Harry muttered, "We should go back to workin' the Holloway road, ya know. We did well there and the ale at the Boarshead Pub is the best around!" He burped loudly for emphasis.

His partner, Mike, retorted, "No, there are more post boys on this road, and richies too. One good hit here is worth three on the Holloway."

"Maybe, but them 'post boys' have a partner riding with 'em now, carrying a blunderbuss and a pair of pistols an' all, you ninny."

Jacques chewed on his bottom lip and ignored the banter between the other two. He concentrated on watching the roadway. Traffic did seem unusually low tonight, both in and out of London was typically steady at this time of night. But something was coming. He held up his gloved hand and the banter stopped. All three listened intently, their eyes peeled on the roadway.

Inside the carriage, as Willy chafed his shoulders to keep warm, a loud thud was heard. The carriage came to a sudden stop, and in the silence, the coachman turned to bellow, "You summoned, M'Lord?" anticipating that His Lordship had knocked because one of the travellers had to take a break.

"I did not summon you, Daltrey." Sir William paused, "There was a bang."

"I'll have a look, sir." Daltrey got down from his station, stretching his legs. He walked slowly around the carriage, inspecting as he went.

Daltrey was a fine coachman, loyal to his Master and to his trade. Like the two footmen who accompanied him, he was well-trained, including in the use of weaponry (primarily the blunderbuss and its accompanying bayonet), to ward off highwaymen. Past challenges – and there had been a few – were typically dealt with simply by a show of force, such as firing the gun in the general direction of attackers.

His master's carriage was a Berlin Troika; a covered carriage drawn by three horses, with a raised coach box from where he drove it and a basket in the rear. One of the finest and largest private coaches, it was able to carry up to six passengers. He was proud to operate it. Highwaymen knew of it and of its defences, so they typically allowed it to pass.

But the vehicle's immense size also made it hard to handle, and slow. There was no hope of escaping from mounted robbers by speed, which also increased the chance of the carriage flipping while cornering. The two footmen were employed to right the carriage if and when it went over. Two was a low number for such a magnificent carriage, but Sir William refused to hire more. So, speed was not an option, given the increased chance of a flip.

Each of the three hired men was armed with a blunderbuss. Normally, the two footmen rode at the back, in the basket. But Sir William had insisted that his staff use the trip into London to secure any necessary supplies for the household, while the family attended the theatre. Daltrey had therefore arranged to purchase weapons and ammunition at a Carnaby Street weapons shop. These were stored in the basket, covered in a waterproof tarpaulin but loaded and ready to be used when required. With no place to stand in the back, the footmen had to ride up front with the coachman.

A few lingering raindrops fell as Daltrey walked slowly around the carriage in the mud, checking for damage. He thought that perhaps a branch had fallen from a tree, or more likely, there was a problem with a wheel. He removed his glove, tossed it on the mud and kneeled on it to check the undercarriage.

The footmen got down to stretch their legs, leaning their weapons against the wheel of the carriage. They proceeded to adjust their clothing and scratch themselves, as travelling men are wont to do. In doing so, they politely turned their backs to the carriage in case one of its occupants might chance to peer out and see a churlish manipulation of breeches.

Leaning under the carriage, Daltrey ran his bare hand along the long, mud-caked leather braces that supported the body. Everything seemed to be in good repair. What could have possibly caused that bang?

Unbeknownst to him, he was being watched intently.

Despite having their prey stop directly in front of them, the highwaymen knew that they had to move fast. With a nod, Jacques brought his neckerchief up over his nose, as did his two partners. Each carried a pistol – a type of blunderbuss, in its handgun form – called a dragon. All three drew their pistols from their holsters, holding the barrels skyward, and spurred their horses on down the grassy, wet embankment next to the road. They quickly reached the flat of the road. The two footmen, who had had their backs turned, frantically lunged for their blunderbusses at the sound.

Too late! The footmen fell, easily dispatched by three shots at close range.

Startled by the sounds of approaching horses and shots fired, Daltrey bumped his head hard on the carriage as he tried to get up. His wig fell to the ground. He stumbled to his feet, cursing and rubbing his head in pain. He thought he could feel the lump growing larger as he rubbed. He could see the upright barrel of the blunderbuss leaning against the far wheel, but he was closer to the weapons stashed in the rear basket.

"No need to move, driver!" Jacques pointed his pistol as he used the more derisive word for coachman to ensure that the man knew his place in this exchange. "Hands up! Stand over there. And, make your way slowly, for I am prone to making quick mistakes – and when I do, they usually take the form of lead."

He motioned with the gun to a place near the rear of the carriage, not far from the bodies of the dead footmen. Hands high and head low, Daltrey walked slowly to the assigned spot. The barrels of the dragons held by Harry and Mike followed his every step.

The occupants of the carriage heard the commotion and rose from their seats to peer through the window. They saw three masked horsemen, each armed with a smoking dragon. They saw the bodies of the footmen and the dark stain under each body. Rachel shuddered. Her brother sat down again, breathing heavily and shivering. He had always been timorous of highwaymen.

One of the thieves, dressed in fashionable clothes, dismounted and approached the carriage on foot. With a French accent he bellowed, "You in dere, come down now! Stand and deliver your purses."

"Oh botheration!" Sir William had had his carriage threatened by highwaymen before. But the liberal use of the blunderbuss had always scared off would-be assailants. This time, his footmen were down and his coachman had been caught without a weapon. He would need to hire more footmen after this.

Aggravated, he opened the door and made his way slowly down the small steps to the tall grass beside the muddy ruts in the road. Behind him lumbered his son. His daughter followed, taking his hand as she stepped down.

The rain had stopped, but it remained cool in the waning evening light. The three stood in a line, with the father in the centre. After smoothing her dress and adjusting her hat, Rachel stood defiant, chin raised.

"So, who, or should I say, *what* do we 'ave 'ere?" asked the leader of the robbers, to the hoots and whistles of his henchmen. Jacques' eyes did not leave the young woman, who was a vision of loveliness against the backdrop of the mud and trees. The other men's catcalls took stock of the effeminate young man.

Steely-eyed, the Duke cleared his throat. "I am Sir William Mansfield, the Duke of Chestney. This is my son, Lord William, and my daughter, Lady Rachel. Leave us to continue our journey home or I swear to you, sir, you shall hang by your neck at Tyburn!"

The Duke was referring to London's notorious Tyburn Tree, from which tens of thousands of highwaymen, robbers, murderers and other convicted men and women had met their end.

Jacques shuddered at the thought. As a teenager, he and some 250,000 others had been there to witness the hanging of two men; one a celebrated thief and the other a talented escapee who had somehow avoided an earlier hanging. Books had been sold at the gallows, songs were sung and hawkers sold souvenir portraits of the prisoners. Well-to-do spectators sat in galleries erected for the occasion, or in rented rooms in neighbouring houses and pubs.

Jacques had pushed through the crowd to get to a good vantage point as the horse-drawn cart, called a tumbrel, carried the condemned men to the tree, where nooses were secured around their necks. The gigantic crowd of spectators had gone silent, holding their collective breath.

Then, the tumbrel was driven away, leaving the prisoners suspended. The crowd erupted in cheers. The worst part for young Jacques had been when the friends of the condemned had run up to tug at hanging men's feet so that the men would die quicker and suffer less. After the corpses were cut down, there was a rush to grab the bodies: some people believed their hair and body parts would be effective in healing diseases.

Jacques quickly recovered from his remembrance. "I, sir, am Jacques DuTemps, a gentleman of the road. And I am quite attached to my neck, thank you!" He looked to his partners, who were chuckling under their kerchiefs, and made a mocking choking motion with his hands. "I am about to relieve you of the weight of your purses, so that you may fly home quicker. I do not wish to resort to using this firearm again, but my friends and I will do so if you do not now comply. Now, your purses!"

Sir William immediately recognized the name. Being robbed by an infamous highwayman was regarded by some as something of an honour. On the other hand, he considered any highwayman or footpad (a thief on foot) as scum to be brought to justice. Nevertheless, he had no choice: he withdrew his purse from his waistcoat pocket and threw it onto the wet ground at Jacques' feet. He indicated for his son and daughter to do the same, which they reluctantly did.

Jacques smiled at Rachel as he and Mike dismounted. Mike stooped to retrieve the purses, and handed them to his master before getting back on his horse. "Rachel... such a beautiful name for an even more beautiful young woman! Come 'ere, let me feast upon your beauty." He held out his hand and beckoned her closer with his fingers.

Rachel wrapped her gold shawl tighter around her, looked at her father and brother, and with her head held high, stepped boldly toward the highwayman. Despite her trepidation, she had to suppress a smile; she too recognized the name. Her social circle was abuzz with rumours about highwaymen, their escapades, victims, lovers and ultimately, their hangings.

Jacques' eyes missed not a detail. Softly, he cooed, "Ah, you are truly beautiful as you stand before me."

His deep, foreign voice was like liquid honey dripping slowly over weathered leather. With confidence, he slid down his mask in the dim light and stepped as close to Rachel as her voluminous skirts would allow.

As he approached, Rachel realized that she had had no idea just how handsome this infamous highwayman was. He seemed familiar. His black wavy hair, tied with a black ribbon under his tricorne, matched the shiny colour of his well-kept moustache, and his aquiline nose made him look strong and intelligent. But, as she would recall privately later, it was his soulful brown eyes that left her knees shaking. Thankfully, her dress covered her. At her next tea, her friends would be so envious!

Jacques brazenly removed his leather glove and caressed Rachel's cheek, then took a lock of her silky auburn hair in his hand. He leaned forward into her petticoats, and sniffed it. Rachel's father and brother looked on in horror. Seething, Sir William repeatedly clenched his hands into fists. He could not take much more.

Undaunted, Jacques continued, "The fragrance of lilies from France graces your 'air. Coincidence? I think not. I digress. Before we leave this party with your money, I believe that you owe me a party piece: a joke, a song or a dance. If you please, you may save *ton père* further problems if you have a good one for me."

"Leave her, man! Leave her alone." Sir William moved threateningly toward Jacques. Both horsemen tensed and raised their dragons.

"Father, never mind," Rachel said gently to her father. "His is but a simple request. I have a song to sing. And then, we will go," She turned back to face Jacques and sighed. "It is called *Vive la rose*, and it goes like this…"

Rachel hummed the key and began to sing. Her sweet voice caressed the evening air, taking all that heard her to another time and place.

43

"Mon ami me délaisse
Ô gué, vive la rose
Je ne sais pas pourquoi
Vive la rose et le lilas
Il va-t-en voir une autre
Ô gué, vive la rose
Qui est plus riche que moi
Vive la rose et le lilas
On dit qu'elle est plus belle
Ô gué, vive la rose
Je n'en disconviens pas
Vive la rose et le lilas
On dit qu'elle est malade
Ô gué, vive la rose
Peut-être qu'elle en mourra
Vive la rose et le lilas
Mais si elle meurt dimanche
Ô gué, vive la rose
Lundi on l'enterrera
Vive la rose et le lilas
Mardi, reviendra me voir
Ô gué, vive la rose
Mais je n'en voudrai pas
Vive la rose et le lilas." [1]

Rachel knew that she was taking a risk singing *en fran-çais* to a charming Frenchman. But she felt it was worth the risk to appease him, and hopefully win her family's freedom without further loss.

Her hands were coupled gracefully at her waist for most of the performance, but she artistically stretched out her

---

[1] Adapted from an 18th century French Canadian folk song, composer unknown.

arms as the song reached its climax. The song was about unrequited love. The first line is roughly translated as "My boyfriend dumped me."

Completing the song, Rachel hung her head and waited for their fate to be decided. Jacques said nothing for a short time, still enjoying the sweet melody that resonated in his ears. The scene, controlled in its entirety by Jacques, was very quiet. As Sir William glared anew, Jacques stepped close to Rachel to once again take her chin in his hand and look into her brown eyes. It was at that moment, in the relative quiet, that he heard the slight ticking of her pendant watch.

"*Très magnifique*, M'Lady. I have known that tune since I was a stable boy in Rouen. Your former boyfriend must not only be blind, but deaf as well. That is good news for your future suitors. *Merci*! Now…", the highwayman smiled and motioned with the barrel of his gun to her petticoats, "Do you have something for me 'idden in your accoutrements? Something that ticks to the beat of my 'eart?"

Reluctantly and with some effort, Rachel pulled out her beloved pendant watch, and holding it by the chain, handed it over.

∞

1

Fraserdale
Summer 2018

THE MORNING AFTER THEIR meeting with Beatrice, Zac was standing inside the K2 telephone booth – the time machine, that is – next to Skypilot; his heart racing and his eyes glued shut.

Zac opened one eye, then the other. He saw Sky's aunt through the glass panes of the booth, sitting at her computer. She was not keying in anything, but seemed to be simply waiting and watching nervously. She seemed to have completed her preliminaries: taking fingernail measurements and photos of each of them – their faces, their right hands and a close-up of each of their right middle fingers.

Zac impulsively grabbed his friend's hand.

"No, dude," Sky said. "That ain't happening. You're on your own for this part of the journey." Sky purposefully removed his hand from Zac's firm grip, as a strange noise increased all around them.

Zac crossed his arms in acknowledgment that his life-long buddy had a point. Zac was raised by his single father, after his mother suddenly left when he was nine years old. He never fully understood her reasons for leaving, but he knew that she was now living with a woman in southern California. She had never made an effort to contact her estranged husband or son. Zac's father, stunned by his wife's actions, never remarried. Zac understood the importance of independence.

As before, the process began with a bright, pulsating light inside the booth, accompanied by the now-familiar low and undulating sound.

Later, Zac remembered only some initial discomfort associated with what seemed a rhythmic stretching of his body. This was quickly displaced by a lifting sensation. He felt as if his body was being gently lifted away from the floor, his clothes seemingly hovering around him. Seconds passed, then minutes ticked by. Or did they?

Again, Zac slowly opened one eye... then, the other. No panes of glass, no Aunt Bea. Total darkness surrounded him, punctuated by pinpoints of light darting past. A dim light, originating in the direction that he seemed to be travelling in – if in fact he was travelling in a single direction – slowly and inexorably replaced the darkness.

Suddenly, he came to a violent stop, hitting his head on something. When he gathered himself, he found himself lying on what appeared to be a wet, oily tarpaulin. Groggily, he began to get up, pushing with his arms. But his head hurt too much, and darkness overcame him.

The sharp report of guns firing stirred him to semi-consciousness. He heard voices, at first angry, then conversational in nature. He thought that he heard someone call his name. Couldn't be...

And that didn't matter at the moment. He appeared to be in a box, on top of some bumpy material covered by the oily tarp. The dimness told him that it was evening or early morning. He lifted a corner of the tarp to reveal old-fashioned wooden rifles. Under the rifles, he could see what appeared to be knives.

He listened carefully to the conversation outside. He pushed himself up and peered cautiously over the side of the box. As his head cleared, he realized that he was in the rear of a carriage on a muddy road, surrounded by trees. Seven people were visible in the dim light, three of whom were close by. Two of the three were on horseback and wore strange hats and masks. They appeared to be guarding the third person, who stood between the horsemen and Zac, beside a steep hill that bordered the road. Two bodies lay crumpled at the base of the hill. As Zac listened, the others, further away, spoke in subdued tones.

"Rachel…" said the male voice with a French accent, "Rachel, such a beautiful name for an even more beautiful young woman! Come 'ere, let me feast upon your beauty."

There was further unintelligible conversation, then Zac watched as the woman, dressed in a fancy hat and a huge dress, hesitantly moved toward the man. Then, of all things, she began to sing! She had a strong, sweet voice; a voice that Zac could not fully enjoy under the circumstances.

He felt that he had to act, and soon. He was not sure about what was happening, but what with the masked men, he figured he had happened upon a robbery. He shuffled noiselessly – but not painlessly – from his position, into a crouch.

Out of the corner of his eye, the man closest to him – the one with his hands over his head – saw the slight movement. At first, Daltrey assumed that the robbers had a fourth member who had snuck up from behind the carriage. Then, he remembered the thud that had brought the carriage to a stop. This young man was obviously a stowaway. How he got in the basket, Daltrey could not fathom. He had checked it at the theatre just prior to leaving, as he habitually did. Vagrants often tried to get a free ride when they could. Now, this one might be of some assistance. It would be the least he could do to help pay for his ride. The two made subtle eye contact; the dim light acting to hide the contact from the highwaymen and hinder mutual acknowledgment by Daltrey and Zac.

As Rachel's song distracted his guards, Daltrey motioned with his eyes and a slight downward jerk of his head to the pile of weapons under Zac's legs. Zac had only held a gun a few times before, when his dad had taken him shooting quail. He had loved the adventure, and as it turned out, he was a good shot. But that was a couple of years ago. Or was it? Zac looked at the clothes these people were wearing.

He nodded to the man and carefully peeled back the thick tarpaulin. The singing covered up the muffled sounds he made to extract two rifles. Zac was surprised to see that the knives he had noticed earlier were actually bayonets attached to the barrels of the rifles.

Quietly taking a rifle into each hand, Zac slowly stood up in the basket, watching the two men on horseback. They were leaning forward in their saddles, engrossed with both the song and the woman who sang it. Their weapons, while pointing more or less toward their prisoner, were held limply and without purpose. Just then, the woman finished her song. There was a prolonged silence, followed by the compliments of the man standing closest to her. And perhaps, a demand: the woman reached under her dress and handed something on a chain to the Frenchman.

At that moment, Zac threw one of the bayonetted rifles to the outstretched arms of the nearby man, who caught it by the barrel. Daltrey quickly cocked the blunderbuss, aimed, and fired up at the closest horseman.

The single-shot blunderbuss, an early form of the shotgun, was ineffective at long range, but bloody effective at downing short-range targets like poor Mike. The lead balls tore through the man, killing him instantly and propelling his shredded body off the horse. The loud blast and the sudden loss of its rider startled the horse. It bolted between Jacques and Rachel, knocking both to the wet ground.

Now armed with only the bayonet on the spent blunderbuss, Daltrey ran the few paces to the other horseman.

Lunging the bayonet toward his torso, Daltrey screamed, "Drop your weapon and get down, now! For I'm also a devil at a quick mistake, but when I make one it takes the form of a wicked blade shoved deep inside a foolish man."

Harry nodded and held up his weapon by two fingers before dropping it. As it fell, Harry lifted his leg slightly to deflect its fall. This simple action was enough to divert Daltrey's attention for a split second. Quickly, Harry spurred on his horse, shouting "Giddy up!"

Daltrey lunged with the bayonet at the departing rider, stabbing him in the leg. Harry howled out in pain. He rode to where Jacques was getting to his feet, and slowed to help his leader onto the horse. Zac aimed his gun at the fleeing felons, but could not risk shooting them with the other people in close proximity. Daltrey ran toward them but had to go around Rachel, who remained indelicately sitting on the muddy road, but seemingly intact.

Before Daltrey could get to them, the two highwaymen rode off into the darkness – but not before Jacques shouted, "Farewell, Lady Rachel, we shall meet again! Look for a red rose in my lapel! And listen for the ticking of your beautiful watch!"

The sound of his laughter and the galloping horse faded into the damp summer air.

∞

8

LIKE ZAC, SKY FELT compelled to close his eyes inside the K2. Nevertheless, he could see the bright light penetrating his eyelids. Tiny lights streamed by, slowly coalescing into one above him. Or, below him – he wasn't sure.

An unseen force pulled at his body. He was uncomfortable with the sensation. Then, it stopped suddenly, as did his body.

Regaining his senses, Sky realized that he was lying amongst wet bramble bushes, in a gulley under a tree. A few raindrops fell. Holding his arms in front of him, he smiled. He had landed in one piece. Getting to his feet, he checked that he had all the items that he had entered the K2 with: all the coins were there; the recharging unit, the cord, the smartwatch and his Mickey Mouse pocket watch.

He stretched, then shouted: "Zac! Zaaac!"

Sky could smell smoke. In the dim light, he could not see very far. He carefully extricated himself from the gulley and the brambles, but not carefully enough as he ripped his pants. He had a few scrapes from the sharp thorns of the bush, but nothing serious. His ears were ringing, although the journey had been relatively quiet, save for that popping sound.

The tree was a huge oak, and it appeared in the dim light that someone had carved initials in it. He ran his fingers along the gashes in the bark; it looked and felt like a "J," or maybe an "I" and a capital "D."

He stood looking around, unsure of what to do next. Was that singing in the distance?

Feeling woozy, Sky felt compelled to walk, using his sense of smell to locate where the smoke was coming from. Maybe that was the source of the singing, too. But, the singing – if there had been any – had stopped. This sniffing method worked well, and he soon saw the faint glow of a distant fire. He walked on through the wet underbrush, toward the glow. The bottom portion of his ripped jeans was now soaked.

Closer now (he hadn't walked very far), he realized that the fire was hardly a fire, but just glowing embers in a handmade pit. The rain, he guessed, had been heavier earlier and had extinguished the flames. In the distance: another odd noise. This one sounded like a firecracker. He held his breath, listening for more.

Sky trudged through the underbrush into what appeared to be an overnight encampment, He was not able to see much in the half-light. Whoever had been here had left some kindling and a leather satchel under the cover of an old oak tree. Sky opened the satchel to find three blankets (two were stained and holey); some thin thread on a spool; a rusty needle; three metal cups (two of which were filthy); and a small metal pot. A little fabric package held a leafy substance. Sky sniffed it: tea.

The night (or early morning) was not cold and the rain had almost stopped. Sky hunched over the dying fire and held out his hand to gauge its warmth. He was tired. His body ached, and despite devouring Gramma's delicious breakfast just a short time ago, he was hungry too.

If this was evening, it could get colder. In any case, if he was going to use the fire he had better do so quickly, or it would soon be out. He needed some dry moss or straw to get a spark. Under the protective canopy of the oak tree, he found some moss. He placed it where the embers seemed hottest, and used a stick to position it perfectly. Blowing on it, the wispy smoke became billows that became a little puff of flame! He fed his fire with some of the kindling that had been cut, and sat back, watching and thinking.

Sky didn't drink a lot of tea, although his Gramma did. But a hot cup would be great right now. He had the tea, but unfortunately, no water.

He would sleep now beside the fire until morning, whenever that came. The camp had not been abandoned, it seemed. If someone came by as he slept, he hoped that they'd be friendly. In the morning light, he could look around, get his bearings; maybe find a stream and decide what to do next. He hoped that Zac was close by and that he was thinking the same way. Sky gathered some grass and foliage for a bed, and using his vest for a pillow, fell asleep beside the crackling fire.

∞

9

RACHEL TRIED TO GET up from the drenched ground, but her skirt proved to be too wet and too hooped. Her brother scurried over to help her up. Her expensive dress was muddied and ruined.

Her father was beside himself. "That man will hang, by God!" Sir William fumed. "I don't care about his crony, HE will hang! Daltrey, let's go before they decide to return." He stomped through the mud toward the carriage.

"Leave the dead one for the footpads. And leave the horses. We must make haste." He turned, sighed, and extended his arm in a sweeping motion, "And fear not, I will arrange to have the bodies of the footmen recovered immediately when we get back to Mansfield."

Daltrey acknowledged his master and motioned toward Zac, who had jumped down from the carriage, looking perplexed. Daltrey knew the weapon was loaded. He motioned for Zac to hand over the gun. The weapon safely in hand, the carriage man asked, "What of this vagrant, Lord? I believe that he was a stowaway, riding in the rear basket, likely all the way from London."

Sir William nodded his head slowly, thinking that more likely, the vagrant happened to be passing when the robbery occurred. He remembered Daltrey checking the carriage prior to them leaving the theatre, as was his practice. In any case, the vagrant had helped them escape.

"He will ride with us to the estate, if he so pleases," Mansfield looked at Zac, "What say you?"

Everyone's attention, including that of Rachel, turned to Zac. "I say, umm Lord, I will ride with you. Perhaps you can help me find my friend." Zac had not counted on being separated from Sky.

"You do not sound like an Englishman, or a Scot or a Mick, for that matter. Where are you from?" The nobleman held up a hand. "But, not now. Tell me about yourself and your lost friend as we go. We'll have time, although home is not far from here."

Zac followed as Sir William and his family made their way back into the carriage. With a rap on the roof by Sir William and an acknowledging cry from Daltrey, off they went. Rachel and her father again sat in the forward-facing seat, and Wee Willy (such a moniker is somehow justified when a father named William names his son William) sat beside the vagrant, Zachary.

Zac thought it pertinent to introduce himself with his given name, Zachary, rather than the more familiar Zac. He shook hands with each of his fellow travelers, and particularly enjoyed shaking Rachel's outstretched, gloved hand. To tell the truth, he didn't know whether to shake it or to kiss it! She was wearing a low-cut dress, now quite muddy, from which Zac tried valiantly to avert his eyes. She had a lovely smile too.

Rachel's initial impression of Zac was that he was very strange, with his clothing, his speech and his haircut. With her basic knowledge of the world, she classified him as exotic. She had to learn more about the vagrant. Willy felt the same way.

The carriage was, of course, in perfect condition, other than the small dent in the wood above the basket left by Zac's head when he fell. Daltrey never did retrieve his glove or wig, but the estate later replaced them both, somewhat to his dismay: Daltrey hated wearing the damn wig.

Sir William wanted to know where Zac was coming from and going to. Zac explained that he and his friend had been travelling to London, looking for work, when they were separated. Thankfully, he had heard Daltrey mention London earlier.

"Well, times are tough everywhere, Zachary. Work will be hard to secure in London. As you helped us in time of need, so too can I assist you. I am, as it turns out, in need of a footman. Are you interested?"

"Yes, sir. I would be interested in employment." Zac had no idea what a footman did. He knew that his hosts' home was not far and that Sky couldn't be far from here either. He jumped at the chance to be in close proximity. "But I am most interested in finding my friend."

Sir William ignored the implied request. "I'm glad that you have accepted my offer. You may address me as Sir William, or simply, Lord. Now Zachary, you do speak with a strange accent. Where are you from, the colonies?"

Zac's knowledge of history was being tested. "Yes, Lord, I am from the colonies," he replied. And, for emphasis he added, "Indeed."

"And, your clothes! I've never seen anything like them – and I've travelled extensively, including to Africa. Is that the way they dress in the colonies?"

The mention of Zac's clothes prompted Rachel to blurt out, "Yes, please tell us, Zachary, about your strange clothes. Father, look at his footwear. So strange!" She looked down to his Nike sneakers, and he crossed his feet shyly. Rachel giggled.

Sir William extended an arm. "I'd like a better look at the footwear. Please remove one."

Reluctantly, Zac untied a sneaker, and waving it slightly to air it out, handed it over.

Holding the sneaker, slowly turning it in his hands and bending it, Sir William seemed taken by it.

"Are these some type of... sporting shoes?" The nobleman reluctantly handed the Nike back to Zac, who nodded as he slipped his foot back into the sneaker and re-tied it. Zac was dressed in the everyday clothes of his generation the free world over. Like most young men of his age, he didn't think too much about what he was going to wear that day. Perhaps he should have. Or, better, he should have accepted the handmade clothes as offered by Beatrice; she had warned him and Sky.

But he sat there now in his red Nike sneakers, baggy jeans, white tube socks, and a plain grey hoodie. Under the hoodie, he wore his favourite T-shirt; a black one with a big red cross, with two lacrosse sticks in front forming an X. The words "DONATE BLOOD" were written above the cross; "PLAY LACROSSE" was written underneath. Under the hoodie, he wore the smartwatch on his wrist. He could not let his hosts see the smartwatch.

"Yes, sporting shoes. This is typical for the colonies, I guess, pretty normal clothes for me." Zac responded truthfully. There was no need to lie – so far.

Boldly, Rachel stood and reached over to grab the hood portion of Zac's hoodie. "And, this flips over your head to keep the rain off and your head warm?" She playfully lifted the hood over his head, letting it fall comically in front of his eyes. Sitting down with her delicate hand over her open mouth, she stared at Zac. Then, she laughed. They all laughed at Zac and his hood as he peered out from under it.

Giggling, Rachel persisted. "What's under there?"

"Under where?" Zac pushed the hood off of his face, fearing what might happen next.

"Under your hooded garment, of course. Do you wear something under it?"

"Yes, sure I do."

Rachel looked at her father, trying to read his face for a clue as to how far she could go with her interrogation. Seeing a positive wrinkle or two around his eyes, she said to Zac, "Quite. Can you show us please?"

Zac looked at Sir William for any possible support, but found none in his still-mirthful face. Willy was, of course, of no assistance either. His hand conveniently covering his smile, Sir William simply wiggled a finger, indicating that Zac should proceed.

"Okay, but please know that we dress differently in the colonies." Zac slowly removed the hoodie, freeing his right arm only and keeping the garment hiding the smartwatch on the left wrist. He held up his free arm and smiled nervously, revealing the T-shirt and, if you had asked Rachel or Wee Willy, wide shoulders and muscular arms.

"Your shirt has words emblazoned on it! Why on earth?" asked Sir William, leaning closer to read the T-shirt. "'DONATE BLOOD'? Why would anyone wish to give perfectly good blood? 'PLAY LA... CROSSE?' What devilry is this?"

"Lacrosse is a game that I play, with a ball and sticks that have pouches to catch the ball. Those," Zac pointed to his chest, "are two lacrosse sticks in front."

Zac knew that he had opened the proverbial can of worms. Making things even worse, he blurted out, "First Nations... err... I mean, North American Indians taught us the game!"

Sir William sat back in his seat and looked inquiringly at his children. Thankfully for Zac, it was at that moment that Daltrey turned the carriage through the massive front gates, complete with a porter's booth under an impressive gatehouse, and onto the pristine gravel driveway of the estate (the driveway was raked every morning).

Zac quickly pulled the hoodie back on. Sitting backward in what was now full darkness, he could see little. His companions seemed deep in thought, so he took the opportunity to ask if he could stick his head out the window. Sir William pursed his lips and nodded.

Even in the darkness, the estate seemed immense. If the light were better, Zac would have seen a fieldstone wall that surrounded just a small portion of the 40,000-acre estate. Zac couldn't wait to see more of it in the light of day.

The carriage pulled up to the main entrance, and a footman tethered the lead horse as the party disembarked. At the top of a wide staircase and opening one of the two huge doors was a snappily dressed, but seemingly dour man. His bald pate was fringed by a crown of silver hair. His well-groomed sideburns were long enough to be fashionable, but short enough to be more than presentable to the most discernable of visitors.

"Ahh, Jamieson!" The Duke seemed genuinely happy to see him. "We've had a spot of trouble on the road. Highwaymen detained us, and sadly, Ames and Pitt have been killed. Please work with Daltrey to ensure that their bodies are recovered immediately. I will advise the household tomorrow morning.

"And this…" Sir William hesitated, wondering himself exactly what "this" was, "… is Zachary. He assisted us greatly on the road, and consequently, I've hired him on as a footman. Please disregard his colonial clothing for the time being." Sir William turned to his young guest. "Zachary, I will have our butler here, Jamieson, brief you on your new duties in the morning. And, I want to talk to you at that time as well. Jamieson, see that the new footman has lodgings for the night." Sir William turned to walk away. "For now, to bed. It has been a regrettable night. Come, children!"

While the horses and carriage were led to the stables, Willy and Rachel followed their father through the main entrance… but not before Rachel turned to smile at Zac. who of course, smiled back.

"Don't return her smile, footman!" With the family now gone, Jamieson scowled at Zac.

"Why not? She's beautiful!" Zac stretched out his arm toward the door through which Rachel had just entered, in a "see for yourself" manner.

Jamieson had been in the employ of the Mansfield family for years, after being hired as a page by the Duke's father. The duties of the page included seeing to the needs of visitors, which in many cases, were visitors of high social order. Jamieson had used his innate social skills and haughty demeanour to his advantage, and had quickly risen through the household ranks.

As butler in the frequent absence of the steward, Jamieson presided over all 44 – no, with the addition of Zac and the loss of two footmen, make that 43 – of the servants in the house.

Jamieson grabbed Zac's outstretched arm and forcefully lowered it to his side. "'She' is the Lady Rachel; the daughter of Sir William Mansfield, the Duke of Chestney; which is a hereditary title of highest rank below only the monarch himself. I'm sure that you have heard of the Duke. And you – *you* are a mere footman, or at least you are striving to be. And I am the butler of this fine house, so you will address me as Mr. Jamieson – and you will not use that impetuous tone with me. Now, come. I will see you to your lodging."

His new place in the order seemingly established, Zac followed Jamieson into the immense building; not through the main entrance, but through a side door. "This way to the servants' quarters," directed Jamieson, still incensed by the newcomer's impetuousness.

Jamieson led Zac down a long, panelled hallway and down a flight of stairs. They passed a young girl on the stairs; a scullery maid, who couldn't help but stare at Zac, his clothes and especially, his Nike sneakers. The men proceeded down another hallway past a series of doors that were close together, indicating small rooms inside.

Jamieson opened the last door at the far end of the hallway, "Here you are: your new lodgings. Mr. Ames' personal effects will be removed from your room tomorrow. Please place any of your possessions – although I understand that you have few – on the bed in the morning, so the staff know what not to remove. I will personally wake you at 6 a.m. to brief you on your duties. The Duke will speak to you after the staff meeting. Oh, and what is your surname so that I may properly address you?"

After Zac told him, Jamieson closed the door behind him, after muttering, "Mr. Burling, it shall be," emphasizing the "B" sound as though it were a weight that he now had to bear.

∞

10

THE RAIN OF THE previous ill-fated night had begat a beautiful clear morning. The sun was rising as Jacques DuTemps and Harry Moody approached their camp; both on foot.

Jacques led one horse and Harry, limping, led two others. They had been unable to immediately return to their camp, due to its proximity to the scene of the crime. So the men had shared the horse, riding around until they could return to retrieve the two remaining horses. They had wandered, but were close by.

Harry reached over and grabbed the reins of Jacques' mount, bringing both the horse and its dismounted rider to an abrupt halt. He pointed ahead through the trees, to rising smoke. "I thought I put that fire out. Look, someone's there. 'E's stoked the fire, now 'e's sleepin' like a baby." Harry stroked his chin. "The usual approach?"

Jacques nodded, almost imperceptibly. When Harry had stopped him walking, Jacques had been thinking about the previous night; a night of grievous loss, but considering the weight of the purses and the pendant watch in his pocket, one of substantial gain.

The Duke and his party had left the three bodies where they fell. Jacques and Harry went first to their friend, Mike, whose mangled corpse lay crumpled beside the roadway. They took his few items: a ring, a pipe, some coins and ammunition. Nearby, squished into the mud, was his dragon.

Other than their leather boots and belts, the dead footmen had few personal items to pillage. Their wigs were now encrusted in mud and were, in any case, useless for highwaymen. One footman wore a gold wedding band that was too tight to remove, so Jacques had to remove the finger. Using the broad-blade knife he kept in a sheath on his belt, he grimaced as he cut through the bone. Thankfully, there was little blood as the body had been dead long enough. This one also had a few coins in his pocket.

The other, older man appeared on first glance to have nothing to take, but further inspection revealed a mouthful of silver teeth – which Harry proceeded to pull out, one by one, using pliers from his saddlebag. He had done this before, and had modified his pliers with a firm wire to make the gruesome job easier. He secured the wire around each tooth, and with a quick tug and twist, out they popped – usually. He had, in past operations, broken a few jaws when the molars proved to be too stubborn. "Dead men tell no tales and ya couldn't unnerstand this one if he did," Harry had joked over some poor sod's broken jaw in a previous extraction.

The extracted teeth were plunked into a small pouch for later selling to a silver merchant. The merchant would pay the highwayman the estimated value of the silver, while neglecting to inquire as to the teeth's origin. Of course, he usually underestimated their value. He would then mix the teeth with flux, and using a heavy crucible, melt the mix in an induction furnace, creating an electro-magnetic field that separated the metal from non-metal.

The men had gone to find their horses, leaving the bodies where they lay. Someone would see them in the morning light and arrange for their disposal.

Whispering, Jacques and Harry discussed how to deal with the sleeping visitor. While most men would approach cautiously, Jacques was not most men. He strode through the clearing toward the sleeping figure. He thought it important that his men – now down to one – see him as fearless.

Jacques approached with gun drawn while Harry, his own gun ready, hid behind a tree. His wound, a deep gash in his calf, was still bleeding despite his best efforts to staunch the flow by wrapping it in the legging from his other pants leg.

"'Ey, wake up, sleepy 'ead!" Jacques kicked Sky's butt. Sky woke quickly, looking around, wondering for a moment where he was. He stood up and turned to face Jacques.

The Frenchman cocked his head to one side, looking the stranger over. The tall young man was wearing the strangest clothes he had ever seen, here in *Angleterre* or on the continent.

Sky was wearing his favourite blue jeans, now ripped, and a brown vest over a black and brown paisley shirt with an oversized collar. On his feet he wore the cool, red paisley Vans sneakers that he had received last Christmas from his grandparents. Not exactly the "beachwear" he should have been wearing to fool his grandparents when he had left, ostensibly for the beach, that morning. But the Fraserdale morning had begun overcast with threatening rain, so a wardrobe change had been in order. "Besides," he had told his Gramma as he kissed her goodbye and patted his pack-pack, "I've got all my swim stuff in here." As he left, tears had welled up in his eyes. He hadn't known what the day would bring, or even if he'd see his Gramma again. If she had sensed that something was amiss, she didn't show it. "Hope the sun comes out!" she'd said. "Have fun. And, don't forget the sunscreen."

But, that was this morning. . .

"What are you doing in my camp?" Jacques barked, trying to ignore Sky's clothes.

"I'm doing fine, thank you," Sky replied. "Sleeping by the warmth of the fire. It was a damp night."

"Hmph! You used some of my wood, I see." The high-wayman motioned with the barrel of his gun.

"Yes, but I can cut you some more."

"Did you also steal some tea?" Jacques motioned to the satchel under the tree.

"Tea is only good in water, eh? No water," Sky said.

Jacques scowled. "You talk funny! Where are you from?"

"So do you. Where are you from?" Sky felt that he had to be aggressive, or he would be pushed around. Besides, this guy had just jolted him out of a sound sleep.

Despite the stranger's insolence, Jacques was enjoying the exchange. "They say 'Never answer a question with a question'. Makes sense, don't you think?"

Sky continued to stand steadfast, hands on hips, ready for action. But he was scared and at the mercy of this armed stranger. Getting no response, Jacques sighed at what seemed to be an initial stalemate. "I'm going to search you now, to ensure that you're not armed."

Sky knew that this man would surely find the smart-watch and/or the battery pack, so he quickly raised his arms in a surrender manner, saying, "That's not necessary. I am unarmed and… I come in peace."

Sensing that this strange young man was indeed not a threat, Jacques motioned for Harry to join them. Harry limped out from behind the tree, bringing the other two horses with him and tying all three horses to a nearby tree branch.

"Are you 'ungry?" asked Jacques of the stranger. Sky nodded. Jacques said, "We 'ave food. We will share some with you when you have shared something about yourself. Again, where are you from?"

Sky knew that eventually he would have to share personal information with these men. He knew that he'd have to make a lot of it up, however. Despite the stranger's accent, he had to assume for now that the target of Middlesex,

England had been successfully achieved. So, he began, "I live in America. I took a long voyage to come here."

"So, you're an American. The English 'ATE the colonials!"

"Well, not exactly American."

"But, dere is nothing else dere!"

"Not exactly. The English have a colony, too."

Jacques had limited knowledge of the colonies and had never met anyone from there. "You…" he said, pointing a wagging finger, "… are an English Loyalist, living in America!"

Sky thought about that, and had to admit that that was pretty close to the truth. "Yes, let's go with that."

"Hmmm, yes, let us 'go with that', as you say." Jacques was confused, but needed to start sewing up his partner's oozing leg. "So, what's your name?"

"Sky."

"Sky?"

"Yes, Sky. Just Sky." His full given name was too confusing to explain back home, let alone here.

Jacques smiled at Harry. "Just Sky, 'uh? Maybe that is where you dropped from, eh? Dat guy Sky!" For some reason – perhaps to do with the French translation or just the simple rhyme – Jacques found this to be very funny indeed, laughing and poking at Harry to join in the merriment. Harry, wincing in pain, was less impressed. He moved close to the fire and lay on his right side.

Sky found a small stick nearby and offered it to Harry. "You can bite down on it – for the pain."

He had seen that in the movies and it always seemed to help cowboys, if not their teeth. Harry nodded, took the stick and proceeded to put one end in his mouth.

"No, no, sideways," Sky used his index finger to show Harry the proper cowboy way to bite a pain stick.

With a drooly grunt in protest, Harry grudgingly turned the stick. He rolled down his frayed and bloody legging to expose his punctured left calf. Blood continued to ooze from it; the red stain ran all the way down to his shoe. He felt himself lucky: leggings are cheap to replace, but the stab had just missed his more expensive breeches.

As Jacques left to fetch water from a nearby stream, he told Sky to get the needle and thread from the satchel. When Jacques returned and finished washing his partner's wound, Sky showed him how to sterilize the needle. He stuck the end of the needle with the eye into the soft wood at the end of a stick, then waved the stick with the exposed sharp end of the rusty needle through the fire. Sky had to say something about the needle.

"Do you have another needle? This one is rusty and might cause an infection."

Jacques and Harry looked at each other quizzically, then at Sky, before casually returning to what they were doing. Harry closed his eyes tightly and bit down on the stick. As Jacques sewed, he asked Sky more questions. Sky had to continue to be evasive; he didn't even know where or when he was! Gradually, he turned the conversation around to focus on Jacques. That in itself was not difficult, as it turned out that Jacques loved to discuss Jacques.

"I 'ave been 'ere for 12 years now. I was born into a family of nobility only to 'ave it unjustly stripped from us. I 'ad to work from a young age, mostly with 'orses. I was even, for a time, a stable boy, then groom to Sir William Mansfield, a local nobleman of some repute. But I am sure that Sir William would not remember me; at least, not as his employee. Perhaps he will remember me after last night, eh, 'arry?"

Harry managed a grunt, the biting stick lodged tightly in place.

Sky had some difficulty watching the procedure so he turned away, looking into the fire. Jacques noticed the stranger's uneasiness and gave him an inquiring look.

"I'm okay," Sky assured him. "But I might faint. I come from a long line of fainters."

"Ya mean, ya come from a long 'orizontal line of fainters!" Jacques laughed so hard that he had to stop his stitchery.

Sky could still hear Harry's groans each time the needle sunk in for a new stitch. Jacques went on, nonchalantly wiping blood with a dirty rag as he worked.

"Mike was a good partner, we worked well together. Ey 'arry? 'old still! Mike was good, eh? *Merde!* We're going to need a new man. Pity, *non?*"

Jacques stopped sewing. He wiped the wound one final time and rinsed it with water. It appeared that the slow trickle of blood had stopped. There was a long silence. Even Harry stopped grunting and groaning. He opened his eyes to see why it was suddenly so quiet. Sensing that they were staring at his back, Sky turned from the fire to face Jacques.

The handsome highwayman smiled and asked, "Ave you ever ridden a 'orse?"

∞

11

SKY HAD LITTLE CHOICE but to join the small band of highwaymen, led by the infamous Jacques DuTemps. He could steal a horse and ride into the night as the others slept, but where to? And, if they caught him as he escaped, or afterward, they would likely kill him. And, if he somehow got away, he might go from a bad situation to worse. Still, he thought that by having his own horse, escaping from his partners might be easier if and when he needed to do so.

Sky was unexpectedly alone. He hoped that Zac was alive and well. Knowing his buddy, he was thriving. He had no idea how they gotten separated, other than some type of glitch in the GPS. What he could not know was that the two time travellers had actually entered this space-time in close proximity to each other – as close as the process would allow – but that Zac had been immediately carried down the road in the carriage, leaving Sky further up the road in the brambles and out of earshot, more or less.

Sky, Jacques and Harry camped there for two more nights, waiting for Harry's leg to heal enough for him to ride to London. Sky could honestly tell Jacques that he had ridden a horse before. What he didn't say was that it had been only on a daylong trail ride with friends in the Okanagan Valley in British Columbia. While he had enjoyed the ride, his most vivid memory was of sore leg muscles and a sorer butt for several days afterward. At least he had learned that a rider must show a horse who's boss.

Sky was also honest when he told the men that he had never fired a gun. So, for two days, both Jacques and Harry taught Sky how to clean, load and fire a handgun; the deceased Mike's dragon.

Jacques advised Sky that they worked only every second or third night, as part of a verbal agreement with another gang of "land pirates."

"We do pretty well that way, making a decent living without having to worry about the other 'gentlemen of the road' coming after us," Jacques explained.

Camping on the final night prior to leaving for London, Sky used his cunning to learn the current date. He began a conversation about birthdays, providing his date (not the year!) and asking for those of each of his companions. Harry did not know his birthday; he wasn't even sure how old he was. He lay beside the fire and closed his eyes to sleep. But Jacques, apparently ever loquacious, proudly stated "August 2, 1735! *M' mere* was so proud of her beautiful boy and so glad to be rid of me in the summer 'eat. Ha!"

Sky thought about the date. "So, your birthday is in, let me see, how many days?" He pretended to count in his head, using fingers too.

"Well, today is Sunday, May 25, so I will be 31 years old in… less than three months! *Mon Dieu*, how time flies." Jacques shook his head.

"That it does," Sky responded with authority, remembering his own flight through space and time. He calculated that meant it was May 25, 1766. He was glad and relieved to have used a bit of deception on Jacques in a seemingly meaningless way, and to have landed in the intended time-place. It bode well for future encounters. Jacques was sharp and always wary. In his business, he had to be. Sky would have to match him.

His success in determining today's date – two days into his 39-day adventure – meant that he had to be ready for transference back to Fraserdale in 37 days, on July third – which was, he calculated, a Thursday. He wondered if Zac would be with him.

The three men slept until the early afternoon. So, after breaking camp, they began their slow ride to London later than planned. They rode slowly due to Harry's wounded leg and Sky's lack of horsemanship.

Harry's leg was still aching as they approached the outskirts of London on a warm, cloudless evening. Even though the wound was on the outside of Harry's calf, the ride was hard on it. And, not being used to riding, Sky's butt was sore. And his legs ached.

Jacques told Sky that they were headed for a part of the city called Covent Garden; specifically, the Shakespeare Head Tavern.

"The Shakespeare – people call it 'The Bard' – has the finest ale in all the city, and the most buxom waitresses, eh 'arry!? We will drink together there. But before we go too far into the city, Sky, you will need to change into some regular clothing. We must blend in; we cannot have you dressed like a... a colonist! 'Arry, we'll need to secure our tall friend some clothes. Let's try to find a suitably tall donor."

Typically, the riders rode their horses at a gallop on the open road, slowing to a canter or trot to rest the horses. Now on cobblestone in a west London suburb, the horses were walking as their riders scanned pedestrians for potential victims. Sky knew that he was going to have to participate in the upcoming clothes theft. After all, it was clothes they were obtaining for him. More importantly, he had to prove to his partners that he was a worthy member of the gang – at least for now.

They were riding through a remote part of town, with few people out walking. The few who were, seemed to be dressed poorly; rendering them unsuitable. Harry, in his preferred position of being in the lead, turned 'round in his saddle and motioned to a man walking in the direction in which they were travelling. The man was dressed in the manner of the middle class; perhaps he was a merchant or an artisan, shopkeeper or tradesman. He appeared to be fairly tall and about the same build as Sky.

The horses slowed to the pedestrian's pace. Their hooves clip-clopped. The man, who was elderly and used a cane, was returning home from an appointment at the Royal Society of London for Improving Natural Knowledge. He sensed danger. Without so much as a glance behind, he picked up his pace and abruptly turned down an alleyway.

The horses followed.

Walking fast now, the man turned to see three riders quickly dismounting. He began to run, awkwardly using his cane for support. The three pursuers followed on foot. Jacques and Sky soon caught him. Harry, limping to catch up, led the three horses.

There were no others around. Any that appeared turned the other way when they saw what was happening ahead. The old man cried out, "Leave me be, you thieves you!" He tried to hit one of them with his cane, but the assailant – a younger man wearing strange clothes and footwear – easily grabbed the cane and snatched it from him.

"Thieves, are we? Nay, we simply want to exchange your breeches and coats for some of our own. Take all your clothes off, old man. Now!" Jacques commanded.

The bespectacled man seemed to contemplate the strange request before slowly beginning to remove his clothes and shoes. He piled them on a cleaner part of the cobblestone and stood in his underwear, arms outstretched before his assailants.

"As much as I hate to say it, keep going," Sky told the man. Harry and Jacques grinned and pretended to hide their eyes. The man complied, removing his shoes and his underwear. He stood naked with both hands covering his groin.

After Sky spoke, he began to remove his own clothes. He had forgotten about his two watches: the smartwatch on his wrist and his beloved Mickey Mouse pocket watch! Plus, the recharger and cord. It would mean disaster if Jacques or Harry saw any one of these.

Sky moved nonchalantly so that the old man was between himself and his partners, hoping that the man's frail, naked body and the extra distance in the dwindling evening light would provide sufficient cover. With Harry limping and Sky virtually naked, Jacques was the only one of the gang who could run after the old man should he try to bolt, so he was keeping a close eye on him.

Under the circumstances, Sky couldn't be too concerned about what, if anything, the old man happened to see. More importantly, his new partners must not see any of his electronic items. He positioned his body so that it too blocked the highwaymen's view.

Sky sat down to remove his sneakers, then everything else. He deftly unclipped and removed the Mickey Mouse watch, recharger and cord from his jeans pocket and slipped them amongst the pile of clothes left by the old man.

He sat naked beside the man's clothes, holding his wrist with the watch underneath his hand. He was able to put on the linen shirt first, which now hid the smartwatch, although it continued to emit a slight glow through the thin shirt. The other items were more of a challenge. Sky moved to put on the old man's breeches, and stooped to pick up the pocket watch, recharger and cord, which he quickly stuffed into the pocket of the breeches. But not quite: as he stuffed them into the breeches, the Mickey Mouse watch clattered onto the cobblestones.

"What's that, then, Sky?" asked Jacques, as Sky picked up the watch and deposited it in the pocket of his new breeches.

"It seems the man had a pocket watch, which is now mine!" Sky was emphatic. The man, wanting only to be spared his life, said nothing about a watch that was not his.

"Or mine," said Jacques gruffly, "You will show it to me later." He acted as though he might have seen something.

Far worse than this exchange of words was the exchange of underwear. Sky had no choice but to pull on the old man's stained and smelly knickers. He winced as his new partners suppressed a laugh. Perhaps they felt that it was part of Sky's initiation into the gang. Then he finished dressing in the old man's clothes, which thankfully fit pretty well, including the shoes. Sky turned and faced Jacques with outstretched arms, indicating he was done.

Jacques nodded and turned to the old man. "Now, you may go. Keep your coins and the contents of your pockets. You can dress in those colonial clothes, if you wish, or go forth as Your Creator made you. Well," he pointed at the sad figure, waving a finger up and down, "you were likely less wrinkled when 'e made you those many years ago."

The man looked so forlorn and – when he was forced to remove his hands from his groin – apparently, cold. He said, "I have no choice, I'll dress in your castoffs."

He sat on the stone road and held up each strange piece of clothing. Realizing which piece goes on first, he dressed. When he had finished, he stood, picked up his cane and turned to continue his journey. Off he went, quickly, wearing Sky's torn jeans, his paisley shirt, the brown vest and the Vans sneakers.

"It is done; we go!" Jacques and Harry turned their mounts to leave. Sky followed on his horse, feeling less comfortable in his new duds, and as Jacques intended, less conspicuous. As comical as the scene had been, Sky realized now why Aunt Beatrice had wanted them to wear period clothing. Giving this man his clothes was dangerous. It could mean a change in fashion. Was the world ready for vulcanized rubber? It surely wasn't ready for paisley sneakers.

The excitement of the clothes exchange over, Sky realized just how smelly his new clothes were. At the time, Englishmen bathed perhaps twice a year. Those who could afford to would visit a mineral spa at Buxton or Bath or perhaps a seaside retreat, where they enjoyed the medicinal and cleansing properties of salt water. But most people kept clean, but not very, with periodic sponge baths. The old man, he decided, definitely got the better of the exchange, even with the tear in his jeans.

The deeper into London they travelled, the thicker the stench became. Not the stench from the old man's clothes, but the stench of the city itself. The world's greatest city was filled with the smell of horses and their waste – and worse... much worse.

Sky could not believe his senses. He covered his nose with his arm as they passed the rotting corpse of a horse. He had no way of knowing that, in the darker parts of the city in which he was soon to reside, human corpses were occasionally found. As they continued they passed dead dogs and cats, and many dead rats. Those still alive scurried through the muck into dark crevices.

A bold rat scurried across the cobblestone directly in front of the horsemen. The barrel of Harry's dragon followed its path. He had been aiming his gun at would-be targets, stray dogs and rats, and pretending to shoot; even mimicking of the sound of the gunshot.

"*Poomb!*" Harry amused himself with another fake shot. Each one was, of course, deadly in his fantasy. As he, ever in the lead, turned in his saddle to gloat about yet another "kill," a stream of water began to flow down the slope of the street toward them. Harry holstered his pistol and cupped his hand to his mouth. "Water main burst! Calm your horses." As he turned and stroked the neck of his mount, the trickle became a torrent.

Cascading water enveloped everything in its path, splashing up to window ledges and doorways. One lad, trying to escape, slipped onto his backside. The foul liquid enveloped his head. Cursing, he got up with some difficulty and ran. The roadway quickly became a fecal stream of purple, putrid water. The horses and the few pedestrians were forced to slosh through the ankle-high soup: a fetid amalgam of biological waste from the local butcher shops, pigsties, dyeworks, and slaughterhouses. The jetsam included human waste and household garbage that had been tossed into the street to accumulate and rot in piles until the "night soil" men came to clear it all out. If they came.

Sanitation was rudimentary if it existed at all. Underground pipes – some just hollowed-out tree trunks – were poorly constructed. A network of crude storm sewers carried rainwater, but the system was often overrun with biological waste.

Even under normal conditions, pedestrians had to dodge the slop underfoot, projected from the wheels of horse-drawn carriages at intervals: the likely cause of the custom of gentlemen walking on the roadside when accompanying a woman.

To add to this urban quagmire was the combination of the oft-falling rain, fog and thick clouds of black soot that homes, factories, tenements and shops belched into the filthy air. Wood was scarce and expensive, so coal was the main source of energy. The resultant soot mixed with the rain to coat everything in a dreary, toxic grey, and caused profound damage to vegetation and buildings, which had to be repainted often to cover their soiled surfaces.

Washed clothes set out to dry – even the clothes of a person on the street – were "smoked," and an entire industry of refurbishing soiled clothing had resulted. White clothing was to be avoided because it quickly turned grey.

This combination of pollution and foggy weather often proved lethal. Parish clerks had for many years compiled "bills of mortality": documents that listed birth and death rates, including the causes of deaths, and had identified a correlation between particularly high death rates and severe fogs.

People usually kept their windows shut tight, but not because of the soot. There was a fear of fresh air, which was believed to spread airborne diseases like "consumption." Even buildings were taxed according to the number of windows, so landlords often boarded them up. Tenants' health suffered as a result.

Sky calmed his horse the best he could. It seemed to take its lead from the other horses, which remained calm as the surge pushed a few sizable objects into their legs. When the flow receded, there hung in the air an odd silence as the shock of the event took hold. Except for the highwaymen, the street was now deserted. The few faces that appeared in adjacent windows quickly disappeared again.

The only sound was that of a kitten, soaking wet and meowing, which Sky saw washed up against a building.

Jacques took quick action. He dismounted, and kicking aside objects in his path, strode to the kitten. Sky grimaced, wondering what the highwayman would do next. Jacques gently picked up the wet ball of fur and raised it to his chest, stroking it and whispering to it in French. Sky watched in amazement and some admiration as the notorious highwayman gently tucked the feline into his waistcoat pocket before remounting his horse. Jacques and Sky fell into line behind Harry. They were close to their destination.

But the kitten was but a distraction from the olfactory chaos that was consuming Sky. The combination of the dead horse, the stench of the water main break and the old man's clothes proved to be too much for the gangly Canadian. His stomach began to convulse in protest. Gagging, he called out to his companions, "Stop! Give me a minute."

As Jacques and Harry watched from their mounts, Sky dismounted and ran to a deserted alleyway, where he leaned on the wall and vomited violently. Just at that moment, a woman in a second-floor window directly above Sky shouted something unintelligible to him.

To Harry and Jacques, however, it sounded like "Gardyloo!" Jacques' hand shot up but before he could intervene, the woman dumped the contents of a chamber pot out the window, right onto Sky below as he stood doubled over, waiting for the next stomach contraction.

After that, he did not have to wait long.

Predictably, Sky's partners reacted differently to the smelly scene. Harry buckled over on his horse, laughing uproariously. Jacques correctly muttered, "*Merde!*" before dismounting and running to Sky's aid. Sky's clothes, with the possible exception of the breeches, were soaked.

"My God!" Jacques recoiled. He covered his nose with his arm and took a few steps back. "She was trying to warn you, *mon ami*, by shouting 'Gardyloo'." The Frenchman shook his head. "Yet again, the English have bastardized a perfectly good French expression: "*Garde a l'eau!*"[2], which means, as you know now, 'Look out for the water!'" His voice muffled by his arm, Jacques directed Sky, "If only it were water, eh? There is a public fountain just up the road. Come, let us ride. You can clean up before we go to *Le* Bard."

The two rejoined Harry, who was trying hard to keep a straight face, on their mounts. Faster now, the trio cantered along the streets of central London.

---

2 The English slang for toilet, the "loo," probably derived from this practice.

As Jacques had said, the fountain was not far. Sky washed his head and neck while Jacques bathed the calico kitten, despite its protestations and tiny sharp claws. He then used a rag from his saddlebag to gently dry its fur, an irresistible combination of black, white and copper. Feeling somewhat better, Sky and his companions made their way to the Shakespeare Head public house.

The flickering candlelight inside the pub was a welcoming beacon as darkness descended. The three tired riders tied up their horses on Carnaby Street. They stretched and scratched themselves before entering the tavern, not far from where Sir William Mansfield and his children had watched the play at the Royal Theatre three days earlier.

The bustling Covent Garden neighbourhood was home to "lesser" theatres than the Royal, and to other pubs, coffeehouses and brothels. But The Bard was the epicenter of the action, some of which was culinary. The kitchen of the tavern was renowned for miles around London. So great was the demand for the chef's turtle soup that the proprietor bought 50 turtles at a time.

But most of the action was carnal by nature. Dining customers were potential customers of the many prostitutes that frequented the pub. And vice versa, one may suppose, if one's appetite had first been whetted upstairs.

And at the center of The Bard to arrange all things carnal, was one Jack Harris.

∞

12

Covent Garden area of London

THE SMOKY TAVERN WAS noisy and crowded, but a wave from Jacques caught the eye of a tavern boy, who smiled and motioned them to a less-crowded table near the unlit fireplace. Throughout the public house, patrons sat at long, heavy wooden tables on matching benches, or stood about the bar.

The boy waved some seated patrons further down the table, making space for the thirsty highwaymen. The displaced patrons mumbled their protests but complied.

"'Ello, JACK!" Jacques DuTemps called to the man behind the bar, emphasizing the English pronunciation of his name.

Jack Harris[3] threw a rag over his shoulder and came to place a big hand on Jacques' shoulder. "Hello *Jacques!* Your regular? Harry? What'll your friend have?"

Jacques formed a circle with his outstretched fingers. "Ale all round then," Jack said. "Be right back."

Jack was a talented publican and a part-time pimp, as well as the self-professed author of the *List of Covent Garden Ladies,* a popular guide book of the area's prostitutes. Printed every Christmas from 1760 to 1793, it detailed the appearance, sexual skills and fees of around 80 prostitutes,

---

3 His real surname was Harrison.

reviewing them as one would a movie or a restaurant for the benefit of the common London rake. Many men met that description: a man of aristocratic or upper class background who indulged in any pleasurable activities he so desired, social mores be damned.

Known as the Pimpmaster General, Jack proudly admitted to being a pimp. He also took pride in supplying the city with a stock of fine whores, all of whom paid him for an entry in his famed parchment list. He had agents stationed throughout London, including major points-of-entry, who would meet the arriving stagecoaches and wagons, hoping to recruit the fresh young women come to find a new life in the big city. Jack travelled annually to Ireland, which, he claimed, produced the most beautiful young lasses. In addition to these activities, he somehow found time to operate a "Whores Club" from a private room in the tavern – on Sunday evenings, no less.

"Jack is the 'ead skinker[4] 'ere at De Bard," Jacques said to Sky. "But, 'e does much more than that, doesn't 'e 'arry?"

Tired after the day's events and of spending too much time together, the three men had little to say. Harry never said much anyway. He just grunted and looked around, waiting for his ale. He had removed his overcoat and topcoat. He rolled up his sleeves to reveal a dark tattoo on his broad, hairy forearm: a tribute to "Annibell," her misspelled name emblazoned in perpetuity on a banner flowing across a heart, shaded to provide a 3D effect.

Harry's thirsty eyes wandered around the room, stopping at each of the ample bosoms that seemed so plentiful here, as Sky couldn't help but notice. After awhile, Jack returned with a tray full of six ales in silver mugs. Jacques was also enjoying the view. "So, Jack, any exciting new wenches?" he asked.

---

4 A server of drink; the landlord of an alehouse or tavern.

"Oh, many, my friend, many. Do you not have the latest copy? It's been out since Christmas, you know."

The book, known simply as *The List*, was called the "essential guide and accessory for any serious gentleman of pleasure." There was little censorship of prostitution, and *The List* provided a vital service in describing the celebrated ladies of pleasure who frequented Covent Garden. In many ways, it set the tone for the depravity of the neighbourhood, the city and indeed, for the times. While the list contained some famous prostitutes, most were not so famous. However, it ensured that they would not be entirely obscured by history.

Jacques had not bought the latest edition. "I may have lost my copy; I move around a lot, as you know. I'll need to purchase another, won't I?"

"Aye, Lord love you when you do; just two and six. One name not on *The List* is my niece's – Helena. The courts have entrusted her to my fatherly care, so to include the young beauty would not be appropriate. Instead, I have her workin' here at the Head. But," Harris leaned in and whispered, "Betwixt you and me, she and her virginity are available to a curious gentleman, for the right price."

"Sounds tempting, my friend. You say she's a beauty?" Jacques asked.

"Indeed, sir!" replied Jack. "She is but a simple farm girl, but perhaps not so simple; she can read and write. But you need not be concerned, Jacques, you can't afford her. Hoy, there she is now, by God!" Harris put the tray on the table and pointed to a young lass who had just then emerged from the kitchen, carrying a tray of empty mugs.

He need not have pointed. Jacques and Harry, who had simultaneously raised their mugs to their lips, did not drink. Instead, despite their thirst, they put their mugs back on the table, spilling the foamy contents. They stared intently over

Sky's shoulder. A few other patrons – those still able to see clearly – had a similar reaction.

"Mon Dieu," was all that the usually talkative Jacques could muster.

Sitting with his back to the kitchen, Sky turned to see. His jaw dropped and his life changed in that moment.

She was a sleek vessel of loveliness floating in a sea of debauchery.

Sky first noticed her blonde curls, which bounced as she worked to stack the mugs. An off-white apron over a long brown skirt with hooped petticoats covered her long legs. Worn leather thongs, strapped around her ankles, covered her delicate feet. Sky may have been interested to learn that she, like most women of the time, did not wear knickers. She wore a tight-fitting, laced vest over a red linen, off-the-shoulder blouse that was not particularly low-cut by the standards of the day, but her curves were apparent to any who appreciate that sort of thing.

Sky appreciated that sort of thing. He felt that he had to meet this beautiful, tall young lady.

"Nineteen and just arrived," smiled Jack, enjoying the men's appreciation. "Lived on a small farm a good day's ride from London, till 'er parents, my brother an' 'is wife, were murdered just last year – 'ccused o' witchcraft!"

The court – not fully aware of Jack Harris' activities, it seems – had assigned her to her Uncle Jack, her only known relative, to mind her. She was now his legal ward.

Oblivious to the attention being paid to her, Helena stopped to wipe the perspiration from her brow, and her pink cheeks puffed as she breathed out. Glancing toward the table where her uncle stood, she smiled an innocent smile. Sky hoped that the bright smile was meant for him.

She had not smiled much recently, having lost her parents at the hands of vigilantes. The practise of witch-hunts was subsiding. Political leaders and the educated elite rejected the belief, and the last government-sanctioned execution for witchcraft in England had been 50 years ago. But it takes longer to change the masses, and so there remained the threat of mob justice for accused witches.

It was commonly believed that witches had the power to curse people, cast spells, turn food poisonous, make livestock ill or crops fail, all of which Helena's parents were accused of by a neighbouring farmer who had bickered with them for many years. His bad luck and bad planning had created a series of unlikely events that he vehemently blamed on his innocent neighbours.

In his twisted state, he successfully convinced other farmers of the couple's witchcraft, and with the tacit approval of the local sheriff, raised a large lynch mob. The noisy mob mustered at his farm, complete with pitchforks, scythes and other impromptu weaponry. Some carried hemp sacks filled with rotten fruit and garbage.

They marched *en masse* to the neighbouring farm, raising a cloud of dust as they went on that hot summer morning. With them they brought a newly-made ducking stool, which they left beside the small lake that formed, in part, the boundary between the properties.

Seeing and hearing the approaching mob, the terrified couple implored their daughter to ride their only horse into London and to seek out her Uncle Jack, who they knew only as a well-known businessman in the Covent Garden brewery trade.

Teary-eyed and sobbing, Helena kissed and hugged her parents, then quickly rode away, not daring to look back. She knew only that she was headed in the right direction, having been to London just once, when she was thirteen. She shivered, remembering some of the images of that visit.

The mob stormed the small farmhouse, and after a short search, found her parents hiding under the floorboards of the main room. They were stripped, and with their hands tied behind their backs, were taken forcibly to the ducking stool made for two that the mob had left beside the lake. With their right thumbs tied to their left toes, the couple were strapped in and dunked repeatedly into the frigid lake water, while the agitated crowd threw handfuls of rotten fruit and garbage and roared in approval.

The ducking stool was a sure-fire way to determine if the user was a witch. If the person floated and lived, she was considered to be a witch, as she rejected the "baptismal water." If she drowned she was deemed innocent, but most unfortunate. On that hot morning, at the mercy of an angry mob, neither floating nor sinking was going to help Helena's parents.

Watching Helena in the pub, Jacques stroked his chin. "Jack, your niece is an incredible beauty, but she is not of my taste. Too young. I prefer my women more… experienced."

"Well, that is a good thing, *mon ami*, for I plan to sell the 'deflowering rights' for her to a nobleman. If I am able to do that, I could make a huge profit, perhaps £150! I'd be a rich man and able to buy you an ale now and then."

Sky could not believe his ears. Any girl deserved a better fate than that. And this girl, this Helena, seemed special.

"Errr, is SHE in the latest edition?" Jacques was preoccupied now with staring at a shapely, mature woman sitting on the lap of a large, red-faced man. The man's hands were wandering all over the woman's body. She made no attempt to discourage him. Despite being otherwise occupied, the ginger-haired beauty gazed back at Jacques and tilted her head with an artificial type of coquetry. She smiled provocatively.

"Caramel? Of course she is. She possesses a fine Irish countenance indeed, which makes her one of my top girls, still. I have 'Mel minding Helena for me when I am too busy, which is my usual state." Jack laughed as he slapped Jacques on the back.

Jacques now stroked his moustache. "And, 'ow does a gentleman procure 'er services for the night?"

"Well, you can talk to me. But…", Jack jerked his head in the Irish woman's direction, "it looks as though she may be busy tonight." Just then, Caramel stood and, with her eyes still fixed on DuTemps, pulled her red, low-cut dress down into place. The red-faced man rose from his seat, wobbly but determined. He tugged her by the hand and led her on a staggering route to the stairway that led to private rooms upstairs.

Downing a gulp of ale, Jacques slammed down his mug and rose quickly from the bench. He dodged and side-stepped through the crowd, and intercepted the red-clad woman and the red-faced man at the base of the stairs.

Harry and Sky watched as Jacques, gesticulating and smiling, spoke to the red-faced man, as though telling a story. The story included a part that had Jacques turn a pirouette and a pratfall to the floor. As he got back to his feet, many in the pub were now watching with amusement. The red-faced man, sufficiently drunk and laughing at the pirouette and subsequent fall, did not anticipate the quick and hard kick to the groin administered by the fully func-tioning Frenchman.

The red-faced man was now even more red-faced. In the relative quiet that surrounded the scene, the man made an unearthly noise, fell to the floor with a thud and lay there moaning and writhing. Jacques stood over his adversary, pirouetted once more for effect, and with his tricorne in hand, he bowed low – left, right and centre – to the clap-ping, cheers and whistles of the patrons.

He then reached into his waistcoat pocket, and to a collective gasp from the crowd, produced a mewing, multi-coloured kitten. He held it high in both hands before pre-senting it to the woman in the red dress. She accepted the gift with a small curtsey. He then took her hand and led her, victoriously, upstairs to a cacophony of lewd suggestions.

Grinning from ear to ear, Harry turned to anyone who would listen. "That's my friend, that's my friend…" As the red-faced man left the building, doubled over in pain, Harry grabbed his two ales and grunted a semblance of a "good night" in Sky's general direction. He then got up and walked toward a group sitting by the window. The group included at least four women, two of whom seemed to be as yet unattached for the evening. For good reason. Sky watched as Harry whispered into a particularly nasty-looking wench's ear. Shaking his head, Sky quoted to himself, *Was she ever more lovely, was she ever more radiant? I sure hope so!* He chuckled at his new friend's attempts at courting.

Alone now, Sky sat and sipped his ale. He wasn't a big drinker, but here he was in an authentic London pub, rubbing elbows with every kind of merchant, thief, harlot and vagabond. He didn't see Harry or Jacques again that night.

The evening's excitement seemingly over, Sky gazed down the table at a group playing a card game. The cards they held were large, and rather than hearts and spades, they featured pictures of humanized animals. To get a better view of the game, but mostly to get a better view of the kitchen, Sky slid down the bench closer to the group.

At first, the man holding the cards beside him drew his cards closer to his chest, hiding his hand from Sky. After a time, though, the man realized that Sky was not a threat. He smiled and showed him his cards, asking Sky if he'd ever seen the game. Sky just shook his head.

"The game is called 'John Bull'. There are 64 cards, organized into 16 family groups of four. You've been watching us, so you've seen me ask another player if they have a card that will complete a set. That's called a 'trick'. Unless the player is cheating, like Frank over there," he raised his voice for the benefit of Frank, who quickly became the face of innocence, minus the halo. "You have money? You want to play?" The man looked at Sky as though Sky might be lost.

"No, but thanks. I'll just watch for a bit, if I could."

"Suit yerself, mate."

Sky watched as the tricks were made; Mr. John Bull and his family, Dr. Crow, Poacher Fox and Mrs. Quack, and the others. But Sky could not concentrate on the game. He watched the kitchen door, hoping to get a glimpse of Helena. He did, but only glimpses, as she moved gracefully to and fro. He thought she must be almost as tall as him.

Glassy-eyed, he remembered the look of terror in his mother's face on that night long ago as she fell, urging him to run; the African night hanging heavy around them. That was his most vivid memory of that horrid night. Consciously or not, he had forgotten most of the other details.

As was his habit in times such as this, he began tapping his foot and humming Led Zeppelin's *Ramble On* to himself.

As the night drew on, Sky realized that he needed a room for the night. Groping around in his waistcoat pocket, he found the coins from Aunt Bea. He was tired and hungry after the ride, after everything. Mostly, tired. He'd eat breakfast tomorrow.

Sky sat, looking around at the famous pub and reflecting on the days' events – the sights, the sounds, the… smells. He watched as yet another man relieved himself in the corner, a corner that contained a number of chamber pots for that purpose (there were no toilets in the building). It was late, and the man's aim had likely been better earlier.

It was much different than his fantasy life, with his mansion, carriages and prancing white horses. The filth, the stench, the depravity… he couldn't wait 'til tomorrow to see more…

∞

13

AS ONE OF THE "celebrated ladies of pleasure who frequent Covent Garden," Caramel had a regular room at the top of the stairs. Designed for hosting gentlemen, the room was shared with three other girls. She opened it with a key that she somehow found deep in her voluminous cleavage, while holding the purring kitten in the other hand.

Smiling, she released the kitten, which quickly found a spot under the dressing table. The room was spartan, with the dressing table, a dresser and two end tables the only furniture other than the large bed. A board festooned with hooks for visitors' clothes was on the wall next to the door.

The bed was, of course, the focal point.

Beds were status symbols. This four-poster was a gift from a rich benefactor. He had also purchased one for Caramel's own apartment. For both locations, he had included expensive silk bed curtains, which hung from the ornate wood framework. When closed, the curtains held in warmth, prevented drafts and enhanced privacy. There would be no need to close them tonight.

Closing and locking the door behind them, Jacques took Caramel's outstretched hand, kissing it and working his lips up her arm to her shoulder and long, shapely neck. She sighed seductively and turned her head to expose more of its fragrant length for his practised lips and tongue.

His moustache tickled and he knew how to use it, making the fine auburn hairs on the back of her neck tingle. She was soon tingling all over.

Ever the gentleman (and mindful of what he was paying her), he resisted the urge to take her standing there. Enjoying the chase as much as the conquest, Jacques slowly removed his black leather gloves, finger by finger. Folding them together, he lit the candle on the table beside the bed. He then laid back on the bed, arms propping up his head, and watched as Caramel slowly and purposefully removed her frilly red dress and hooped petticoats.

Earlier that day, her dressing process had taken almost an hour, as it did every day. So, she did not take the undressing process lightly; she needed a purpose, which was usually payment for services rendered. Looking at the handsome villain lying on the bed, Caramel knew that Jacques provided a delightfully higher purpose.

Now, she stood at the foot of the bed before the highwayman, wearing nothing but her shift. She was naked underneath it, with the notable exception of fine silk stockings, held up by garters tied just below her knees.

Walking flirtatiously to the bed, she had his full and growing attention. Gone was the lithe, leggy look of her past. That look had been replaced with a look that was even more erotic, more tactile; a mature, curvaceous woman of unqualified experience.

Yet somehow, the characteristic that he noticed the most at that glorious moment was the colour of her eyes. She batted long black lashes over deep brown eyes. The last time he had seen eyes as beautiful was a few days ago, on the road, when he had gazed into those of Lady Rachel.

Now, in the flickering candlelight, Caramel's eyes resembled limpid pools in which he could swim for hours. Standing beside the bed, she ran a finger up his thigh. As her hand lingered, she kissed his lips and their tongues danced momentarily. His hands began a tactile exploration of her curves. But she took control, perhaps sensing that for a man usually in control, he wished to relinquish that role for now.

She removed his boots, waistcoat and shirt before pulling down his breeches. She left his hat on, for now.

She leaned over, licked her lips and blew.

The candle was thereby extinguished.

Afterward, they lay together, her head on his chest. She had seen him a few times before at The Bard and knew who he was by his reputation. He was as handsome and charming as the other girls had told her. And as skilled. She was happy to have finally bedded the infamous highwayman.

As you now know, Jacques loved to talk. Caramel, on the other hand, tended to be a quiet person. She didn't say very much that night. He, on the other hand, told her the story of the band's attack on the carriage, the loss of Mike, the injury to Harry and the "hiring" of a new man; a colonist with the odd name of "Sky." He told her of Sky's need for proper clothing, and he chuckled as he told her about the clothing switch with the old man. He laughed loudly as he related the "Gardyloo" part.

He did not mention whose carriage he had robbed.

As he paid Caramel the agreed upon amount, he told her about the strange device he caught a glimpse of on Sky's wrist as he was exchanging clothes with the old man. "I've never seen anything like that thing!" he said. "Some type of talisman, I'd wager. The evening light was dim, and the device 'ad an unearthly glow! I'd steal it in a pinch, but I am sure that it would be cursed."

Caramel didn't think much of it at the time because Jacques admitted to seeing just a glimpse of the thing that resembled a talisman. But, it interested her, as it would interest other cunning folk.

∞

14

Mansfield Castle
Middlesex

ZAC WAS EXHAUSTED AND sore from his crash landing in the back of the carriage. So he slept well that night, despite his excitement. Jamieson had assigned him to the small bedroom of the now-deceased footman, Ames. Ames had kept few personal items in his room, but a letter of employment from the estate found in a drawer of the only dresser in the room confirmed his identity.

In the privacy of his small room, Zac recharged the smartwatch. He kept the coins from Beatrice in his pocket at all times. He understood their value and realized that he would have to keep them hidden, along with the smartwatch and battery pack.

Before dropping off to sleep, Zac inspected his new bed. Lifting the sheets revealed a wooden frame with canvas tightly laced across it. On the canvas was a thin, straw-stuffed mattress and on top of that was another, equally thin but firmly packed feather-stuffed mattress. The fabric of the top mattress had been burnished in places by the movement of a bed-warmer. Zac was amazed that such a contraption hadn't burned down the great house.

He had assumed that the bed would be noticeably shorter than his at home, but when he got in, he was able to stretch out comfortably. He was soon fast asleep.

Later, the muffled sounds of servants preparing for their daily routine gently woke him. He was awake and sitting at the end of the bed when Jamieson rapped on his door, as he had promised. "Mr. Burling! It is 6:30 a.m. Meet me in my office in 10 minutes."

"Yes sir!"

Zac did not want to dress in a dead man's clothes, nor did he want to upset Jamieson by doing so – so he slipped on his Nikes, hoodie and jeans. He hid the smartwatch and charger under the mattress. Within minutes, he was briskly walking down the long hallway, politely asking servants along the way directions to Jamieson's office. The two servants that he met looked at his strange clothes and timidly pointed down the hall.

He found Jamieson through the open door of an office next to the kitchen, decanting wine for the evening meal. Jamieson managed the entire household, with the assistance of an underbutler. As the butler, his duties included supervising all aspects of the household, particularly the dining room; managing the wine cellar, decanting wine; and serving spirits. He was in a position similar to the housekeeper, an office held by a female – but being male he was, naturally, her superior.

Zac knocked on the doorframe and waited.

Jamieson turned and looked up. With his mouth full of wine – he seemed to be gargling with it – he could only manage to crook a "come in" finger at his newest footman. He swallowed. "Ahhh Mr. Burling, I need to brief you on your duties as a footman in the service of Sir William Mansfield and his family. The Duke will be addressing the household about last night's incident after the staff meeting. Come in."

Jamieson continued to decant both red and white wine, tasting it occasionally for quality.

As Zac stood beside an empty chair, Jamieson described his responsibilities as a footman both in- and outside the house. On all days, he was to rise early to get through his morning duties prior to the family waking. He may be required to pay his master's respects to his master's acquaintances and friends, when the master was unable to attend an event. He would also enquire as to the health of those he visited, while hand-delivering messages. When in-house, Zac was to set the clocks, wait on the family's table, and lay out the tablecloth and cutlery. He was to serve tea and shine the cutlery. Zac was to walk behind his master or mistress, open doors, carry parcels and the like.

Outside, he would work as an escort or messenger. As an escort, he would ride on and if required, defend the carriage; a duty of which Zac was already keenly aware. He was required to ride a horse when delivering messages. He had never ridden one, but he had to claim that horses were the most popular way to get around in the colonies.

He would be paid eight pounds per year. He was not informed that this compared to the £18 that Daltrey received and the seven pounds a housemaid received. The estate provided their food, clothing and lodgings. An independent person needed to earn substantially more – in the neighbourhood of £40 – to keep a family for a year.

Their master, Sir William, on the other hand, earned an annual salary of about £4,700.

"Every day, you will wear the livery of this house. It is representative of this proud household and you will bear that in mind at all times," Jamieson said sternly as he approached a closet and pulled out a garment. He held it up to Zac's frame, then replaced it in the closet and grabbed a bigger one. "Try this on in the stillroom, there." He pointed to a room adjacent to his office. "The maids have gone to the meeting – thank God they're prompt for some things – so it's empty for you. Return with it on. Oh! And take this and try it on as well." Jamieson plucked a silver wig off the top shelf and pushed it toward Zac's chest.

"It is the largest wig I have, so I trust it will fit atop that generous head of yours." Jamieson stared at Zac as he spoke, and tried, unsuccessfully, to suppress a smile.

The stillroom was where most great houses distilled wine or brewed beer. Closing the door, Zac could see that cleaning products and even medicines were also made therein. It was also used for the storage and production of liqueurs, preserves and cakes and for the storage of tea and coffee.

Zac did as he was told, dressing in the highly-starched linen shirt, black breeches and black coat. He transferred the coins from his jeans to his new breeches. With a scowl of private protest, he arranged the wig on his head, fastening the attached clips to clumps of his hair. Zac returned to the office in the assigned livery, still wearing his red Nikes. Again, he waited for Jamieson.

Jamieson had his back turned, conducting further quality control on a fine bottle of Chardonnay. He turned, took one look and shook his head, "Oh, your footwear! Here, put these proper shoes on." Standing, Zac removed his Nikes. Jamieson selected a pair of leather shoes with a large buckle from the floor of the closet. He handed the shoes to Zac, who in turn handed over the offending sneakers. Jamieson weighed the sneakers with an up and down motion. Secretly, he marvelled at their design and light weight.

Finally getting permission to use the chair, Zac put on the leather shoes.

Not bothering to inquire as to how the shoes fit, Jamieson forged ahead. "Fine. Now, I must tell you that Lord Mansfield has requested to borrow your footwear – *this* footwear, from the colonies – as you will no longer have use for them. I am sure that you will agree to that, am I correct?"

Zac did not want an 18th century duke running around in his Nikes, but again, he had little choice. "Of course, Mr. Jamieson." He started to nod, which turned into a type of bow, which turned into a semi-curtsey, which turned his face red.

Jamieson digested the entire sorry display and paused before saying, "Quite. Now, regarding your behaviour as a footman. I must tell you that His Master has been very generous to you; the position you now fill is usually acquired only after a long apprenticeship. I can only surmise that you were instrumental in warding off the highwaymen." Then he muttered, seemingly to himself, "I'll have to ask Daltrey about the event."

He continued, "Oh, and you report to me, of course. So, it will be to my credit if you are able to keep things in good order."

Absentmindedly, Jamieson made a steeple with his index fingers. "The master, long ago, imposed a strict dictate of celibacy for staff, banning girlfriends and boyfriends, whether those friends are of the staff or otherwise. Your wages may be deducted for breaking a household item, making a mistake, forgoing church or other offenses such as drunkenness. Grounds for dismissal include breaking the code of celibacy, theft (guilty or suspected), insubordination, dishonesty or any grounds at the master's convenience. To gain employment in another house, you will require a character reference from myself – so be sure to behave with the utmost professionalism at all times. Am I speaking clearly?"

"Yes, Mr. Jamieson."

"All right, let's be off." Jamieson corked the bottle, and with a silk handkerchief, dabbed aggressively and with a practised motion at the corners of his mouth. Then, the men briskly made their way to the hall with Zac wearing his new livery, wig and shoes. The shoes were comfortable enough, but heavy. Jamieson carried the colonial Nike sneakers in the same disdainful way he would have carried a dead rat.

∞

15

BY THE TIME ZAC and Jamieson entered the hall, all of the estate's staff had arrived and was standing and waiting. Some were in murmured conversation.

The staff at Mansfield Castle adhered to a hierarchy, which was based on a firm division between "women's work" and the work performed by skilled labourers (men). At the top of this hierarchy was the house steward, who supervised the maintenance of the house and other properties on the estate. He also acted as the duke's secretary. The steward was often in absentia, dealing with affairs of the estate elsewhere. So, daily management typically fell to Jamieson, the butler. Under his watchful eye worked the underbutler; the valet Mr. Quering, and four footmen, including Zac.

Female servants included a housekeeper (she was essentially Jamieson's equal, but because she was a woman she reported to him), 14 housemaids, two seamstresses, a cook, a confectioner, two kitchen maids, a vegetable maid, three scullery maids, two stillroom maids, a dairy maid and seven laundry maids.

All of these 43 full-time staff lived in the servants' quarters. Most never saw the entire castle, spending most of their daily lives in but a small part of the household.

Other workers would visit daily, including the upholsterer, two scrubbing women, a laundry porter, a porter, two window cleaners and various others who kept the household. The upholsterer wore a number of hats; not only did he provide and repair the fabric and leather seats of furniture, he saw to all the furniture needs of the estate. He was the interior decorator of the day, buying and selling pieces in order to keep the interior up-to-date. The recent conversion of the Tapestry Room to a decidedly feminine tea room was his greatest accomplishment to date.

Outside were the clerk of the stables, the ostler, two grooms and two gamekeepers. The clerk was responsible for the operation of the stables, but also for the other "outdoor" pets that the Mansfield family owned.

As he entered the immense room, Zac was taken aback. The hall was the second-largest room in the estate after the gallery, which hosted the largest galas and balls. Here in the hall, the walls were bedecked with gold-framed pictures and huge tapestries. Entranced by the room, Zac didn't see Jamieson hand the offending Nikes to Sir William's valet, Quering.

If it were somehow possible to show more disdain toward the footwear than did Jamieson, Quering managed to do so. Quering was responsible for every aspect of his master's person. His primary role was to see to his master's appearance, including the care and selection of clothing. Quering prepared the master's toilette and brushes, and cut his master's hair and wigs.

At night Quering undressed the duke, and in the morning he dressed him in attire appropriate for the day's activities. The master does not prepare for bed, nor get out of bed, until his valet is present to assist. Quering's training had been as a master of fashion, so Sir William was always appointed in the finest, most fashionable gentlemen's attire.

The intimate nature of this role meant that Sir William might have been inclined to share sensitive information with Quering. This was not the case. Outside the house, His Lordship's confidante was Caramel; inside the house it had always been Jamieson. Quering was, in fact, Wee Willy's confidante.

Sir William entered the room shortly thereafter, followed by his son and daughter. To Zac, Rachel looked even more beautiful in the morning light. She wore a yellow taffeta dress, with a matching ribbon in her hair and a mauve choker around her delicate neck. William the III pranced in, looking very satisfied with himself in a shimmering nautical-inspired jacket and breeches. His high silver wig was balanced somewhat by his high-heeled leather shoes.

Any remaining conversation stopped immediately when Jamieson raised his hand. Clearing his throat and speaking with authority, Sir William provided a summary of the altercation with the highwaymen, the loss of the footmen and their upcoming burial. He noted their exemplary service records and noted that there would be a funeral service in the chapel on Sunday for any staff who wanted to pay their respects. He thanked Daltrey for his decisive action. He also briefed the staff on the upcoming masquerade ball, which got some of the staff at the back of the room whispering amongst themselves.

His Lordship paused; the signal for Jamieson to bellow, "Quiet, please!"

Sir William walked closer to where Zac stood and, extending his hand toward Zac, introduced him. "This is Zachary Burling, who heroically assisted Mr. Daltrey in subduing the highwaymen. Consequently, Mr. Burling is now employed as a footman here at Mansfield Castle."

Not wanting to stumble into another semi-curtsey, Zac waved awkwardly instead and fidgeted under the attention. He couldn't help but glance toward Rachel, who smiled, seemingly pleased to have him on staff.

The staff again whispered amongst themselves. Sir William continued, "He is new to his duties and is from the colonies, so he may sound a bit... foreign. Please ensure that he is treated well and that you assist him with his duties. That will be all."

The meeting over, the staff dispersed to resume their duties. Rachel and William left the room, leaving just their father, Jamieson, and Zac. Jamieson stepped over to confer quietly with the Duke, who seemed to suddenly remember something.

"Oh yes! Thank you, Jamieson. Zachary, come here please." He paused as Zac approached. "Now, I want you to teach my cricket friends and me this 'cross' game from the colonies. From your description, it sounds like much fun. What would we need in order to play?"

"Well, Lord. That is a tall order, indeed." Zac was having some fun trying to copy local speech patterns. "We'd need two goals and two goalie sticks and at least 12 sticks, depending upon the number of players per side. We'd need a ball and likely a spare ball, too."

Sir William seemed to think that these requirements would not be a problem. He went on to describe how they could play "cross" on the cricket field, adjacent to the stables. He wasn't sure how many of his friends would be interested in playing, but he had perhaps 25 cricket players to ask. He said that the game seemed similar to football, the game of the working classes, but with sticks that somehow catch the ball.

"It seems to me that football gives the working classes an opportunity to channel their grievances and hostilities. Matches, I've heard, often become violent; with limited rules and usually no referee." The duke surmised, "I trust that 'cross' is less violent."

Zac didn't know what to say to that. Lacrosse is a much more violent sport than football (soccer, to Zac). So he said, "I believe, sir, that we may need some protective equipment."

"Fine, if that is possible. If it is not, then please fashion a cross outfit for me; one like the North American Indians wear. I'm still looking for a suitable masquerade costume and that might be the ticket." Sir William stroked his Van Dyke. "We could play at the time of our next scheduled cricket match, a week from Thursday. Ask the gardener, Mr. Munn, for help in making the required equipment. Jamieson here will write a note to Munn to that effect. He often has to repair or replace tools, so making the sticks and goals can't be all that different. Jamieson, this will take Zachary from his duties for a time; please arrange for a replacement."

Jamieson smiled cursorily and said, "Very good, sir." His eyes darted to Zac, and showed his annoyance.

Sir William began to walk away, then turned to say, "And, while playing cross, we can talk more about life in the colonies!"

Zac was not going to question His Lordship. Creating lacrosse sticks and goals is quite different from repairing a hoe. But he simply bowed in the manner in which he had seen others, said "Sir," and left the room behind Jamieson. He'd go see Munn that afternoon, after noting on paper what would be required. In the meantime, he went with Jamieson to tour the kitchen, the servant's quarters and other parts of the household in which the new footman would work. He was then briefed on his duties for an upcoming event hosted by Rachel in the Tea Room.

Finding Munn in the garden was easier than trying to explain what was required in order for the duke and his friends to enjoy a game or two of lacrosse. At least he was able to provide Munn with the note from Jamieson, which made his request "official."

Munn was a busy gardener, with three junior gardeners under his guidance. But upon reading the note he complied, understanding that His Lordship wanted this strange task completed for next week. Zac had never made a stick from scratch, but he had an idea about how to proceed.

So, referring to Zac's note of requirements, the two men worked together over the course of the next four days creating 20 sticks, including two large goalie sticks out of a stock of round hickory that was intended for garden tools. They had to bend them, thankfully in much the same way that Munn bent tool handles; that is, by steaming the end of each stick for about 40 minutes until soft, then bending the wood by using a steel form. Then, they wired the sticks to hold the shape, and used a hand brace to drill small holes for the webbing.

Munn had a good supply of leather, which he complained about having to replenish after this. "Oh botheration! His Dukeness better not resent having to get more leather soon. I mean, it's his fault, ain't it?"

They cut the leather into strips for the webbing and proceeded to string the bent sticks. For the goals, they nailed and lashed together frames of the right six-foot by six-foot size, and hung a burlap cloth for the mesh around each goal. Munn complained again about the price of nails, which, he reminded Zac, were handmade and expensive.

Munn didn't know much about cricket, but went to retrieve a cricket ball to see if it could be used for lacrosse. He tossed it to Zac, who weighed it in his hand: it was too big and heavy. So Zac cut some of the leather into pieces, sewed the pieces tightly together, leaving a hole into which he stuffed horsehair – a lot of horsehair – so that the resulting balls were hard and about three inches in diameter.

They did not have enough leather to fashion protective equipment for each player, so Zac got to work on an outfit specially designed for the duke to fulfill his request. He thought that Sir William might want to play with something specially designed for him. So, he used leather to fashion a helmet and some padding.

Then, with devilish zeal and a lot of blue dye, he customized a "uniform" for the duke.

∞

16

SKY WOKE UP EARLY. It was his first full day in the City of London; the greatest city in the world!

He had stayed the night at the same cheap inn where they had stabled the horses; the Wander Inn. The sign at the front desk had said that a room for the night could be had for twopence.

Thankfully, Beatrice had given Zac and Sky a crash course in 18th century British currency along with their coins. Modern British currency was complicated enough, let alone that of the 18th century. Pounds, shillings and pence ("the plural for penny," Beatrice had reminded them) made up the basic currency, with a relationship of 12 pence to the shilling and 20 shillings to the pound. A farthing was valued at one-quarter of a penny.

The coins in his breeches pocket totaled almost £10, approximately what it cost to rent a house for a year. In other words, he was carrying a lot of cash in the middle of a crime-filled city. He would have to be very careful.

When he'd arrived last night he'd met the innkeeper, a surly man at the best of times, and his wife, who sat writing in a ledger at a desk behind him. The twopence advertised at the front desk would get him a shared bed in the lodging house, but he needed privacy to see to cleaning his clothes and keeping his smartwatch and charger from curious eyes. And, he could afford it.

Sky carefully counted out and paid the innkeeper five-pence for a private room for the night, telling the man that he'd likely stay longer. He did not notice that one of the coins that he gave as payment was dated 1769, although it was currently the spring of 1766. Luckily, the innkeeper did not notice either; his bad mood had him quickly count and pocket the coins while he growled under his breath.

"Oh, stop being churlish. Leave the young man be." The woman, who had just confirmed that she was indeed the innkeeper's wife, turned and pointed her feathered quill pen toward her husband. "Give 'im 'is room, you ninny."

The innkeeper had obliged, with a well-practised grunt. He grabbed a bronze key from the rack, and in a final gesture of defiance, tossed the key into Sky's outstretched palm. He pointed up the stairs and growled, "Third door on yer left."

A single tallow candle was provided in the small room. Before retiring, Sky recharged the smartwatch, using the charger. He reminded himself to be sure to recharge the watch every night. He also handwashed his clothes – the shirt, underwear and breeches – and left them to dry in the breeze by the window, wishing that he had access to his Gramma's washing machine and dryer.

As he drifted off to sleep, he wondered how she and Gramps were doing. If Aunt Bea was correct – and he had to have faith in her vision – then his grandparents would not even realize that he was gone for a long time.

As was her habit, Sky's Gramma had insisted on giving him a full breakfast of eggs, bacon and fruit before he and Zac left for "the beach."

Looking out the window at a grey morning, Grampa had mused, "Sure hope it clears up. Girl-watching on the beach won't be the same in this weather." Grampa had then glanced at his glaring wife as she whipped the eggs, adding gruffly, "At least, that's what I've been told!"

He woke with the feeling of having a full, satisfying sleep. He checked his laundry. Most of Sky's clothes had now dried sufficiently, but the breeches were still damp despite a stiff breeze. Undaunted, Sky pulled them on and pocketed the recharger and cord. He'd had the smartwatch on his wrist all night.

He had tentatively arranged to meet Jacques and Harry tomorrow at the Wander Inn stables. So, he had a full day now to explore. His goal was to see as much as possible without bringing attention to himself.

Sky descended the stairs into the common room of the inn. There were just a few customers having breakfast. He took a small table at the front window so he could watch the street and the passers-by on a brisk, windy morning. Inns like this one offered a variety of food, including meats, fish, dairy products, vegetables and desserts, with the most common being bread, cheese, fish and meats.

This particular menu – or "Bill of Fare" as the title proclaimed – was a single sheet of stained vellum paper; the prices shown in shillings and pence. The menu described breakfast, lunch and dinner selections, with the latter featuring boiled mutton with caper sauce. A customer could also choose from a selection of fowl, such as partridge, quail, goose or duck.

At this time in England, dinner typically included cold meats, sweets and wine. Hot food was generally only served in restaurants or pubs, or when guests were visiting. Fruit was not on the menu; only the wealthy had access to fruit. The unwashed did not mind. Most people turned up their noses at uncooked fruit; they thought it would give one indigestion, or even the plague.

The breakfast selections were, thankfully, simpler than dinner and more familiar to Sky's Canadian palate. He passed on the gruel; that is, boiled oatmeal with a bit of butter or, for dinner, wine. This food would take some getting used to.

"What'll it be, luv?" The plump server asked as she grudgingly approached his table.

He ordered eggs, bread and cheese.

Listening to the young man place his order, the server seemed suddenly invigorated. "Bust me if that ain't the strangest accent I've heard! What part of Scotland you from, lad?"

Remembering the song, Sky blurted out, "Kintyre, near the Mull."

This seemed to, somehow, placate her. She slowly walked away, absentmindedly nodding her large head.

Sky sat and gazed out the window again. His breakfast arrived a few minutes later, which he gobbled down despite its odd taste. He had not eaten since breakfast at Jacques' camp, which was yesterday morning, but it seemed like days ago.

Again, he sat back and enjoyed watching the throngs of people walk by, the carriages pulled by clip-clopping horses and all the other activities. He watched as pretty young girls, hired by vendors of small shops, tried to entice potential customers inside. Street vendors loudly hawked their products. Prostitutes, with their bright red lipstick and rouge-covered cheeks, plied their wares even in the breeze of the early morning; and workers, mostly male, bustled off to work, holding their hats in the wind. The contrast between the gentlemen's drab clothes and the women's colourful dresses was stark.

It was then that he heard a sickening crack, like the breaking of a large piece of timber. Across the street, a big shop sign: "Nicholson's Rainwear and Umbrellas" – itself shaped like an umbrella – had fallen, pinning a man underneath it.

After the Great Fire of 1666, much of central London had been rebuilt, quickly and haphazardly. The new buildings were thrown up using second-grade materials, and yet many of them still stood 100 years later. Their accompanying signage was heavy, in part because of the need for large pictures for those people – about half the population – who remained illiterate. So, streets could be hazardous; particularly in windy weather.

And, that wasn't including the flying contents of chamber pots.

Finishing the last mouthful of breakfast, Sky found himself standing with his nose against the window as he watched a curious crowd gather around the stricken man. The incident even slowed road traffic, as carriage drivers gawked to catch a glimpse. A bystander stooped as though to help the dazed man, but instead quickly reached inside the victim's coat and grabbed his purse. The thief burst through the circle of onlookers and ran off down the crowded street. No one went after him.

No one, that is, except Sky.

He leaped past the startled waitress and ran out the door. Like his hero Superman, he had to intervene in an obvious crime! He heard the innkeeper yelling after him to stop; he hadn't yet paid his breakfast bill. The innkeeper started to run after Sky but quickly gave up the chase, figuring that other customers may get the same idea in his absence. Sky would pay his bill later.

Sky ran past the fallen man and the small group that stood around him. He could see the escaping man running through scores of pedestrians. He seemed to be slowing down, until he looked back. He must have seen Sky, who was rapidly closing the gap between them, because he knocked an elderly man to the ground in his renewed efforts to escape.

It didn't matter. With his long legs, Sky was able to catch up to the man after two blocks or so. He jumped and tackled him, sending the pickpocket flying. Then Sky landed on top of him. Pickpockets were legion in London. Unlike this one, some were well-dressed, so they could be mistaken for people of good standing. And some *were* of good standing, but had lost their savings due to an extravagant lifestyle or a bad bet.

Sky sat on top of the young man – a boy, really. "You'll be giving his purse to me, buddy," he said. "And I will return it to its rightful owner."

"Awright, gov', awright! 'Ere it is then…" The boy, lying face down, awkwardly produced the purse and Sky yanked it out of his hand. It was then that he noticed a man standing next to them, short of breath and puffing. He evidently had followed the chase, watching the whole scene; including the tackle.

The uniformed man in blue smiled, and with what Sky thought was an Irish accent, said, "Well done, lad. Not many would have done that."

"Well, where I come from, we are polite and law-abiding. I felt that I had to stop this thief."

The man nodded and introduced himself. "Patrolman Leddy of the Bow Street Runners, sir!" He was a member of the fledgling professional police force – the first for the City of London.

For a runner, Leddy was a big man. Under his police-issued, reinforced top hat – designed to be stood upon when extra height was required – his red hair was cropped short. His short waistcoat attempted to, but could not hide, a protruding belly. He was equipped with a baton, a rattle, handcuffs and a cutlass.

The Runners were outfitted in smart blue tunics with gold buttons; they were blue because it kept clean longer, and because an officer working at night in a navy blue tunic can more easily sneak up on criminals.

"I know this boy. He is not a serious offender... yet." Leddy put his hand on the handle of his baton, but did not pull it out. "Be off with you, Jerry O'Flarity! Next time I will bring you before the magistrate. Or worse, I'll tell yer mother!"

Sky got off the boy. Jerry O'Flarity quickly got up, and picking up his hat that had fallen off during the tackle, ran off down Bow Street.

"We have far too many to convict; I'm not going to take him in today, even though, in addition to my retainer, I would be entitled to the government reward if he was convicted. Say, let's get that purse back to its owner, shall we?"

The two began to walk back to where the sign had fallen. As they walked, Leddy explained to Sky who the Bow Street Runners were. "We're few, but effective. We patrol within the parish of Bow Street, mostly, and are paid a decent wage to arrest any wrongdoers – especially thieves, and in particular, the serious offenders. As you may not know, being from out o' town, prior to the Runners," Leddy paused to retrieve a man's hat that had blown off in the wind, "there was no organized law enforcement. The idea of a uniformed policeman patrolling the streets to prevent crime was considered 'too French'; an affront to the Englishman's liberty."

Handing the hat to the man with a nod, Leddy continued: "Every man was expected to contribute to policing, just as every citizen was expected to report and prosecute anyone they witnessed committing a felony, and serve by rotation on the night watch. They were even expected to apprehend offenders and bring them to the watch house." Leddy tipped his hat to a well-dressed woman. "It was a heavy responsibility. So now, their taxes pay our wages instead."

When they returned to the scene of the crime, the stricken man was on his feet but still bent over and woozy from a cut on his head. Leddy produced a handkerchief that he used to wipe the tall, thin man's wounded forehead. He whispered, "Hold still, mate. It looks like the bleeding has almost stopped."

Sky handed over the heavy purse, asking, "Are you all right?"

Opening his purse, the man sighed, "Yes, yes, I'll be fine. Thank you for returning my purse. Y-you are one of the few honest people in this city. My name is C-Cavendish, Henry Cavendish. Please take this as a t-token of my utmost… appreciation."

He held out a fistful of large coins toward Sky. Leddy's eyes looked like they'd pop out of their sockets.

"No, I cannot accept a reward." Sky placed his hand over the man's outstretched hand. "My name is Sky – Sky Sewell. I'm from the colonies; I hope to represent the general honesty there."

"My g-good man, the colonies sound like a remarkable place, with remarkable inhabitants. Still," Cavendish stammered, "I-if there is ever anything I can do for you, you can contact me through the Royal Society."

"The Royal Society?" asked Sky and Leddy in unison. They turned and looked at each other, quizzically.

"Yes, the Royal S-Society of London for Improving Natural Knowledge. I'm a f-fellow there. I dine there every Thursday with the other m-members." Henry had a halting speech pattern, and, it appeared to Sky, an aura of timidity and reserve that was almost comic.

Sky had no way of knowing that the soft-spoken Henry Cavendish was a respected, if misunderstood, scientist. The Society was the extent of Henry's social life. Now 35, he was soon to be left a fortune that would make him one of the richest men in London. For the time being, however, he enjoyed a generous allowance from his father, Lord Charles

Cavendish. Nevertheless, his dress was old-fashioned and consistently drab.

Henry had never married. In fact, he seemed to have an aversion to women. At his palatial home, he ordered his dinner by placing a note on the hall table, and his women servants were instructed to keep out of his sight or be dismissed. Many of his discoveries and groundbreaking experiments took place in his well-appointed laboratory; the "garden shed" of that home in London's Clapham Common neighbourhood.

Henry painstakingly tried to avoid the attention of others, which made his current predicament all the more unpalatable. Most of the attention had, fortunately, subsided and people were now walking by without staring. The huge, fallen umbrella sign had been moved to a nearby alley.

"So, what do you do at the Royal Society?" asked an ever-curious Sky.

"I am a ch-chemist and physicist. In fact, I am now bringing to the Society my initial findings on the chemistry of gases…" Henry first tapped a small leather carrying case, then his forehead, "… if I don't collapse on the way. I also conduct experiments concerning electricity." In fact, Henry wrote comprehensive papers for the Society on the theory of electricity that were based on precise quantitative experiments. His quiet, understated work was distinguished by its accuracy. His genius was not known until a century later, when his experimental results were finally revealed. During that time, many others had been credited with Henry's discoveries.

Suddenly, as if one of those bolts of electricity had hit him, Henry blurted out, "Say, since you cannot accept a c-cash reward, you should join me for lunch! As a small token of my appreciation."

Sky wanted to collect as many experiences as possible. Any experiences or people he met could only help to locate Zac. He nodded and said, "I'd like that. When and where?"

"This Thursday, at 11 of the clock. The Society is located at the c-corner of Fleet and Bow streets. Well, again, thank you very much. And to you too, officer."

Henry extended his hand, and both Leddy and Sky shook it. "I m-must be on my way. See you Thursday, Sky!" The scientist turned and faltered down the busy street, rubbing his head as he went. Leddy and Sky turned and walked the other way.

Leddy couldn't contain his excitement. "I could not believe the King's Pictures he was offering you!"

"King's Pictures?"

"The coins, man, the coins! There must have been three pounds in his hand."

Sky gingerly stepped over a particularly putrid pile of filth as they carried on. "Oh, he is a generous man."

"He is, indeed. And you, my friend, are an honest one. I say, the Bow Street Runners are hiring; would you be interested?" Leddy held up a large finger, "Before you answer, walk with me to John's house; it's not far."

"John" was Sir John Fielding, a local magistrate and the younger half brother of the late magistrate Henry Fielding, author of the recently published book, *The History of Tom Jones, a Foundling*. His was one of the first of the genre called a "novel."

The innovative Fielding brothers had created the Bow Street Runners in response to rampant crime in London. Sir John had been blinded at a young age, and as Leddy whispered to Sky as they entered the building, "they call him the 'Blind Beak'. He can recognize some 3,000 thieves and others, just by listening to their voices!"

Sir John had turned his appointed house from being the mere house of a magistrate to being the Bow Street

Magistrates' Court. In it, he created a setting that could attract and accommodate a large audience for his examinations of suspected offenders. The court was open for the most of the day and evenings on most days of the week, even when Fielding himself was not in the office. There was usually a clerk or assistant in the office to whom one could report offences.

Leddy paused at the base of a wide staircase and whispered again. "John is an admirable man. He encourages the London press to attend court, and he provides newspaper readers with a weekly report on his legal activities. The King must think so too – John was knighted five years ago."

One of the court's functions was to act as a central collection point for information about crimes that occurred all over the country. At a time when statistics were not typically recorded and documents not kept, Fielding was providing a vision of the future.

Leddy led Sky up the stairs and into the front room, now transformed into a courtroom. A crowd of perhaps 40 onlookers sat quietly in raised bench seats around the perimeter of the large room. The magistrate sat on a raised dais, while a nearby scribe took notes. Leddy and Sky stood in the crowd against the back wall, shuffling into place in the unanticipated silence.

They had obviously arrived at a key moment. The tension was palpable. Sky watched in awe as two patrolmen stood on each side of an alleged murderer, while Magistrate Fielding loudly pronounced his declaration: "I find the evidence against you sufficient to hereby sentence you to death by hanging, one week from this Monday at Tyburn. Take him away."

The patrolmen escorted the prisoner, his head hung low, out of the courtroom; another murderer to be hung at London's notorious Tyburn Tree. Fielding and the Runners dealt with thieves to the best of their limited ability, but crime remained rampant. A large, vulnerable and generally newly-arrived population was often victimized in dark alleys. That combined with the frequent shroud of fog to make London a criminal's paradise. Murders, robberies and assaults were commonplace.

Despite Leddy's good intentions, Sky didn't want any part of it. He couldn't be a lawman; he was already a highwayman… of sorts.

But maybe joining the Runners would provide him with protection from Jacques, if the highwayman came looking for him. And, it might be an interesting way to see London while looking for Zac. Hopefully, he could somehow cast the eyes of the law in Zac's direction.

Sky had an idea. "What if I joined you on your rounds as an observer, at first, to see how a true constable does his job?"

Leddy thought that that was a fine idea and that his superior, the Justice of the Peace, would likely agree. "Join me next week at the constabulary," he said. "We'll patrol. Lessee if we can't catch us some criminals."

∞

17

"THAT WILL BE ALL, Beulah," Lady Rachel dismissed her maid, whose duties included dressing her. She gazed with satisfaction into the looking glass. She was now ready for her morning appointment; a tea party with her lady-in-waiting, Abigail, and three other female friends of sufficient social status. She wore a bright pink Brunswick gown accented with royal blue trim. The gown was actually made up of two pieces: a thigh-length jacket featuring a high neckline and a faux hood, and a matching petticoat.

A lady-in-waiting is a personal assistant, providing companionship and attending to the needs of a high-ranking noblewoman. Like most others, Abigail was also a noblewoman, from a family in "good society"; but one of lower rank than Rachel. Although Rachel selected Abigail as her lady-in-waiting, her father heavily influenced the selection. After all, the Mansfield household compensated Abigail for these duties. But, as she secretly told Rachel, Abigail would gladly see to the needs of her mistress for free.

Rachel loved tea parties, more than she liked the tea itself. She would have been appalled to know that the tea that she and her friends were about to drink was probably contraband. Being high in demand and light and easy to transport, tea was a profitable smuggling commodity. It continued to make its illegal way to the island nation by way of the sea, and even by way of seaside tunnels dug expressly for that purpose.

The feminine culture of drinking tea, as Rachel had lectured her father, demanded an appropriate environment. Thus, she had her father convert the Tapestry Room to a tea room, resplendent in its hand-painted *chinoiserie* (Chinese-inspired) wallpaper. When the estate was built, wool and silk tapestries had a utilitarian function; protecting rooms from damp and cold weather, covering otherwise austere walls and insulating big rooms. The ornate tapestries were huge, expensive and a display of the family's wealth.

Rachel was part of a trend that had wallpaper replacing tapestry wall coverings. The upholsterer had worked with Rachel to select furniture pieces and the *chinoiserie* wallpaper, along with porcelain and decorations; all of which were the latest in interior fashion. They also reflected the British desire of the time to create appropriate settings for drinking tea; a ritual that had its beginnings in the growing trade with China.

Intimately ensconced within this decidedly feminine room, Rachel, along with her three good friends and Abigail, her lady-in-waiting, could confidently and safely discuss topical events, rumours and innuendo. And by far, the biggest topic of interest was the attack of the highwaymen, in which Rachel was intimately involved. The story had already made the rounds locally, but the women were anxious to hear Rachel's story firsthand.

As Rachel and Jamieson waited inside, the white-gloved Zac directed the four young women into the room. Abigail led the way. Matilda, Charlotte and Elizabeth followed, bubbling with excitement. The three were also, of course, from prominent local families.

Rachel greeted each woman with a hug and her ravishing smile. "Oh, do come in. Let us have a comfortable coze."

With visible resignation, Jamieson advised the visitors that the footman, Burling, was at their disposal while they visited the estate. With a warning glare at Zac, Jamieson took his leave. Zac remained standing by the door, arms behind his back, as he had just been taught. He did not know that Rachel had instructed Jamieson that none other than Zac was to be the attending footman for the tea.

The women stood chatting for a time, until Zac carefully rolled in the tea service cart. Then, the blissful group moved slowly, with the alluring rustle of silk, brocade and fine linen, toward the two shapely chesterfields placed just for this purpose, adjacent to the large windows. There they sat, their full, brightly-coloured dresses contrasting the grey and black stripes of the chesterfields. They sat close together, talking endlessly and giggling.

Valiantly, they tried to discuss topics other than charming highwaymen. Elizabeth's father owned a coalmine in the West Midlands, an area that had seen local rioting due to the shortage of food. The shortage was widespread and many other areas in southern England were also experiencing rioting, as they had for many years. The year had been particularly bad, as mobs seized grain and other foodstuffs, commandeered markets, marched in force, and attacked and often destroyed corn mills.

Sipping her tea with her pinky finger properly extended, Elizabeth said, "Father has demanded that the local magistrate deploy troops to suppress the rioters. He says that he'll have to close the mine if the riots continue."

Outwardly, Elizabeth seemed concerned and her friends were able to sympathize. She knew, however, that her lifestyle would not change very much even if the mine were to close; her father had extensive holdings elsewhere. The riots, which would end a few months later, were a precursor to more severe agrarian rioting yet to occur.

Changing the subject, Abigail intoned, "I've just finished Henry Fielding's *The History of Tom Jones*. Some call it crass, but I enjoyed it, every word. It's the first of its kind, they say, the first *novel*. Sad that Fielding died; he wore so many hats."

Ever the practical one, Matilda noted, "Well, the novel will do well. My father says that even though only about half of the population is literate, the written word is becoming very popular. It's not just boys attending school any more, more girls can too."

The young women in the Tea Room need not fret about that; their families ensured that they would always attend the best schools. Most children were not as fortunate. Their families could not afford to have them go to school at all.

Matilda went on, "There's even a new type of school – the Charity School – for working class children. My maid's children attend one in Hounslow. They are taught religion, and how to read and write. Both her son and daughter are learning trades such as cobbling shoes, carpentry and straw plaiting. They even sell the resulting crafts to help the school."

Elizabeth said, "Perhaps, but everyone knows that children do not have to attend school if they did not wish to. And, their parents usually want them to stay home and work in the shop, the field or the mines – like my father's – to contribute to the family income."

Nevertheless, literacy was increasing rapidly. Just a few years earlier, in 1755, the writer Samuel Johnson had published his *Dictionary of the English Language*; the first of its kind. Even women shared in the literacy boom: females were the target of weekly magazines and romance novels, all of which encouraged chastity and sobriety.

Abigail continued to endorse Henry Fielding's novel. "The hero, Tom, is a vigorous young lad and Sophia, the beautiful heroine, is virtuous, and smart too. She reminded me of you, Rachel. And Tom reminded me of Ward Hampton. You'll have to read it!"

Rachel regretted her friend bringing up Ward's name. Her father had tried to bring her and Ward together last year. Ward's father and Sir William were friends who shared an interest in cricket, foxhunting and business. Both men thought that a marriage of their children would not only solidify their business interests, but would be good for their lineage.

A formal meeting had been arranged. Ward had taken Rachel into London for the day. As a surprise for Rachel, Ward had included a tour of Bethlehem Royal Hospital, also known as "Bedlam." The hospital was actually an asylum which was open to the public until 1770 as a, well, human zoo. Visitors who paid a small admission price could spend hours gawking at the inmates. Thousands toured Bedlam annually, wandering through the wards, poking, prodding and teasing the patients to their hearts' content. What fun!

But it was no fun for Rachel. For her, the hospital visit confirmed that Ward was, frankly, a cruel, pompous ass – quite self-centred and conceited. He was a few years older than she, and he had used his charm and handsome face to seduce many women, young and old, over the years.

Although they had courted only for a short time, Ward had tried to deflower Rachel on numerous occasions. Rachel had had to metaphorically and physically push him away. When she told her father that she wanted no more to do with Ward Hampton, her father seemed displeased. But secretly, he understood his daughter's feelings toward the brash young man. Ward Hampton's reputation as a rake was well-known. There would be other suitors for his beautiful daughter. But time was moving on for her. While life at the estate was, of course, grand, she was isolated from her peers by sheer distance.

But enough about Tom Jones and Ward Hampton. The gigglers all leaned forward – they could not wait a moment longer.

"Tell us, Rachel, tell us about the highwaymen!" Charlotte was ebullient.

Zac could not hear most of their conversation, but thought that his name might have been brought up, given the quick glances coming his way and the following titters and giggles.

They sipped from dainty cups as Rachel told them the story of the carriage ride, a strange thud outside the carriage, the charge of the highwaymen, the fatal shootings and the heroism of the new footman. More glances Zac's way. His abbreviated training in mind, he tried – and succeeded somewhat – to look straight ahead and not at the group of attractive young ladies.

Rachel purposefully saved the best part for last. She leaned in close to her friends and whispered, "It was Jacques DuTemps, you know."

Elizabeth gasped, "The famous highwayman? I heard rumours that it was he. Oh, I entreat you to tell us more, Rachel! Is he as handsome as they claim?"

Rachel spoke with a dreamy, faraway look in her eyes, "More so, I wager. He removed his mask just for me. His deep, accented voice, dark wavy hair and, especially, oooh his deep brown eyes had me enraptured." Whispering again: "I dare say, I thought my knees would surely buckle as he spoke to me." She paused for added drama, before adding, "I was fortunate to finish my song."

"You sang for him?" Charlotte inquired, reaching for a biscuit.

"Well, yes Lottie, at his gun-wielding request, I felt somewhat compelled." The quartet giggled once again.

At this point, Rachel fanned her face with her gloved hand, "As he rode off, he said that we shall meet again." She dropped her chin and looked up at her friends, coquettishly biting her bottom lip, "I'm hoping that he is right."

Abigail concurred, taking Rachel's hand and exclaiming, "It would be so exciting for you, Rachel!"

Matilda saw it differently. She pointed out that Rachel was approaching the age when young women seek a husband, not a swashbuckling lover. She reminded her friend that Jacques DuTemps was a ruthless highwayman bent on robbery, and that he would likely be brought to justice soon.

"He'll probably hang before he is 40 years old," Matilda muttered.

Rachel sighed, *"Quel gâchis ce serait[5],"* before taking another sip of tea. As her friends continued their animated conversation, Rachel daydreamed – and her eyes lingered on the handsome footman standing by the door.

His eyes, seldom failing in their duty, remained forward.

∞

---

5 "What a waste that would be."

18

SKYPILOT SPENT THE DAY with Constable Leddy, fighting crime while seeing the sights of London. Or vice versa – Leddy was content to walk and talk; crime fighting could perhaps wait a day. The accompaniment was sanctioned by the Justice of the Peace, on the condition that Sky would assist the constable in any way needed to fulfil his duties.

When the day was over, Sky was glad to have seen many of the sights of central London. But his tour guide had shown an unfortunate predisposition to focus on the darker, gristlier side of things.

On the main streets, carriages, hawkers, horse carts, dogs and throngs of people were ubiquitous, creating a cacophony of urban sounds.

The two passed many coffeehouses, all of which were crowded with men. It was common knowledge that coffee increased the reproductive capabilities of men. So, hopeful men dominated the coffee houses, with only a few brave women facing the dirty looks and shaking male heads that came with their own desire to sip a hot coffee.

Rather, women who had the means gathered in tea rooms or, more typically, they went shopping. The city had much to offer those with disposable income. Numerous shops offered all kinds of products, though most of the city's inhabitants could not afford to shop, except for necessities.

As they walked the streets, Sky was able at times to see the skyline. St. Paul's Cathedral dominated, creating an upper tier all of its own. The spires of lesser churches reached skyward, creating a middle tier of almost 50 edifices reaching closer to God, with all other buildings on the lowest tier.

But Constable Leddy told Sky of tiers even lower than that. When Sky turned to walk up a street, Leddy grabbed him by the arm and pointed in another direction, saying, "You don't want to walk by the cemetery, especially today. This breeze will carry the stench of the 'poor's holes' toward us."

"Poor's holes?" asked Sky, now walking with the constable in the right direction.

"Communal graves, Sky. Some are seven tiers deep. They leave 'em open till they're filled with bodies. Oye! Even the minister has to conduct the burial service at a safe distance. This way is a tad less pungent, my friend."

They walked on, passing Buckingham House, which was owned by King George III. The King was planning to use the building as a retreat for his wife, Queen Charlotte. Sky knew that Buckingham Palace now occupies this space.

They came to London Bridge, the main crossing of the River Thames. Most Londoners had to depend upon the polluted waters of the Thames for drinking water. The river doubled as the primary source of water for the city, and the repository for virtually all of its discharge. That discharge included the filth thrown overboard by the hundreds of ships and barges that crowded the harbour. It would be another 100 years before any attempt was made to filter the river water or protect it from pollution.

The wealthy in the city, on the other hand, typically purchased spring water from private companies. With a number of clear streams flowing on their property, the Mansfields enjoyed fresh water at no cost.

With water an unattractive drinking option, most urban dwellers opted for a safer, albeit more potent drink. Gin was cheap, delicious, intoxicating and unregulated. Street corner hawkers of the spirit would sell gin to anyone who was thirsty. There were a staggering 8,000 places in the city where gin was openly sold.

A few years prior to when Sky and Leddy toured the city, Henry Fielding warned, "Gin… is the principal sustenance of more than a hundred thousand people in this metropolis. Many of these Wretches there are, who swallow Pints of this Poison… the Dreadfull Effects of which I have the Misfortune every Day to see, and to smell too."[6]

As Sky then saw, even London Bridge featured gin sellers. Up until just a few years ago, the bridge had been festooned with wooden houses and shops, buildings that were erected in a haphazard way. The bridge was choked with traffic and the buildings exacerbated the problem. They were then deemed a fire hazard and a risk of collapse due to the increased load on the bridge's arches. So, all the bridge buildings were demolished through an Act of Parliament.

The southern gatehouse was Leddy's favourite part of the bridge. Pointing across the structure and yelling against the noise of traffic, he enthused, "That is where we mounted the severed heads of traitors, impaled on spikes. But not before they were dipped in tar and boiled – that kept the rain and snow off 'em! If you're lucky, you might get to see some; heads are still displayed."

To his relief, Sky did not see any severed heads that day. But, he did see an unfortunate man being tortured in 'the rack.' Knowing that the prisoner was on public display not far from the bridge, Leddy brought Sky to see.

"At least he has a chance to live," Leddy said. "Better that than 'the head crusher,' which is a vise tightened over the head. It'll crush your head, teeth first, then your eyes

6 An Enquiry into the Causes of the Late Increase of Robbers, 1751.

pop out, then your brain." Leddy loved to watch Sky's face contort as he described the gory details.

To further disgust his visiting friend, Leddy had to add, "Witches have it as bad with 'the pear'. That's a thin metal device on a thread." He held out his hand, palm up and fingertips together. "It's fluted at one end, which is inserted in any bodily orifice, and the thread is slowly turned, expanding the fluted part of 'the pear'." Wide-eyed, Leddy slowly separated his fingers, "Makes hanging at Tyburn look good, eh?" By now, Sky knew that the rotund Bow Street Runner often assumed the classic position of both hands on his belly when he laughed.

They walked by the Tower of London, which, Sky discovered, was more castle than tower. It was a complex of buildings set within two concentric rings of defensive walls and a surrounding moat. The Tower has had many uses in its long history, but during Leddy's time it was primarily a fortress, a storehouse and a prison.

The Tower must have looked imposing for invaders on the Thames. As Leddy and Sky stopped to gaze at the edifice, a conspiracy of ravens flew up against the white façade of the wall, symbolically ensuring that the kingdom would endure. Sky resisted the urge to tell the constable that the kingdom would endure through many wars, pestilence and political upheaval for at least another 250 years.

Apart from his affection for spiked heads and various forms of torture, Leddy was an enthusiastic guide, with lots of stories and jokes. "I arrested a pickpocket just the other day. He was robbing a dwarf." Leddy looked at Sky with a straight face, shook his head and lamented, "I mean, how can you stoop so low?"

If he knew his companion's source of distraction, Leddy would forgive Sky for not laughing. Sky's mind was firmly on Helena. He had to warn her about her uncle's perverse intentions.

That afternoon back at the constabulary, he waved goodbye to Constable Leddy, hoping he'd see the officer again. He hurried back to the inn, his mind churning with ideas.

More than pure physical attraction, he felt something of a commonality with Helena unlike any feelings he had had in the past – well, before now. He hoped that she too would feel something. But he resolved to tell her of her uncle's plan, in any case. No one should be subjected to that.

But not yet – they had not even met! He had to get Helena alone, away from the glassy-eyed admirers of the public house and more importantly, away from Jack Harris.

Sky needed a plan.

Perhaps he could rely on his innate Canadian politeness and charming accent to ask her out. No, he knew that wasn't possible. The only Canadian charm in England right now was embodied in Zachary Burling, wherever he might be.

Sky had a better plan.

∞

19

OUTSIDE OF THE WANDER Inn was a weathered public notice board. Sky glanced around before ripping down a poster that advertised an upcoming concert at "Vauxhall," wherever that was. The back of the poster was blank, as he had hoped. He rolled the parchment, stuffed it in his borrowed topcoat and headed into the inn.

He hoped to see the innkeeper's wife, not the surly man himself. In Sky's comings and goings, she had proven to be much friendlier than her husband.

He was in luck. She was behind the counter, again making entries in the ledger with her impressive quill pen. She wore a white, bleached linen cap with lace ruffles. This type of cap was ubiquitous, being worn by women of all classes almost all the time except for formal occasions.

Hearing him approach, she glanced up from her work. "'Ello luv. Enjoying your stay?" She knew that he was, in some unique way, foreign.

"Very much. I'm having a great time," Sky said. "I have a small request." He leaned on the desk, smiled and unconsciously pushed the poster deeper into his pocket.

"Yes, what is it?" the woman stood straight and put down her pen.

"May I borrow…" he pointed to the pen, "… that?"

"You want to borrow my quill?" she responded, with just a hint of indignation.

"Well, yes, if I may." Then he playfully added, "I'd like to write to a young lady."

"Lordy! Won't she be the lucky one, I daresay." The innkeeper's wife grinned, dropped her two chins and batted what was left of her eyelashes. "I'm using this one, luv, but I can loan you a spare."

She opened a drawer and pulled out a feathered pen similar to the one she was using, and an inkwell. She handed both to Sky. "Return them by morning, if not before. I'm 'ere till midnight."

Sky thanked her and bounded up the stairs to his room.

There, he lit the candle and deposited his acquisitions on the small desk. He got to work. He had never used a quill and ink before, but after some practise blotches on the front of the poster, he caught on. The front advertised the "Vauxhall Pleasure Gardens" and the outdoor concert soon to be performed by one Thomas Arne. He'd keep that in mind.

That evening, he returned the quill and ink well to the front desk, sliding them across with a hurried "Thank you" to the innkeeper's wife.

Then, he jogged back to The Bard to seek out Helena. Carrying his completed work, he boldly walked to the back of the pub to the kitchen, past seated men lifting mugs of ale, showing their "Bacchanalian propensities". Thankfully, Helena's uncle was not in sight.

Sky saw her there doing the same tasks she was doing the other night, wearing the same clothes and still wearing them well. Glassy-eyed and with a love-struck look on his face, he stood watching her work for awhile.

After a time, she noticed him looking at her. Back from his daydream, he summoned the courage to motion her over. She put down the mugs, drying her hands on her apron. She walked toward him, smiling broadly. Sky's heart missed at least three beats.

"What can I do for you, luv?" she asked, looking him up and down.

"Hi Helena, I…" Sky stammered. She was tall; the two stood almost eye to eye.

"How do you know my name?" she asked, taken aback.

"Your uncle is a friend of my… fellow employees."

"Oh, I see. My notorious uncle, eh? So, what's it to ya, then?" Helena looked anxiously back into the kitchen. "I don't have much time to chat."

"My name is Sky Sewell. We, my friends and I, were here the other night. I was… I am interested to make your acquaintance."

"You're not from 'round here are you? All right, we are acquainted. Now what?" Helena felt like she needed to challenge this presumptuous yet interesting young foreigner.

Sky was prepared. "Now, I have some quick questions for you." He pulled the poster from his pocket and sat down at an empty table. He had written on the back of the poster. His plan was based entirely on what Helena's uncle had revealed about her; that she could both read and write.

He placed the rolled up parchment paper on the table, revealing his handiwork with the borrowed quill pen. He anchored the paper with the mugs that had been left by the previous patrons. He motioned for Helena to sit.

"No, I couldn't possibly! I am working." She glanced toward the kitchen.

"This won't take long. Your uncle told me that you can read. I have six written questions for you."

Intrigued, Helena moved closer, but did not sit down. The questions read:

"What is the short form of The Bard's given name?
What is the name for a female sheep?
What is the opposite of "stop"?
What sound does an owl make?

To find the area of a rectangle, you multiply length by _____?
Do re _____ fa so la ti do?"

Helena was genuinely pleased. "Oh, this is a puzzle. I love puzzles!"

She looked down at the paper, deep in thought, accentuating her naïveté by sucking gently on her pinky finger. "Well, William Shakespeare would have been called 'Will' by his friends, I suppose."

"Correct!" Sky knew now that she would enjoy answering the questions. He filled in the first blank with the word "WILL".

Helena correctly guessed the next three answers: "EWE," "GO," and "HOOT." She thought for awhile about the rectangle question, but finally, her eyes widened and she blurted out, "WIDTH!". Sky filled in the blanks as she responded.

The last question was easy for her, as Sky had hoped.

"MI," she said excitedly, "Do re MI, as in music."

"Correct again. Now…" Sky pointed to the six assembled words at the bottom of the page, "read the words together."

Helena leaned over and ran her fingers over each word, still clutching her apron with her other hand. She read the words, but too slowly.

"Faster, and as though you're asking me a question," Sky directed.

She nodded and read again, "WILL EWE GO 'OOT (he had anticipated that she'd drop the "H") WIDTH MI? She raised her voice at the end to indicate a question.

Realization spread across her pretty face and she raised her hand, apron and all, to cover her mouth.

Triumphantly, Sky nodded and said softly, "Yes, Helena, I will go 'OOT with you!"

Her eyes dancing, she smiled at being so delightfully deceived.

Forgetting his planned rendezvous schedule with his "fellow employees," Sky turned the poster over and pointed. "We could go to Vauxhall. Do you know it?"

"Yes, of course I know it; who doesn't? The Pleasure Gardens, silly, in Spring Gardens, across the Thames. I've always wanted to visit."

"It's settled then, I'll take you to Vauxhall."

Despite appearances, Britain was enjoying a period of unprecedented prosperity. As like no time in the past, successful merchants, businessmen and other professionals had the time and money to indulge in leisure time activities. As the focus of much of this leisure time was music, the growing middle class would often visit opera houses or music clubs. In London, a "pleasure garden" like Vauxhall was the place to go to hear the latest concertos. The bourgeoisie would go to "people-watch," or to simply be seen there.

For Helena, a visit to Vauxhall was a grand adventure. Upon her arrival in the city, she had lived with her uncle. So far, Jack Harris had kept her and her honour locked up at home when she wasn't working in the kitchen at The Bard, where he could keep his eye on her.

Consequently, she spent most of her time at home reading, sewing, and doing the household chores. She, too, had just finished reading a borrowed copy of *The History of Tom Jones*.

Helena thought this chap was peculiar, but exciting in an exotic way.

"Meet me outside The Bard at 6 of the clock next Sunday," she said. We'll walk there together. And to think that Thomas Arne is playing that day! You've made my day... Sky." With a smile, Helena returned to the kitchen.

Sky knew and loved music, but his knowledge did not extend to the composer Arne, nor the fact that he had written both *Rule, Britannia!* and the catchy *A-Hunting We*

Will Go. If it had, Sky would have been humming the latter tune as he left the pub.

He was smitten. He could not wait until Sunday. In the meantime, he would rejoin Leddy, if the officer would have him along during the day. He stuffed the poster into his pocket and left The Bard. Later, he could not recall his feet actually touching the cobblestones on the way out.

∞

20

SO, WHILE MANY THOUGHT that Jack Harris was protecting his sweet niece from his sordid world of prostitution, he was actually protecting her virginity for the substantial monetary gain it would bring him.

Many were interested. Tavern customers were generally entranced by Helena's uncommon beauty while she performed her duties as a kitchen maid. Many would leer at her, with or without a whore on their lap.

Jack had had some offers, but none were serious enough or, more likely, large enough. So he waited.

One such offer had been made in April, when a young rake had visited The Bard in the company of three peers. These well-to-do young Englishmen were in the final stage of a two-year European tour; the objective being, of course, to gamble, drink and fornicate to their hearts' content.

This particular rake, one Weldon Blimely, was the *de facto* leader of the quartet. The mustachioed and married Weldon had led the assault on pretty young lasses through France, Savoy, Genoa, Tuscany and Switzerland. It mattered not if those lasses were "professional" girls or not. Weldon took particular joy in seducing innocent girls as opposed to simply bedding a prostitute. The gents kept score, of course, and all women counted for one point. Except a virgin; she was worth five.

Down by four points to his mate Hugh, Weldon would need to deflower a maiden to win the contest and the £60 from his mates. Time was of the essence. When the four entered The Bard, their journey was literally coming to an end. Alas, so was their money.

Like scores of men before them, though, they sat at their table slurping turtle soup and swilling beer, only to be eventually captured by the beauty that was becoming known as "Helena of the Kitchen." Weldon decided that the kitchen wench would be the next notch on his bedpost. He had no way of knowing that she was indeed worth five notches.

Watching her with rising interest, Weldon had only to inquire of the skinker – others called him "Jack" – as to how to bed her.

Jack, who seemed to have more than a passing interest in a potential transaction, was direct. "Ahh, mate. Ain't she lovely? Yes, she can be had. She is a virgin, don't you know. So that, combined with her obvious youth and beauty, means that she can be had for 150 quid. Tonight, upstairs." He cocked his head in that direction.

Weldon knew that even he could not afford such a price at this moment. But he toyed with the idea and with the waiter, asking him to bring the wench over to his table. Jack spoke to Helena in the kitchen, quietly explaining that he had four young lads that wanted to meet her. This wasn't the first group of "lads." He pointed to their table and instructed her to join him there in a few minutes. He neglected to explain that he had pledged her virginity for £150.

Jack then returned to the rakes' table, where he further detailed Helena's farm background, her naïveté and, most importantly, the presence of her hymen. Weldon questioned her purity, working here amongst all these lustful men.

"Of course she is a maiden, sir! I have personally seen to her celibacy since her arrival from the farm, untouched as driven snow. At the farm, she'd milk the cows and collect apples from the orchard. Oh!" Jack pointed at Hugh, who sat with a broad smile and a dreamy expression. "I can see you imagining her milking a cow as we speak, sir. 150 quid and she is yours for the night. But speak quickly, as that price I cannot guarantee for long. And, no talk to her about money! Oye, here she comes now."

Helena walked cautiously to the table, as many of the glassy-eyed imbibers paused to watch her do so. Shyly, she stood at the end of the table.

"This, gentlemen, is Helena," Harris raised his arm in a sweeping motion. "She is desirous to meet young people like yourselves and to… uhhh… perhaps spend some time together."

Weldon leaned back on the bench and wolfishly looked the fair maiden up and down. In a loud voice he intoned, "I am pleased to meet you, Helena. I hope that we are able to 'spend some time together' – close together, may I say – very soon."

One for the spotlight, he stood and walked around the table to stand next to Helena. He had underestimated her height; she stood a full head taller than the diminutive Weldon! He looked up at her comically. Sadly, and with pity in her blue eyes, she looked down at him.

Weldon's mates and even Jack, who knew that he would not be making any money now, burst into uproarious laughter. Some sitting at tables close by realized what had happened, and joined in the merriment at the expense of Weldon Blimely.

Weldon trudged back to his seat, sat down and crossed his arms, defeated by his shortcomings and attempting to take it in his stride.

Tears now rolling down his cheeks, Hugh stopped laughing long enough to bellow over the din, "Money or otherwise, mate, you're a little short!"

∞

21

AS SOON AS HE saw the barn, the colt bolted. Out for a long morning ride on her favorite palfrey, Rachel lurched back in the saddle and was almost jolted off the horse. But she had been expecting the charge, so she leaned forward and held on tightly to the saddle.

Rachel rode the horse "astride" rather than "aside." That is, she rode like a man would; with a leg on each side of the horse rather than in the annoying "sidesaddle" style in which most women rode: aside, with one foot in a stirrup and a knee over the pommel. Riding astride was considered to be indecent for women… everyone knew that riding aside protected a woman's virginity.

Everyone but Rachel, that is, who would have none of that. As she had told her riding instructor years ago, it was simply more comfortable and less dangerous riding astride! And, there was usually nobody around to witness her wanton misbehaviour.

Rachel wore a riding habit custom-made for her by a reputable London tailor. Like most women's outfits, it adapted elements of men's wear, modified with a waist seam to fit tightly over stays and a wide petticoat. It was finely tailored of sturdy broadcloth used in naval uniforms, and included mariner's cuffs.

But, rather than maritime blue, Rachel wore emerald green. A narrow straight collar attached at the back of her neck, and the buttoning in front that normally kept her warm on chilly rides had been unbuttoned for the ride home. The outfit was trimmed with silver braiding, imitating a military uniform. Rachel found that she could turn a few heads wearing this stylish outfit informally when travelling, visiting or just walking between shops in London.

She let the colt take her, and he galloped through the long grass in the field in the waxing sun. The morning was still cool enough to allow the dew on the long grass to moisten the legs and flanks of the horse. The rider's long auburn hair flowed in the wind under her fashionable hat, and she smiled widely. She breathed deeply. *This is riding!* she thought.

The palfrey snorted and slowed as it approached the barn. Seeing a young man – a footman, perhaps – at the barn door, Rachel sat up in her mount. The man seemed to be holding an envelope, tapping it against his thigh. She may have a message waiting for her. Most likely, a note from Abigail or one of the other girls, thanking her for her hospitality yesterday.

As Rachel approached, she recognized the messenger as the new footman, Zachary. She found herself gazing down, checking that her outfit looked as good as it felt. Then, she asked herself why she had done so.

When given the task of bringing a message to Rachel, Zac was excited to perhaps have a chance to speak with her. He knew that he had made something of an impression on her, as Jamieson had insinuated in a moment of weakness after the tea party. As he decanted wine while providing further instructions for the tenderfoot footman, Jamieson had conceded that Lady Rachel had instructed him that Zachary was to be the attending footman for the tea party.

But Zac also wanted to do something about the smartwatch. While he understood why Aunt Bea had insisted that he and Sky keep the watches on, he had to hide it better and conceal it from prying eyes. Also, the battery pack was uncomfortable; its weight constant in his pocket. He felt it now, a constant reminder of where he was and of the imminent danger.

But, in order to enact change, he had to find some leather. This task was the perfect opportunity.

Jamieson had handed Zac the envelope with strict instructions to deliver it "with no fanfare." Taking his leave while attempting to look less than ecstatic, Zac ran out to the stable, wanting to get there in lots of time.

He ran through the immense gardens that surrounded the estate house. Past the corral, a small grotto and a lake with a bubbling stream had been created. The grotto, as you will see, was occupied.

The ostler – responsible for the horses and tack – was in the adjacent corral training a gelding. Jamieson had spoken to him earlier, telling him to keep an eye on the new footman and in particular, his interactions with Lady Rachel.

When he saw the ostler, Zac slowed from a run to a more refined walk. He adjusted his livery and entered the empty barn. Inside, hanging in the corner and covered in dust, Zac found a dusty old dressage saddle.

In addition to cricket, the duke also loved fox hunting. He had a special fox hunting saddle designed; one with a low pommel and cantle (the rear part), which allowed for more freedom of movement for both horse and rider during the chase.

This dressage saddle, Zac surmised, *is no longer being used.* He lifted it and examined it closely. It had engravings on the sides and on the cantle, but there were bigger pieces of leather underneath where the saddle rests against the horse, hidden from view. He grabbed a nearby knife, a mallet and an awl from the tool shelf. He found some long leather laces hanging with the rest of the tack. He began to cut the inner leather of the saddle into usable pieces.

Using the battery pack to measure, Zac cut one big piece of leather and two smaller pieces for the sides of the pouch. He cut two vertical holes for his belt. Working quickly, he used the awl and mallet to punch holes near the edges of all the pieces. Through the holes, he weaved the leather laces. The big piece wrapped around the battery from the bottom, with the ends coming together near the top. Cinching the laces brought the three pieces together into a pouch. He left enough leather to allow for a flap at the top, which was then tied with a short piece of leather lace.

Zac removed his belt and stood wide-legged (so that his breeches stayed up!), then looped the belt through the vertical holes in the back of the pouch. He positioned the pouch so it rested just below the small of his back. The shirt that Jamieson provided should provide adequate cover for the watch itself, with lots of frilly fabric in the sleeves.

Satisfied with his creation, Zac turned to see a horse and rider approaching fast. *Just in time* he thought. He grabbed the envelope and left the barn quickly, not noticing the ostler who had left the corral and had quietly entered the barn. The ostler had watched for some time from behind a stall half-wall, as Zac used leather cut from a saddle to fashion some kind of pouch.

"Say there, Zachary! Do you have a message for me?" Rachel was out of breath as she skilfully brought her energetic colt to a stop.

"Hello, M'Lady. Yes, I was told to wait for you here, to give you this." Zac held up the envelope. "Here, allow me to help you off your horse."

Zac offered his hand, but Rachel hesitated at first; a footman need not provide this service unless told to do so. Realizing that he was new, she smiled, took his hand and dismounted. Once dismounted, she continued to hold his hand and he continued to provide it. Their eyes locked in a stalemate until Rachel failed to suppress a smile.

With a slight bow (a vast improvement over previous attempts, due to practising in his room), Zac handed her the envelope. It was addressed to "Lady Rachel Mansfield" in a large, flowing script. The ostler emerged from the barn to take the horse's reins from Rachel. Zac looked at him, thinking *Funny, I thought that I was the only one in the barn.*

The ostler walked off into the corral with the horse, cooling it down. He peered over his shoulder at Zac as he did, making a mental note to request an audience with Lord Mansfield. The Duke himself should be told about that strange white box, and about the footman's need to hide it in a handmade pouch. A pouch made from a usable dressage saddle, no less! He would simply report to Jamieson that nothing seemed to be awry between the footman and Lady Rachel.

Perspiring in the most feminine of ways, Rachel used the envelope to fan her face. A competent footman would have, at this time, said "good day" to the lady and run back into the house to assume his numerous duties there. Zac was not yet a competent footman, so he stood, waiting to be dismissed.

The dismissal did not come, at least not immediately, as Rachel found the young man to be at once odd, charming and truth be known, quite handsome. Not in a dashing highwayman type way, you understand, but in a familiar boy-next-door way. And that in itself was somewhat odd to her because here at the estate, the nearest boy-next-door was three miles away.

In any case, she needed to speak with Zachary.

"I have not yet been able to thank you properly for your assistance on the road. It could have gone even worse, if not for your actions. I am happy that my father was able to employ you as a result." Rachel found herself to be embarrassed when she would normally be confident. Her embarrassment seemed to enhance her beauty. Zac could only smile.

"You really must return to the house now, Zachary. Jamieson will soon be wondering as to your whereabouts."

"Very good, M'Lady." Zac bowed slightly, "I, errr… look forward to seeing you at the ball on Saturday."

"Oh! You do, do you?" Rachel was removing her gloves. "You may not recognize me, you know. I plan to dress as a troll!"

"Oh no, M'Lady, I'd recognize you anywhere. And," Zac paused, "you are no troll."

He turned and began walking briskly toward the mansion, the battery pack now virtually weightless and invisible in the new pouch located at the small of his back.

Rachel smiled. This footman was so honest and brazen! After Zachary had left, she began to open the envelope. On a whim, she held it to her dainty nose and sniffed it. Her delicate nostrils flared. The smell of perfume filled her senses. Could it be from Jacques?

She wanted to savour the letter, in the privacy of her own room. She hurried back to the estate, entering via a rear door; the quickest route.

Back in her bedchamber and perspiring once again, Rachel removed her jacket. She closed her eyes and sniffed the envelope once more. She sat at her writing desk, and used her silver letter opener to open the envelope. It was from Jacques! He had written her a poem. She read:

"The Lovely Lady Rachel:

Your fragrance and sweet voice have been on my mind constantly since our chance meeting on the road. The delicate ticking of your timepiece (which I keep next to my heart) always reminds me of you; its beat seems to perfectly match the beating of my

heart — that is, until I think of you, then my heart
outpaces it. I am compelled to write you a simple
poem proclaiming my feelings.

Ticking, ticking
It seems that Father Time moves at different rates
When we are apart, he moves too slowly;
When we are lovers, he will move too fast —
When you are in my arms, I will have little time
To show you how much I love you
Before it is time for me to go

Father Time will catch up with you… at the masquerade ball.

Jacques"

∞

22

And do whate'er thou wilt, swift-footed Time,
To the wide world and all her fading sweets;
But I forbid thee one most heinous crime:
O, carve not with thy hours my love's fair brow,
—William Shakespeare,
Sonnet 19

OUR OWN FAIR YOUTH, Zachary, had fallen into the daily routine of a Mansfield Castle footman.

He rose early each morning. He would shave, have a sponge bath and dress, inspecting his livery in the common mirror at the end of the hallway. He would complete most of his duties prior to the Mansfield family breakfast, with which he would assist. Before serving lunch, he had numerous other mundane duties to attend to, such as polishing silver and managing candles.

Zac enjoyed his afternoon duties more than the morning ones. That was when he would often provide a carriage escort for family members, or deliver messages on horseback on behalf of his master. As an escort, only on one occasion did he have to point his blunderbuss. An ill-advised pair of footpads had tried to rob the carriage while it had stopped for a wheel repair. Nary a shot was fired as Zac, the other two footmen – yes, the duke had hired an additional footman after the attack by Jacques – and Daltrey simply had to threaten the robbers before they lost their nerve and backpedalled into the trees that bordered the roadway.

There was a weekly routine as well. Every Sunday morning prior to the service in the chapel, household staff would gather for inspection. Jamieson typically inspected his charges in the hall, while the housekeeper conducted her inspection in the kitchen. The inspections included a review of livery (its condition being the responsibility of the employee). Also reviewed were personal grooming – hair, teeth and fingernails. Staff requiring a haircut or fingernail trimming were sent immediately to see the attending barber (who trimmed nails in addition to hair) prior to the mandatory church service.

Jamieson moved slowly down the line, comprised of the four footmen and underbutler, their hands extended for inspection. His Lordship had excused Quering, who also reported to Jamieson, from all future inspections. Lord Mansfield knew that Quering was fastidious with regard to personal hygiene, and that he felt himself above all that, in any case.

Each of the footmen held in his right hand the silver wig that he was required to wear while on duty. The other three footmen kept their heads shaved for ease of fitting the wig every morning. Zac was the only footman with a full head of hair, but thankfully it was relatively short and his wig was easily accommodated, generous head or not.

The inspection was completed with but a single transgression: Zac's fingernails required an immediate trim. He was sent to the barber, who was waiting in the stillroom. Beatrice would have to depend on the measurement of Sky's fingernails when they returned to Fraserdale. Zac sighed. *If we return to Fraserdale.*

In addition to his regular duties, he had "other assigned duties," such as setting the pendulum clocks throughout the estate. A recent invention, the pendulum was more accurate than its mechanical predecessors, but still required physical adjustment of its big hand of up to 10 minutes per day.

The well-known clock maker and museum proprietor, James Cox, had made an exquisite clock for the hall in Mansfield Castle. Cox's "Peacock clock," while difficult to say, was not difficult for visitors to enjoy. Encrusted with shimmering jewels, the peacock was able to turn its head when the hour was struck. It was positioned next to a large window that made the jewels glitter by day. Candles strategically placed near the base made it glitter by night. The Peacock clock was not set by Zac or by any of the other footmen, Jamieson had charged himself with this duty.

The irony of this daily clock-setting exercise was that Zac got the "accurate" time from the large sundial in the front garden. On cloudy days, he secretly referred to his smartwatch, which kept time "within 50 milliseconds of the definitive global standard, with the same precision of GPS satellites." That standard, he felt, was sufficient for the purposes of the Mansfield household.

Mansfield Castle boasted a number of pets, including six English foxhound hunting dogs, two lapdogs (a poodle and a bulldog), a number of brightly-coloured goldfish in the Drawing Room and a gorgeous scarlet macaw parrot. Zac hardly ever saw any of these, with the exception of the parrot, which was usually in its huge gilded cage in the Billiard Room right beside the clock that Zac set daily.

The bird had been assigned to that most masculine of rooms for an expressed purpose. To the amusement of all, Lord Mansfield and his male guests had taught the bird a few choice words and phrases. These lessons usually took place late in a game of billiards, with its attendant cigars and port.

Zac couldn't resist teaching the bird a few choice words of his own. Every day while making his rounds, Zac would take a few furtive minutes to talk to the mimicking macaw.

He had only a few moments each day, but the bird got to recognize him, knowing that Zac usually carried a few pecans, cashews or other nuts pilfered from the kitchen.

"That's what she said!" and "Canada Rocks!" The bird really got into that one, rolling the "R." *And no one*, thought Zac erroneously, *will know about Canada for another hundred years!*

But, the bird had a favourite saying. One that confused Zac: "He's a witch!"

Zac's confusion was somewhat alleviated the next morning, when he routinely entered the Billiard Room to set the clock. Already in the room was Chiku, the house-maid, cleaning the fireplace. She had rolled up the decorative hearth rug after shaking it out, and had laid canvas to protect the area in front of the fireplace. She had swept up the ashes and was just finishing the job by wiping down the marble hearth when Zac walked in.

Zac had gotten to know only a few of the domestic staff; mostly just the other footmen, who he knew only casually. Chiku was the exception, as Zac would run into her when he made his daily rounds. She was also exceptional in another, more superficial way, as she was the only black servant in the household.

Africans had been in Britain since arriving as troops in Roman armies. Chiku and her sister had arrived as slaves, their capture justified by the claim that blacks were simply barbaric savages who did not even have their own language.

The sisters were separated when the slave ship docked at Liverpool. Chiku was fortunate in that she was sold to a trader who sold her to the steward of Mansfield Castle. The steward knew that it was fashionable amongst the elite to possess a black servant; Chiku was to be something of a status symbol for Lord Mansfield. She would never learn what became of her sister.

Although their encounters were always brief and fleeting, Zac and Chiku always enjoyed each other's company – perhaps because they were each, in their own way, different from the others.

Chiku was now in her late 40s, and the physicality of her daily routine was growing increasingly difficult. Recognizing this, Zac had given her Ames' bedwarmer.

"Let me get this right, Chiku," Zac had asked at that time. "One takes hot embers from the fire and places them in this little pot, then one puts the pot – full of the burning embers, mind you – into their bed? I don't think so!"

Chiku had laughed and laughed at that, but she prized the bedwarmer. She had put it to good use for many cold, wet winters. Her spirits always rose when she came across "that sweet, funny boy from the colonies."

Chiku, whose Swahili name meant "chatterer," had lived up to her name as a young girl. Enslavement had initially caused her to be silent. But as she had grown accustomed to her new surroundings and language, she again found her voice. And despite her past, and the long working days and virtually no free time of her present, that voice was often filled with merriment and joy.

The free-spirited Zachary was a catalyst for her voice to run free, as least for awhile.

He quietly entered the room, seeing her wiping the marble hearth while humming softly to herself. Unable to resist, he snuck up behind her.

"Hello Chiku!" he bellowed. "Are you cooking me eggs for breakfast?" He pretended to look for his eggs in the fireplace, sniffing for the aroma.

Startled, Chiku turned to face him. "You! Zachary, you are a scoundrel, scaring a poor woman like that." She made a fist and hit him, half-heartedly on his hard shoulder. Then she smiled and laughed.

Zac opened his arms and the two embraced briefly, before letting go and standing awkwardly, face-to-face.

To end the awkwardness, Zac held up a finger and said, "Chiku, watch this." He took something from his pocket and walked slowly to the birdcage, from which the parrot had been watching the shenanigans.

Chiku crossed her arms and watched, wondering what the boy with the funny accent was up to now. He opened the large wrought-iron door of the birdcage and leaned in, hands behind his back and the cashew from his pocket now lodged between his teeth. He hoped that the parrot would take it gently.

He looked and sounded comical as he mouthed the words, "Don't bite me…" with the cashew preventing him from speaking clearly. The bird looked interested, and craning its feathered neck, inched forward on its perch.

Neither Chiku nor Zac saw Lady Rachel walking by the open Billiard Room door. Rachel stopped and watched in amusement as Zac mumbled, "Don't…"

The parrot then filled in the blank, "Bite me!" before snatching the nut and nipping Zac on his lip while doing so.

With an "Owww!", Zac jumped back, holding his mouth. Rachel entered the room, trying to suppress a laugh. Chiku curtsied and, using the canvas like an emergency bag, picked up her cleaning tools and quickly left the room. Rachel stood there, arms crossed, tapping her foot under her blue silk dress while Zac remained buckled forward in pain. He looked up at her, licking his cut lip and tasting the trickle of blood.

Finally, Rachel could not hold back any longer. A slender gloved hand to her mouth, she started to giggle. Then laugh. She was laughing as she walked over to where Zac was standing, still a little hunched. She lifted his shoulders so that he stood straight. No longer laughing, she gently removed his hand from his mouth, and looking at his slight wound, used her tongue to make that "tsk, tsk" sound.

She then did something that Zac would never forget. She took his cheeks in her hands and kissed and licked his lips, blood and all. She licked her own lips now, and then she pursed them, saying in a childlike voice, "Poor, poor boy. The bad birdie nipped you, didn't he?"

"Yes, Ma'am," Zac was aghast. He was about to explain, when Rachel moved her finger to his lips, silencing him. She whispered into his ear, her warm breath making the hairs on his neck tingle. "You know, my father thinks that you are a witch. He thinks that you hide somewhere on your person a talisman of some bedevilment. Where is it, Zachary? You can tell me."

Maintaining eye contact, Rachel began to touch the footman's uniform all over, feeling for, and finding, some bulges, "Is it here? Perhaps here…"

He stepped back abruptly, stopping her overt sexual advances. She took a deep breath and after a long pause, scolded him: "You had better be very careful, Zachary."

Then, she turned and stormed out.

∞

23

THE CRICKET PLAYERS ASSEMBLED on the pitch at Mansfield Castle, as they did at 9:30 a.m. on every second Thursday throughout the summer. They had all received word from the duke that they should come prepared to play a new game from the colonies.

They were advised in the hand-delivered letter that they would be trained to play by a young man proficient at the game of "lacrosse"; a game from the colonies.

While delivering the letters of invitation on horseback, Zac got a chance to enjoy the fresh air of the beautiful, rolling English countryside. He could not know that on bad days, with a proper wind, London could be smelled from here. He could not know the extent of Sky's experience with that powerful stench and all that was associated with it.

Sky! He had to somehow find Sky and soon. Beatrice's 39-day window was dwindling. By his calculation (each night, he added a tally mark to the wall behind his mattress), he had been here for 20 days. That left just 19 days to find Sky and prepare for the journey home.

Zac would soon have to abandon his employment at Mansfield Castle and, he supposed, journey to London. There, he could make inquiries and post notices. He had enough money to offer a reward.

Lord Mansfield seemed to think that his debt to Zac had been paid in full through the offer of employment. He had ignored or forgotten about Zac's request for help to find Sky during the carriage ride. And, Zac hadn't had another opportunity to ask His Lordship since that evening. Perhaps during the game…

Had they made a grievous mistake in coming to this time and place? Mistakes, he knew now, had been made. He was beginning to think that he might not get back to Fraserdale. If only he could speak to Sky. He always seemed to know what to do.

On the pitch, a few men bowled the ball and some played batsman, but most stood chatting and stretching in the bright sun. The bowlers threw underhand, as the overhand throw for cricket had not yet been developed.

Zac was to provide the lacrosse training. So once again, Jamieson had to make alternative arrangements for the completion of Zac's regular duties. He did so grudgingly.

John Wedgwood was there with his father, Josiah. Many of the wives and families of the participants had come along, curious about this new game and always happy to visit the beautiful Mansfield Castle. Rachel, Wee Willy and Abigail were in attendance, as they had heard about the extent of the required preparations for this unique new game. And, they wanted to see the handsome footman, Zachary, in action.

Zac had had an opportunity to practice throwing the ball with Munn, using the new sticks, after they had completed their preparations. Munn spent much of the time retrieving dropped balls and complaining. However, Zac now felt somewhat prepared to teach the game, using this rickety equipment.

Sir William finally arrived, but he was not wearing the outfit that Zachary had made for him. As Zac later learned, Sir William did not want to have any advantage over his friends. "If they are unprotected, then so shall I be! But, I think I've found my masquerade costume – a gift from the colonies. Ha ha!"

At the duke's command, Zac gathered the group of 17 men in front of one of the two goals that had been set up about 80 yards apart on the cricket pitch. Although smaller than a regulation lacrosse field, the field was appropriate for a training session. With Munn's grudging assistance, Zac marked off a rudimentary goal crease, brushing white paint on the grass that had been freshly cut with scythes.

Excitedly, Zac summarized the game, focusing on the fundamentals. Using the two leather balls, he showed them the "face-off," passing, receiving, shooting and defending. John Wedgwood showed some interest in goal, making some athletic saves, when the shooters were able to hit the net. He also was on the receiving end of a few shots to the legs, and a particularly painful one to the "groinular" area.

The players, however, wanted to play. So, they assigned teams and split into two groups. But both teams looked similar.

An idea hit Sir William like a bolt of lightning, "Perhaps we can divide the group by 'shirts and skins'."

"'Shirts and skins'?" asked John, still rubbing his groin.

Thankfully, his health that day was not affected. John went on to become a noted horticulturalist and heir to the Wedgwood pottery company. And, perhaps as importantly, the uncle of Charles Darwin.

"Yes – one team removes their shirts, leaving a team of 'shirts' and one of 'skins.' Zachary here and I volunteer to be skins…" Sir William walked a line of demarcation, making two teams, "… with these lads." While removing his shirt, he motioned for one team to join him and Zac.

To the audible delight of some in the audience, the "skins" removed their shirts. Zac knew that Rachel was watching as he peeled off his already sweaty linen shirt. He may not have been the most muscular of 21st century young men, but he was one of them. Here in the 18th century, his chiselled physique – honed by regular exercise and advanced nutrition – dramatically contrasted with those of the other players.

While removing his shirt, Zac remembered the pouch that held the smartwatch, the portable charger and the cable. Too late – the pouch was now visible in the small of his back. In his excitement he had forgotten about it! Had Sir William assigned him to the skins team on purpose? Zac hoped that its presence was not considered strange for anyone seeing it; perhaps, he thought, it could have been considered a money pouch.

Sir William was one of those who did notice the pouch. And, remembering the ostler's story, he did think of it as strange. He'd get to the bottom of it later. But now, he had a "cross" game to play.

The scrimmage began. The sides were evenly matched and although the skill level was low, the players put out a lot of effort. There were a lot of flubbed catches and even more flubbed shots, but these led to guffaws and chortles.

After playing for almost an hour, the players took a break. Sweating, puffing and backslapping, they walked toward the audience, which greeted them with polite applause. The sound of gentile clapping was replaced by the sound of a line of approaching teacarts, if you can imagine what that sounds like.

Josiah Wedgwood had surprised the group by providing tea, despite the heat of the day. Twelve of his servants carefully pushed and pulled six carts to the sideline. Each cart displayed the latest china from the Wedgwood Company, founded just seven years earlier.

Water was provided in large buckets with communal ladles. Zac quenched his thirst and encouraged the other players to drink up, but some still opted for tea. The shirtless Zachary captured the attention of the collective audience that day and, in particular, of Rachel and Wee Willy.

Throughout the game, Zac was content to pass the ball rather than dominate play. True to his word, Sir William sought out Zac during the game to ask about life in the colonies. Zac was being tested; he knew it. This also absorbed the limited time that Zac thought he might have to ask Sir William to help find Sky. Despite knowing that he was under scrutiny, Zac was unable to definitively answer most of the duke's rather pointed questions.

Toward the end of the game, some of the players requested that Zac display his full skill with the ball. So he reluctantly did so, moving fluidly across the field, a zig here, a zag there, dodging players who flailed at his stick. Using his favourite inside-outside move, he backhanded the ball past the fallen goalie into the yawning cage.

Other than Josiah's groin and a few scrapes and banged fingers, there was only a single injury. One of the goalies took a hard shot and left the game holding his shoulder.

As Sir William proclaimed later, "Even more fun than I had anticipated! Too bad that we cannot use the sticks to throw the cricket ball; the cross ball seems to go much faster propelled from the stick."

Zac cringed at this, not wanting to change the game of cricket for eternity. But then, he thought about and was comforted by Aunt Bea's words: "Anything a time traveller does in the past must have been part of history all along."

Game over, the small crowd clapped and cheered their appreciation. As Zac walked by with the other players, Rachel beamed and tugged at Abigail's elbow. Wee Willy turned and walked slowly back to the estate house, hiding a sly smile.

∞

24

GAZING ABSENTMINDEDLY AT THE calico kitten that peered back with suspicion from under the dressing table, Sir William continued to express his agitation.

"He is a *witch*, I tell you!" He sat at the edge of the four-poster bed putting on his borrowed "sporting shoes." As he spoke, Caramel dressed.

"Rachel told me that he is behaving strangely, although she would not elaborate. He seems to know little about the colonies he claims to come from. Why, since the Stamp Act was repealed in March, I have been reading the papers about goings-on there, so I know of what I speak. He knows little of the Thirteen Colonies, or of other parts of British North America!"

He finished tying his shoes and stretched out his legs, again admiring his new footwear. "My ostler saw him making a pouch to hold some type of talisman. And, I saw the pouch on his person at the game. That was no money pouch. And look at these shoes! Indeed, how can one help but look at these shoes? What devilry is this? If they weren't so damned comfortable! We have to do something, 'Mel."

They were in Sir William's Edward Street townhouse in London, which he kept as a convenience for obligatory meetings in the city. But it was mostly a convenient place to meet Caramel. In fact, she lived there most of the time when she wasn't otherwise engaged.

For her, this relationship came down to simple economics. While Sir William never actually paid Caramel, he lavished her with gifts in addition to allowing her to live in his townhouse. As a prostitute of some renown, she could earn two guineas, or pounds, per coupling; that was over £400 a year if she worked hard. Plus, she obtained additional income by robbing unsuspecting customers – "a little here, a little there." In her former profession as a housemaid in Mansfield Castle – a fine household – she earned only eight pounds a year for a roof over her head and a life of drudgery.

Many young women did the same simple arithmetic, and thousands of girls flocked to London each year for the purpose. About one in every five women in London was a "Covent Garden nun." For some it was a supplement to a day job, if they were fortunate enough to have one. But most could find no other form of employment. Prostitution was not a "last resort"; it was the norm.

Caramel the housemaid had become Sir William's lover when she was just 17.

It had been easy to find an empty room or use the gardeners' shed for a few hours for their trysts, even when Lady Emily was at home. Their domestic relationship lasted until Caramel fell pregnant and had to leave the estate at the age of 20. Jamieson had found out about her condition from the housekeeper, who had found out from Caramel's roommate. Jamieson had to, of course, invoke the household rule of celibacy: release from employment without a letter of reference.

Sir William certainly did not want his good name tarnished by a scandal, so Caramel was released. The chances of His Lordship being linked to a common housemaid were low, but he took no chances.

Like those other young women, Caramel made her way to London. Without a reference from her last employer, and unmarried, she had to hide her pregnancy while looking for work. Finding nothing, and living in Covent Garden, she turned to a life of prostitution to earn a living, starting by offering such services as a "threepenny upright" in squalid alleyways as other girls worked nearby.

She dabbled as a professional practitioner of folk medicine; healing the sick, telling fortunes, creating herbal remedies and enacting anti-witch measures. When her baby girl was born, she continued to sell her body. Her co-workers pitched in when they could to mind the baby when Caramel was working, usually not far away. With regret, Caramel could remember many times hearing her baby crying as she serviced a customer.

A natural Irish beauty, Caramel was now 41; past her prime but maintaining her "regulars," and via a complimentary description in *The List*, still acquiring new, curious clients. The publication for that Christmas listed Caramel "nautically" thus:

"Miss Calhoun, No. 26, Edward Street, Cavendish Square

This is a fine tall lady, about five and thirty, a very fine figure, just returned from Brighton, has been in dock to have her bottom cleaned and fresh coppered, where they have washed away all the impurities of prostitution, and risen almost immaculate, like Venus, from the waves. A cunning one, she is now fit to carry any burthen, and sails from the rate of ten to twelve notches an hour. If the spring and even the summer of her beauty be past, she is not without hope of a fruitful autumn. She at present has a distinguished man who is her favourite, and lives on the second floor. Her footing is rather superior to the common run, and expects five pieces, but being disappointed, is very well pleased with three or four."

Over the years, Caramel had risen among the ranks of harlots to become something of a celebrity. But that celebrity was waning as "Miss Calhoun" aged.

Other celebrities made *The List*, and all had their apparent amorous encounters chronicled annually. Sir William made the list, as did kings and dukes, earls and clergymen. After all, it was a time when men of every rank frequented popular bathhouses. All the propaganda was designed to enhance the credibility of *The List* and improve on its annual circulation of about 8,000 copies.

Caramel remained Sir William's mistress; his courtesan – that is, a lover and confidante to the royal, noble and wealthy men of society. Courtesans were socially acceptable; even accompanying a man to a social function, taking the place of his wife and often with her acknowledgment. Nevertheless, courtesans could be persecuted at times or even accused of witchcraft, which could in turn lead to imprisonment and execution.

Although not as educated as some, Caramel's "street smarts," striking beauty and sophisticated charm more than made up for her lack of formal education. But she had never accompanied the duke to a social function; he saw no reason to publicize their relationship, thereby exposing it to his children and others.

Now, however, the duke no longer had a wife (Caramel had seen to that).

She was a member of the "cunning folk." Other members of the cunning folk had a family heritage of professional magical practitioners, but Caramel only professed this type of background. She, like many others, had no formal training. And yet, she claimed to be proficient in folk magic – specifically love magic, offering services pertaining to sex and relationships. She would tell fortunes by reading palms, or she would divine the name or appearance of a clients' future lover. Or, she would cast a spell to ensure a spouse's fidelity, preventing them from committing adultery. Though Caramel was doing well financially and did not need to work as often as before, no pension awaited her, so her side-line was a useful one in more ways than one.

Having cleared her competition, she treated the widower Sir William very well indeed, hoping to become more than simply his mistress one day. But Sir William was content to have his cake and eat it too, visiting Caramel whenever he so desired and leaving his home life less… complicated.

But Caramel remained optimistic, and perhaps this endeavour would prove the fruitful one.

Pulling an expensive silk stocking up her shapely leg, Caramel purred, "Do something? What do you have in mind, M'Lord?" She excited him, especially during sex, by calling him "Lord."

"Here, here is a drawing of his talisman." Sir William handed Caramel a piece of paper with a rough sketch on it resembling a smartwatch, but only slightly. "Look in your book. Look to see if there is something like it; anything. See if we can use something to positively identify him as a witch."

Lord Mansfield had lost his Lady Emily and their unborn third child almost 20 years ago, seemingly the victim of a witch's potion. Ever since, Sir William had taken an interest in ridding the world of witches in his attempts to avenge his wife, whom he had so loved. He enjoyed seeing them hanged, dunked or burned at the stake, although these events seldom occurred anymore. More was the pity.

"I must go now," Sir William sighed as he embraced Caramel, his hands running down the length of her back and beyond, so as to more easily recall the gentle curves of her body during his return carriage ride to the estate. He held her tight and kissed her full lips passionately.

Grabbing his hat, he positioned it properly – at a rakish angle – and said, "I'll be back next week. I hope that you will have found something by then."

∞

25

FOLLOWING HER LABORIOUS DRESSING process, Caramel fruitlessly searched all of her textbook of magic, called a *grimoire* (grim-WAR), and elsewhere for a picture that resembled the talisman.

As she turned the pages, she snapped each one in disgust. She had to have something – anything – for Sir William next week.

One of the most common services that Caramel and the other cunning folk provided was to fight the effects of malevolent witchcraft and curses. She combined folk magic with elements of ceremonial magic, which she had learned through the study of the grimoire. The book contained instructions on how to create magical objects like talismans and amulets, how to perform magical spells and charms and how to summon supernatural entities such as spirits and demons. As well, therein were instructions on how to identify witches.

Some cunning folk claimed to be able to locate treasure, and were employed to do so. In some of these cases, people believed that a supernatural entity, such as a demon, spirit or fairy was guarding the hidden treasure, and that a cunning practitioner was needed to overcome them using magical means. This ability, with which Caramel claimed to be blessed, might help her locate the talisman.

Cunning folk could use a variety of methods in order to cure someone of sorcery, including physically tackling the witch, breaking the spell over the afflicted by magical means and by using charms or potions to remove the witchcraft from the person's body.

Caramel had used a potion to kill Lady Emily all those years ago. She'd had an accomplice of the highest order; one who held a grudge.

It was simple, really. From Sir William – who loved his wife and knew nothing of the plot – Caramel had learned that Lady Emily travelled to London every Tuesday to meet in a favourite coffee shop with three friends. This group had been subject to the masculine wrath of the coffee shop regulars, especially at first. The men saw the regular visits as an assault on their male bastion, grand ladies or not. However, they soon learned to tolerate the "Tuesday Trollop Troupe," as the ladies unfairly came to be known.

Leaving the coffee shop, the women would go shopping. Well, they would usually go shopping. On her doctor's orders, extended shopping trips, with all the necessary walking, were forgone for a few months during the latter half of Lady Emily's pregnancy. Her doctor had discouraged her from taking the bumpy carriage ride. To no avail; Lady Emily travelled against his advice.

Stanley worked at the coffee shop. He was also a regular client of Caramel's and a fellow member of the cunning folk. Stanley had been in the employ of Lord Mansfield as a groomsman, until he fell into disfavour after two horses died in his care. Stanley had been dismissed with a poor reference. As a result, he had been unemployed and living in squalor for almost two years. For retribution, he had agreed with Caramel to add a little "spice" to Lady Emily's coffee.

Stanley put the poison in Lady Emily's coffee at his regular station behind the bar. As usual, he worked with his back turned. Unusually, he reached into the breast pocket of his waistcoat and pulled out a small vial of clear liquid. With furtive glances this way and that, he emptied the vial into Lady Emily's coffee cup before returning the empty vessel to his pocket.

Stirring her coffee and purposely leaving the spoon in the saucer, Stanley brought the tray of four coffees and a small plate of scones to the aristocratic women. The four of them were having an animated conversation. Holding the tray, he placed a cup and saucer in front of each woman. Only in Lady Emily's saucer lay the spoon.

He knew that she'd not recognize him now. With a contrived smile and a nod, he returned to his station with the empty tray. The four continued their conversation, sipping their hot beverages and nipping into the scones.

The owner of the coffee shop had been suspicious of Stanley for some time now. He had been made aware of his affiliation with the cunning folk, but in general the affiliation proved a boon to business for the clientele it generated. Nevertheless, the owner kept a wary eye on Stanley. He felt that, despite their reputation as being "anti-witch," the cunning folk shared many traits with witches.

So the owner watched with interest from across the crowded room, as Stanley reached into his pocket and produced a suspicious-looking vial. Head down but eyes peeled, he watched as his employee emptied the vial and served the coffees to the "Tuesday Trollop Troupe." He noted the spoon in the saucer, and that the coffee was destined for Lady Emily Mansfield.

Like most people, the owner knew of Lady Mansfield. He did not know, however, that she – or, more properly, her husband – was Stanley's former employer.

He decided that he had to intervene; to remove all four coffees because they were "not of a quality to Her Lady's high standards," or whatever other excuse he could provide upon removing the offending drinks.

The high-strung owner, who enjoyed sampling copious cups of coffee, quickly made his way toward the Lady's table. A sharp pain in his chest and arm stopped him in his path. With a groan and a look of anguish, he fell to the wooden floor. It was not the first time he had felt such pain and it would not be the last.

A crowd gathered around him; some attended to the shopkeeper while others continued to sip their coffees. Lady Mansfield did not stand to leer at the fallen man, choosing, rather, to continue to sip her coffee with her friends, who declared "Poor man!" and "I hope he'll be all right."

The entire scene simply encouraged the women to finish their coffee and scones a little sooner. They left the coffee shop, having agreed to do "just a little shopping," what with Lady Emily's pregnancy in its eighth month.

They did not shop that day. Emily died on the street, her friends by her side. The doctors assumed that her death had something to do with the pregnancy, and perhaps, the carriage ride.

The shop owner survived his heart attack. One week later, he visited Mansfield Castle and requested an audience with the grieving duke. In the Drawing Room, the owner related his story to Lord Mansfield, who was still in mourning and was thus clad in all black. The owner concluded, "That man, my employee, poisoned Lady Emily. I daresay that he is a witch! Lord, he should be arrested."

Two days later, on the recommendation of Lord Mansfield, the Duke of Chestney, Stanley was arrested and charged with practising witchcraft and committing murder. With Jamieson's assistance, Sir William recognized his name as that of a released former employee; one who may have been seeking retribution. Jamieson recalled reports from other staff about the man dabbling in the Black Arts, even while in the employ of Mansfield.

Sir William's sworn statement included these points and the fact that he believed that the accused worked alone, seeking revenge for his perceived wrongful dismissal, despite the man's claim that he had an accomplice.

Caramel Calhoun's name was never entered into any of the official documents regarding the case.

Caramel had thought that, by eliminating Lady Emily, she would take her place. She received only part of that wish: her beautiful auburn-haired daughter, born in a back room of a London brothel with the help of a fellow "nun" acting as midwife, arrived just a few months after Caramel came to the city.

Distraught at the death of both his wife and his unborn child, Sir William accepted Caramel's offer of her own newborn daughter to fill the huge hole in his heart. The babies' ages were within weeks of each other and the death of the unborn child was easily covered up when Sir William came home to Mansfield Castle holding a newborn baby girl, whom he called Rachel, after his mother.

Caramel slammed the book shut. The grimoire search had left her with nothing to show Sir William; nothing that resembled the description of the footman's talisman.

Giving up for the moment, she fondly remembered her intimate conversation with Jacques. She recalled his post-coital account of the young man he'd come across, and with whom he was now working – a strange young man who appeared to possess a strange talisman of his own…

She tried to remember the young man's odd name. Oh, what was it?

∞

26

"SKY!" HELENA CALLED OUT happily as she saw him approaching, a head taller than the general crowd.[7] She stood on her tiptoes and waved over the heads of the people who filled the pavement outside The Shakespeare's Head tavern at 6 p.m.

She could not have been more beautiful, even in her modest clothes. Her grey dress, cut fashionably low, was trimmed with simple white lace. She had pulled up her long blonde hair under an unassuming hat.

After her afternoon sponge bath (none but the very rich had bath tubs), she had used a bone toothpick to clean her teeth. She did not have one of those expensive new bristle toothbrushes that people were talking about. She had heard that the bristles were actually the coarse hairs from the back of a hog's neck, attached to a bone or bamboo handle.

I'm not sure that I'd want to have that in my mouth in any case, she had thought as she rinsed her mouth with a mint and vinegar mixture. Then she had chewed a mixture of mint, cloves, cinnamon and sage to freshen her breath. Lastly, she had checked her appearance in her hand-held, wood-framed mirror. Upon reflection, she was sufficiently pleased.

---

7 Average heights, of around 5'6" for men and 5'1" for women, were at an all-time low, reflecting poor overall health and economic hardship.

Helena had then left the flat and hurried to meet her beau. Sky was a suitor, and she suspected that he felt the same way.

As Sky approached he saw Helena talking with a tall, well-dressed older woman who, like Helena, possessed a rare beauty. The two made quite a sight, apparently, as many passers-by glanced back once or twice. But the older woman did not have Helena's youthful verve.

Not knowing whether to peck his cheek or not, Helena relied on a dainty handshake to greet Sky. She also wanted to appease Caramel, who needed assurance that Jack's ward would be safe at Vauxhall in the company of this young man.

They exchanged pleasantries and laughter. She introduced him to the other woman, whose name was Caramel. She smiled and asked him to repeat his name.

"Sky," Caramel repeated. "That is an odd name for a tall young man who speaks in an equally odd fashion. You're certainly not Irish! Whatever you are, you take good care of Helena today. Her uncle wants you to know that she is to be home by 11 of the clock; no later."

They bade Caramel a good day and walked down Carnaby Street. Had he not been lovestruck in the presence of the lovely lass, and had he turned to look, Sky might have caught a glimpse of Caramel's icy stare.

Sky again felt like he was walking on air as he and Helena crossed Westminster Bridge and strolled along Fore Street toward the Vauxhall Pleasure Gardens. It was a long walk, but Sky felt it was too short.

Too often, he would look over at her as they walked. A few blonde curls had escaped from under her hat, and bounced along as they went. Her smile was ravishing, so he used all the means available to him to make her smile. Sky was so entranced that he failed to notice the glances that other men gave to his walking partner. Simply put, Sky was too busy falling in love.

As they walked, the number of pedestrians walking in the same direction grew, particularly on the far side of the bridge. Most were destined for Vauxhall; a crowd of about 15,000 was expected today. Sky had no idea what the admission charge was to be. He cared not; he had enough money to last until he had to leave.

As they walked, they talked. Sky had to tell Helena the truth. He explained how he had heard her uncle Jack Harris boasting about the money he would make by selling her virginity to the highest bidder.

"I don't want any harm to come to you. I had to warn you. No one should be subjected to…" He was so engrossed in making his point, gesticulating as he walked, that he didn't notice that Helena was no longer walking beside him. She had stopped.

He ran back to where she stood – a sad, defeated figure. As the concert-goers shuffled past, she said quietly, "I have no option other than to let him do with me what he will. I am his court-appointed ward."

Sky draped his arm over her shoulders and whispered, "I am from the colonies. We do many things differently there. For one thing, we dress differently. For another, we treat women with respect."

Even with a tear running down her cheek, Helena couldn't help giggling at that, "Respect, eh? There's not much of that here. The colonies sound like somewhere I'd like to visit one day."

They rejoined the crowd of walkers. Helena related to Sky her story, in her own words, of growing up on the farm and her parents being accused of being witches. Sky prickled when she spoke of witchcraft. It evoked thoughts of his own parent's fate; memories that he had repressed for years. He wanted to share his story with her in return.

She described her flight to the city as the angry mob drew closer to their farmhouse. During the two-day journey, Helena had evaded highwaymen and other brigands through the use of speed and stealth. That is, she kept her thoroughbred horse galloping whenever she saw other travellers on the road, or at places where the road was curvy.

"My father," Helena began, "believed that a fast horse could outrun any threat made to him or any member of his family while on our rare journeys to London or elsewhere. When I reached the age where I could ride, he had saved enough money to make the substantial investment in a thoroughbred filly. Helena's lip twitched and her eyes pooled up.

"We named her 'Velocity'."

The filly lived up to her name.

For the one night that Helena needed to camp, she made no fire. She slept in the hole created by the root of an uprooted oak tree. Wild berries were all she had to eat.

She had never met her uncle, and at her young age had only heard that he worked in a popular public house. An avid reader, she remembered the name well: The Bard.

Arriving on her weary horse on the streets of London, she had to make only a few inquiries about Jack Harris and The Bard. Most knew one or the other, and pointed her toward Covent Garden.

Immediately upon her arrival, Uncle Jack had arranged for the sale of Velocity, telling her that the proceeds would "help to pay for your room and board until you can find work." In fact, it was he who had got her work, at the Shakespeare's Head, where he could keep his eye on her. "He practically locks me into his house when I'm not working in the pub."

The family farm – the proceeds of witchcraft – became the property of The Crown. The entire case – the fate of the farm and of the daughter of the deceased – was brought to the court and dealt with simultaneously. Helena sobbed as she explained how unfair the court-ordered arrangement had been. "The courtroom was a dreadful place. I wish to never enter one again!"

Sky comforted her, and to ease the weight of her tale he then shared his own story as best as he could without revealing that the events had happened in the future. They were a distant memory that he had never shared before, not even with his grandparents. He, too, cried as he told Helena of running through the darkness down the embankment and into the thorny acacia bushes. As he spoke, Helena sniffled and gently rubbed his arm in support. Then, she held his arm until he stopped walking. They embraced, as others walked around them.

Teary-eyed, Sky said simply, "Thank you for letting me share my grief."

Helena used her handkerchief to dab away a tear from his cheek. "It seems that we bear a similar burden, Sky. Sharing the load makes it lighter."

Prior to the Thomas Arne concert, the couple toured the immense fairgrounds, which had large fountains and stands offering refreshments. Other couples strolled by, all promenading their finery.

The concert was jammed with revellers, but Sky and Helena managed to find good seats on the grass, not far from the stage.

In the darkness of the audience, Sky thought that he would impress his new friend by identifying Arne's songs using the Shazam app on his smartwatch. He was just about to activate when he thought better of it; too dangerous. But just the feel of his smartwatch in this setting served to remind Sky of his life in Fraserdale and all of its comforts – comforts that he had taken for granted. He wouldn't any longer, if he ever got to enjoy them again.

After the concert, fireworks lit up the night sky as the two sat close together on the grass, surrounded by other couples and some families. Up until then, the only contact they had enjoyed were brief touches and Helena's empa-thetic tear-dabbing. But now, they sat hand in hand, oohing and awing with each explosion.

Sky summoned the courage to take Helena's hand to his lips and kiss it lightly. Their eyes met. He gently took her chin in his hand and kissed her full, pouty lips. She responded by wrapping her arms around his neck and kissing him passionately in return.

The night was moonless and dark, so the two young lovers only fully appeared when the fireworks lit up the field, causing those around them to anticipate what the next explosion would reveal.

Vauxhall Gardens was mostly comprised of public "genteel" areas, where people walked and chatted and chil-dren played. But the gardens also contained more intimate places where couples could enjoy some private time together.

It was to one of these quiet, dark places on the banks of the Thames that Helena led Sky. The fireworks continued awhile longer.

∞

27

BOUNDING UP THE STEPS two at a time, Sky arrived at the Royal Society of London for Improving Natural Knowledge. He was a few minutes late, as the many sights and sounds had distracted him on his walk.

The valet at the door had been expecting him, and showed him into a large, darkened room. The room served as both a restaurant and a lecture theatre with large, round tables scattered throughout and a raised platform at one end, where scientists could report their latest findings to their peers.

Sky walked slowly between the tables, looking for Henry Cavendish and hoping that he'd either recognize the scientist or that the scientist would recognize him.

There were about 50 Society members in the room, all men of course. Some of the hallmarks of being a gentleman at the time were a strong sense of honour and civility. These men, at least on the surface, seemed to embody these. Sky thought he felt just a little bit smarter being under the same roof with this esteemed group.

Henry looked very pleased indeed to see the young man enter the room. He waved Sky over and introduced him to the four distinguished-looking men at his table.

After completing the introductions, Henry leaned toward Sky. "I have a bit of a s-surprise for you after lunch, if you choose to partake," he said.

"Oh? What do you have in mind, Henry?"

"Oh, my good man! If I told you, S-Sky, it would no longer be a surprise now, would it? Let's enjoy lunch together first." Henry motioned to the white-haired man across the table.

"Clive Rock here recently completed some important work in the area of Factitious Airs, a subject that interests me as well. C-Clive, if you please, relate to us your findings."

As Clive proudly described how he had produced hydrogen gas through extensive experimentation, a hardy lunch was served. Today's lunch consisted of potato soup and cheese, with an entrée of doe venison. Finishing up, Henry excused himself and Sky listened as Clive pontificated. No doubt, Clive enjoyed talking about science in general and about chemistry in particular; a bit of a "hydrogen gas-bag," thought Sky.

Clive was not known to be "fashionable." Rather, he was the personification of scientific functionality. The archetypal wire-rimmed glasses that he always wore were functional; the proof being that his glasses were an early facsimile of today's.

Clive's eyeglasses made him, dare we say, a visionary.

Eyeglasses as we know them, held by the partnership of ears and nose, were developed some 50 years prior to this meeting of the Royal Society. However, early designs were not immediately successful or popular, leaving other styles with attached handles such as "scissors-glasses," and lorgnettes (the ones with the handle at one side) as more fashionable.

As he listened to the scientist, Sky began to think that Clive looked vaguely familiar, but he could not place him. He had seen so many people in the streets of London, from all walks of life. And all of them within a very short time. But only a few who wore modern-style eyeglasses. Sky scoured his memory.

As dessert was being served – Empress pudding with wine – part of Henry's surprise was revealed. One of the scientists stood on the platform and announced, "We are pleasantly surprised to say that Henry Cavendish will be demonstrating his recent findings in the area of electricity."

The Society had reason to be surprised; the timid Henry rarely addressed the group. Today, though, he had an ulterior motive.

The curtain on the stage was drawn back to reveal Henry and a menagerie of equipment.

Obviously nervous, Henry seemed excited as well. He introduced the experiment as the "c-conversion of a mixture of dephlogisticated and phlogisticated air into nitrous acid by the electric spark."

He then asked Sky to join him onstage. The other part of the surprise! Reluctantly, Sky made his way onto the stage as the audience clapped sporadically.

Not a comfortable orator, Henry hurried through his introduction of Sky Sewell, saying that the lad "is from the colonies, where few scientific experiments are conducted as they are too busy defending themselves from b-bears."

The joke fell flat. Deafening silence.

From the back, someone shouted, "We can't *bear* any more of your jokes Cavendish. Get on with it!"

With a weak smile and a weaker wave to the voice at the back of the room, Henry bravely forged ahead. In his characteristic stammering voice, he explained to the audience that, for the purpose of the experiment, Sky would fire a mixture of common air and hydrogen by electricity, hence the spark. Simultaneously, Henry would gather the resulting water in a dish. His hypothesis was that the water would contain nitric acid, which must be due to the nitrogen present as an impurity in the oxygen, the so-called common air.

"This will be the first time that I have conducted this experiment, which requires an assistant. My thanks to Sky for p-providing that."

He whispered to Sky, "All you have to do is provide the spark, using this," he handed Sky a flint spark lighter, "applied here." He pointed to the confluence of two beakers and a nasty-looking, curly copper wire.

Sky held the lighter at the designated spot and rubbed the flint...

The instant that the spark appeared, Sky felt the surge of electricity through his body; a horrible sensation. He was overcome and fell, unconscious, to the floor.

With a high degree of athleticism or perhaps premonition, Henry managed to lunge toward Sky and soften his fall somewhat.

With Sky unconscious on the floor, Henry ran over to the stage curtain cord and quickly pulled down the curtain. The startled audience saw only Clive, who had risen from his seat and quickly walked toward the stage to ostensibly assist his friend Henry. His cane could be heard tap-tapping above the murmurs of the audience.

Some in the audience then noticed what Clive was wearing on his feet: strange, red paisley cloth shoes. Society members who were close enough could clearly see the word "Vans" emblazoned on the shoes. One of the members leaned toward his neighbour, and with an elbow to the neighbour's flank and a finger wagging at the shoes, declared, "First, those ridiculous eyeglasses; now his footwear!"

Henry worked quickly now. He turned Sky's limp body face-down on the floor. He ran his hands along Sky's limbs, apparently searching for something, then lifted the sleeve of Sky's linen shirt and gasped.

Using his cane to part the curtain, Clive stepped through and stood over Henry. Eyes wide, Henry looked up at his accomplice and whispered, "W-we were right."

When the curtain was again raised, the audience saw Henry holding the revived, but still wobbly, lad by the arm.

"He's fine. H-he's fine! He just received a jolt of electrical current through his b-body. The experiment needs to be re-worked before I present it to the Society again. Now, enjoy your lunch!"

Henry and Clive each took an arm and slowly accompanied Sky down the steps from the stage. They resumed their seats in the dining hall. Henry's presentation was the only one that day. As lunch ended and members left the hall for the day, Clive, Henry and Sky were left in privacy.

Henry said, "I don't p-present to the Society often, for obvious r-reasons. The members will consider my apparent failure to be a function of stage fright."

"Apparent? What went wrong?" Sky needed to know.

"Well, nothing really went wrong; it went p-precisely according to p-plan," Henry was unapologetic.

Sky was taken aback. Henry explained that he and Clive had discussed the recent theft of Clive's clothes, and their reappearance on Sky. At one of their frequent meetings, they had compared the physical description of Sky the highwayman with that of the young man who had come to Henry's aid on that windy day. And, they had used all the resources in Henry's well-appointed laboratory to analyse the materials found in the highwayman's discarded clothes and footwear. They then devised a plan to stage the presentation, knowing that Sky would likely and conveniently faint from the electrical shock.

Sky was perplexed and annoyed, but Henry seemed unconcerned. "We knew that you'd likely succumb, but that you'd be fine afterward," he said. "The electrical current was administered in a measured amount. We had to have you unconscious in order to prove our hypothesis."

"Prove what hypothesis?" demanded Sky, his head spinning less now.

Henry glanced at Clive, then back at Sky. He sighed. "To prove that you are from the f-future."

∞

28

SKY HAD TO LOCATE Jacques DuTemps, and quickly. Going out with Helena yesterday meant that he had missed his arranged meeting with Jacques and Harry at the Wander Inn stables.

He inquired at the inn. Jacques had left him a sealed note:

> *"It is important that you act together with Harry and me. We depend upon you! Be at the Wander Inn stables at eight of the clock tonight. We will work. Also, I have an invitation for you. JD"*

Relieved, Sky pocketed the note and thanked the innkeeper. In response, the innkeeper managed to nod slightly and mutter a terse "Hrrumff!"

Sky arrived back at the inn stables before the noted time and leaned against a hitching post, waiting for the highwaymen to arrive. It was a blustery night already, with wind driving spattering rain. It threatened to get worse. He resisted the urge to "play" with his smartwatch; most of the apps did not work here, in any case. But he did take out his Mickey Mouse pocket watch to run his fingers over its familiar patina and open it, just to remind him of home and to see if it was keeping correct time. Mickey was off again. He shook it and tapped it gently against the post.

Just then, around the corner of the inn came Jacques and his partner Harry, striding with purpose toward Sky. Harry walked with a slight limp. At first, Sky was alarmed and ready to run, but the smiles on their faces told him that everything seemed fine. He may have abandoned them, but they remained friends, for now.

Jacques removed his tricorne hat and shook the water from it. "There is that guy Sky!" he said. "Are you ready to work now?"

"Yes, sorry I missed last night," Sky said. "It won't happen again."

Jacques came closer and his tone changed. In a low, menacing voice he growled, "It 'ad better not. You missed a good night. We 'it a stagecoach, a private coach, and some pedestrian. Now, to the 'orses."

The weather worsened as the night went on. It worked against them. Although it did not prevent them from working, it seemed to have a drastic effect on road traffic. They waited at their usual spot under the tree. They saw no one on the road, other than a few footpads, who they recognized as regulars.

The waiting gave them time to talk. Harry's leg was getting better, but he hoped that he would not retain a permanent limp. Harry spoke at length about his sexual exploits that night at The Bard. Sky thought they had the ring of fiction rather than fact, but he humoured him anyway.

Sky reminded Jacques about the invitation he'd mentioned in his note.

"Ahh, yes, yes. I saw an advertisement in the newspaper. There is to be a masquerade ball at Mansfield Castle next weekend; my former place of employment. 'Arry does not want to attend – sore leg – so I am asking if you would like to come with me."

Sky sniffled in the cold rain, but was intrigued. "A masquerade ball? Tell me more."

Jacques explained that in recent years, Sir William Mansfield had hosted an annual masquerade ball at his estate to celebrate the birthday of "that poofter son of 'is". The event was highly anticipated by everyone, rich and poor. "People call him Wee Willy, but I care not to find out why," joked Jacques, at which Harry chuckled. "I know only that this type of celebration allows 'im a 'igh degree of *expression personelle*... 'ow do you say, oh yes, self-expression. Any costumed guest is welcomed. And the price, a mere shilling, is right. Getting a costume is the 'ardest part."

Jacques did not seem daunted by the dangerous prospect of attending an event at the home of one of his recent victims. In fact, just the opposite: he was excited by the danger. He had once worked at the estate as a young lad and had watched Rachel from afar. He had spoken to her only a handful of times in his position as groomsman.

He was hoping to speak with her again at the ball. He had let her know in his note that he would be dressed as Father Time. His heart raced at the thought of seeing her again. It raced even faster when he thought of charming her anonymously, in costume, right under her father's snooty nose.

His thoughts of Rachel kept him warm on the following few unseasonably chilly summer nights. Jacques had a flare for selecting vulnerable targets, and he and his men did well, without having to fire their dragons. They split the take 50-40-10. Harry was pleased; his take had improved by 15 per cent with the death of Mike.

Sky was happy with 10 per cent, but he feigned wanting a greater share. Jacques shook his head. "You 'ave to *earn* more, Sky! You need to impress me as a budding gentleman of the road. Maybe you should lead the next attack. I will give that some thought. But enough about business; what about the masquerade?"

"Count me in, Jacques. It sounds like fun." Sky was thinking that maybe, just maybe, Zac would be there as well. He already had a brilliant idea for a costume, and he happened to know of a very good seamstress.

He would pay her well.

∞

29

"A 'SUPERHERO'? I DON'T understand what that is," lamented Helena. "I know what a hero is, like a war hero. But, how can a hero be 'super'? He's already a hero."

Sky had gone to visit Helena at her uncle's house the day after their tryst at Vauxhall. They were sitting together on a small couch in her uncle's second-floor apartment. Jack was, of course, at work.

Sky explained about the upcoming masquerade ball and how he was obligated to attend with Jacques. He hoped that Helena would be able to attend as well. He would help her with the admission charge, and would pay handsomely if she would sew him a special costume.

"This hero is big in the colonies. Well, he is big wherever he goes! He is a superhero because he has special powers. His name is Superman. I can draw a picture of him for you."

"Before we talk about your 'superhero', Sky Sewell, we have a more important matter to discuss." Helena, with a look of bliss in her blue eyes, took Sky's hand in hers and sighed. "Last night with you was incredible. I loved spending time with you. Our time in the shadows by the river was my favourite." Helena blushed. "And you know now that you were 'my first'." Helena blushed redder and continued, "But during that time, I felt something sitting upon your wrist. Later, your linen shirt was all that covered it, and in the darkness I could see it glowing through the linen! I have never seen anything like it. Is it some kind of magical talisman? You must show it to me, whatever it is. I cannot be with you if you are dishonest with me."

Sky involuntarily began to touch the smartwatch through his shirt. In the short time that he had known Helena, Sky had fallen deeply in love. Moments away from her seemed like eternities. The similarities and the strong feelings they shared for each other had become almost immediately apparent. He trusted her implicitly. It felt right to share more with her.

With that in mind, Sky unbuttoned his cuff and rolled up the sleeve of his shirt. He showed her the watch, and touched the face to change the display for her. Seeing its bright, moving colours and changing face, she was awe-struck. She read the words on the screen and she mouthed them, quietly, "Calendar, weather, YouTube…" Entranced, she whispered, "May I touch it?"

"No, actually, not yet. Touching parts of it will make it do different things. Accurately telling the time of day is just one thing it can do. It does things that you cannot imagine." Sky looked suspicious as he peered out the window. "I stole it from a magician that my friend and I met on the road to London."

Looking closely at the device, Helena's pretty face was obscured by the locks of blonde hair that fell onto Sky's arm. Through her hair, she looked up at him and with purpose, said, "I know that you are no thief. There was no magician. And this is not magic; this is some type of device. Tell me the truth!"

Sky placed a crooked finger under her chin and gently lifted her head until their eyes were level. He stroked her hair out of her eyes. "You are right, my love. There is no magic here." He paused. "It is science, but science from the future!"

Helena gasped.

His eyes watery pools, Sky continued, "I am not of this time, Helena. I am visiting from the future. This device – we call them 'smartwatches' – helped us get here."

Helena was quiet for a time, trying to take this all in. Then she asked, "What do you mean 'us'? There are more of you? How many?"

"Just my friend, Zachary, and me. We were sent to prove that time travel could be accomplished. But, in finding that it could, I also found you – my true love! – and now...now, I want you to come back with me."

"Back with you? To the... future?" Helena sat up rigidly.

"Yes! Come with me, Helena! Come with me to the future! Well, what I mean is I will come back here for you. We have only two of these devices; one for me and one for Zac. So, I will have to come back here to get you. You are not happy here."

Sky stood up to emphasize his point. "Your uncle is keeping you like a pet that happens to clean and work for him until he can sell your virginity to the highest bidder! I am glad that you no longer have your virginity. It is not a commodity to be sold. But he will only turn worse – much worse, I suspect – when he finds out. Come with me!"

He sat down again beside her. They embraced, kissing passionately.

After awhile, Helena spoke. "I'll need some time to think," she said, her eyes wide.

Even now in his arms, in her heart she knew that Sky was right; her life was going nowhere. And now, no longer a virgin, she would not be subject to her uncle's version of "cloistered protection" any longer, if he were to find out. He'd likely cast her out onto the street. Would she revert to what so many other young women of her age had done and become a prostitute? She would have to survive somehow.

Then she thought of her future; maybe one spent *in the future* with a man who she was quickly growing to love. Her imagination exploding like the fireworks at Vauxhall, she asked quietly, "What is the future like?"

Thinking about his life in Fraserdale, there was too much to begin to describe. So, he teased, "You're used to a little rain, right?"

They curled up and talked for hours about life in the future, life in 1766 England, and life in general. Sky told Helena about how he came to arrive in this time and place. He told her about Zac, how they got separated, and how he needed to re-connect with his friend. He told Helena about the importance of him and Zac being together in less than three weeks, to successfully travel back to the future.

Sky asked Helena again if she would sew him a Superman costume to wear to the masquerade ball.

"Of course I'll sew it for you!" she said. "I have time. You said you'd draw me a picture of this Superman hero?"

They agreed that Sky would draw a couple of pictures of the Man of Steel for Helena's reference, and that they would visit the textile merchant to purchase the needed fabric. Helena took some of Sky's measurements to ensure a good fit. Then, she provided him with a quill, ink and paper.

As he was drawing some rough sketches, he asked if Helena would be able to attend the masquerade.

"Attend a ball? Me? I never have and I likely never will. In any case, I am scheduled to work at The Bard that night. I'd love to attend, though. I've not told anyone, but sometimes, alone in my room, I dance," Helena admitted. "I love music. It makes me want to move. And, dressing up would be so much fun. I've never done it, but I dream of dancing in a grand, hooped dress, with petticoats and lace."

She quickly got up and demonstrated, humming a tune and moving gracefully around the room. Then just as quickly, she sat down, dejected. She sighed. "Pray hold me excused; I cannot come."

∞

30

AS HE HAD DONE in previous years, Sir William hired a well-known London impresario, Mr. Pickett, to work with Jamieson to organize this year's ball. Pickett, in turn, arranged most of the details of the event, including the advertisements published in journals and newspapers a month before the big date.

Some of the journalists who worked at these papers, as well as clergymen and others, opposed the masquerade ball due to its debauchery and perceived damage to English morals. The "others" included strong and vocal opponents such as Henry Fielding, until his recent death. Consequently, the concept of the masquerade ball was soon to suffer a rapid decline in popularity.

The writing was on the wall for the masquerade ball, as it were. But the message on that wall was not to be read just yet; the attendees were simply having too much unbridled fun. There was much revelry yet to be had.

The summer masquerade at Mansfield Castle, in celebration of Wee Willy's birthday, was contrary to the norm. Most balls were held during the winter months. But that worked to its advantage, as both the rich and the poor sought a summertime soirée.

Reading one of the newspaper advertisements for the upcoming ball, a reader might get the impression that the event was to be exclusive; a gathering of those of sufficient social class. But the reader likely also understood that one of the central facets of the event was the concept of social mixing.

Besides, the ads targeted anyone who could afford a costume and a ticket. Ticket prices – a shilling – were still within the range of the lower class. While the ticket price for many masquerades had recently increased in an effort to limit access to the poor, Sir William felt it important that everyone have the opportunity to attend. The ball was his way, he claimed, of "giving back to the community" – although his motivation had recently changed, with the agrarian riots and the seeds of social discord being sown. He was now aiming to placate the masses, but publicly he stuck with "giving back."

His feeling was in keeping with the theme of the masquerade ball; that is, once masked, the rich and the poor became indistinguishable. The masquerade offered the opportunity for the poor to rub shoulders with the rich. In this way, the upper echelons of society and even royalty looked through their masks at other masked partygoers, playwrights, peddlers, prostitutes and pimps, making rich fodder for gossip. This was the essence of the attraction of the masquerade: anonymously enjoying the ability to engage with those whom they would otherwise be forbidden to do so.

Such faceless mixing, further mixed with copious amounts of food and drink, led to a sexually-charged environment. A woman could attend a masquerade unescorted; the only other place she could do so was church. So, as at all masquerades, courtesans and prostitutes were prominent at Mansfield Castle.

Like much of the "lower class," the prostitutes thoroughly enjoyed the anonymity behind the mask. They could overtly flirt and tease young men, especially those with protective mothers or wives. The "upper class," on the other hand, often felt anxious not knowing the class of fellow masqueraders.

An honourable gentleman's wife might shame herself by associating, knowingly or not, with a lower class man.

Pickett, the impresario, was a guest of the estate for the week preceding the event. He hired the orchestra and singers. He even made costumes available for those attendees without a suitable one. All attendees at a masquerade ball had to be in costume. This rule was well-known, strictly enforced and usually adhered to. Pickett would station a man at the door of Mansfield Castle and, as required, refuse entry to anyone not attired in a true costume.

Children were not invited. And at the command of the duke, any witch's costume was to be turned away.

A masquerade dripped of a carnival, if not carnal, atmosphere. Loud music, conversation, laughter and lavish food and drink played crucial roles. Wine was the drink of choice for the gentry, while the lower class preferred beer. The duke offered, for the first time, a new brew from Dublin called Guinness.

Gambling was available in the Billiard Room, although a player had to be wary of professional gamblers who did not identify themselves as such. The room had been the Games Room for years until Sir William's father developed a fondness for billiards, which itself evolved from croquet. To this day, the green felt on the table is designed to resemble grass.

The festivities would be hosted in the Gallery; the Grand Ballroom. The room was huge, spanning virtually the entire length of the building, with a central raised area where the orchestra would play. Being the most visible, it was also the most decorated, displaying a higher level of opulence than any other room.

The mood of this opulence was eclectic, matching the varied tastes of the host. The duke had visited the Netherlands, France and northern Italy with Lady Emily, and the couple had returned to England with the latest decorating concepts, which had changed slightly over the years. The dominant colours of The Gallery were white and yellow, which contrasted in a pleasing way with the warm elegance of the polished oak floor and the mahogany and teak furnishings. Graceful Doric columns lined the feature wall and served to extend the room vertically. The niches in between the columns held statues of stone, bronze and marble.

Zac had worked with the other staff to decorate the ballroom with additional candles, so that participants could enjoy the festivities late into the night. All the lighting added to the heat in the crowded room, and combined with copious amounts of wine and beer, it encouraged masqueraders to remove clothing as the night progressed. Skimpier costumes led to late-night debauchery.

∞

31

THE PARTYGOERS STARTED ARRIVING an hour or so before sundown. Most expected to be at the ball until daybreak.

Some carriages were huge and garishly decorated, like Sir William's. Others were smaller, drawn by a single horse, and austere. Humbler guests arrived on horseback, and a few on foot. Many had travelled all the way from London; others came from the neighbouring estates and hamlets that dotted the rolling countryside.

Approaching the 40,000-acre estate through the massive arched gates, guests would marvel at the grand scale of the stately house. Designed in the rare English baroque style, the monumental building featured a U-shaped design, with the main building forming the bottom of the U and a wing on either side that extended toward the front. This design appealed to the Georgian love of symmetry. The dominant feature of the main building was a domed tower over The Hall, itself flanked by smaller decorative towers on the front façade.

Expansive, manicured lawns bordered the driveway. Only the rich, like Lord Mansfield, kept lawns. To further prove his wealth he employed many gardeners to cut the lawns, using scythes.

While the poor had no land, of course, the middle class may have owned a small plot. Any land was used for crops or raising animals. This land holding, acquired piecemeal over several generations, was the basis for Lord Mansfield's vast wealth. Land provided the family with status, security and a voice in the dealings of the rural community.

Sir William, his father and grandfather had bought out smaller neighbouring landowners, known as the gentry. This upper middle class group had recently found that land was no longer the secure source of income it had once been, particularly with the high taxes imposed on it to finance Britain's recent wars. In contrast to Sir William and other members of the aristocracy (who held many of the top political positions), the gentry were unable to adapt to these changing market conditions, so they were forced to sell. Many made their way to London, looking for, but often not finding, employment.

Ironically, Sir William had recently taken advantage of rising land values by increasing the rents of the remaining tenant farmers. These farms were, naturally, located far enough from the estate to ensure that the family might enjoy the highest quality of country air, without any farmyard odors.

In one corner of the lawn, for the entertainment of guests, Sir William kept a hedge maze. Unlike a labyrinth, which has no cross-paths or branch-offs and always leads to the center via a twisted routing, a maze is designed to confuse. Following a trend, Sir William had reduced its size while maintaining four quadrants with a central, elevated pavilion from which onlookers could enjoy the confusion of the walkers below.

The air was electric with excitement; even the servants were ebullient. The highly-anticipated night was finally here, promising to be an intoxicating combination of propriety and passion.

As a footman, one of Zac's tasks on this auspicious night was to greet the guests and provide them with two options prior to commencement of the ball. Each option was designed to showcase Lord Mansfield's wealth.

The garden comprised about 10 acres of the estate. The first option was to tour – under the guidance of the gardener, if desired – the gardens and grotto.

Sir William was proud to tell guests that Lancelot "Capability" Brown, the most renowned landscape architect of the time, was responsible for the design. Sir William enjoyed telling guests just how the landscaper had earned his nickname: he was in the habit of viewing a subject plot and saying, "It has great capabilities."

Under Brown's guidance, the landscapers at Mansfield Castle simplified the garden by replacing most structures with rolling lawns and expansive views of isolated copses of trees, thereby expanding the landscape.

The gardener, Munn, while he had only limited knowledge of a game called "lacrosse," had extensive knowledge of trees, flowers, vegetables, fruits and landscape design, developed over years of training and by direct consultation with Brown.

With the enthusiastic approval of the Duke, Brown had included a meditative grotto in the garden. The grotto was designed to draw visitors into its seclusion, and provide them with a quiet environment amenable to thoughtfulness and meditation. For summer visitors – the time of year for most wanderings in the garden – the grotto provided cool shade, punctuated by the relaxing trickle of a picturesque waterfall.

As lovely as that sounds, the grotto itself was not the highlight.

Therein lived a hermit; the grotto functioning as a hermitage. The hermit was a middle-aged man, hired and cared for by the estate, whose five-year "job" was to be a live diorama, entertaining guests by just being there.

Three costumed guests strolled through the gardens that evening, prior to joining the others at the ball. One, a mature woman, was dressed like Mrs. Quack from the card game "John Bull." The other two seemed to be a matching pair, wearing traditional Chinese dress. The older man, Mrs. Quack's husband, wore a *changshan* or "long shirt," while the younger woman wore a tight-fitting silk *cheongsam*.

In keeping with masquerade protocol, all had carried their masks into the garden. The Chinese masks were yellow, with Asian eyes painted in black.

The visitors happened upon the grotto; all paths seemed to lead there. They decided to sit on the large bench that was perfectly positioned for users to gaze into the grotto below. From there, they could rest and enjoy the cool tranquility.

The man, a wealthy tradesman, said, "If we're lucky, we may be able to view Sir William's hermit as he goes about his business, such as it is, before it gets too dark."

The young woman had to ask, "Why in the world does he keep a hermit?"

The man responded knowingly, "Well, that's the very point of a hermit; he has no business, other than to entertain passers-by, like us."

"But he doesn't tell jokes, juggle or even dance. He's just…" the young woman shrugged, "… there."

Just then, the hermit – perhaps roused by the sound of distant conversation – slowly emerged from the cave.

"No, he's THERE!" joked the man as he pointed toward the slovenly, middle-aged man below. The hermit wore no shirt; just a dirty scarf around his neck, sandals and tattered breeches. He stretched, then proceeded to scratch his filthy, matted hair and beard in what could have been either a daily ritual or performance.

The tradesman stretched out his legs and placed his mask on his chest. "You've nicely summarized his life during his contract with Sir William. He's just there."

He clasped his hands behind his neck and continued, "Let's say that an average working man makes about £60 per year, these days. That man below, living here continually for five years, through all types of weather, receives nothing until the completion of the contract. At that time, he will receive a pension of £50 per year, for the rest of his life. Most lords make the pension payable only upon completion of the five-year contract."

The young woman ran her gloved hand slowly down her thigh in a fruitless attempt to smooth an already-smooth *cheongsam*. "I still don't fully understand."

Mrs. Quack rolled her eyes.

The tradesman was not concerned. "Most people, my dear, do not. Supposedly, the hermit symbolizes Sir William's spirituality. I, for one, will not be remarking about how deeply soulful our friend Sir William is."

The older woman, who had been quiet since sitting down, simply stared at the hermit. To his credit, the hermit had taken up an item that looked very much like a human skull. He was now standing, one foot perched on a boulder, gazing at the skull, contemplating… something.

The tradesman leaned forward, his elbows on his knees. "Ahhh, look at him now! Deep in thought. Good for him. Sir William tells me that this particular hermit has been living here for the past four years. See his hair and beard? A stipulation of employment is that he not cut his hair, beard or fingernails. Nor is he allowed to bathe, so it's a fine thing that we are up here and he down there."

The young woman absentmindedly waved her hand in front of her nose, "I'm quite sure that I'd stay well back if I happened to be down there, in any case. A hermit is a hermit, after all."

The man responded, "Indeed. Sir William's employees are not as fortunate as we three; they have to bring him two meals a day and empty his chamber pot."

The young woman looked at the man with admiration, "You certainly seem to know a lot about hermits, Mr. Ladner."

"Well, I myself considered acquiring one at one time."

The young woman paused, enjoying the moment. When she asked with a smile, "And, why didn't you?" Mrs. Quack recognized the sly smile as one from Poacher Fox himself.

Without hesitation, the man replied, "Oh, I decided that having you as my courtesan was much more important."

The serenity of the garden was suddenly made even quieter. The mature woman got up, and with a glare at her husband and a "Harruff!", Mrs. Quack waddled quickly back to the estate house. The other two suppressed their cruel laughter until she was out of sight. They lingered a while longer.

The second option presented to arriving guests was to tour a portion of the interior of the house under the guidance of Jamieson; viewing Sir William's collections of art, tapestries and furniture, some of which were personally made by Thomas Chippendale. It was Zac's responsibility to escort guests desiring this tour to join Jamieson's group. In addition to the recently redecorated Tea Room, guests were able to view the immense Dining Room and the Garden Room, with its expansive view of the garden.

Adjacent to the Hall, visitors could also see the Drawing Room where, during a typical evening, Sir William, his family or a distinguished guest could "withdraw" for more privacy.

For the masquerade ball, the Drawing Room was a place where a smaller number of visitors could be entertained. Tables had been laid out for card games such as whist. Chess, draughts and backgammon were other options. A new game from China, called dominoes, engaged other guests in a corner of the room, under a huge tapestry depicting an equine event.

Guests might marvel at the presence of a small chapel for the private use of the Mansfield family, their servants and guests. This, however, was not the night for the reverence of the chapel.

Costumed guests politely accepted the invitation to either of these tours, but most just wanted to begin the evening's festivities. Thus, the tour of the home was the most popular, providing anxious guests with the ability to easily "slip away" to the Gallery.

Zac was kept busy that night. He thoroughly enjoyed his duties as escort and later, as server in the Gallery. Aunt Bea had teased him about "getting used to" items like silver *cloches*. But she could not imagine just how familiar Zac had become with that particular silverware. He had already carried many such platters, although actually opening them was not his duty. That was the responsibility of the waiters.

As darkness descended, he had to light candles. But not just any candles. As Jamieson's charge, Zac was responsible for lighting/extinguishing the pricey beeswax candles. The cheaper tallow candles (rendered from animal fat) were the responsibility of the housekeeper and her staff. Zac quickly learned how to tell the difference between candles: contrary to the tallow candles, the beeswax burned pure and clean, produced a smokeless flame and emitted a pleasant odour.

Zac and the other footmen had been seconded as servers. Speaking with them, Zac was told that some costumes included painted faces and risqué dress. Pickett had also seconded male staff from neighbouring estates to ensure that there were many hands to provide the food and drink. Staff were also required to wear identical masks.

Zac was told, however, of an upcoming duty that he was hesitant to accept, although refusal would likely mean his termination. Even Jamieson, who had to inform him and three other footmen of their particularly heavy evening task, seemed genuinely distraught in having to do so.

As host, Sir William wanted a unique costume. He had asked Zac to create an outfit for him that would resemble what the North American Indians wore while playing the 'cross' game. He summoned Quering and Zac to his dressing room, asking that Zac bring the new outfit and certain other items. The duke insisted that Zac help him and Quering put together his costume, much to the latter's chagrin.

On his head, the duke wore a customized leather helmet, complete with earflaps and chin strap. His exposed skin had been dyed a light brown, ostensibly just like the Indians. Zac knew that this may be considered offensive in the future, but was encouraged by Sir William, who wanted "a realistic portrayal." One eye had been darkened underneath with a black substance; a mask was not required of the host. The breeches and leggings were still there, but the breeches, dyed blue, had leather padding added underneath at the knees and thighs. A tight-fitting blue vest over a linen shirt helped keep shoulder pads, themselves fashioned from bedding, in place.

On the vest, Zachary had painted a thick white cross, with the word "DUKE" above and "LACROSSE" below it; an homage to the Duke University Blue Devils, Zac's favourite field lacrosse team.

Lastly, he pulled on the "sporting shoes" and held one of the lacrosse sticks that Zac had helped build. He held in the mesh of the stick a leather ball. The completed costume made the duke look like a cross between Indiana Jones after a fight and a pirate on steroids.

"Sire, it's an abomination," lamented Quering, staring at his master's reflection in the gold-trimmed mirror. Holding the dripping paintbrush, Zac nodded his satisfaction.

Sir William gazed at himself, stroked his Van Dyke beard and smiled. "An abomination, Quering? Nay, a handsome, cross-playing devil, indeed! I must go and greet my guests now."

As the duke and his entourage made their way to the Gallery, Zac had to smile. The likeness between this duke and the university mascot was uncanny!

Try as one might, one could not remove the devilish grin from Sir William's face that night; at least, not until much later.

∞

32

ONE OF THE LAST to arrive in the Gallery, Sir William was awed by the variety and colours of the costumes. They were exquisite, as cost was not a concern for many. One of the first that he recognized was a stunning fairy princess across the room, fanning herself with a green fan inside a circle of costumed men. He had paid a king's ransom for her costume, but it was worth every penny.

Most guests had planned what they would wear far in advance. They ranged from the simple "domino" to lavish regalia. The mysterious domino was the most common costume for both sexes, made typically of a simple black cloak and mask. The domino was the most common because it was the simplest and the cheapest. A black domino (other colours were available) could be bought for just four shillings at a London warehouse. A person bedecked in the domino costume displayed intrigue and adventure. And, he or she often remained mute for at least part of the evening.

Across the vast, crowded room a female masquerader asked, "Do you know me?" in a low, sultry voice. She had chosen to come as an Egyptian queen; a fine choice for the tall, stately woman. Her simple sheath linen dress featured broad shoulder straps decorated with gold thread and brightly-coloured beadwork. Her headdress was of white lace, trimmed with a border of pearls. The human hair of her black wig was tightly interwoven with tiny ringlets of gold.

Around her long neck she wore a shaped cone of decorative metal and gemstones. And, she was barefoot.

"Yes, I know you!" responded a smiling gentleman dressed as a Turk, with a scimitar at his belt. Introductory interactions were subject to certain verbal codes. Only specified phrases, well known by all, could be used when masqueraders addressed each other to begin a conversation. These rules established a semblance of order in what could otherwise be a chaotic environment.

Despite the potential for chaos, the masquerade had a strict code of behaviour. For example, a gentleman could ask a woman to dance only after he was formally introduced to her. If a woman declined one request for a dance she must turn down all others. To say no to a man early in the evening meant that she could not dance for the whole night! A maximum of two dances was allowed with the same partner.

Masked guests were supposedly dressed so as to be unidentifiable, creating a type of game to see if guests could determine each other's identities. Masks were usually removed after midnight.

There were a number of scantily-dressed guests representing warm, exotic locales. One man, wearing only a black Afro wig, black mask and sarong-type pants, was allegedly from Africa. Any exposed skin (of which he had a lot) had been darkened. In the crowded room lit by hundreds of candles and oil lamps, the heat could be overwhelming. This became a concern for those with elaborate, layered costumes, particularly as the evening progressed. The African kept cool.

Sir William's neighbor and friend, Josiah Wedgwood, was dressed as a gondolier. From a distance, Sir William waved at his friend and chuckled at the brilliant irony of the costume. Mansfield had recently helped Wedgwood finance the construction of the Trent and Mersey Canal. His burgeoning pottery business had been plagued by transportation problems; that is, the stoneware was subject to frequent breakage in shipment via conventional means, such as packhorse or carriage. The canal – for which construction had recently begun – would provide smooth sailing for his stoneware to market. The gondolier costume was Josiah's comical way of saying thanks.

Even Father Time was there; a white-bearded man dressed in a grey mask and robe, carrying a scythe. An hourglass and a gorgeous pendant watch were draped around his neck, and a red rose on his lapel provided the only vivid colour in his otherwise drab costume. The man was looking around the room, anxiously searching for something or someone. He too spotted the fairy princess, who he immediately recognized: her costume and mask could not hide – in fact, they embellished – her curvaceous body, a body that he had recently partaken of.

Father Time was accompanied by a gangly young man who wore a unique, tight-fitting, three-coloured costume. The blue outfit – the likes of which had never been seen before – garnered much attention that night. It was worn tight to the body, due in part to thumb holes for the sleeves. It was paired with a large, bright red cape that hung almost to the floor, in the bottom of which was sewn a pouch containing a portable charger and cable. Sky wore red knee-high boots over blue tights. In his red briefs, he had apparently endowed himself with some needed padding. On his chest and on the cape was a stylized letter "S" in red on a yellow background. His belt and a mask were the same bright yellow. His long, curly dark hair had been oiled down – really oiled down – to stick close to his head. A single ringlet of hair encircled his forehead.

He spent much of his time crossing his skinny arms in front of himself, his hands behind his biceps to make them appear larger. Father Time appeared to reprimand him several times, ushering him to follow.

There were a few medieval court jesters, with their multi-coloured, mirthful attire. Their distinctive "cap 'n' bells" hats consisted of three bouncy points with a jingle bell at the end of each point. With their frenetic movements, they worked the crowd into uproarious laughter. One of their favourite routines was to copy the walk or dancing style of an oblivious victim. They seemed to be merely jovial participants but in fact, the impresario had hired the troupe.

Most of the merrymakers were shrouded in gaudy resplendence, but the most gaudy was yet to come. Wee Willy, the birthday boy, had yet to make his appearance. Rachel was well aware of her brother's need to make a grand entrance. In contrast, she preferred to informally enter the Gallery with her lady-in-waiting, Abigail, to greet and mingle with everyone else.

Abigail came as a pirate, complete with a musket, a "stolen" navy blue Admiral jacket, breeches and high leather boots. Like Blackbeard the pirate, she, with Rachel's help, had tied her wig into very tight braids and lit these on fire, to terrorize victims upon boarding their ship as the slow-burning braids smoked harmlessly. Unlike Blackbeard, she proudly displayed her ample bosom in a low-cut bodice.

Rachel did not come as a troll, as she had teased Zac that she would. She had changed her costume after she had read the note from Jacques, deciding to come as Mother Nature. She hoped that the costume change would improve her chances of meeting Father Time.

Dressed in a grass-green dress, Rachel's costume was simple. On her head she wore a crown of fresh-cut flowers and leaves. She wore no wig, choosing to display her natural dark red locks. As was the fashion, she too wore a low-cut bodice. On her feet, she wore sandals decorated with white daisies that laced up her slender calves. A green mask lined with small mint leaves completed her costume.

Father Time saw Mother Nature before she saw him. He excused himself from his yellow-masked friend and moved adroitly through the crowd, his hourglass and pendant swaying from side to side. He moved around the dance floor, slowing only long enough to pirouette as he feigned a dance with a nubile nymph. He approached Mother Nature as she stood chatting with a buxom pirate.

Under his mask, he smiled and purred in a low voice, "Do you know me?"

Mother Nature seemed very pleased. In fact, she gasped audibly before exclaiming, "Yes, I know you!" She turned to her friend and, with a deliberate and prolonged wink under her mask, asked, "Abigail, could you excuse us please?"

Abigail left the two chatting side by side in a relatively dark corner of the room. She watched as Mother Nature took Father Time's pendant watch in hand. The two will likely ignore the dance protocol (of a gentleman asking a woman to dance only after being formally introduced), thought Abigail, but dancing was perhaps not the evening's favoured activity.

No mask can hide desire.

Abigail then became engrossed in a lively conversation with a leprechaun that professed a rising interest in pirates and their booty. So, she was unable to watch as Mother Nature led Father Time out of the room and down the corridor.

But another interested party watched intently from afar. The fairy princess, still surrounded by masked gentlemen, fanned herself faster as the heat in the room increased. Like Mother Nature, the fairy was clad all in green, dressed in light fabric to stay cool while displaying her natural endowments. Her tiny costume consisted only of a short skimpy dress tied at the waist, with taffeta "wings" protruding from her shoulders. The laces of her simple green sandals had been wrapped around her calves and tied just under her knees.

The fairy princess excused herself from the conversation and then stealthily followed the couple down the corridor.

Sir William had arranged, through the impresario, for a chamber orchestra to play for the evening. The 32-piece orchestra included string sections (the violin, viola, cello and bass) and percussion, brass and woodwind instruments. The harpist was left plucking, off in a corner.

The music reflected the popular dances, such as the minuet. Its well-known, delicate steps were often flirtatious: a man and woman start holding "proper" (that is, their right) hands; they retreat in order to touch right hands again and quickly change to touch left hands; they again retreat and return to meet face to face, and finally, hold both hands.

Subtly erotic, the minuet had been the most popular social dance of the courts for years. But other dances were now gaining popularity, particularly with young people like Rachel. Dances like the allemande, wherein its rhythm, steps and embrace is accented by a plethora of complicated handholds between partners. Like many of the dances of the time, the allemande's handholds and movements required a great deal of practice. So, books were published to guide beginners.

Rachel's piano had been moved into the Gallery in her father's hope that she would sing and play later for the entire group. The piano was regarded as one of the most technologically advanced musical instruments, but it was also the costliest. Thus, it was regarded as the precinct of the aristocracy. Rachel was not unique in this regard; most daughters of the gentry were taught to play piano. Some played as well as she, but none could match her charming voice or coquettish beauty.

Rachel's father had hosted many social events at the estate. Thinking that visitors would find it captivating, he had employed a voice teacher from Paris to train his pretty daughter to sing to complement her instrument playing. Visitors enjoyed her "impromptu" concerts in the Music Room or, when the guests were many, in the Hall. Hearing the talented young woman sing and play was a highlight for many visiting courtesans.

Unbeknownst to him, Rachel's recital at the masquerade would be completed, *sans* piano, and to an audience of one.

The ball had gained comfortable momentum, with the crowd of some 250 in the Gallery fully engaged with their favourite libation. Forty others played games in other designated rooms, or simply enjoyed the gardens in any way possible.

Others were dancing, eating and flirting, when the orchestra suddenly stopped playing. Everyone's attention was directed to the orchestral stage, where the host, Lord Mansfield, stood holding his lacrosse stick and accompanying ball in his bizarre blue outfit. No one, save for two, knew what or who he was trying to be.

Beside him, assuming a regal pose, was Pickett the impresario. He was dressed like King George III, the young reigning monarch. "George" wore a gold topcoat with matching breeches, gold shoes, and white leggings to match the leopard skin cape draped across his shoulder and clasped with a gold medallion.

Pickett blew a whistle for silence, then shouted: "My Lords and Ladies, Beggars and Thieves," he paused and smiled at the truth to his joke. "Welcome all! Without further ado, I give you Lord William Mansfield the Third, on the occasion of his 23rd birthday!" With a sweep of his hand, he directed the audience's attention to the main entrance door.

The trumpet section of the orchestra stood and played a heraldic fanfare. A grand entrance was about to occur. After an attention-getting pause, the huge double door opened and in came a garishly-decorated, covered lounge chair for a single passenger, carried on two horizontal poles, supported by four masked footmen. The chair, or *palanquin*, was open so that all could take in the splendor that was William III, who sat and waved and smiled. With him was a golden harp, which he strummed randomly. As was his intent, his costume topped them all.

Cross-dressing was a common form of disguise at this, and indeed, at most masquerades. Women were able to dress as men and men as women, all in a way that would normally be disgraceful. Like the class roles that disappeared at the masquerade, gender roles were subject to reversal. While he and his father were the only masqueraders to be identified, Wee Willy stuck to the rules and proudly wore his mask: a decidedly feminine one.

The footmen carried the *palanquin* into the centre of the room and placed it down. They approached the chair in unison and knelt as Willy rose. Taking the hand of the first footman, he descended the two steps onto the Gallery floor. This, in itself, was a challenge, for Willy was dressed in a woman's formal hooped gown, complete with fresh-cut red roses in the many petticoats of the skirt. The bright yellow dress was low cut and padded.

His silver wig, standing almost two feet above his head, brushed against the top of the door as he ducked while leaving the *palanquin*. Any exposed skin had been powdered white, and a large beauty mark was placed high on his left cheek. He pranced back and forth, so that his admirers had ample opportunity to enjoy him.

Apart from a few low wolf-whistles, the crowd at first seemed dumbstruck, but soon began to clap and whistle. A white-faced courtesan near the stage, a disguised and longstanding member of the Macaroni Club, was almost apoplectic with her – actually his – clapping.

Noticing the courtesan made Willy prance more, enjoying all the attention. Many in the crowd thought, correctly, that he must have been drinking before entering the Gallery. For his birthday, the crowd started singing *For He's a Jolly Good Fellow* and clapping rhythmically. Some in the audience soon changed the lyrics to "For He's a Jolly Good Woman" which soon had everyone in gales of laughter.

Still holding the hand of the footman, Wee Willy ascended onto the stage in front of the orchestra. The footman had to use both hands to hold him and keep him from falling, as the dress and his inebriated condition hampered his progress. This started another wave of uproarious laughter.

Only the Birthday Boy's father found little humour in the display. Sir William Mansfield had never fully understood his son. Since Lady Emily's death he had tried to accept his son's condition, which seemed to grow more flamboyant every year.

Barely achieving the stage, Wee Willy turned to face the audience with a wide drunken smile. Teetering, he turned to the closest footman. With a devilish sneer, Willy ripped off the footman's mask and flung it into the crowd. He then grabbed the startled footman's cheeks and forcibly kissed him on the mouth, to the gasps and wild cheers of the raucous audience.

The footman, visibly shaken, began to descend the steps, leaving the stage. He rubbed his mouth on his forearm as he went.

A cry, barely heard in the din, rose from across the gallery: "Zac!"

Seeing that the de-masked footman was his friend, Superman raced through the crowd toward the stage, his cape finally released to take full flight behind him. He got to Zac at the foot of the stairs, held out his arms and hugged him.

At first, the dazed Zac did not recognize his friend dressed as his childhood hero, with his hair slicked back. But when he did, Zac hugged him back, shouting over the din, "I'm happy to see you too, but if you try to kiss me," Zac held up a shaking fist, "I'll knock you back to Fraserdale!"

∞

33

WITH THE EXCITEMENT OF being reunited and the noisy masqueraders who surrounded them, the two young men did not realize what had just happened. When they hugged, the thumb strap holding the tight sleeve of Sky's Superman costume had broken. The sleeve rode immediately up Sky's arm, exposing the smartwatch to the gathered crowd!

Those closest gasped and pointed, and then slowly stepped back. The collective attention was switched from Wee Willy on the stage to the two young men standing in the middle of a widening circle.

From the stage and with a clear view, Sir William pointed and cried, "Look, he bears a lighted talisman upon his wrist! His friend there, a footman in my employ, also possesses such a talisman! What sorcery is this? Witches! Seize them!"

The three footmen who had helped Zac carry in the *palanquin* moved forward, as did some of the crowd. At that moment, a strange pinging noise – unlike anything ever heard in this house – emanated from the lighted talisman on Superman's wrist.

Keeping his hand on the smartwatch, Sky shouted, "We have cast a spell. That's right, that's right! Stand back! Back! Let us go!"

Removing his hand from the watch momentarily, Sky grabbed the bottom of his cape and moved his arm over his head, so for a moment, the cape looked like a big red balloon.

They made their way cautiously through the gaily-dressed crowd, which parted in fear of another spell as the two headed for the main door. Faster now, and still pinging, they ran down the hallway and out the front door, down the stairs and past the startled attending footman onto the front lawn, which was totally shrouded in darkness.

In the dark, Zac fumbled for the charger. Finding it, he flipped on the LED flashlight. Now, they were able to see the many carriages parked on the front driveway and lawn, and the horses tied to temporary posts – they had many to choose from.

Behind them though, the crowd surged forward, led by Sir William. In the excitement, no one noticed that Father Time, Mother Nature and the fairy princess were absent. In fact, they were in a room not far from the parrot, though too far to hear the bird squawking, "He's a witch! He's a witch!"

Zac began to climb up on a nearby stagecoach; four sleek black horses at the ready.

"No, no, too big. This one!" Sky waved his friend over to a lighter, single-bodied open carriage that carried only two people. He untied the horses; an anxious quartet.

Although Superman was not aware of it, the carriage was known as a Phaeton – considered the sports car of the age. Aristocratic gentlemen used the Phaeton in races; it had the fastest wheels around. The young men would need them.

As their eyes got accustomed to the dark, the large group at the front door descended the stairs. They could see a strange light dancing amongst the carriages. The Gallery had essentially been emptied, leaving only the orchestra and a few – mostly haptic – others, like Willy.

Shouting commands to ready the carriages and get the horses, Sir William found himself pointing with the lacrosse stick. It was then that he remembered the ball that was loaded in his cross stick. He ran toward the dancing light...

Angry shouts, then commands and the sound of horses neighing and of riders urging their horses on, grew louder. They had no time to lose! No longer needing the flashlight, Zac turned it off.

Luckily, the carriage had been positioned in a prime location by the footmen in the same way that young men admire a sports car parked at the school dance.

"Haaa!, shouted Zac, who had taken the reins as Sky untied the horses. "Haaa!" The reins ricocheted off the horses' backs, spurring them on.

"Ouch!," yelled Sky, as a projectile hit him square in the neck and dropped into the basket of the carriage. Luckily, his blowing cape seemed to have cushioned the impact somewhat. He rubbed his neck with one hand and held on tightly with the other.

A large gatehouse bordered the massive gates of Mansfield Castle. The gatehouse functioned as a post for the gatekeeper, a jail and in an earlier age, a viewing platform to watch the movement of nearby game. The gates were typically kept closed and were opened only as required. Tonight, with all the anticipated comings and goings, the duke had had the gates left open.

The Phaeton flew through the gates as the gatekeeper looked on, perplexed. He saw two people in the carriage; one, who may have been dressed as a footman driving the horses and the other, who had on a most bizarre costume; the cape of which kept billowing up into the driver's face.

Minutes later, more carriages drove to the gates, led by Sir William himself. He was accompanied by Pickett, who looked decidedly awkward. He wished that he hadn't had a momentary lapse of cowardice when, back at the estate, the duke had grabbed the reins of a carriage and shouted, "Come on then, Pickett!"

The procession of carriages stopped momentarily.

"Which way?" the duke hissed at his gatekeeper through the dust.

The gatekeeper simply pointed east, down Bath Road toward London.

Away flew Sir William and Pickett, followed by at least a dozen other carriages of all types. Three single riders on horseback came some time later, as it had taken the footmen some time to prepare their mounts. All were determined to track down and arrest the witches so that they could be brought to trial.

They were all too late. The fleet Phaeton flew fast, far into the night.

∞

34

RACHEL HAD INTENDED TO take Jacques to her bed-chamber, thinking that no one would suspect such brazen behaviour. Everyone was otherwise occupied, in any case. Rachel could not wait to kiss Father Time with his mask on. So, in the hallway, a few doors away from her room, she turned and kissed him.

Caramel, the fairy princess, followed stealthily. She hid in a doorway alcove close to where Rachel embraced Jacques. Peeking around the corner, she watched as they kissed passionately.

She was well-hidden, but didn't realize that the tip of her green, fairy princess wing was exposed. From down the corridor, as he hungrily kissed Rachel, Jacques saw the wing tip. He recognized the wing; he knew its owner intimately. Being French, he was able to maintain his concentration with Rachel while formulating a plan.

Inflamed, Rachel took Jacques by the hand and turned to walk, faster now, the few steps to her room. Behind her, he unclasped the hourglass from around his neck and dropped it quietly to the floor.

Rachel opened the door and began to lead the highway-man into her bedchamber. He paused, saying in a whisper, "Fair Lady, I need to retrieve my hourglass which has fallen just there, down the 'allway. I will join you shortly."

Rachel smiled and whispered in his ear, "I will begin to remove my costume, but I may require assistance with some parts."

That was a lie; she knew that her selection of the simple costume had been made to ensure ease of undressing. She entered her bedchamber and closed the door behind her.

Father Time passed down the corridor to where the hourglass lay. Pausing over it, he then ran to the alcove where he had seen the tip of the wing. There, he found Caramel.

Expecting her to be somewhat aroused at having watched the embracing couple, Jacques was surprised by her protest.

"You cur, you! You are planning to bed Lady Rachel! How dare you?" Caramel was livid, hitting his chest with her fists.

"Caramel, my love, calm down. Calm down! Yes, of course I will. And," he paused to lift her chin. Looking deep into her eyes with longing, he purred, "you should join us."

"Join you? Not tonight, not with her. Perhaps under different circumstances."

"And, what is wrong with these circumstances? These circumstances are *parfait*! You do not find the fair Lady Rachel attractive?"

Her will almost gone, Caramel slowly stopped beating his chest. She went limp, letting the highwayman take her in his arms. Jacques' nostrils flared; the bouquet of the fresh-cut flowers that made up her crown was intoxicating. He wondered if Rachel would agree.

"No, she is very attractive," Caramel sighed. After a time, she looked up at him. Teary-eyed and barely able to mouth the words, she exclaimed, "Lady Rachel is my daughter!" Caramel slumped to the floor.

"Mon Dieu..."

He turned, picked up the hourglass, and looking back at Caramel once more, he hurried down the corridor and slipped into Rachel's chambers, closing the door behind him.

Caramel removed her mask, hung her head and cried.

∞

213

35

"NO, VASSI. WE DO not share our cup with anyone."

Vassi's mother scolded him as she took the cup from Vassi's little sister's hands. "As 'Romanichal' people, we must keep clean always, or we will get sick and pass the sickness on to all the other Romani."

Vassi, his little sister Nico and their mother were nomads, travelling throughout southern England. Their people were wanderers who often travelled on foot, but this family group had a horse-drawn, covered cart.

At night, if the appropriately supple trees were close by, they would sleep in a temporary "bender" tent made from the branches they bent to support a tarpaulin. Sleeping under the cart was not an option; it was occupied.

But now, it was early morning. 11-year-old Vassi had stayed up late the previous night past his bedtime to enjoy the fire, singing songs with his family. His pretty mother, Mika, had perfect dark skin, but blonde hair and bright blue eyes beneath her headscarf.

Vassi's father, Leopold, was not Romani but was originally from Germany. The sound of snoring from the tent confirmed that he was sleeping in, tired after yesterday's ordeal with the footpad.

The family was en route to London.

Leopold had no choice; he had to return to London. Two things drew him and his family there.

The first was his desire that his growing family worship at a German church. He had recently heard from a German merchant, a sugar baker in Salisbury, that a new Lutheran church – St. George's – had been built in Aldgate just east of London. His wife had agreed when they got married to have their children raised in a Lutheran church, while retaining her Romani customs.

Romani never shared eating utensils with anyone, not even with their own husbands or wives. These items were always washed in running water, never still; and then soaked in a bowl of boiled water. Then they were dried with a towel used only for that purpose, and then washed again in running water before being reused. This was seen to be essential because of the risk of disease from contact with stagnant water. It had been that way for as long as Mika could remember.

With this in mind, she had helped to select yesterday's campsite. The site was beautiful. Far enough from the main road – Bath Road – to prevent passersby from seeing their campfire at night, the site was beside a fast-moving stream that emptied into a small, tree-lined lake.

The stream made the lake water particularly cold, as Leopold and Vassi had discovered that afternoon when they had ventured in for a swim. Father and son frolicked together for as long as they could in the frigid water, before emerging naked to warm up by the fire, then splashing back in.

Leopold had shown Vassi how to make a simple breathing tube using a bulrush, plucked from the shallows. The father bit off the top and the bottom of the stem, and making a face, submerged his large body, leaving only the end of the reed exposed.

Vassi stood quietly nearby, waist-deep in the water. He was fascinated, watching as the reed moved into deeper water. As his mother and sister looked on, the reed moved slowly back toward him. The reed was right beside Vassi when the crouching Leopold exploded out of the water with a roar, trying to startle his son.

Vassi was a little startled, and Nico giggled. But Vassi was mostly taken by the breathing tube. For the rest of the afternoon, he and his dad took turns submerging and breathing through the bulrush tube. They made a few spare tubes, hoping that Mika would join them when Nico was asleep.

But, that was yesterday.

This morning, a loud growl erupted from the cart! The horse tossed its head, snorted and shuffled its legs.

"Leo, you need to feed your bear again!" Mika yelled toward the tent, then shook her head in annoyance. The horse relaxed. The snoring stopped abruptly.

The family was in the business of bear-baiting. The main bear-garden in London was the Paris Garden, at Southwark, on the south side of the Thames from London. Leopold and family would head there in the hope of securing a time to bait their bear against dogs, usually large English mastiffs or bulldogs.

Leopold got out of the tent with a theatric grunt, in protest for being woken. He left his daughter inside, sleeping soundly. Plodding to the front of the cart, he stretched before scratching himself unapologetically. Mika watched her husband and grinned.

Leopold removed the curtain that had covered all three exposed sides of the cage, revealing a huge black bear with a grotesquely damaged snout. Elderberry branches, bereft of berries, littered the floor. The man and the bear scowled at each other.

Leopold went to the back of the cart, where he opened a small pen to extract a live clucking chicken. Grabbing it by the neck, he returned to the front of the caged cart where a long stick lay on the ground. He stooped to pick up the stick, then he opened the pen, keeping the bear back with just the sight of the stick. He threw the chicken into the pen and watched as the bear quickly killed and ate his breakfast.

The bear had been a valuable investment for Leopold, so he took great care from show to show to ensure that the bear was not killed or maimed and rendered useless. But he also had to file the bear's teeth short in order to reduce injuries to the dogs. Thankfully, this laborious process – which involved Leopold, stout ropes and four strong men – was only required annually.

Leopold's bear had gained notoriety throughout southern England; so much so that he even had a name: Brummbär, which means "sore head" in German. The bear's snout and ears had been badly scarred from previous bloody events. In fact, the bear was missing most of his left ear. To date, Brummbär had kept both of his eyes, which was a good thing: blind bears, their owners knowing that they are doomed, were whipped to amuse the crowds before being destroyed.

It was then that Leopold saw the fancy gentleman's carriage approaching. He motioned for Mika to hide. She ran behind the cart with Vassi. Leopold grabbed his only weapon; a sword, from behind the driver's seat – and, already in a surly mood, went to meet the carriage.

He made quite an imposing sight. He was very tall, with a thick neck and heavy shoulders; well-muscled, mustachioed, with a shaved head. As he had just got out of bed, he was shirtless in his breeches.

"Vat do you vant?" he shouted with his German accent and in his deepest voice, as the carriage approached.

"Food, if you have some. We mean you no harm." The riders were young men. One was dressed like a footman, perhaps. And the other – well, he was colourfully attired…

"Ve have little, but ve vill share vat ve have for some news about conditions on the road to London," Leopold said.

By this time, the impressive carriage had slowly entered the campsite. The four horses had obviously been ridden hard. Zac and Sky got down, looking tentatively at the bear in the cage.

Leopold was relieved; these two seemed harmless. Perhaps they were lost. He stared at them, especially at the one who wore a brightly-coloured cape. "Don't let ze bear scare you. He's eaten now, von't be hungry for a few hours." He had to ask, "Vat in God's good name are you vearing, boy?"

Tired and forgetting what he was wearing, Sky looked down at his costume. He gave an exhausted laugh and said, "It's a long story."

"Ve have some time. Ve vant to be back on ze road tomorrow. But come, sit vith us by ze fire and break your fast. Zere's plenty of fresh vater for your horses." Leopold waved his sword to encompass both the lake and the stream. He decided to keep the sword close for the time being. Mika and Vassi came slowly around the cart to stand beside Leopold.

Sky and Zac accepted the German's invitation, and introductions were made. With some difficulty, the weary travellers removed the four harnesses. Driven hard for most of the night, the horses first drank heavily at the stream, then moved slowly to the fresh, tender grass nearby.

Mika prepared a breakfast of scrambled eggs covered in onions and cheese with mashed potatoes over the crackling fire, while the boys sat down with Leopold by its warmth. On his lap, Leopold held Vassi, who couldn't keep still – he was fascinated with the visitors' clothes. He tugged at his dad's arm.

Leopold again asked the men why they were dressed the way they were. The two explained about the masquerade ball, the false allegations against them and their night flight. They didn't, of course, mention anything about the Man of

Steel costume or the smartwatches and accessories, now carefully hidden, in Superman's cape pouch and in Zac's leather pouch.

They said that they were from the colonies and headed to London to find work. Sky's eyes never left the flickering flames as he said quietly, "I'm pretty sure that we are being followed. With your permission, I'd like to hide our horses and carriage."

Leopold knew that Mika would feel the same way about these tired strangers – as strange as they were – as he did. She would welcome them as insurance against any land pirates they may encounter.

"You have my permission," Leopold rose to his full height, "and my help."

The men worked together, leading the horses through the underbrush and down an embankment into a damp, wooded depression. There, the horses would have plenty to eat. Any neighing would not be heard, they hoped, at the campfire; muffled by both the topography and the gurgling brook.

They pushed the Phaeton carriage into the shallows of the lake, fully submerging the wheels amongst the bulrushes and overhanging branches of the surrounding trees. Over and around the carriage, which was already nicely hidden, they spread bushes and branches.

Wet to the waist but breathing easier now, Zac and Sky returned with their host to the campfire.

"Brrrr! So cold," muttered Sky, standing with his back to the fire and lifting his cape to distribute the warmth to where it was most needed.

They sat and chatted, getting acquainted and losing track of time. The heat of the day was gradually replaced by the coolness of twilight. In the growing dimness, the fire brightened.

Zac asked Leopold why he and his family were here, which was really asking why were they travelling with a bear. Leopold told them about their life as bear baiters, travelling from town to town, entertaining the people.

"Ours is not an easy life; always on ze move. Our fate hangs on ze vell-being of a vild animal. If ze bear is badly vounded or dies, ve are lost. But, for now, ve have no choice." Leopold looked at his pretty wife and said thoughtfully, "One day, maybe, ve vill be able to settle down, to join a good church and earn a living by my own hard vork."

He continued, "London is calling all of us. I suggest that ve travel together, for protection zrough zese foul voods. Ve can share vot meager food ve have viz you."

"But, we have no weapons or money," Sky said. He still had his coins, of course, as did Zac; but wisely would not share that information.

"You can re-pay your debt ven ve get to Southvark," said Leopold with a dismissive wave of his big hand. As his father waved, the little boy found his opportunity to escape from his lap, where he'd been pinned for much of the day. He tried to pull away from his father's firm grip. Finally, straining against the lad's pulling, Leopold let the rambunctious Vassi go.

The boy giggled as he launched directly at Sky's Superman outfit, outlining the 'S' on Sky's chest with his fingers until Sky feigned being tickled, falling over in a heap with Vassi laughing on top. Leopold laughed and looked at Mika, who was smiling broadly.

As he watched his son wrestle with Sky, Leopold shook his head in disbelief. He had an old coat to lend this one, in his brightly-coloured suit. He left the group at the fire and went to the cart to retrieve it. He searched for and finally found the old tattered topcoat. Returning to the fire, he handed it to Sky, saying, "Here, this vill cover most of your costume until you can buy regular clothes."

Leaving the topcoat and little Vassi, Sky ran to the semi-submerged Phaeton. He climbed in while trying not to get too wet. Through the covering branches, he grabbed the ball that had hit him as they fled Mansfield Castle.

Rubbing the back of his neck in remembrance, Sky returned to the group at the fire. He tossed the ball to Vassi, who caught it with delight. now had a new toy for a boy who had a few.

The boy had been taught well and he remembered his lessons. One lesson in the Romanichal tradition was to reciprocate when you could. Still holding the ball, Vassi ran to his tent, returning after a time with a broad smile, the ball and something he had gotten from the tent. Timidly, he handed the new objects to Sky, a small pencil and a few tattered pieces of vellum paper.

Sensing that the gift should not be refused, Sky simply smiled and said, "Thank you, Vassi." He was just stuffing the paper and pencil into the pocket of the topcoat when they heard the clip-clop of an approaching horse and the squeal of carriage wheels.

Leopold leapt to his feet. He ran to his son and lifting him to his feet, told him, "Vassi, show zem ze breazing tubes. Hurry now, into ze vater!"

Dropping his new ball beside the fire, Vassi knew what had to be done. Leopold pushed Sky and Zac, who were now standing, toward the darkness of the lake. They followed the boy's lead, each one taking a bulrush stem from the small pile at the lakeshore. Out of the revealing glow of the fire, they quickly waded in.

"Sky, your smartwatch!" Zac knew that Vassi would not know what he was referring to. Zac quickly removed the strap that held the leather pouch at the small of his back and threw it into the bulrushes beside the lake.

"Almost forgot. Thanks buddy." Sky unbuttoned the cape and threw his electronics close to where Zac had thrown his.

"Over there, past the carriage," whispered Sky as he waded in, indicating where they should rendezvous.

The water, now above Zac's waist, seemed even colder than before. Its sting was exacerbated by the memory of the warmth of the campfire.

Just then, a carriage slowly entered the campsite, firelight flickering off its metal parts.

Vassi demonstrated the underwater breathing technique he himself had just learned. Under he went, leaving Zac and Sky to see only the exposed end of the boy's bulrush stalk. They watched as the stalk moved miraculously to the arranged meeting place.

Now it was their turn. They had to act quickly. Just as their heads were going under, both chanced a glimpse toward the carriage. While they were too far away to recognize the two occupants, they easily recognized the costume that the driver wore. On the driver's chest, they could see a large white cross, with words above and below. Zac knew the words; he had painted them.

Simultaneously, they lowered themselves into the icy cold water, leaving only innocuous reeds should searching eyes peer out over the lake.

Leopold greeted the visitors in the same way that he had greeted the Canadians earlier. He fetched his sword and stood, defiant, in front of the carriage. "Vat do you vant?" His voice boomed through the twilight, causing the horses to snort and fidget.

The driver brought the rig to a stop and leaned forward. "We are looking for two men in a stolen carriage. We believe them to be witches. As such, they may be dangerous to you and your fine family."

Sir William looked to where Mika held her little girl. "Have you seen them?"

In the water behind the foliage-covered Phaeton, Zac, Sky and Vassi were able to surface and watch the drama unfold before them. All three were dreadfully cold and Vassi began to shiver. They hoped that the visitors would leave soon; the water was far too cold.

"Ze only person zat ve've seen since yesterday morning was a footpad who tried to rob us," Leopold stated with conviction. "I zreatened to open zis cage," he threw back the tarpaulin, revealing a sleeping bear, "and he took off faster zan a cat after a rat."

"I trust that the bear was awake when you made your threat," chortled the visitor. "I am Sir William Mansfield, the Duke of Chestney. This is Mr. Pickett. I apologize for the intrusion and for our costumes, but you see, we left a masquerade ball rather abruptly last night and we have been searching ever since. We would pay handsomely for information about the young men we seek."

Not being a local, Leopold had not heard of this duke or a Mr. Pickett. Their mention of a masquerade ball was corroborated by the costume of the one called Sky. The weight of a handsome reward would feel good in his pocket as they entered London.

But no, the presence of the young men would serve him well when they resumed the road. Leopold could not, in good conscience, betray them. Besides, they now held, and could easily harm, his son.

"I vish zat ve could be of assistance, Sir... Villiam, but you're not looking for a mere footpad, it seems. Good day to you, sir."

Leopold turned and walked purposefully to sit at the fire beside Mika, who cradled the sleeping Nico in her arms. At that moment, Mika noticed the ball. In the rush to hide, Vassi had dropped the ball beside the campfire.

Mika gently placed the swaddled toddler on the ground, where she adjusted the blanket to cover and pick up the ball. She had no idea of the ball's history; she only knew that it had come with Sky, and for that reason, it had to remain hidden. She picked up her little girl and deftly dropped the ball into the pocket of her dress.

The newcomers in the carriage watched with interest. Mika could not tell whether they had seen what she had done or not.

Sir William was determined; he was not going to be denied. Leaving Pickett, he climbed down from the carriage and walked slowly toward the campfire. There he stood, ominously.

By this time, Vassi was shaking uncontrollably. Zac and Sky, themselves shivering, had to somehow keep him warm. Leaving the cover of the Phaeton and the water was not an option. So, the three huddled together in a tight ball. Vassi's teeth chattered loudly and Zac had to quickly close the boy's mouth, while holding a finger to his now-blue lips.

Sir William was not in a hurry, but he did not wish to enrage the large man who had greeted them, sword in hand, and with a bear for company. He knew that married partners could often disagree. That was the stratagem that he decided to employ.

"What about you, kind lady?" He moved a step closer, removed his cross headgear and crooned, "Have you seen anything extraordinary today?"

Mika looked at Lord Mansfield and then at the man sitting uncomfortably in the carriage. Unlike many people, she was able to read. Although she could read the words "DUKE" and "LACROSSE" painted with a cross on the duke's blue vest, she had no idea why anyone would care to paint words onto perfectly good clothing.

While she did not have a perfectly clear view of the man in the carriage, his gold-coloured topcoat made him look extraordinarily like the English king. Oh what was his name… George! she remembered.

Mika responded to the duke's question with a question of her own. "Extraordinary, you ask?" She paused. "Yes, I certainly have."

Leopold had been gazing into the fire, thinking about Vassi in the cold water. He wouldn't last much longer. But now, he turned to stare at his wife. *She wouldn't*, he thought. He held his breath.

"And what extraordinary thing did you see today, kind lady?" Sir William took a couple more steps toward the fire, anticipating a positive response.

"I've seen a footpad run away from a caged bear and two fools dressed up. One thinks that he is King George and the other, who claims to be a duke, obliged to identify himself as one by labeling his very clothing! Both fools now know that my husband and I cannot be bribed. To repeat for you my husband's wishes, good day to you, sir!"

With that, Mika left where she was sitting and sat down again with her back turned to the duke. She gently rocked Nico. Leopold exhaled. Only he could see her face in the firelight, her eyes sparkling above a tight grin.

Finally defeated, Sir William pulled his helmet back into place, turned and re-joined Pickett in the carriage. He began to turn the vehicle in the tight space, but had difficulty in doing so. Pickett sat uselessly beside him. Sir William cursed in frustration, which caused Mika to giggle softly to herself.

Leopold was mindful that time was of the essence for Vassi and the others still in the water. He jumped up, and grabbing the lead horse by the bridle, easily turned the carriage. With a slap on the horse's rump, Leopold watched the carriage lurch forward to Bath Road. The receding sound of the horses and carriage soon turned to ominous silence.

"Vassi!" Leopold shouted absentmindedly, immediately hoping that his voice wouldn't carry too far.

He didn't know where in the lake they were. He ran to the Phaeton where he thought they would try to hide. He was right. Throwing foliage aside, he found the three bedraggled figures shivering on the lakeshore. They had watched the carriage leave and had slipped out of the water. All three were curled up in a ball, with Vassi in the middle for maximum warmth. Each still held a bulrush.

"Come, come to ze fire. Mika, fetch blankets." Leopold held the limp body of his son to his massive chest, willing the heat from his body into Vassi's frail form.

Zac and Sky had never been so cold. Dripping, they made their way to the fire.

"Take off those wet clothes," commanded Mika. "You'll warm up much quicker without them. I'll fetch firewood. But first, take these."

She handed each of them a blanket that they used first for modesty while removing their clothes, then for warming by the fire. Leopold had removed Vassi's clothes and was now hugging his son under the blanket.

The boy shivered, his teeth still chattering, "Your breathing tubes worked well, Father." Leopold couldn't speak, so he just hugged his son tighter.

Mika returned with an armful of wood. She soon had a large fire crackling. The night was not particularly cold, thankfully, and the three from the lake slowly regained their body temperature.

Perhaps in understanding that they had barely skirted disaster, no one spoke for a long time. When they began to realize that all three were going to recover, they began to relax and converse.

After awhile, Mika excused herself and took Nico to bed. Leopold, carrying the sleeping Vassi, followed his wife into their bender tent. He then went to the cart and returned carrying a bottle and three tin cups.

"Zis vill varm your blood." He poured the clear liquid into the cups and passed a cup to Zac and Sky.

Zac sipped the gin. He had had hard liquor, but never gin. Leopold was right, Zac could literally feel it warming his blood, radiating into his limbs.

"I'll help you set up a tent tonight. Ve'll be on ze road to London at first light."

With Leopold's skilled assistance, the bender tent was erected quickly. Later that moonless night, with the sound of Leopold's snoring coming from the other tent, Zac crept out to retrieve the electronics. Knowing approximately where he had tossed his, he found his pouch first. A quick check revealed that all three – the smartwatch, the charger and the cord – were intact. Using his flashlight app, he quickly found Sky's close by.

Returning to the tent, he whispered to Sky, "Got 'em."

"You da man, dude. Thanks." Sky rolled over and was asleep before his head hit his rolled up cape.

∞

36

BACK ON BATH ROAD to London, the Canadians found that Leopold smiled often and large; his eyes squinting shut in glee. And, when he was trying to be funny or he was just stressed, he'd make a unique "BRRRTT" noise by blowing air out through his pursed lips. He was as kind as he was big. Here was a guy that they wanted to keep on their side.

How he, with his content family, could be involved in a blood sport like bear baiting, they could not fathom; but for over 100 years, bear baiting had been popular. Even royalty loved a good show; King Henry VIII was such a fan that he had a pit constructed at his palace of Whitehall. And Queen Elizabeth I was so fond of the entertainment, she would ensure that a show was included everywhere she went. When Parliament tried to ban bear baiting on Sundays, she overruled them.

In ancient Russia, bear-baiting was a contest between the bear and an unfortunate man wielding either a mace or a knife. If the bear did not tear him to pieces, spectators would throw him a spear, and he would try to kill the animal. By Leopold's time, the sport of bear-baiting was in decline, in part because of the scarcity of bears. Bears were extinct in Britain and rare in western Europe. Leopold had received help from relatives in Germany to import Brummbär.

Leopold, Mika, Vassi and little Nico sat on the bench of their horse-drawn carriage, with Brummbär caged and covered behind them. Behind them rode Sky and Zac in the stolen Phaeton, pulled by four sleek horses that were freshly watered and fed. Londoners gawked as the procession clip-clopped toward the infamous Southwark grounds.

Outside of London's boundaries, Southwark was beyond the control of city administrators. This made it a haven for nefarious activities such as bear-, badger- and bull-baiting, prostitution, and – heaven forbid – unlicenced acting.

Sky was wearing Leopold's old waistcoat over his Superman costume. They had arranged to stop at a tailor's to purchase a permanent suit of clothes for both himself and Zac, who still wore his footman's livery.

While Leopold, Mika and the children waited with the carriages outside the small haberdashery, the tailor displayed a selection of breeches and topcoats made of various fabrics, including silk, cotton, linen, wool and leather. He also carried a selection of men's purses, which Zac and Sky thought would be in keeping with their new outfits.

The guys decided that in order to meld with all levels of English society, it would be wise for one of them to be dressed as a common man while the other dressed as a gentleman, though without any element that may make them stand out in a crowd. After a quick game of "rock-paper-scissors" – a game that the tailor had obviously never seen – Sky won the right to purchase the more expensive gentleman's attire.

Thus accoutred, they paid for their new clothes and purses and secured their electronics within.

Leopold and Mika smiled and clapped when the two emerged from the shop. Holding his new black tricorne hat, Zac took a deep dramatic bow, looking resplendent in a chocolate-brown woolen waistcoat with matching breeches and a tan-coloured silk shirt, frilled at the cuff. Sky followed Zac out, looking less happy in his labourer apparel: a dark grey waistcoat, grey, plain linen shirt and tan breeches.

Despite winning at the game, Sky had convinced his friend to "take the better clothes, for a change." He felt that his friend had played the servant for long enough on this adventure.

As she sat on the carriage, looking up and down the dirty street, Mika remembered how she hated London. She preferred to be on the road, where personal hygiene was easier. To her, London was the place where dirty people lived – washing only twice a year! As she saw now on her way to Southwark, people relied on public fountains to bathe. But her family had to be here, unfortunately. She understood that, and she loved and trusted her husband.

The motley procession arrived at the main gate to the Southwark fairgrounds. The fair itself had closed down three years ago. Tavern keepers had replaced the vendors, who had hawked their goods at the famous fair every September since 1550.

Leopold and Mika got off the wagon to stretch their legs and to speak with one of the tavern keepers, who had been seconded to work the gate. His job was to collect a fee for the right to camp on the fairgrounds. He also conducted a head count of campers and assessed any potential animal acts on the spot. Acts that he permitted inside would then be further reviewed by a committee.

The gatekeeper told them that there were still show times available: bear-baiting took place every day of the week except Sunday, the Lord's Day, which was decreed a day of rest. Despite this, a show of another sort was available on Sunday.

Behind the wagon sat Sky and Zac in the Phaeton. They watched as the gatekeeper walked slowly around Leopold's wagon, scratching his beard.

"So, you say you've got a bear in there for the baiting, eh?"

"Zat's right." Leopold crossed his big arms. "He's had some success."

"Let's have a peek at 'im, then."

Leopold shook his head, "I vouldn't, if I vere you. He doesn't like to be disturbed before breakfast." He looked at Mika for support. She nodded toward the gatekeeper.

"Well, 'tis my job to check all the animal acts, so I need to see 'im." The man approached the covered wagon, grabbed the tarpaulin that covered the cage, and with one quick motion, threw back the tarp.

There was a tremendous roar, which startled the horses and the people. The gatekeeper had unfortunately chosen the corner where the great Brummbär was dozing, dreaming of his next meal. The bear turned as he roared, thrusting a massive paw out between the bars of the cage.

The gatekeeper had time only to take half a step back, but that half step saved his life. Brummbär's claws knocked the tricorne off his head and ripped through his topcoat. The man flew backward, landing on his rear in a cloud of dust directly in front of Leopold and Mika.

The man, still in shock, remained on the ground where he had landed, "Does he have a name?"

"He does," Leopold helped the man to his feet and handed him his hat.

"And what would that be?" asked the gatekeeper, dusting off his hat.

"He is called. . . " Leopold paused, anticipating the man's response. He looked at Sky, Zac and Mika before saying, "Brummbär."

"Brummbär," the man repeated quietly, "The great Brummbär ..." he inspected his torn coat and walked back to his post at the gate. "He'll do." He pointed behind him without bothering to turn. "You can camp over there, by the bear-garden. Come see me later to set up a show time."

As Mika set up camp with the help of Zac and Sky, Leopold went back to meet with the gatekeeper. He selected a show time on Saturday, a day of promise as more workers had the day off. And it provided the show organizers a full week to advertise.

The bill went out, tacked up at public notice boards and distributed to businesses throughout central London and south of the river:

> *"This is to give notice to all gentlemen gamesters, and others, that on this present Saturday is a match to be fought by Brummbär, a bear of some repute, baited against a number of dogs, for a guinea, to be spent. Five let-goes out of hand are planned. Also on the playbill is rat-baiting and a cockfight, so bring your finest gamecock. The prize for the winner is a large pink sow and ten piglets. To begin exactly at ten of the clock, with the bear-baiting at two of the clock."* [8]

Performers camped in the field adjacent to the bear-garden, so Leopold and his family selected a site close to a big oak tree, joining the merchants, hawkers and other vagabonds who had assembled. As part of Leopold's entourage, the young men were allowed to camp in the field directly beside his camp.

The first task for Zac and Sky was to pull a huge tarpaulin over the Phaeton and secure it with ropes and spikes at the four corners, thereby hiding the vehicle they had stolen. The six horses were corralled nearby with those of the other travellers.

Their second task was to bury their purses. They still had a king's ransom between the two of them, and carrying that amount of money to a raucous bear-garden did not seem wise. Zac looked at Sky, then at the oak tree and nodded.

---

8 Adapted from "The Gentleman's Magazine", Vol. CCLXX, January to June 1891

The bushes around the tree provided sufficient cover for one of them to dig while the other kept watch.

They buried all but a few coins. When done, Sky used a stick to scrape the dried moss off a large rock in the shape of a cross.

∞

31

SKY WOKE TO THE sound of the tolling of the bells of St. Paul's Cathedral. He had heard the bells chime before, but this chime – a higher tone – had been rung for the 8:00 a.m. Sunday church service.

With no suitable trees in the city, Leopold's family had brought with them enough "bender" branches for two tents. Sky and Zac slept in one beside the family in the other, the oak tree providing shade for much of the day.

Emerging from the tent into the coolness of the morning, Sky could easily see across the river the silver dome and tower of the cathedral, gleaming in the morning sun. The tallest structure in the city, St. Paul's was built on Ludgate Hill, the highest point in the City of London. Sky recognized its majesty from books and Google images, even from this vantage point south of the River Thames.

Sky and Zac had less than a week to "look for work" before the bear-baiting performance on Saturday. While the seeking of employment could act to excuse them from attending the bear-baiting, they both felt obliged to be present for Leopold and his family. They were, however, not looking forward to the anticipated brutality of the upcoming show.

Sky told Zac about Constable Leddy and the Bow Street Runners. Anxious to see the city, Zac gladly agreed to go with Sky to the constabulary on Bow Street. It should be easy to find, as Leddy had described it as being "just across

Castle Street from Pott's Vinegar Manufactory." They hoped that both of them could join Leddy on his rounds.

They bade goodbye to Leo and his family, who were just rising to face another day. Rather than the lengthy walk via the bridge, the two chose to take a "wherry boat" across the Thames; a more pricey option. But, if they were to walk with Leddy on his rounds, they were going to have to get there on time and conserve some energy on their way.

The boat was rowed expertly through the crowded harbour by two grizzled wherrymen with long oars. The wherry was about 22 feet long, and narrow – just four feet wide amidships. It carried Zac, Sky and three other passengers, all of whom held on tightly to the gunnels through the choppy waters.

They arrived at the constabulary shortly before the pre-arranged time, and were pleasantly surprised to meet Leddy at the entrance in his "plain clothes," making his way to work. Sky introduced Zac to Leddy, and asked if he and Zac could join Leddy on his rounds.

"I'll ask His Worship about Zac now. He should be in his office. Pray take a seat over there and wait for me. I'll be about 15 minutes." Leddy motioned to a nearby bench.

Leddy came skipping down the steps some 20 minutes later, wearing his police blues, his top hat and a smile. He simply said, "Let's be off!" confirming that Zac was able to join him and Sky on his rounds.

As Leddy walked along, he said, "You're in for a treat today, lads. The wise Justice of the Peace has ordered constables to provide to him the names of people who are gamblers, profane swearers and cursers; and those who work today, on the Sabbath. We'll visit a few businesses and knock on the doors to ensure that the Lord's Peace is being upheld. The first order of business, however, is to execute this warrant issued by the J.P." Leddy withdrew an addressed envelope from his breast pocket and slapped it against his thigh as he walked.

Zac couldn't resist. "So, people can't work today – Sunday – but you're working?"

Leddy furrowed his brow at the newcomer. "Constables are the exception… and clergymen!"

Leddy explained that the Runners could arrest anyone guilty of a crime, whether petty or serious, including vagrants and the "idle and disorderly." "Like that one there," Leddy pointed to a heap of dirty clothes on top of the roof of a shed in a refuse-filled alleyway. Neither Zac nor Sky had noticed that the heap was actually a sleeping man.

Leddy prodded the heap with his baton. The heap groaned and rolled over. Leddy growled, "This one is quite drunk; he's no threat. How he crawled up there, God only knows. Maybe he was thrown up there. But, we gotta take him in off the street. He can sleep it off in a cell. Help me get him off the roof."

The roof was high enough to present a challenge for Zac and Sky. There was a lot of garbage strewn about, but nothing firm to stand on. It was then that Leddy showed them the usefulness of his reinforced top hat. Removing the hat, he placed it beside the shed and stood on it! He was then able to grab the man, now somewhat conscious, and drag him to the edge, where Sky and Zac caught him as Leddy pulled him over the edge.

They nudged and shook the drunk until he regained semi-consciousness with a squawk. He could almost walk, so Leddy took his arm around his neck and led him back, legs a-wobble, to the constabulary. Sky and Zac helped with the awkward burden when Leddy needed a break.

To keep the drunk conscious and walking, Leddy peri-odically planted an elbow in the man's ribs. Each time, the man cried out in pain and Leddy grinned.

"He's drunk enough gin to float a king's ship, I'd wager."

∞

38

FINALLY, SATURDAY DAWNED BRIGHT and sunny and the crowds began to fill the Southwark grounds. A slight breeze from the south kept the festive banners billowing toward London, helping to keep the stench of the city away.

The place bustled with activity. Some guests arrived with "learned" pigs, which performed fantastic feats of arithmetic, played cards and even told fortunes. Others arrived carrying their caged gamecock, specially bred and sporting attached metal spurs on their legs for the morning cockfight. The cockfight was to be held in a specially-built pen, from which the birds (or anything else) could not escape.

Prior to the cockfight, another event took place in that pen: a trained Old English bulldog sat waiting patiently, his nostrils flaring as a familiar scent approached. Throughout the surrounding stands, the large, raucous audience was placing bets. They were betting how long it would take the dog to kill 100 rats.

The dog's interest was piqued when eight men carrying four large crates approached the pen. The bulldog strutted back and forth, watching as the men positioned the crates on the top of the pen wall. With a nod from the foreman, the crates were simultaneously opened and the squeaking contents were dumped into the pen. A few of the rats managed to stay inside the upturned boxes, but these were quickly thrown in to join the others. The rats squeaked and scurried for cover but found none, other than momentary cover under other rats; an undulating wave of fur and rubbery tails.

The dog got to work, teeth flashing and head shaking. The audience stood to watch, cheering on the dog, then cheering on the rats, depending upon their bet.

The winning bet? Nine minutes and 30 seconds.

The much-anticipated main event, however, was the bear-baiting in the afternoon. The fighting was to be done in the bear-garden, which was essentially a round pit, surrounded by a high fence. Tiered seating surrounded the pit for spectators who paid a penny for the bottom tier or two pennies for the higher tiers. A sturdy post was set in the ground near the edge of the pit and the bear would be chained to it, either by the leg or neck. Spectators would wager on whether it would be the dogs or the bear that would survive the vicious fight. Leopold and his family were praying for Brummbär. He was their meal ticket.

Wee Willy did not profess to thoroughly enjoy watching bear-baiting; he associated it with the lower classes. Apart from the brutish nature of the entertainment, he felt that poor men were wasting their money at Southwark. He attended regularly though, because a friend of his worked there.

Maurice Morris, a successful tavern keeper, enjoyed an intimate relationship with the young Lord Mansfield. He, like Willy, enjoyed dressing in any type of finery, men's or women's. He had recently attended the Mansfield ball dressed as a courtesan. He was delighted when Willy had entered on the *palanquin* and even more delighted, albeit a tad jealous, when he had kissed the startled footman.

Consequently, William III had arrived early on that Saturday, as he had many times before. He had arranged to meet Maurice under the same large oak tree where they had met before. Maurice was uncharacteristically late, so Willy found himself snooping around.

Most campsites were occupied, as campers kept at least one of their party there to keep a wary eye on their belongings. Willy, of course, had no reason to steal anything; he had everything he could possibly desire, except perhaps Maurice.

Since his birthday masquerade, he had been on the lookout for the stolen Phaeton. That is why the only covered carriage in the field was of particular interest to him this bright Saturday morning. The good weather meant that carriage owners need not cover their vehicle. In any case, most never bothered to. One owner, or perhaps thief, apparently thought it was in his best interest to cover his.

Whistling casually, hands clasped unthreateningly behind his back, Willy approached the covered vehicle. He looked around furtively, noticing that a few campers stared at him.

Undaunted, he untied one of four ropes that secured the tarpaulin. He then crouched down and pulled back the tarp to reveal a magnificent Phaeton – the stolen carriage! Willy gasped, his hand covering his mouth.

Walking toward Willy from a distance, Maurice saw his friend throw back the tarp. The look on Willy's face told him that something was amiss.

When Maurice got to where Willy stood, the two men hugged, but did not – could not – kiss in such a public place. Willy explained why he had uncovered the Phaeton and that he still needed to find the horses that had pulled it. A short walk to the corral revealed many candidate horses, but Willy told Maurice that he had no way to identify the four stolen steeds.

"This means that those two witches might be here – Zachary and his friend from the masquerade. Did you see his friend's colourful outfit, Maurice? Outrageous!"

Maurice placed his hand on Willy's arm. "Don't worry about that now. You can tell me all about it soon. Come, I have a place where we can have a quiet coze before the show."

They re-tied the tarpaulin and smiled at the few people who continued to watch. The two men then boldly walked arm in arm toward the buildings that surrounded the bear-garden.

Meanwhile, Leopold was meeting with the dog owner and the event organizer. The men agreed that four dogs, Old English bulldogs, would be released five times to attack the bear. The first attack (or "let-go") would be with the youngest dogs. The dogs would be changed for each subsequent attack, with the most experienced ones used in the final release. The performance, it was agreed, would continue until the bear was exhausted.

Returning to the bear-garden just before 2 of the clock, Leopold asked Sky and Zac to help him prepare the bear for his fight; yet another for his very life. The two young men were hesitant, as could be expected, to enter the pit with the bear.

Zac said to Sky, "That bear is huge, man! Are you sure you wanna do this? It's like my dad always said: 'The only good reason to ride a bull is to meet a nurse'."

Sky ignored both Zac's question and his joke, choosing to follow Leopold into the bear-garden through a gate in the high fence. Reluctantly, Zac followed. He could hear dogs barking, not far off. He asked Leopold, "Can Brummbär hear the dogs?"

"Aye, but he's heard zem many times before. He seems to like a challenge."

As the crowd looked on in anticipation, Leopold and Zac held the bear with a specially-made pole tethered around a stout post, while Sky secured the chain to the bear post. They secured the bear, not by his neck but by his leg, so that he could move more easily.

The stands were almost full as the bear-baiters exited the enclosure and the last few stragglers filed in under the hot afternoon sun. Most of the attendees were men, middle-aged or younger. There were a few wide-eyed children. Maurice led Willy to their reserved seats midway up the wooden bleachers.

The breeze had died down, subjecting the crowds to the full stench of the city across the river. Flies buzzed everywhere, but especially around Brummbär. They relentlessly landed on his eyes, ears and snout. Long ago, he had given up shaking his great head to momentarily rid himself of the bugs. Now, they feasted undisturbed.

Some bear owners also owned the fighting dogs. These owners usually chose to remove the teeth of their bear by smashing them with a hammer, and removing the claws by ripping them out with pliers. This barbaric act took many men to complete but, they felt, would make it more fair for the dogs; thereby extending the lives of both bear and dog.

Brummbär, on the other hand, still had most of his teeth and claws. Leopold had no dogs, so tavern keepers were aware of the bear's physical attributes, and through word of mouth, his tenacity and stamina. He was one of those bears unfortunate enough to have long and bloody careers, becoming stars in their own right.

But, even the renowned Brummbär could not defeat his greatest enemy: time. The bear was aging.

The crowd roared its approval when the fight announcer entered the bear-garden, carrying a huge speaking-trumpet. He swung the bullhorn to his mouth and swivelled from side to side as he bellowed, "Welcome, one and all! Today, we will witness the great Brummbär, a bear of some renown, baited against a number of dogs. Five let-goes are planned. Have you placed your bets? I hope so because the show is about to begin! I give to you... Brummbär!"

He motioned toward the beast, then bowed and walked through the gate in the surrounding fence. Again, the crowd roared and collectively sat forward on the benches. Leopold, Sky and Zac watched nervously from behind the fence.

Mika remained at the camp with the children. Like some of her neighbours at the camp, she had watched as Willy and Maurice discovered the stolen Phaeton. Like her neighbours, she didn't know what to make of it. She would be sure to tell Leopold when he returned.

Brummbär was leaning against the fence, panting and trying to get out of the merciless sun. His left rear leg was tied to the post. He seemed to have about 15 feet of chain to work with. The dogs were kept behind a small wooden gate that opened upward. Their barking could almost be heard over the audience of about 300 cheering, blood-thirsty onlookers.

The noise of the audience, the barking dogs and the growling bear was excruciatingly loud when the dog gate was slowly raised. Some of the children watching covered their ears; others covered their eyes. The slow opening was designed to increase the fear of the bear, the blood lust of the dogs and the excitement of the crowd. The first two dogs scratched at the dirt to clear space to get into the pit. The gate fully open, four young muscled dogs charged, teeth bared, through a cloud of dust, toward their prey.

With an opening roar, Brummbär stood on his back legs, towering over his assailants. He swatted the first two unfortunate dogs unceremoniously against the fence; the first one way and the second, the other. Both dogs lay still, blood pooling underneath one. It didn't move again. The other stirred, but only enough to sit, shaking and whimpering, to watch the remainder of the fight.

The other two dogs fared better, for a time.

One bold dog pinned the bear by the nose and tugged, pistoning with his powerful rear leg muscles. His partner bit away at the bear's huge neck. The bruin shook his broad head in an attempt to dislodge his foe. It did not, but it did break the dogs' teeth. With the snap of the teeth, the dog lost its grip and turned away, yelping. With a roar, Brummbär turned to the dog's partner, and his jaws now free, bit him on the neck – taking hold and shaking him until the dog's lifeless body bobbed like a ragdoll.

The first let-go completed, the dog-handler entered the pit to retrieve the two living dogs, such as they were. The crowd booed, wanting the bear to finish off the wounded dogs.

The second, third and fourth let-goes, as you might imagine, went progressively worse for the bear. The shouts of encouragement for the dogs seemed to grow with each let-go. Leopold could see that his bear was exhausted. Soon, the animal would suffer irreparable harm. Perhaps he already had.

Leopold left Zac and Sky, running around the enclosure to where the event organizer stood watching. Seeing the huge German approach, the organizer turned his head slightly, and with an almost imperceptible nod, had three large, rough-looking men stand threateningly behind him.

Undaunted, Leopold screamed, "Stop ze fight! Ze bear is spent. Stop ze fight now!" The German's large finger prodded the man's chest. The bodyguards took a collective step forward.

Despite Leopold's protestations, the organizer insisted that he "had promised five let-goes, not four!"

Leopold knew now that his protest had come too late. In a final act of defiance, he placed his large hands on the organizer's chest and pushed him back, hard, into the arms of the three thugs. All four men were thrown backward over a row of boxes.

Before they could decide how to react, Leopold was gone.

As each group of dogs was more experienced and trained than the last, the once-magnificent animal was exhausted as the final let-go was about to begin. Part of Brummbär's pink tongue had been bitten off; the remainder hung out of his open jaw, dripping blood. Half of the dirt floor of the pit was stained purple and red. This held down some dust, thereby improving the view for the spectators.

The scent of new, barking dogs seemed to make the beast realize his fate. He plunked himself down on the purple dirt, no strength left to move, other than to raise his battered head.

If you ask a child to make a noise like a bear, the child will roar. Bears do roar, when enraged, but they can make a number of sounds. They can make a purring sound when content, and a coughing sound when frightened. In his long life, Brummbär had purred just a little and roared a lot.

Now, for the first time, he coughed.

The gate was raised.

∞

39

THE AUDIENCE LONG GONE, Zac and Sky watched somberly as workers secured ropes and pulled the hulking lifeless mass of Brummbär out of the bear-garden. Leo couldn't watch. He sat on a log with his back turned, his head in his hands.

Finally, he made his "BRRRT!" noise and slowly rose to his feet and dragged himself back to the family camp. Sky and Zac followed in a funereal procession.

Back at camp, Mika knew what had happened as soon as she saw her husband's tear-lined face. Sky placed his hand on Vassi's shoulder and Zac took little Nico in his arms as Mika and Leopold hugged, crying silently together.

The loss of the bear was devastating. Getting another was out of the question. They had no idea what they would do.

In the wagon, Leopold reached to the back of the highest shelf. He pulled out a half-full bottle of gin, swirling its contents. His last.

That would have to do.

40

DURING THE FOURTH LET-GO, Wee Willy stood up and screened his eyes from the glaring sun. Maurice thought that his friend was finally seeing how much fun bear-baiting could be. But no, he seemed to be looking beyond the action, in the direction of the fence on the opposite side of the pit.

"They're there! They're there!" Willy screamed, yes, like a girl. But, he resisted the urge to point.

The crowd roared as the dogs scored another point.

"Who's there? Where?" asked Maurice, having to yell in the din.

"There! The witches, the footman Zachary and his strange friend. They're standing behind the fence. See? They've changed their clothing, of course, but I recognize that handsome footman."

Maurice remembered only the footman, who Willy had kissed. Looking down – yes, that could be him. The young man standing beside him had curly hair, whereas the footman's accomplice at the masquerade had had his hair slicked down.

"Well, it's them, both of them!" Willy exclaimed. Then, quietly to himself, "What to do, what to do?"

Maurice heard his friend's lamentation. "You could contact the Bow Street Runners," he suggested. "They'd come and pick them up for the young – and charming – Lord Mansfield."

"Oh, the Runners don't have jurisdiction here in Southwark!"

Just as the crowd roared again, Maurice had to yell again. "My dear man, nobody has jurisdiction here in Southwark! Send a runner to the constabulary. Your father knows the J.P. personally, does he not? You have no time to send a message by Royal Mail, you duck!"

"A runner to bring the Runners – yes, yes, of course," Willy shrugged.

He opened his valise and wrote a note on a sheet of fine vellum paper, under the letterhead of Sir William Mansfield. Signing and folding it, he looked around and spotted a lithe young man two rows up, who looked in need of some money after a long run. He beckoned the young man over, briefly spoke to him and handed him the letter. Pocketing the letter, the man quickly made his way through the crowd and disappeared through the gate.

Constables McCracken and Leddy were dispatched to Southwark by special permission of the Justice of the Peace, who knew he had to act when he saw who had signed the hand-delivered letter. He was already short of men, so two would have to suffice.

They arrived near the dinner hour in the waning light, and met the younger Lord Mansfield and his friend just outside the bear-garden. The young man who accompanied them was given a guinea for his troubles, as promised. He left, with a smile for the generous payment and with a bow to Wee Willy. Perhaps not a bow – more of a curtsey as a final impertinence to the effeminate aristocrat.

The younger Mansfield took no notice. He briefed the constables on the scene at the masquerade ball: the strange talisman, the pinging sound, the theft and flight of the Phaeton and the fruitless search for the escapees – fruitless, until today.

"There's more," said Willy, thinking about Zac's strange accent, the hidden pouch and the light in the darkness where there were no candles. "But believe me, you need to take them into custody. They are witches!"

McCracken retorted, "That's for the Crown to decide! Take us to them."

Earlier, while their runner had gone, Willy and Maurice had stalked the witches back to their camp, so they knew where they were. Willy had paid another camper a generous amount to keep an eye on the two and to report if they moved.

All the members of Leopold's group had gone to bed already, except for Leopold, who sat looking soulfully into the campfire. An empty bottle was propped against the log he was sitting on. Startled as four men approached, he dropped his mug and stood up, as if to challenge them. This must be the event organizer returning with his henchmen...

McCracken immediately diffused the situation, waving his hand in a downward motion. "Hi there. Constables McCracken and Leddy here, from the Bow Street Runners. This is Lord Mansfield and..." McCracken had forgotten the other man's name.

"Maurice, just Maurice will do," Maurice interjected.

Having not spent a lot of time in central London, Leopold had never seen a Bow Street Runner before. But he was not going to argue, given the official-looking uniforms.

McCracken explained that Lord Mansfield had called them out on suspicion of witchcraft by two young men in Leopold's acquaintance. They were here to take the men into custody, pending a trial.

"Is this your tent?" asked McCracken, as he pointed to the first bender tent.

"It is mine, yes."

"Well, do you know where they are?" McCracken asked, while staring in an obvious way at the second bender tent.

Getting no immediate response, the officer prodded, "What say you, man?"

Leopold was speaking loudly now. "Vell, zey're supposed to be here, but you know young men. Zey are probably out sniffing around for girls. Vhy don't you try zat campsite over zere?" He pointed toward a neighbouring campsite. "Zey showed some interest in a couple of young lasses zere. You may vant to interview ze girls yourselves. BRRRT!"

McCracken hesitated, having never heard a man make a noise quite like that. He knew better. "No, man, we will check this tent first," pointing at the Zac and Sky's tent. The constables moved simultaneously toward it.

At that moment, the back of the tent seemed to explode and come tumbling down in a heap. Zac and Sky, in their attempt to escape out back, had brought it down on top of themselves. The canvas tent continued to gyrate, the men's legs and arms inside flailing helplessly.

All the noise had woken Mika and Vassi, while Nico continued to sleep. Leopold took Mika in his arms and watched.

The movement under the fabric seemed to stop. "We have batons at the ready, so come out with your hands up!" shouted Leddy, a hand on his baton. Other campers, awoken, slowly stepped forward into the firelight, clutching bedding and watching intently.

Finally, Zac and Sky emerged from the fallen tent. Sky tripped over a pole and had to be held up by Zac.

Leddy stepped closer, his mouth open. "Hey, it's you two. I cannot believe my eyes! You are the witches?"

"No, we're not witches. We're just... far away from home," Sky said, his head hanging down. "Maybe you could put in a good word for us, Constable Leddy."

"Well, I'd like to, Sky, but it looks to me like you just tried to escape from under our noses. That don't look good, lad. We have to take you in now. Say your goodbyes."

Zac and Sky, still disbelieving what was happening, said goodbye to Vassi and Mika. They hugged them and thanked them for their friendship and help. Sobbing, Vassi ran into the tent.

They turned to Leopold, who had had a terrible day – the worst in his life. Zac placed his hand on the big man's shoulder and said, "Goodbye, Leo. You helped us when we needed it the most. Thank you very much."

As the constables reached for their handcuffs at their belts, Sky embraced Leopold. No further words were needed. Sky found that none were possible, at any rate.

As he was hugging him, Sky quickly stuffed a small piece of paper into the pocket of the big man's breeches. Leopold felt the movement but his face remained steadfast.

McCracken stepped forward, carrying the cast-iron set of handcuffs. He approached Zac, who extended his arms. The constable secured the cuffs around Zac's wrists and placed him under arrest by the Crown on suspicion of witchcraft.

"Your turn, Sky," said Leddy with a sigh, displaying his set of handcuffs.

Shackled, Zac and Sky were led out of the camp. Before disappearing from sight, Sky turned to see the huge figure of Leopold, his arm around Mika. A few steps further, Sky thought he heard "BRRRT!"

∞

41

ZAC AND SKY SPENT the next fortnight in separate, dank cold cells in the Tower of London. *Only days ago*, thought Sky, Constable Leddy had shown him the outside of the tower. It seemed like months ago. Sky never dreamed that he'd see the inside, other than perhaps as part of a tour group from Canada.

All their personal effects had been removed, including what remained of their money along with the chargers, the smartwatches and cords – and Sky's Mickey Mouse pocket watch. As prisoners, they were kept in their windowless cells the entire time. They were fed twice a day from a tray passed through a slot in the solid wood door. The door remained shut for their entire stay. There was a chamber pot, but no candle.

Sky felt as powerless as Superman with a slab of Kryptonite sewn into his cape. The dark cell was excruciatingly uncomfortable and the bench was not wide enough for a bed, so he curled up in the corner where the stench of urine was less. With no way to tell time, the hours extended into days.

Sky passed the time by sleeping, mostly, but also by exercising regularly: doing push-ups and using the bench to hold his feet for sit-ups. Down the corridor, Zac was also exercising, but he also lifted the bench for arm curls.

When the cell doors were finally opened, both men were disoriented and thoroughly disillusioned. Both were relieved and heartened by the sight of the other in the corridor, though that was quickly tempered by the guard's command: "No talking!"

Despite their physical activity, the act of walking was, at first, a challenge for the two. The early morning sunlight stung their eyes and momentarily blinded them as they left the Tower.

They were taken by horse-drawn tumbrel in the early morning to the Bow Street Magistrate's Court for their much-anticipated trial. A witch trial had become a rare event indeed, and Londoners lined the streets, craning their necks to watch the procession. Designed to provide a clear view of prisoners, the tumbrel had only a wooden railing on all four sides. Zac, Sky and two guards were the only occupants of the slow-moving cart.

Upon arrival, there was much jostling both outside and inside the courtroom as the accused, their hands shackled behind their backs, were shuffled to the front of the court-room and into the prisoner's box.

The bailiff shouted, "All rise!" as Sir John 'Blind Beak' Fielding, magistrate, appeared from a side door. Standing, the audience watched as he slowly made his way, unassisted, to his seat.

Collectively, the crowd sat and began talking amongst themselves, the noise gradually increasing until they practi-cally had to shout to make themselves heard.

Fielding, who had only just taken his own seat, quickly grew annoyed. Despite his immediate calls for order, the audience remained boisterous and loud. In fact, the crowd seemed to be getting louder, not quieter. The crowd outside was pushing to get a glimpse of the happenings inside. Spectators nearest the entrance were being jostled and shoved. There was no order in this court.

The oddities of this particular case had spread rapidly through the city. The strange defendants who wore strange clothes and bore strange items; their escape from a masquerade ball in a stolen vehicle; their discovery at a bearbaiting in Southwark – these tidbits had brought people out in droves and were now being discussed both outside and within the courtroom, where whispers had blossomed into loud, animated conversations.

Fielding summoned the bailiff and they conferred quietly under the din. With a nod in the direction of the bailiff, Magistrate Fielding slammed down his gavel, breaking its handle. The shattered head hit the wooden floor and skittered to a stop in the middle of the room.

The room suddenly became quiet as attendees wondered what the blind magistrate was going to throw next.

Most were able to hear him bellow, "Enough! Enough! Obviously, order cannot be had here in this court. Thankfully, another venue is available, one that has been enclosed to limit the influence of *disrespectful* spectators."

Boos and catcalls ensued.

"These proceedings will be moved to the Old Bailey, to reconvene tomorrow morning at half past 8 of the clock."

With a wave of his arm in the direction of the prisoner's box, he commanded, "Bailiff, remove the prisoners."

And with that pronouncement, the magistrate steamed out of the courtroom. The prisoners were removed and returned to the Tower of London to wait yet another day.

∞

42

DAWN BROKE WITH THE promise of another hot day; perhaps the hottest day of the year. Again, the tumbrel rolled through crowded streets. This time, however, it rolled west to the Old Bailey, the Central Criminal Court of England and Wales, so named for the street upon which it has stood since the late 1500s.

A few of the onlookers outside the Old Bailey were better-prepared this morning, bringing rotten fruit and garbage to toss at the witches as they were led off the tumbrel and through the entrance door to the one and only courtroom.

The accused were led to stand at the dock, facing the witness box, where witnesses for both the prosecution and defence were to testify. There was no need for them to wait in the prisoners' quarters in the basement as other prisoners throughout the day would do, as they were the first case of the day; the queue of cases having been modified to accommodate the witch trial.

Above the dock hung a looking glass – a mirror, carefully angled to reflect daylight onto the youthful faces of the accused. In this way, jurors and others could better see their facial expressions in order to ascertain the validity of their testimony. Also overhead, a large, hand-carved sounding board was ready to amplify their voices.

Lawyers, bailiffs and clerks of the court sat at a large mahogany table in the middle of the room; their down-turned, bewigged heads seldom rising from the copious notes they were taking. As had become the practice, the magistrate had ordered a clerk to spread nosegays[9] and aromatic herbs around the room to mask the stench of all present, and to prevent infection. Typhus, or "gaol fever," had taken the lives of two judges and the Lord Mayor not long ago.

As in most jury trials since the Middle Ages, there was no defence lawyer. The defendants were expected to refute the evidence presented against them. Needless to say, this provided the prosecution with a huge advantage. The evidence against the young foreigners was mounting and seemed, at this time, irrefutable.

Prisoners fortunate enough to not be convicted to death were subject to many alternative punishments. One of these was branding; so two wrist irons for restraining convicts' arms were placed ominously at the centre of the table: a subtle reminder that law-abiding citizens don't get burned.

The jurors sat together in stalls on the right of the accused. From this optimal vantage point, they were able to consult each other and efficiently arrive at a verdict, without leaving the room.

The spectators' gallery was behind and just above the jurors. Unlike at the Bow Street Magistrates' Court, a fee was charged for those wanting entry to the gallery. Today, there was no problem filling all the seats – and, at a higher price to match demand. This also improved the quality of spectator: those who could afford to attend were, by nature, more genteel – and better behaved.

In an era defined by the marked differences between rich and poor, one of its contradictory characteristics was that all social classes could attend a masquerade, bear-baiting, play, court ceremony or public execution.

Nevertheless, today the gallery was mostly comprised of those who could afford such a self-indulgent pleasure; others

---

9 Tied bunches of fragrant flowers

attended because they had a compelling reason to be there. Despite her reluctance to re-enter a courtroom, Helena was present, along with her Uncle Jack and Caramel.

Also in the gallery sat a rather timid-looking man, dressed in an old-fashioned waistcoat and breeches that seemed too big for his thin build. Not wanting to miss a thing, he had arrived early and secured a front row seat. But when a young woman entered and sat next to him, the man cleared his throat nervously, quickly rose and found another seat at the back of the gallery.

Sir William, Lady Rachel and Wee Willy sat with the Lord Mayor and the Sheriff of London. The Mayor, who was entitled to sit on the judge's bench, elected to sit with his friend, Sir William, in the witness' bench.

The London press was, of course, in attendance to ensure that readers received a full report. The press corps included journalists from Ireland, Scotland, Wales and France. Journalists toyed with headlines for the next edition; headlines like "Witch Hunt not Dead Yet!" and "Tyburn to be Readied for Witches."

The door to the judge's chambers opened and the bailiff shouted, "All rise!"

Amid the clamour of everyone rising from their seats, Magistrate John Fielding made his practised and efficient way to his bench. He stood at his seat for a time, seemingly getting a sense of the room, before folding his robes under himself to sit.

The bailiff then read the charges to the prisoners and the magistrate asked both to plead to the charge: "How do you plead?"

First Zac, then Sky responded, "Not guilty, Your Honour."

∞

43

FOLLOWING PROTOCOL, THE PROSECUTION began the proceedings with a summary of behaviour on the part of the co-accused to be "in keeping with that of witches in the practice of witchcraft". This behaviour included speaking with an unrecognizable accent. Counsel assured the judges and jury that the accents were not of European origin and in fact, no one from the Americas spoke in this fashion either.

Counsel contended, "The 'accent' then is perhaps not an accent at all. Rather, it can be used as an incantation while conjuring a spell. Of this, we will all need to be mindful if and when the accused are cross-examined."

The pompous demeanour of this particular prosecutor belied his excitement; that is, he was pumped by the prospect of prosecuting witches. Recently called to the bar, the young man wore his black ensemble – robe, waistcoat, silk stockings and buckled shoes – with considerable and unadulterated pride. A guilty verdict, he was keenly aware, would bolster his career as well as public interest in the state of witchcraft and the legal profession. Not that he anticipated being short of work. There continued a steady flow of legal work in London, a city that was only now developing a police force. Witch trials served to provide much public amusement, and, based on their rich history, usually ended with a condemnation of the accused. He anticipated a relatively easy conviction here today.

Easy, apart from the heat of the day, that is. He was sweating profusely. He could feel it run down the middle of his back. To dry his face and neck, he held a handkerchief that was already too wet to be of much use. His grey, braided horsehair wig was criminally hot as he stood, with some flourish and sweeping of his robe, to dramatically address the courtroom.

"Your Honour, the Crown requires only a single witness at this time." There were no witnesses for the defence included on the docket, but cross-examination of the co-accused by the Crown was noted as being possible.

The Crown's witness was called to the stand.

Lord William Mansfield was a well-known figure throughout London's elite. He bore a striking figure as he strode across the room and up the three stairs to the witness box.

The prosecutor failed to subdue a smile. Lord Mansfield's very presence as a witness against the co-accused held significant influence on all those present. After Sir William took the oath, the prosecutor began.

"If your Lordship would please describe the clothes that the defendant, Zachary Burling, was wearing the day you met him."

Sir William answered each question with confidence. He provided details when it seemed necessary and was succinct when a short answer would do.

"Describe the noise made by the amulet worn upon Sky Sewell's wrist as they made their escape."

For the first time, Sir William seemed unsure of how to proceed in his answer. Not wishing to embarrass His Lordship, but knowing that a conviction was imminent, the prosecutor pressed his witness to emulate the actual noise. Reluctantly, Sir William mouthed a noise that may not have resembled the pinging sound that the smartwatch had made – but it was a funny noise made by making a funny face in this most serious of places. The onlookers in the courtroom were amused as Sir William stopped his noise-making. His face reddened.

His questioning complete, the counsellor thanked his witness with a pronounced nod that was closer to a bow. Sir William then left the box, still distressed for having had to make that ridiculous noise. As he made his way back to his seat beside the Lord Mayor, from somewhere in the back of the room came a loud "Ping, ping!"

The courtroom exploded in laughter. Even Rachel, sitting next to her father, had to cover her grin with a gloved hand.

Magistrate Fielding tapped his gavel on his desk. "Enough, enough! Continue with your summation, Counsellor."

The din subsided and the prosecutor began to slowly pace around the room. As he strolled, he summarized the damning evidence against Sky and Zac.

"Your Honour, I believe we have sufficient – indeed, damning – evidence to support the conviction of these two young men." He was thoroughly enjoying himself now. "In short, the charges and evidence are thus – " at this point he raised a finger to indicate the numerous pieces of damning information.

"Wearing strange clothes – some with *words* written thereupon – and footwear. Fleeing from the masquerade ball – and, later, from the *law*. Theft of a carriage and four horses…"

He was projecting his voice theatrically now, clearly relishing the stage. He reminded Sky of his history professor back home. *Who'd have thought his memory would ever make me feel nostalgic,* Sky mused as he attempted to remain calm.

"… Possession of matching amulet bracelets, and white boxes that cast forth a wicked and powerful light. Possession of a bizarre pocket watch that features an unfathomable creature depicted thereupon. Conjuring a *SPELL* – to use, if I may M'Lord, the word that the accused themselves used at the time – through the use of one amulet. Concealment of these very items. Theft of materials to conceal said items. And finally, though I repeat it, *attempted escape from police constables* at Southwark."

Almost out of fingers, the counsellor noted, "the aforementioned personal effects, now confiscated by the Crown, are displayed here on the table in the middle of the courtroom, with number placards for reference."

Fruitlessly wiping his brow again, counsel walked to a spot directly in front of the magistrate, where he concluded, "The evidence, it seems, is overwhelming and irrefutable. No further witnesses are called at this time. The co-accused are indeed witches. A suitable sentence is, in the mind of the Crown, death by hanging at Tyburn." He bowed his head in a deferential manner and made his way back to his seat.

There was a surge of noise throughout the courtroom. Magistrate Fielding nodded his bewigged head and turned, unseeing, in the direction of the jury. Sensing that Fielding was about to speak, the courtroom grew quiet. In the silence of that moment, a thin voice could be heard from the spectators' gallery: "Stop!" Henry Cavendish stepped from his seat in the back of the gallery to the railing at the front. He found himself directly beside the woman who had displaced him to the back row. He gulped and took two large steps away from her. He shouted, "They are N-NOT witches and I can p-prove it!" There was a general buzz throughout the room until the collective attention was focused on the man in charge. The blind magistrate tilted his head in a curious way. "Henry Cavendish, of all people!" he proclaimed. The courtroom buzzed again in astonishment.

Fielding continued, "You must have something substantial up your sleeve to make such a public spectacle of yourself! Bailiff, show Mr. Cavendish to the stand." Escorted by the bailiff, Henry made his way to the witness box, holding his tricorne as a symbolic shield in front, and taking small steps on spindly and no doubt shaking legs. With his hat, he carried a bulging burlap bag.

Although not a fellow of the scientific body, John Fielding had friends and associates at the Royal Society and had dined there in the past. One of those associates was Henry Cavendish. Although the magistrate did not know him well, he knew his distinctly stammering voice – a voice seldom heard, but one Fielding found to be worth listening to.

Sensing that the man had completed his laborious journey to the witness box, Fielding shouted, "The court recognizes Mr. Henry Cavendish, scientist!" Then, as if doubting his own abilities, he whispered something to the nearby bailiff, who whispered something back.

"Mr. Cavendish... Henry. What say you?"

By necessity, the courtroom was quiet to hear the soft-spoken scientist. "Lord, f-forgive my impertinence. I did not originally offer myself as a w-witness for the defence due to my trepidation at doing so. But, I stand before you now to prove to the court that these young men are n-not witches. They are indeed..." Stammering more than ever, Henry cleared his throat, "... t-travellers from the f-future!" The courtroom erupted.

Word of Henry's assertion travelled down the corridor and onto the streets, where thousands stood waiting for the verdict. Word literally travelled down the line and else-where, until all of London had heard that the witches were not witches at all – they were time travellers!

Most people were not convinced. Magistrate Fielding met the eruption with rapid and violent hammerings of his gavel on his desk. People were standing and shouting. Some were bent over, laughing. The bailiff and other court officers were rendered powerless. After a time, Fielding gave up hammering as chaos took over. He simply waited until he could finally be heard over the pandemonium.

Some six minutes having passed, he stood and raised his arms, his black robes waving like the wings of a bird about to take flight.

"Silence! Silence! Order in the courtroom now."

Correctly surmising that most in the gallery remained standing, he turned the full force of his knightly wrath upon them, pointing up in their general direction and shouting, "You there, yes you, sit DOWN!"

Feeling his wrath, the gallery obediently sat, and with them sat the others. The room grew quiet, then very quiet. All eyes returned to Henry Cavendish, who, to his credit, had not left his post.

Magistrate Fielding resumed control of his courtroom. "Cavendish, your impertinence is not from your obvious trepidation at speaking in this courtroom, but in making such an impossible assertion. I will give you five minutes to clarify what you mean, which is five minutes more than you deserve! But, like all of us herein, I am curious as to how the co-accused could be, as you assert, travellers from... the future. In Heaven's name, man, speak now! Your good name hangs in the balance."

Henry swallowed. "Lord, business occasioned me to walk on B-Bow Street some weeks ago. At that time, I was the victim of an urchin thief. I came to know of one of the accused, Sky Sewell, when Mr. Sewell not only caught the thief, but returned my p-purse to me intact." The courtroom buzzed at this; Henry Cavendish was known to be rich.

"He refused a generous reward, so I invited him for lunch at the Royal Society where, as you are aware, I am an elected fellow. We, Mr. Sewell and I, performed an electrical experiment for the society. His assistance was a ruse to prove my personal suspicion that Mr. Sewell is a time traveller from the future." Again, the room buzzed.

"The ruse was planned by myself and my associate, C-Clive Rock, who had related to me a story of his being accosted weeks ago by land pirates as he walked home from the Royal Society meeting. The thieves did not take his money, only his clothes – in order for one of the men to divest himself of his own." Henry let go of his tricorne only long enough to point a spindly finger toward Sky. "That thief was S-Sky Sewell."

Henry's statement was met with low and curious murmurs. This time they silenced themselves, clearly eager to hear what was to come next.

"As they switched clothes, Mr. Rock noticed a strange bracelet upon Mr. Sewell's wrist. That b-bracelet you see now before you." He pointed to the smartwatch on the mahogany table. "And, the shoes that were exchanged, I have them here with me." He opened the bag, reached in and pulled out Sky's red paisley Vans sneakers. Sky buried his head in his hands.

Henry opened the bag, "These are not the pointy-toed shoes of a w-witch, by Jupiter! They are of a future design, using materials from the f-future."

Murmurs swelled and quieted again as the murmurers needed to hear more.

"As you can see, the items of c-clothing that my c-colleague was forced to wear home that night are equally strange; not strange in the way of witchcraft, but in the way of advanced science!"

Henry pulled out and displayed the remaining items in the bag: the brown vest, the paisley shirt and finally, Sky's way-cool tie-dyed jeans. The scientist held the jeans in front of himself, showing the audience how the garment should be worn.

There were a few snickers.

"My scientific analysis confirms that the fabrics in these garments and footwear are comprised of materials unknown to any tailor or miller working today!"

He pulled the zipper of the jeans up and down, then again. He thought, and *this closing device is simply genius.*

Henry continued, louder now, "The k-kindness that Sky Sewell displayed when helping me after I was robbed leads me to believe that he was f-forced to join this band of thieves, against his will, and to switch clothes also against his will. That assertion was confirmed when I came upon the contents of his breeches pocket as he lay unconscious in my arms on the stage at the society." Henry shifted his feet.

"Mr. Sewell was in possession of a number of coins – coins that he could not possibly have stolen or wanted to c-counterfeit." The eccentric scientist reached into the pocket of his topcoat and pulled out a number of coins; coins that Sky had not yet missed.

He held them high. "These c-coins appear to be legal tender, minted by the Royal Mint. But, the years they display are…" he read the dates from each as he examined them. "1776, 1779, and 1781 – an incredulity to all of us living here in the Year of Our Lord 1766!"

The crowd gasped and murmured, heads moving from side to side. Sky glanced at Zac. Had Aunt Bea overlooked a detail when she secured the coinage? He hadn't noticed whenever he had looked at them; he was more concerned with the complicated denomination than on the year the coin had been minted.

Magistrate Fielding again banged his gavel. "Silence! Silence! Go on, Mr. Cavendish please." Henry nodded absentmindedly toward the unseeing magistrate and continued, "This is, it appears, the same bracelet that both Mr. Rock and I discovered on Mr. Sewell's wrist at the society experiment, as he lay unconscious in my arms. We also discovered what the Crown now has in its possession; the white b-box and attached cord." Again, he motioned toward the table.

"While on stage at the society meeting, behind the drawn curtain, we did not have sufficient time to f-fully examine the bracelet, the white box or the cord. But, I did touch the bracelet. It has metal bumps upon its side, like rivets in metal. Touching one of these made the item emit strange coloured lights. Many colours and small pictures – incredible pictures – appeared on its face. M'Lord, I was able to move these pictures by simply touching them with my finger."

The crowd murmured as Henry shook his head, "This technology is simply not of our time."

The magistrate rubbed his eyes. "Unfortunately, Sir, I cannot see the lights of which you speak. But, I am advised that they do, indeed, exist as you describe. So, as a scientist, what would you hypothesize, Mr. Cavendish?"

"All of this evidence p-points to something other than witchcraft," Henry replied. "In scientific terms, I hypothesize that these strange objects are from the future – and that these two young men have travelled through time, bringing the objects with them.

"These c-clothes and footwear are the clothes of an advanced design, a design possible only to a future generation. Mr. Rock provided all of the clothes and those incredible shoes to my c-care for the purpose of chemical analysis of fabric and material. There is nothing like this in the world, I can assure you. These c-clothes are not the c-clothes of a witch. A witch may display strange accoutrements, but a witch does not have access to these materials."

Henry continued, "I spoke to Mr. Sewell after our p-presentation to the Royal Society. I c-cannot speak of the circumstances regarding Mr. Sewell's friend, Zachary Burling. But by what Mr. Sewell has told me, and by the similar objects that Mr. Burling had on his p-person, and by association – I surmise that he too, is from the future.

265

"Mr. Sewell t-tells me that they must return to the future on a specific day in order for the t-transference to be successful. This will not only exonerate them as witches, but will assist the future science of m-mankind," Henry paused and seemed to control his stuttering in saying, "A lofty ideal, but one that I believe I am suited for. Quite frankly, Sir, I believe that God has me in mind for this sole purpose."

"Indeed. And when is this 'specific day', Mr. Cavendish?" asked the judge, no longer concerned about the imposed five-minute limit.

The assemblage had its attention firmly rooted on Henry as he responded, "This Thursday, M'Lord."

No one noticed a bearded man edging closer to the central table. He suddenly lunged toward the table and grabbed both white boxes. He bowled over a court clerk who had been seated at the table, and ran through the crowded aisles, stuffing the boxes into a hemp bag as he went.

While Magistrate Fielding could only sit and listen to the commotion, his burly bailiff was stationed like a rock between the fleeing man and the door. The man, shabbily dressed and even larger than the bailiff, put his shoulder down and hit the bailiff hard. The bailiff went down like a sack of legal textbooks. Hardly missing a step, the man flew through the door!

Others helped the bailiff to his feet. He dusted himself off and strode to the magistrate's bench, where he conferred with the blind judge. As the two conferred, Sky and Zac exchanged looks. The white boxes – the chargers – were critical for them to return home.

Again, the courtroom cacophony erupted.

Magistrate Fielding again attempted to restore order – such disruption in his courtroom was unprecedented! In the same birdlike manner as he had employed before, he managed to quiet the crowd.

Mopping his brow, he said, "I... we have all had enough for one day. Henry Cavendish, I charge you with assisting these young men on that 'specific day' to send them on their way. If they cannot or do not return to where – or when – they came, I already have all the evidence required to pass judgment. This court will reconvene on Thursday at half past 8 of the clock. Bailiff, remove the prisoners."

Outside, the bearded man carrying the bag with the mysterious white boxes inside tore his way through the throngs, court officials in pursuit. He bumped into many people as he went, including one elderly man with a cane and a leather satchel.

The transfer went as smoothly as in rehearsal: the bearded man, carrying the bag to his chest, bumped innocuously into the bespectacled old man with the cane, their bodies so close together that passers-by could not see the bag being dropped into the satchel.

Outside the courthouse, other men, including members of the Bow Street Runners, joined the court officials. All of them were focused on their large quarry, who they could see ahead through the crowd.

They ran right past the elderly man, who calmly turned and walked away from the noisy crowds. As the streets grew quieter, all one could hear was the tap-tapping of his cane. Victorious, he was on his way to the palatial home of a colleague in Clapham Common.

∞

44

LEOPOLD HAD FELT THE paper slide into his pocket, but he acted nonchalant. Maybe the gin helped with that. He looked into the eyes of his friend and nodded. Constable Leddy, who was standing closest to Sky and Leopold, did not seem to notice any deception.

Wee Willy cried anxiously, "Enough. Let us go!" He and Maurice turned to leave. The small crowd dispersed into the darkness.

As the constables led the two away from Leopold's camp-site, their legs shackled, Leopold reached into his pocket for the paper. Looking at it was useless; Leo couldn't read.

But Mika could, and she was teaching Vassi both Romani and English. Leopold turned to her, still standing there with their son, and smiled. Sky had to have scrawled the note inside the tent as Leopold was talking to the constables. He handed her the note.

Unfolding the small paper, she recognized it as one that Vassi had given to Sky. She paused to quickly read it to herself. The penciled words were jumbled, as though the writer had written fast and without the benefit of a hard surface to write on. The moonless night was dark, but she could just make out the words. She quietly read aloud:

> *"Leo, no time to writ. Thers a rock wit*
> *a cross undr oak tree, dig undr it*
> *Sky"*

Leopold waited in his tent until the campsite was quiet. Then he snuck out and grabbed his small shovel, a new candle and a flint from the back of the caravan. The oak tree was easy to find in the darkness, but as he felt around with his hands and feet, he found many rocks under it. He lit the candle, knowing the risk he was taking: the campsite – the entire city – was rife with vagabonds and thieves. His big hand shielded the candle flame as he started at the campsite side of the tree and slowly worked his way around, looking for a cross on a rock. It took longer than he thought it would but finally, on the darkest side of the tree, he saw a faint cross scratched in the moss of a cat-sized rock.

Leopold extinguished the candle, pushed the rock aside and dug. The ground had recently been disturbed, so it was easy to dig. Soon, he hit something. He dropped the shovel and started to dig with his bare hands. He found two purses wrapped in a cloth, about a foot down. Unable to see the contents in the dark, he pocketed both. He stood and furtively looked around for any spies in the dark. Then he filled the hole, replaced the rock and returned to the tent.

Mika had put Vassi to bed beside Nico. But, she couldn't sleep, so she was sitting up waiting for him. In the dim light cast by a single tallow candle – one of their last – they counted out the contents of the purses. There was enough money to keep their family housed and fed for the next six months. They could now take up residence in Aldgate and join the new St. George's Lutheran Church. Being a member of the congregation meant job opportunities for Leopold.

Teary-eyed, her bottom lip aquiver, Mika looked at her husband in the candlelight. She would have to get used to living in this filthy city, at least for now; her husband was worth it. They hugged and wept openly now, as beside them, Vassi stirred and rubbed his eyes.

∞

45

ZAC AND SKY JUST wanted to go home. But without the stolen chargers, the confiscated smartwatches were lifeless. As they would be themselves, if they were unable to return home later today.

Today was Thursday! The only day they knew of when a portion of space-time was again in a suitable pattern for time travel. Their space-time shot looked, at this point, like a long shot.

Magistrate Fielding had charged Henry Cavendish with assisting in sending them home.

As Fielding had already alluded to, should they be unsuccessful it would mean a final trip by tumbrel for two witches to the hanging tree at Tyburn. In fact, by judicial order, workers were already building bleachers at Tyburn to accommodate the expected throngs. The high interest in the judicial case of not one, but two accused witches meant that the witches' bodies would likely be 'gibbeted'[10] from the walls of the Tower of London after their deaths.

Now, the day had arrived and the two, arms and legs bound, were again pushed into a tumbrel for the slow journey to the Old Bailey. If anything, the crowds of people lining the streets were even larger than before.

They were definitely more boisterous. Some threw rotten fruit, others just booed and hissed. Some approached the

---

10 Publicly displayed in a small iron cage, suspended above the street.

tumbrel, trying to rock it back and forth. The six guards
– including Constable Leddy of the Bow Street Runners,
who had been seconded to assist with crowd control –
walked alongside, using their batons on a few occasions to
push back the more vociferous or to rap an aggressor on
the knuckles.

Although not in Swahili, the shouting of "Kill the
witches!" was enough to bring back horrible memories
for Sky. He closed his eyes as the tumbrel rocked and
the constables pushed back any troublemakers into the
surging crowd.

Finally arriving at the Old Bailey, the young men were
guided by the constables as they jumped from the cart to
the street, surrounded by the angry mob. In leg irons, they
shuffled into the courthouse as the crowds chanted, booed
and hissed.

Entering the courtroom, they saw that the great mahogany table was now covered with a host of scientific equipment. The clerks and others who normally occupied that
table had been moved to one side. Even the two wrist irons
had been removed. The only other items on the table were
the smartwatches, the cords and the Mickey Mouse pocket
watch, each item numbered for reference by a placard.

The courtroom was already jammed and hot. Most of
the higher-born women cooled themselves with hand-held
folding fans decorated with jewels or feathers. The fans
also served to keep delicate perspiration from causing the
women's carefully applied make-up to run.

One of the viewers was an older man called Gerard, who
had arrived early to get a good seat. He planned to attend
the hangings at Tyburn as well. He couldn't remember the
last time he had seen witches hung. Many thieves and murderers, but witches? It had been too long. He had a great
seat; first row. He had worked for it, rushing into the courtroom as soon as it opened, jostling, pushing and pulling

others out of his way to secure the best vantage point. He was close to the mahogany table and could see and hear almost everything that the accused were doing. And that was what he concentrated on. He did not engage his fellow court-goers in any way.

Gerard was a hat maker by trade, and he unknowingly bore the heavy burden of his occupation. "Hatters" were exposed to mercury, which was used in the production of felt hats. His prolonged exposure to mercury vapour was slowing poisoning him. He sweated a lot, even in cold weather, and was subject to irritability, insomnia, nervousness and especially, to intense shaking. Gerard, the hatter, was going mad.

The gallery included Clive Rock, Jack Harris, Caramel Calhoun and Jacques DuTemps, although the latter wore a disguise (a white wig, strikingly similar to that worn by Father Time at the ball) and an eyepatch. Helena Harrison sat fidgeting, feeling both her misgivings about again being in a courtroom and her concern for Sky.

Sky saw her the instant he was led into the room. She looked beautiful. He knew that, whether he was convicted of witchcraft or not, this could be the last time that he would ever see her.

Sir William Mansfield, Wee Willy and Lady Rachel again sat with the Lord Mayor and the Sheriff of London on the witness' bench. The Mansfield family was richly adorned in outfits befitting of a most public setting.

The blind Magistrate Fielding entered the courtroom on the arm of the burly bailiff. Because of the change in the layout of the room, the bailiff advised the magistrate of every possible walking impediment. Taking his seat, the judge – like everyone else – was expecting a guilty verdict. Everyone else, that is, except Henry Cavendish.

At this time, electricity was a preoccupation of not only Henry – who was primarily concerned with chemistry and physics – but of many learned philosophers and the lay public alike. Electrical instruments and those who experimented with them were found not only in laboratories, but also in public places such as coffee houses and theatres. The production of sparks and the attraction/repulsion of charged bodies were demonstrated in engaging experiments, and became a fashionable form of entertainment for polite society.

Upon the approval of the magistrate, Henry had brought the equipment from his shed to the Old Bailey on the pretense that it might somehow show that the two accused were not witches. Despite the public demand, Henry had never had this particular equipment – which was state-of-the-art – out the door of his shed before. He neglected to mention to the magistrate or anyone else that he was now in possession of the mysterious white boxes, which had been stolen from this very courtroom, and which he had studied in that very shed.

It was well known that Henry Cavendish was reclusive and somewhat strange. He flinched at the thought of speaking in public, and in particular, in the presence of a woman! But, his quest for scientific knowledge surpassed his hermeticism, at least right now with what he had discovered so far. His quest, he felt, was only beginning.

Sensing the time was right, Magistrate Fielding hammered his gavel to begin the proceedings. "Order! Order! Bailiff, please have Mr. Henry Cavendish, scientist, take the stand."

Again, Henry reluctantly took the stand. The burly bailiff, a few paces from the judge, spoke quietly to Fielding.

"Mr. Cavendish, this Court has directed you to assist the accused by way of any possible means to see them back to where they came from if, in fact, they come from where you claim they come from." The judge used a roundabout way to speak in order to avoid using the word "future". "The 'specific day' that you noted in your previous, unsolicited court appearance is now upon us."

He continued, "You are aware of the serious charges facing these men and that, failing a miraculous departure from this courtroom, a verdict of guilty as charged is likely." The judge paused, then continued: "I am told that you have brought with you some equipment today as we previously discussed, and that said equipment lies before us now. Can you describe this equipment for us, please? By that I mean tell the court what it does."

Henry then cleared his throat and described the equipment, which consisted of a cylindrical electricity-generating machine on a four-legged stand. The horizontal cylinder was attached to a vertical turning mechanism that featured two sprockets; a large one below and a smaller one above. A wooden handle on the lower sprocket allowed the user to turn the cylinder. A smaller cylinder, supported by a single leg, protruded from the large one. At the end of this small cylinder, wires were connected via a birdcage-like contraption.

"So, the equipment generates electrical current, correct?" Fielding cut to the chase.

"It does, sir."

"Thank you. And, what is your hypothesis, Mr. Cavendish?"

"It is my h-hypothesis, Sir, that I can send the accused back to their time by simply applying a small electrical charge to their matching bracelets, using their own wire applied to the bracelet. As you allowed earlier this morning, I was able to study both the bracelet and the connecting wire, here in the courtroom. The wire has a magnetic attachment to the bracelet. As you also allowed, my colleague and I spent over t-two hours turning this handle," Henry touched the hand crank, "with the bracelets connected."

Clive Rock rubbed his sore arm and searched in vain the faces of those sitting closest to him in the gallery for people who might know that he was, indeed, the "colleague". He could have told the court that he and his colleague also heard each bracelet make a sound, like a church bell chime, close to the end of the charging session.

Henry said, "I believe that the bracelets may now have sufficient charge to operate as they would under normal circumstances. I may not need to, and I hope that I do not need to turn the c-crank very much at all."

Sky looked at Zac with a glimmer of hope. He had no idea how much voltage the scientist had generated, but he knew that the smartwatch should normally recharge to 100 per cent in about two and a half hours.

"For the sake of all of us, Sir, on this hot day, I hope that you are correct," Magistrate Fielding said. "So, am I correct in assuming that you are ready to proceed with your... demonstration, Mr. Cavendish?"

"I am, Sir."

"Proceed then. Bailiff, please approach the bench." The magistrate needed the bailiff beside him to provide a full play-by-play description.

"I'll need the accused to j-join me at this table," Henry directed.

Two large wooden chairs were already stationed where the wires protruded from the machine. As the burly bailiff leaned over and spoke in subdued tones to Magistrate Fielding, two other bailiffs brought Zac and Sky forward and sat them in the chairs, arms and legs still shackled.

Henry was seen whispering in each of the young men's ears as he took the two smartwatches from the table. He stayed longer with Sky, saying, "I am so d-delighted to have made your acquaintance, Sky Sewell. I hope that I am able to help you on your journey back to the future. I wish that I could travel with you; the science of your time must be... b-breath taking. God knows that I am the right man for the job: may He see you safely home."

Henry attached a smartwatch, already attached to the USB cables via the magnetic panel on the back, to Sky's and Zac's left wrists. The USB cables were, in turn, connected directly to the machine by copper wires, attached by clamps to the USB end of the cable.

"I have instructed the accused to use any means in their p-power to return to their time, including touching the bracelets if required." Henry stood next to the crank, ready to turn if required.

The judge nodded.

They were, it appeared, ready to go.

Zac and Sky sat side by side at the mahogany table, their fate firmly in the odd scientist's hands. An eerie silence fell over the courtroom, as viewers inched forward to the edge of their seats.

The watches had been without charge for most of Zac and Sky's incarceration until this morning, so Sky doubted that anyone could have inadvertently activated one. Although some curious court official may have wanted to try one on, Sky doubted that Henry would have permitted such access under his watch – under his watchful eye, that is.

Sky didn't know if the watches were charged even now. He and Zac were familiar with the use of the smartwatch, knowing that to activate it, one simply had to raise one's wrist. They looked at each other, and with a slight nod of their heads, raised their wrists.

The watches "woke up" simultaneously and the classic watch face was activated: the clock in white on the black background, with the third hand in red. Both watches displayed the red "needs charging" light.

There were not many sitting close enough to see the display come to life, but those who were, gasped, pointed and whispered to their neighbour.

Except Gerard. The hat maker was too engrossed in watching the witches as they quietly spoke to each other, gesticulating and talking about the brightly-coloured bracelets. Gerard saw them follow each other's lead and touch the talisman, changing it magically as other colours raced under their fingers. He had never before witnessed such witchcraft!

Zac, who was closest to Henry Cavendish, asked the scientist to begin turning the crank. Henry removed his waistcoat and placed it on the back of a nearby chair. He then rolled up his shirtsleeves. With a practised motion and a single hand, he began to turn.

At first, the machine made little, if any, noise; a faint whirring. Wide-eyed, Gerard watched as the large cylinder began to turn slowly; he watched as it picked up speed. He heard the crackle of electricity. *"This mad scientist is not going to help these two bastards,"* Gerard thought indignantly. His hands, red with inflammation caused by the poisoning, trembled as he rubbed them together with glee.

The whirring noise increased as Henry, now using both hands, cranked harder. Sweat dripping from his brow, he motioned with his head toward the gallery. Clive Rock knew instantly what was required of him. He rose, and using his cane as both a support and a weapon, jostled and thwacked his way through the crowd down to the courtroom floor, where he joined his colleague. The bailiff tracked his progress in whispered reports to Fielding.

Then, without missing a stroke, Clive replaced the exhausted Henry at the crank, providing a burst of energy. Henry, winded, sat on the open chair and wiped his brow. The whirring and crackling increased. A slight trail of smoke emitting from the large cylinder was quickly transformed into a fast-moving cloud by the wind generated by the cranking motion.

A column of bright sunlight peeked through the second-floor windows, illuminating the centre of the room: the mahogany table, the smoking electrical equipment and

277

the two accused witches. The sunlight combined with the moving smoke to create a surreal, almost biblical scene.

Suddenly, as if on cue, Sky rose slowly from his seat. He reached over on the mahogany table to where his Mickey Mouse pocket watch was displayed as "Item #3," and knocking the paper placard aside, grabbed his beloved watch. He turned to face the gallery where a terrified Helena now stood, looking down.

As the bailiffs moved toward Sky, Zac also stood and looked down at his smartwatch. His hand moved to the watch face.

Teary-eyed, Sky kissed the palm of his hand and threw the kiss to Helena as accurately as he could with bound arms. With both hands covering her mouth in horror, Helena was unprepared to catch the kiss. Sobbing uncontrollably, she felt its effect, nonetheless.

With the touch of a finger, Sky activated the Ticking app. Zac did the same. The Mickey Mouse watch chain, hanging down from Sky's other hand, hit the table.

In the blink of an eye they were gone, leaving only smoke trailing upward in two thin, twisting columns. Witnessing the phenomenon did not help Gerard's condition in any way. He sat dumbfounded, shaking uncontrollably.

As the whirring of the generator gradually stopped, Clive Rock removed his eyeglasses to wipe his brow. He looked toward Cavendish, who was gazing skyward. The scientist turned slowly toward Rock. They both smiled thinly as a deathly silence filled the smoky courtroom.

There would be no hangings at Tyburn today.

∞

46

"HAWKING, GO!" THE CAT meowed and strutted around, stiff-tailed, but didn't leave.

It was now just before dinner on the same Saturday that Beatrice had watched the adventurers disappear in the K2. She had spent the day recalculating and rechecking her previous algorithms, which she had already rechecked again.

Despite her trepidation, she was ready. As long as the transference was made during the narrow time window, Beatrice felt confident that she could bring the boys home as planned.

She sat at her computer and began the sequencing protocol, which would run repetitively until it detected the Ticking app in the smartwatch. "If they are there and they've activated the app, they'll soon be here. Thirty-nine days spent in the past, and just 10 hours of actual time!" she excitedly said aloud. Her pulse rate increasing, Beatrice checked the computer: nine hours, 59 minutes, 18 seconds and counting, leaving about three hours in the transference window. *Be still, my heart,* she thought.

It may have been Beatrice's imagination, but the basement seemed especially quiet just before the K2 began to rumble to life. Her entire focus remained on the computer and on the iconic red telephone booth.

Once again, the time machine began to glow from within with an iridescent light. Beatrice smiled. The interior glow increased, and was joined by a low and undulating sound. The sound increased in intensity until Beatrice had to quickly throw on her industrial earmuffs.

Then, *POP!* And *POP!* The K2 rocked and rumbled.

Beatrice ran to the K2 and opened the door. A trail of steam wafted out from the hot interior. She fanned the air in front of her face and peered in.

She saw Zac first, coughing from the steam and wearing what looked like an 18th century gentleman's waistcoat and breeches. Right behind him was Skypilot, coughing as well and wearing similar clothes, although not as high quality as Zac's. Both had their arms and legs shackled!

As they slowly shuffled out of the K2 and into the basement, the time travellers were dazed and confused.

History had just been made!

Like Neil Armstrong and his "That's one small step…", Beatrice needed a monumental catchphrase to commemorate the moment. One that she could later relate to the media, one that the two chrononauts could tell their grandchildren about and one that embodied this moment for eternity. A simple sentence that encapsulated the astounding effect that a now-proven form of time travel would have on humankind. The world would want such a catchphrase.

Instead, Beatrice hugged them both, clasped her hands together, sighed and asked, "So, how was 1766?"

Zac and Sky embraced, thankful that they had both arrived home in one piece.

With his arm still over the shoulder of his buddy, Sky looked frantically at his aunt. "Aunt Bea, we have much to tell you about 1766. And, we will. But for now, I have to go back! How much time is left in the transference window?"

"Go back? You can't go back. Why do you want to go back?"

Sky blurted out, "I met a girl; Helena Harrison is her name. She is beautiful and I love her. I want to bring her to this time to live here."

"Oh Skypilot, you're such a romantic! You fell in love there? Oh, we have much to discuss. But there's too much at stake for me to allow you to bring anything – let alone a person – back. I mean, clothes are one thing, but a person? Out of the question. Besides, there are only a few hours remaining in the window; not enough for you to go and return."

"I can get back quickly; I know where she is! Please Aunty Bea please!" Sky begged. "Her very life may depend upon it."

Sky explained the situation with Helena and her uncle, who was holding her as a virtual captive to serve his wishes. He knew that her situation was now his responsibility, and he loved her! He had to go after her.

Just a few hours earlier, Beatrice had completed all of her preliminary tasks to ensure a successful transference. Then, she had curled up with a purring Hawking to finish a particularly poignant romance novel. She had used up a full box of tissues.

Hearing Sky's story, her eyes still red, she relented. "Okay, Sky. If she is truly in danger—and of course I believe you— I'll help you bring her back. How can I refuse in light of all you've done? And, to tell you the truth, we'll simply be conducting a future phase of our work a little sooner than planned. What's your plan?"

As Zac listened intently, Sky outlined his plan.

Beatrice was listening as she moved around the basement, lifting this and peering around that, looking for something to remove the iron shackles from their legs. Finding her Dremel tool, she attached a small blade and with some effort through the thick iron, proceeded to cut Sky free, then Zac.

To remain anonymous, Sky said that he would wear the clothes that Beatrice had sewn for him. Beatrice would send him wearing his own and Zac's smartwatch, to land close to the Old Bailey courthouse, which Helena would soon be vacating with the crowds. Sky would connect with her and equip her with the smartwatch. Then, the two of them would be ready to make the time transfer.

Beatrice nodded, "Okay, I can get you to within a couple of blocks of the courthouse. What crowds? And why were you shackled?"

Sky had no time to lose, so he simply told his aunt that there had been a trial with huge crowds both inside and out of the Old Bailey, "Zac will tell you all about it when I'm gone."

Beatrice nodded again and walked to the clothes rack. She grabbed the outfit that Sky had originally refused to wear. She handed it to him along with the black hobnail boots, saying, "I wish these were more comfortable, but this is what they wore on their feet, as you probably know by now."

His shackles removed, Sky visited the bathroom; an underrated comfort of modern living. The guard in the Tower of London had allowed him to go just prior to boarding the tumbrel. Sky changed into the period clothes and shoes. Aunt Bea was right, the shoes were uncomfortable but they fit well enough. He knew that his outfit looked authentic and would pass any test of reasonableness. The breeches were a little tight, but everything else fit well.

"You were right, Beatrice, we should have worn the clothes that you sewed for us," Zac said. "That would have saved me a lot of explaining. Come to think of it, the clothes almost cost us our lives."

Zac would have a lot of time in the coming weeks to think about his adventure. In retrospect, the lack of period clothing was just one of a few errors that the chrononauts had made; errors that had placed them in the prisoner's box at the Old Bailey.

Zac thought that Sky had been right – he usually was – the adventure had been once-in-a-lifetime. But if given an opportunity for another, Zac was sure that they could do a better job.

He thought about his time at Mansfield Castle, his experiences as a footman and mostly, about Lady Rachel. From the moment he met her, he felt a connection. But that connection was tenuous at best, due to his lowly station in life compared to her high social status.

The kiss that they shared in the Billiard Room was not, in fact, shared at all. The confident pressing of her lips to his was simply the aristocratic woman exerting her authority over him. In a similar way, she had had him assigned to the tea party only for the purpose of showing him off to her friends... his was not the epic romance his best friend's had clearly been.

Sky approached the K2, where Zac and his aunt now stood. "I'm ready," he proclaimed.

"Not quite. Did you go to the bathroom?" Beatrice instantly reminded him again of his mom. He nodded.

"Good. Also, you'll need this: a fully-charged battery pack." Beatrice handed Sky another of the infamous white boxes, identical to the two stolen by the bearded man in the Old Bailey courtroom. Sky stuffed the unit into the front pocket of his breeches. Had he been going on a trip of a longer duration, he would have secured it onto his belt. Now, there was no time. No time...

"Now, you're ready! Bring her home to a new exciting life," Eyes welling with tears, the scientist displaced by the romantic, Beatrice hugged her nephew. "I can't wait to meet her."

Sky turned to face his best friend and was surprised to see that Zac's' eyes were watery too. Zac said, "Go buddy – go.

I have never met her, but I already know that she has to be special." He handed Sky his smartwatch, and Sky fastened it to his wrist beside the other.

The two friends hugged and slapped backs in the way that men do when it is necessary to hug another man. Beatrice opened the door of the K2. Seizing an opportunity, Hawking the cat darted from the shadows under the desk toward the open door.

"Oh no you don't!" Beatrice grabbed the cat before he could enter the booth. She scolded him, "The only Hawking in there will be named Stephen. But that is yet to come."

Holding the cat, Beatrice reminded Sky to activate the app at the earliest opportunity. She would have the sequencing protocol running in wait, soon after his departure.

Sky entered the K2 and Beatrice closed the door. He watched through the panes of glass as she and Zac sat down at the computer desk, Zac now holding the mischievous cat. Then he took a deep breath, closed his eyes and prayed.

Having endured the time travel process, Sky was better prepared for the lights and sounds that followed. Again, he kept his eyes closed for the first part of the journey. He slowly opened them, one by one, seeing the same little lights streaming by and merging into a large light as he was propelled forward. Or down, he could not be sure.

He landed, harder this time, on a floor. Rolling, he ended up against a wall. Crumpled up between him and the wall was the bottom portion of a huge purple curtain that extended up to the ceiling. Wincing, he got to his feet and rubbed his sore shoulder.

That's when the applause began.

∞

41

THE ROYAL THEATRE IS not far from the Old Bailey, but it is far enough to compel a time traveller to ask himself what went wrong. Or perhaps, to simply ask the person standing next to him, "Where am I?"

That's exactly what Sky did on the main stage of the Royal. The actor standing next to him looked somewhat perplexed, then annoyed. By this time, the applause had died down and the curtain was being closed. The actor, bedecked like a highwayman, mumbled something about being in a matinee performance of *The Beggar's Opera*.

"And, you somehow ruined my opening scene! Where did you come from?" he demanded.

On shaking legs, Sky wobbled toward the actor and tapped his chest with a single finger. "That's not important right now, buddy. What's the fastest way out of here to get to the Old Bailey?"

The actor was taken aback, but managed to point beyond the closed curtain. "Straight out the main entrance, then left, and left again…"

With a quick "Thanks, eh!", Sky pushed aside the curtain and jumped off the stage, causing the audience to collectively gasp. They had just been told that the play was to resume after a short break. They did not expect to see an actor – obviously a very talented actor who had appeared out of nowhere – running up the aisle and out of the theatre. They enthusiastically applauded his grand exit.

Outside, the street was teeming with people. Sky had to pause briefly to let his eyes adjust to the bright Thursday afternoon sunlight. He turned left down the street and ran toward the river, hoping that the directions from the actor were accurate. And he had many people to ask directions from, which he did.

"The Old Bailey?" he asked.

"Yes, that way," said a woman waving her hand-fan down the street. On he went.

"The Old Bailey?" Short of breath, he asked a merchant; who jerked a thumb in the direction Sky was going. "But you've got many blocks to go, mate. That's at least a 30-minute walk. The Old Bailey is near St. Paul's!" The man pointed to the cathedral dome and tower in the distance.

Many blocks to go? wondered Sky. But Aunt Bea had said she would get him within a couple of blocks of the courthouse. Looks like it was more than a couple of blocks. He had to get there before Helena left. He had no way of knowing where she was going after the trial. But he knew that he had little time.

As he ran, he started to look for unoccupied carriages. He had stolen one before and he may have to again. He saw many, most of which were either occupied or too large to negotiate down crowded streets. He was just about to give up, remove his waistcoat and run the distance. Then, he saw it: a small, light and racy two-wheeled vehicle. Called a gig, the carriage was pulled by a single horse, but looked alarmingly easy to flip.

He stopped to get his breath and watch the gig for any signs of an owner nearby. Soon, a man wearing a light brown robe appeared from within the adjacent shop. He placed a box under the seat of the gig, tied it down and re-entered the shop.

Sky had no time to lose. He ran to the gig, jumped up into the bench seat, grabbed the reins and shouted something like "YAH!" or "HAH!" The chestnut horse, as startled as the nearby people, took off at a brisk canter down the cobblestone street.

Behind him, the robed man – a rather rotund one at that – ran out of the shop, and realized that the cart was leaving without him. He bellowed, "Hey, stop that cart! That's my cart – nay, the Lord's cart!"

Glancing back over his shoulder, Sky understood that the man, who was now shaking his fist, was a clergyman. He had inadvertently stolen a carriage that belonged to a church. Sky mumbled to himself some words that would be unwelcome in that or any other church, as he passed pedestrians and slower carriages.

For most of the journey, the streets were busy and slowed Sky down immensely, almost to walking speed. But portions of the trip, bereft of pedestrians, were made at a canter or even a gallop. During these times, bystanders had to beware of the fast-approaching carriage. Sky yelled warnings most of the way.

One of these bystanders, a gin seller, was unfortunate to follow a potential buyer onto the street just as Sky's gig raced forward. The potential client had just declined the gin seller's offer and, sensing danger, had hurriedly made it to the opposite sidewalk.

The gin seller did not. Directly in front of the oncoming carriage, he ran back to his kiosk, which was stacked with bottles of gin. The gig swerved to avoid a crash. One wheel off the pavement, the gig smashed into the gin stand, narrowly missing the seller, who was sprawled out on the sidewalk.

Gin, wood and glass flew everywhere! While the horse had managed to avoid hitting the gin stand, the gig had hit it sidelong, sending a shower of gin and glass over both carriage and rider.

Sky managed to throw up one arm in an attempt to block the deluge. Nevertheless, he suffered minor cuts to his hands and face. The instant sting of gin in fresh wounds made Sky wince. That was not the worst of it, however; the smell of cheap gin was everywhere: in his clothes, on the cart and probably on the package under the seat.

The package! One hand on the reins, Sky felt for it under the seat and in the box behind. It was gone. It had to have fallen out during the crash.

He urged the horse on – no time to stop. The gin seller was already on his feet, surveying the damage. With his arms skyward and dripping with his product, he seemed to be asking Bacchus, the God of Wine (in the absence of a God of Gin), why. It was then that the gin seller noticed a package, neatly wrapped but partially wet, lying on the cobblestones. Ignoring that it was addressed to the Abbot, Westminster Abbey, he opened it. Inside, he found 12 new copies of *The History of Tom Jones, a Foundling* by Henry Fielding. *A sign from God,* the gin seller thought. *He wants me to sell these to recoup my losses.*

After some time at speed, the gig could only move slowly ahead as the roadway was once again crowded with pedestrians. Most of the crowd was surging slowly toward Sky, perhaps away from the Old Bailey; a good sign. From here, he could recognize landmarks like St. Paul's and individual buildings. He knew where he was! The courthouse was on the next block.

It seemed that the disappointed courthouse crowds were beginning to disperse. All had been hoping for a witch-hanging at Tyburn, but word was that the accused witches had conjured up a spell and disappeared right out of the courtroom. In front of the Blind Beak, no less! Many wondered how the bailiff was going to explain their astonishing departure to the blind magistrate.

He had arrived; the courthouse was mere steps away. Now, to somehow find that vessel of loveliness, Helena, in this sea of humanity. He reined in the horse and stepped off the gig to walk northbound into the surging south-bound crowd.

Luckily, Sky was taller than most people. During his stay in 18th century England, he had had to duck his head many times when passing through a doorway. He had forgotten a few times and had the lumps to prove it.

Thankfully, the young woman he was searching for was also quite tall, perhaps due to genetics and to living outside of the city with a regular healthy diet.

Stinking of gin, he walked upstream into the throng. Some people that he passed pinched their noses and waved their hands in front of their faces, moving the befouled air. Others held an imaginary cup and tossed back an imaginary drink in mockery of the bleeding, gin-swilling but fast-moving man.

As he approached the courthouse, the crowds thinned. Standing next to the main entrance were a number of small groups of people, talking together. One of these groups consisted of a man and a woman, hugging each other. Both of them were tall; a head above the few other people around them.

With mixed feelings, Sky gazed at the embracing couple. Yes, he had found Helena! But she was in the arms of another man – it wasn't her uncle – who was holding her tightly and seemed to be comforting her.

Sky stood dumbfounded in the open for a time. Then, remembering that he was somewhat of an escaped felon, he lunged behind a parked carriage. The horses reined to the carriage got a bit skittish as he peered around the corner. With blood trickling down his cheek and daggers shooting from his eyes, he stared at the man. He could not see his face, which was obscured by a tricorne hat and the back of Helena's head.

The man wore what looked like a white wig and an eyepatch. Sky could make out just snippets of their one-sided conversation; the man seemed to be doing most of the talking.

"'Oney, 'oney, dere, dere... 'e is gone. Gone forever. 'E never amounted to much of a 'ighwayman, I did not 'ave enough time to teach 'im! But 'e was a fine young man. Dere, dere..."

Sky would recognize that accent anywhere. Jacques DuTemps had worn the wig as part of his costume at the masquerade ball. Now, again wearing the wig and adding an eyepatch, his identity had been concealed – so far.

As Helena continued to sob, Jacques produced a kerchief to dry her tears, which he proceeded to do with some aplomb. Sky fumed as Jacques held Helena's delicate chin in his hand and gently propped up her head, revealing tear-streaked cheeks. He dabbed away, leaving only imaginary tears, which he continued to gently wipe – all the while whispering sweet nothings in Helena's ear.

Finally, Sky could hear Helena say, "Merci, Monsieur DuTemps. I appreciate your thoughtfulness. Sky is indeed gone. With him went a piece of my heart. But now, I must go, for my uncle and Caramel await." She motioned up the street. Sky tiptoed to the front of the carriage and looked around the horses to see Jack Harris and Caramel standing and waiting for Helena.

Helena's future literally awaited her.

Just as he was summoning the courage to approach the embracing couple, Sky felt two powerful hands on his shoulders. "Hey, what have we here? Looks like an escaped witch to me!"

Sky turned. Harry stood before him, tightly gripping the lapels of Sky's waistcoat. Apparently, the highwaymen used the strategy (of having one of them hide in case he was required) in a variety of ways. This way, with Harry hiding in the alley as his partner seduced a young woman, had been effective.

Harry leaned in close to Sky and sniffed. "Whoa, you stink! And your face is a bloody mess. C'mon then!" With a jerk, Harry guided Sky out from behind the carriage and toward Jacques and Helena.

Helena pushed away from Jacques. Despite his wardrobe change, she recognized Sky immediately. She smiled and shouted, "Sky! You're alive! But how?" Her sad tears turned to happy tears.

She tried to run toward him, but Jacques held her arm. She could not break his strong grip. Up the street, Jack Harris began a slow walk back to where his niece stood. Jacques might be his friend, but his niece was his way to riches. Jack scolded himself; he should never have allowed the French rake to comfort her. He could not understand why Helena needed comforting, being so upset at the loss of the young man named "Sky." In any case, he wanted her back home now, safe from Sky, Jacques or any other potential suitor. Caramel walked behind Jack.

It was a standoff: Jacques holding Helena by the wrist, Harry holding the escaped witch and Jack, with Caramel close by, formed an odd triumvirate.

His duties of crowd control for the trial officially over, Constable Leddy of the Bow Street Runners casually emerged from the Old Bailey, directly into the drama unfolding on the street. Still in full uniform, Leddy had planned to go straight home to a wee pint and then bed after the excitement of escorting the tumbrel.

Now, he had descended the steps of the Old Bailey into a strange scene. The accused witch – his new friend who had miraculously disappeared from the courtroom – was before him, being held by a man whom he recognized from posters at the constabulary as a highwayman. Sky now wore a different suit of clothes, but Leddy knew it was the escapee. One of the men should be arrested. No, perhaps both of them.

Next to them stood another, more infamous highwayman by the name of Jacques DuTemps. Wearing a disguise, DuTemps would not have been recognizable in the absence of the other highwayman, his partner. DuTemps was holding a very pretty young lady.

And next to them stood Jack Harris, a waiter at The Bard and author of the infamous annual *List*, with a stunning mature woman. Harris should be, but likely would not be, arrested.

Armed with only his baton and his wits, Leddy wondered if the land pirates were carrying firearms. He resisted the urge to draw his baton, relying, rather, on the art of negotiation.

"Jacques DuTemps! Unhand that fair maiden and present yourself and your thieving partner to me. You're both under arrest. I promise leniency with your cooperation."

For Jacques, any barely-begun negotiation was hereby ended. He reached into his overcoat and was about to produce his dragon when an ungodly noise pierced the air. He had not heard it before, but it was the same noise that emitted from the talisman on Sky's wrist at the masquerade ball. Jacques and Rachel had already departed the Gallery for more intimate surroundings the last time that noise was heard.

Jacques – and especially Harry, who was directly beside the noise – was caught off-guard. Harry loosened his grip on Sky's waistcoat. Sky seized the opportunity to turn and punch his assailant, hard. The highwayman went down moaning in pain, blood oozing between the fingers that covered his broken nose.

Jacques struggled to extricate his weapon from deep within his overcoat. Summoning his inner Superman, Sky was upon him quickly, breaking his hold of Helena and grabbing the arm that now held the gun inside the coat. Helena ran to join her uncle and Caramel.

By this time, a few curious onlookers encircled the antagonists. Leddy entered the fray. He felt it wiser to deal with the immediate danger of the two highwaymen first, and Sky later. Drawing his baton, he pulled it over his head and charged DuTemps, poised to strike.

The blow never fell.

A loud bang signaled the start of the race away for the onlookers, who promptly fled. The fleeing group included Jack Harris, who thought it best to maintain his freedom now. He turned and ran cowardly down the street, leaving the two women standing together. He would have a chat with his niece later, reminding her that he was financially supporting her. And, he had a man – a wealthy man – whom he'd like her to meet.

At the same time, five constables and two bailiffs emerged from the Old Bailey and ran down the stairs to assist the beleaguered Constable Leddy. They saw a man kneeling on the street, holding his bleeding nose above a small pool of blood. Another man lay writhing in a much larger pool of blood at Leddy's feet, still holding his dragon at his bloodstained chest. A third man, his face lined with dried blood, kneeled beside the second man, next to Leddy.

Two women stood by. Their very presence indicated that they had been involved in the altercation in some fashion. Three of the constables took a position beside Harry. The other two stood beside Leddy, awaiting the direction of the attending officer.

Groggy and bleeding profusely, Jacques saw Sky looking down at him. Now it was Jacques' turn to sniff Sky. Lifting his head slightly, he whispered, "Whoa, you stink!"

"It is gin, Jacques, just on my outside, not my inside." Sky was almost lost for words; the highwayman had been both kind and ready to kill him. "Thank you for your kindness while I was here."

The older of the two women walked slowly to where Jacques lay. Caramel looked down upon her former lover with tears rolling down her cheeks. She did not go any closer or say anything.

Bleary-eyed, Jacques noticed her standing there. He pulled Sky's ear to his mouth and whispered. Sky looked up at Caramel and, with a huge lump in his throat, said, "He wants you to be the last beautiful thing he sees."

She sobbed heavily, stepped forward and kneeled beside the highwayman. To no avail, he had already gone, his non-blinking eyes looking past Caramel, perhaps hopefully to Heaven. She wept openly. Helena ran to hug and kiss Sky, who hugged and kissed her back. She felt so good in his arms!

As onlookers again gathered around, Leddy conferred with the other police officers. Three lifted Harry up off the pavement, placed him under arrest and led him away. The remaining officers lifted the limp body of Jacques DuTemps, Gentleman of the Road, through the front door of the courthouse.

Constable Leddy shooed the onlookers on their way. Caramel seized the opportunity to slip away with the onlookers, but not before shooting a glare toward Sky. Leddy conducted his crowd control rather casually, taking his time in doing so, even though the escapee Sky stood by. Then, he turned to Sky and with a bewildering expression, said, for all to hear, "I have to take you in now, Sky. You are an escaped felon. Come with me... this way."

Leddy guided Sky by the arm, with Helena alongside, down Old Bailey – the street, that is, not the courthouse. As the three walked together, Leddy spoke quietly. "I know that I am supposed to be taking you in. If I do, you will hang at Tyburn. I'm not going to do that. You are my friend and, I believe, an honest one at that," he spoke with conviction. "I saw what happened in Fielding's courtroom: you are not of this time, as you say. You should go back there, wherever or whenever that is. I will say that you escaped... again! How can I help?"

Sky could hardly believe his ears. Overcome with emotion, he hugged the rotund constable wearing the navy blue uniform with the gold buttons. He stressed, "We don't have much time."

He then turned to Helena. Holding her hands and looking into her beautiful blue eyes, he did not need to speak any words. She just nodded and blurted out, "Yes! Yes! Of course, I will accompany you on this, the greatest of adventures!"

Helena had already had to fly for her very life as the mob approached her family's farmhouse. She was determined to fly again, if flying was indeed required to leave this life of ultimate despair for another life of hope and, looking into Sky's eyes, love.

Sky then led them to where he had left the gig. Thankfully, it was still there. As the three of them clambered up into the gig, Sky said, "We have to maximize our chances of a successful transference by returning to the site of my landing – that is, we need to get to the Royal Theatre."

While not totally comprehending, Leddy nodded and simply said, "Right. Off we go then. To the Royal!"

There was not enough room on the bench seat for the three of them, so Leddy stood in the box, holding onto the bench seat for support. Sky was glad that Leddy had come along. And, he knew the fastest route there. As the gig's horses cantered down the busy streets, Leddy shook his rattle and shouted, "Make way! Make way! Police business here..."

As ridiculous as it must have looked, it worked fairly well as the crowds slowly parted to let the small carriage by. As they went, Sky told Leddy about having to "borrow" the gig, where he had got it from and about the mysterious package under the seat. That story would help to corroborate Leddy's version of Sky's escape when it came time to tell the magistrate.

They arrived at the theatre within 10 minutes. Flying through the front door, the time traveller and his friends encountered the ticket-taker. Again, Constable Leddy exerted his authority: "Police business, Sir! Stand aside!"

"But the play is underway; the final act." protested the ticket-taker.

"As I said, police business!" Police business, it seems, was the only business to Constable Leddy.

The trio breezed past him and entered the crowded theatre. Brazenly, they strutted up the aisle and onto the stage. The same actor who had Sky poke his finger into his chest was pontificating skyward when he was rudely interrupted. Again.

"You! You again? What is the meaning of this?"

Leddy interjected, "Police business, Your Actorness." Leddy bent in a mock bow. "Stand aside while we make the… errr… 'transference'." As the actor took a few paces back, Leddy turned to the audience. In a commanding voice, he directed, "Quiet please! We have a situation happening here!"

Whoever was responsible for closing the curtain evidently thought better of it; the curtain remained open.

Turning back to Sky, the big Bow Street Runner said quietly, "Sky, this is your time – you and Helena. God be with you both."

Leddy took two steps back to stand next to the actor. At first, the audience was annoyed by yet another interruption. But this was getting interesting. Most recognized Sky as the same tall, young man who had interrupted the performance earlier. They settled back in their bench seats, as best as those hard seats would allow, watching intently and murmuring amongst themselves.

Sky stood with Helena in the exact spot where he had landed earlier. He, of course, was wearing both his smartwatch and Zac's. With ceremony resembling the offering of a wedding ring, he removed Zac's smartwatch from his wrist and gently took Helena's hand.

"Here we go, my love. The trip is not difficult, but it is somewhat uncomfortable." He smiled, and with realization said, "I'll see you in Fraserdale."

"Fraserdale, it shall be, my love." Helena's eyes welled with tears.

He brought her arm up and attached the smartwatch to her delicate wrist and pressed the Ticking app. Then he pressed the app icon on his watch. He closed his eyes and leaned over to kiss her.

But, she was gone!

Constable Leddy bowed low to the baffled audience's applause, prior to making his exit, centre stage. He shook many of the hands that were extended on his way up the aisle, as the upstaged actor, hands on hips, looked on.

Moments later, Sky too was again travelling through time and space. He closed his eyes, thinking of Helena. The unseen forces pulled at his body in an uncomfortable way. Then, the light beckoned again.

∞

48

Fraserdale, Canada
Summer 2018

HELENA SAW SKY LEANING in to kiss her, so she closed her eyes and puckered up. But, there was no kiss.

That was her last memory of the Year of Our Lord 1766. Still puckering, she was propelled through space-time, uncomfortably at first, passing bright lights and unworldly sounds; the last one a popping sound. Toward the end of her journey, she opened her eyes. She had nothing to lose on this "greatest of adventures" and everything to gain. A bright light gathered below her as she approached what must be the future. She felt confident that her future would be as bright as the light.

Cast onto the floor of some type of box upon landing, she saw that steam or some type of smoke filled the box. It was made up of a series of windows that made the entire box see-through. Seconds later, Sky landed behind her; he managed to stay on his feet.

The box had a door – a large door – that someone on the outside opened, allowing the steam to escape and the air to clear somewhat. Feeling groggy, Helena slowly rose and looked around. Two people stood outside the box, looking as incredulous as she felt that she must look.

One of the people, a woman wearing odd eyeglasses and a man's white waistcoat, helped her to her feet. Oddly, the woman's legs were showing under the waistcoat. The other person – a young man dressed in a multi-coloured flowered shirt, short pants and some type of sandal – hugged Sky tightly, saying, "It's not beach weather today, dude."

"This… is Helena Harrison," announced Sky proudly, still standing behind her, his hands on her shoulders. In the tight confines of the K2, Sky introduced Zac and Beatrice to Helena. They shook hands with her.

The woman in eyeglasses could not keep her eyes off of Helena; a time traveller from the 18th century, right here in Fraserdale; complete with a pretty dress and an English accent! Ignoring Sky for the time being, Beatrice said to Helena, "Come, come out of the K2. I mean, come out of this booth! Let me look at you."

Beatrice took Helena by the hand and led her out of the box to the old sofa, where Helena sat, her dress bunched up, catching her breath. Zac stood, as awestruck as ever. Wide-eyed, Helena looked around. The four of them appeared to be in a room crowded with items that Helena could not begin to describe. Books on a shelf were one of the few items that looked somewhat familiar.

Another familiar item meowed emphatically and ran between Zac's legs. Beatrice adjusted her glasses and said, "Oh, never mind him. That's Hawking. He's a troublemaker. Zac, please get Helena a glass of water."

As Zac ran upstairs, Beatrice said, "We have so much to talk about. You have made a landmark decision. One that, in the history of humankind, no one else has had to make. You, Helena Harrison, are the first woman to travel through time from your time to this time: the first female chrononaut. You are to be congratulated."

Zac returned with a tall glass of ice water. Helena took a sip and looked up at Zac, Beatrice and Sky, all three of whom grinned vacuously down at her. She felt awkward and confined.. "Is there more to the future than this little room?" she asked.

Sky laughed, "Yes, my love, there is more. Beyond your wildest dreams and more! I suggest that we go outside now for a breath of fresh air. You can look at the future!"

The three chrononauts and their intrepid leader climbed the narrow stairs and were just about to emerge out the front door when Sky, in the lead, turned and stopped them. It was raining hard; not exactly the beach weather that the morning had promised.

He spoke to Helena, "As I mentioned earlier, it rains a bit here."

"That's fine, I am used to a little rain. Let me by!" Helena playfully pushed past Sky, ran out the door, down the stairs and onto the front lawn, as long and unkempt as it was. Already soaked, she spun around; her dress twirling in a happy circle.

A few doors down the street, a brave man stoically mowed his lawn in the rain. Helena would always remember the man in the yellow poncho pushing his lawn mower as being symbolic of completing her journey to the future.

But a more tangible memory would endure, as she spun around and watched as an amazing vehicle – it had to be some type of vehicle – rolled by, almost noiselessly, without any horses to pull it! She was able to look through the glass to see two people inside, one of whom stared at her as the vehicle passed. The vehicle had a front glass that was kept clear of the rain by wiping devices that flapped back and forth.

"That is a CAR!" shouted Sky over the patter of the falling rain. "Short for carriage. But 'carriages' now have motors. There are many – too many – of those here."

As the three watched under the cover of the porch, Helena nodded back at them and watched the car drive away. She twirled her dress once again.

And then, Helena danced. She danced as she had many times before, but always within the confines of her room. She danced to the imaginary music of a minuet, or perhaps the allemande. She curtsied, bobbed and moved sideways; passing imaginary dancers. And, she laughed and laughed. She was free – FREE! Free to be her own person, free to see and experience things unimaginable, and free to fall even deeper in love. Sky was unlike any man, any person, she had ever met.

Her blonde hair pasted to her face, she motioned for Sky to join her.

With Beatrice and Zac looking on, Sky jumped down the steps and took Helena in his arms. They danced together in the rain, laughing and humming an unknown tune. A particularly difficult step had them fall unceremoniously on the lawn, in a pile of laughter.

Breathlessly, Helena pointed to her smartwatch. "All right, dear heart. I'm ready to know now: what is… 'YouTube'?"

"Ha! No, you are not ready for that yet!" Sky put his head back and the rain washed the last of the dried blood off his face. He would need more than a rain shower to remove the lingering smell of gin. He laughed, and kissed Helena again on her sweet wet lips.

From that day on, Skypilot's Mickey Mouse pocket watch kept perfect time. He still had to wind it daily, but it just kept on ticking. He wondered if a fully functioning Mickey would come in handy on his next trip through space and time.

Indeed, it was the best for telling times.

∞

EPILOGUE

TIME TRAVEL?

Really?

The adventures of Skypilot and Zachary are based on the concept of humans travelling through time. But, is that even possible?

Humans have already travelled through time. Astronauts are chrononauts too, through a process called time dilation. When astronauts return to earth, they are younger than what they would have normally been; as if they've travelled into the future. But, only in a minute (that's mī-noōt', for those of you thinking about time) way: an astronaut would have to be in space for over 100 years to travel ahead by a full second.

Time does not tick at the same speed for everybody and, as Einstein discovered, it is affected by gravity. If you were to place extremely accurate clocks on each floor of a sky-scraper, the clocks at the bottom, where gravity is strongest, would tick slower than the clocks at the top.

Gravity helped to deposit Sky and Zac smack dab in the middle of the Georgian era of British history (1715-1837), which takes its name from the period spanning the reigns of four kings, all named George. This was a critical time in which the country shed its rural, medieval cloak in favour of the topcoat of a merchant or, perhaps, a parliamentarian. It was a time of armed revolution in Europe, with Britain teetering on the brink of its own, including the agrarian riots that plagued Elizabeth's father.

The rural economy began a movement toward an urban industrial economy, with incredible advances in science and engineering.

One of the aspects of this movement included the growing interest in electricity. Scientists like Henry Cavendish (1731-1810), along with the general public, became fascinated with its potential through amusing public experiments. Sky and Zac hoped that this fascination would work to get them home.

English society in 1766 was a study in contrasts. On the one hand, the era was the greatest age for the aristocracy. This small group controlled vast expanses of land, on which they built grand estates and employed many servants who saw to their lords' every whim. Their wealth and influence continued to expand, due in part to their domination of the government, improvements in agricultural production and expansion of investment opportunities in Britain and beyond.

On the other hand – the dirty, calloused hand – were the poor. London, the country's greatest city and likely the greatest city in the world at the time, was inundated with destitute migrants seeking work or charity. As a woman, Caramel found work only on the streets, as a prostitute. Some 20 per cent of women at that time in that city were prostitutes.

A few fortunate migrants found suitable work, but most found little but an early death. While the epidemics that had killed huge numbers of people centuries earlier were history, improvements in sanitation, medicine, and food production now allowed people to live longer. Paradoxically, this increased the needy population and exacerbated many social concerns.

The poor turned to cheap alcoholic beverages such as gin and rum to ease the pain. Higher alcohol consumption caused more violence and raised crime rates to unprecedented levels. The amateur neighbourhood watch system employed at the time could not cope; hence, Henry (1707-1754) Fielding's and Sir John (1721 - 1780) Fielding's formation of the Bay Street Runners, the first police force in London.

From the first storm sewers, fashioned out of hollowed-out tree trunks, that often failed in catastrophic torrents of purple slop to the woman tossing sewerage out her window while shouting "Gardyloo!"; from the malodorous hermit who lived in a grotto for the sole purpose of existing to the London "rake" who lived for his own pleasure; from Constable Leddy's hat, which doubled as a miniature step-stool to the grotesque forms of torture, only alluded to herein, that captured the policeman's imagination; from the codified bedlam of the masquerade ball to amusing visits into the original "Bedlam" hospital; from Jack Harris' (-1769) *List* to Helena's toothbrush made from the coarse hairs off a hog's back; from the tumbrels that rolled herein, as they did in Dickens' *A Tale of Two Cities*, to the ravens that fly (to this day) over the Tower of London for the glory of Britannia: the miracle of time travel notwithstanding, most of the temporal peculiarities described in the book are true.

∞

PREVIEW

"TICKING TWO: THE HAWKING SEQUENCE "

"Ticking Two: The Hawking Sequence" continues the time travel adventures of Skypilot Sewell and Zachary Burling after their historic inaugural mission to England in the year 1766.

But, this adventure goes awry from step one. The story unfolds at the theme wedding of Sky and Helena, two young lovers who traversed through time and back to be together. Invited to witness the wedding vows is family friend Sam Richter, the diplomatic agent who had volunteered to see young Skypilot safely home to Canada after his ordeal in Africa, when Sky's parents were murdered. Now a CSIS agent, Sam is not in Fraserdale just for the wedding. He had been directed to find out more about the secretive work of the scientist, Beatrice Westover.

Also at the wedding is Alim, Beatrices' friend, colleague and milquetoast date for the evening.

Beatrice has a mind-numbing mission in mind. She outlines the plan, telling the guys that when one considers all the questions that humankind has had about its own history, many have been answered. A few, however, continue to perplex and fascinate us. She proposes a mission that she knows Sky's missionary parents would endorse; to provide irrevocable proof that Jesus lived; that is, to travel back to Jesus' time, find him and record him in order to prove his existence. And, it is revealed that Alim will travel with them; a third time traveller. But, before travelling to the ancient Middle East, the guys first have to learn the lingua franca of the time. Alim, that "kid from Palestine via the North End of Winnipeg", teaches Sky and Zac Aramaic.

Dressed in the tunics of the ancients, the three are ready inside the K2 to fly through time. But, just as the time travel process is initiated, Beatrices' mischievous cat, Hawking, steps on the unattended computer keyboard, sending the chrononauts into a far different time and space than was intended.

Using a process called "key logging", Beatrice traces where and when the chrononauts have gone. Their only option is a rescue mission. Someone must follow the footsteps of Sky, Zac and Alim and bring them home within the time available.

What they see there, who they meet and what they do might be of interest to you.

Oh! Bring your goggles…

CRAIG ("VANN") WILLIAM VAN ALSTYNE BIOGRAPHY

Craig is a retired planner with the local transit company, where, for 33 years, he happily plotted and planned bus routes and service levels – usually while humming *The Wheels on the Bus*. Researching, writing and editing were enjoyable parts of his job, and not just while researching lyrics of bus-related songs! He has an interest in words, of course, but also in history in general. So, readers of his novels will come to depend upon him for well-researched, thoughtful works.

Craig hangs with his main squeeze, Audrey, who is an educator of some repute in Vancouver, Canada. He has three tall, handsome sons who always support and challenge his sage-like wisdom. When not "R 'n' R-ing" ("riting and researching"), he plays baseball, pedals his bike and tills soil in his garden beside the stream. He recently became a first-time grandparent to Addisyn Louise, who is likely the most beautiful future bookworm in the world.

This is Craig's first published work of historical fiction. He hopes to keep the wheels rolling…